# THE MAIDEN

Kate Foster

# THE MAIDEN

MANTLE

First published 2023 by Mantle
an imprint of Pan Macmillan
The Smithson, 6 Briset Street, London EC1M 5NR
*EU representative*: Macmillan Publishers Ireland Ltd, 1st Floor,
The Liffey Trust Centre, 117–126 Sheriff Street Upper,
Dublin 1, D01 YC43
Associated companies throughout the world
www.panmacmillan.com

ISBN 978-1-5290-9172-4

1 3 5 7 9 8 6 4 2

A CIP catalogue record for this book is available from the British Library.

Typeset by Palimpsest Book Production Ltd, Falkirk, Stirlingshire
Printed and bound by CPI Group (UK) Ltd, Croydon, CR0 4YY

Visit **www.panmacmillan.com** to read more about all our books
and to buy them. You will also find features, author interviews and
news of any author events, and you can sign up for e-newsletters
so that you're always first to hear about our new releases.

*To Margaret Foster, my mum*
*I wish you could have read this*

*She was a woman of a godless life, and ordinarily carried a sword beneath her petticoats.*

*Historical Notices of Scottish Affairs*
by John Lauder, Lord Fountainhall

# Chapter One

# CHRISTIAN

*The Tolbooth Jail, Edinburgh*
*October 1679*

*Y*ou *are sentenced to beheading. God have mercy on your soul.*
*Prepare yourself in prayer.*

The sheriff's words clang, pious as the bells of St Giles', all
the way from the court back into the jail. Six High Constables
haul me across the square, batons braced, just in case. I'm
dangerous, the broadsides say. Their other hands grab for all
the parts of me they can reach. Fingers and thumbs claw at
buttons and bows. Their faces leer too close and blur into a
mess of roar and gawp. All I have left to fight back with are
my feet, kicking everything away that comes too close.

I'm at the centre of the commotion, yet one step removed,
hit by everything in flashes. The sour stench of a vegetable pedlar.
The red plume of a hat. The thought of the slam of a blade.

They'd said the judge might believe me.

*Wear your white lace gown. Fall to your knees and plead your*
*innocence.*

Now the dress hangs from me, dragging in the dirt until I'm
back inside, a thunderclap of bolts sealing the door. I should
have searched for Johanna in the crowd. I should have taken
one last look at the sky.

I'm dragged up the steps into the stink of corridors, past yellow candle lanterns and the debtors and delinquents. They've guessed the verdict by the clamour. 'Chop,' they hiss, brushing their necks with their filthy fingers, eyes agog.

Once the constables have thrown me back into the top cell and wiped the sweat from their foreheads, their faces say, *Well, aren't you wickeder than you look.* They've pulled my gown loose. They stare as I try to put the bodice right. Despite the gloom, their smirks shine. I cringe at the furthest wall near the window, the dank of the stones seeping into my skin.

*You'll be taken up to the Tolbooth platform on Monday to be executed at the blade of the Maiden. Find a minister of the Kirk for your last hours. Murderess.*

Three days. Will they make Mother watch? Will I ever see Johanna again? Or see the rippling fields of Corstorphine, the gorse roaring up its hill, as bright and bold as I believed myself to be?

Now I am just my own hammering heart, each thump of it inside my chest ticking down the minutes until I'm a dark slick of hair in piss-stained lace, bound and barefoot, keening in terror.

I should have begged harder.

I should have tried to look more distraught at the fact he is dead.

The constables are spick-and-span now, coats smoothed down and hats straightened as they rattle out of the room, leaving only me and the guard. He fills the space of the doorway, his head almost brushing the top. The knuckles of his hands touch each side of the door frame.

'That advocate of yours will be waiting downstairs,' he says, not moving an inch.

'Could you fetch him, please?' I say. I have learned to keep my voice meek for this particular guard.

'And what do I get in return?' The silvery light from the barred window slants across his face. His dark eyes glint.

'I'll tell him to pay you the usual two coins,' I whisper.

'Oh, but my price has gone up,' he says. 'Now that you're condemned.'

I will not let him see me flinch at that word. I hold myself still.

'Then tell my advocate your price,' I say, and he folds his arms across his great chest and nods, savouring every moment of our exchange.

'That I will,' he says. 'And remember: you can have anything you want here. Make your last days comfortable. For the right price.' He grins, letting his tongue loll over his lips. His face is flushed with the thrill of being alone with a murderess.

'Thank you,' I say, sounding as grateful as I can.

He brings a key from his chain and leaves slowly, locking the door behind him, whistling with those foul, wet lips as he goes.

And I am alone for the first time since the verdict.

The Maiden. There was a sketch of it, in a pamphlet in our library at Roseburn House. *Scotland's Most Abominable Crimes.* But it was on the high shelf that I was absolutely forbidden to read from, so I only did when no one was around. An execution machine with a wooden frame and an iron blade. *A fearsome contraption the height of two men. Reserved for the beheadings of nobility, its swift mechanism is thought to be less painful than the axe, but none of its victims have lived to bear witness, of course.* The pamphlet included a list of those who had suffered at her blade, eternally damned.

Horrible. I'd pushed it back on the shelf and been peely-wally all through luncheon, with Johanna whispering, 'What have you been up to now, Christian?'

*You did kill Lord James Forrester in cold blood.*

Because, in the end, it did not matter what I said at my trial. No one believed me.

Now they will come and watch in their thousands, at the scaffold at the other side of this prison. Each curled wig and beggar's bowl tilted upwards in unison.

My ears buzz. That high-pitched ringing that comes with shock and precedes one of my vomiting turns. I can't be sick. That guard might strip me again, like he did the day I arrived. His breath hot on my neck. My good cape. My coif. My silk petticoat. *You'll have no need for these fancy clothes here.* I need air. The cell reeks of chamberpot. I rest my forehead on the cold bars of the window, still hearing how Mother used to scold me: 'Christian, no. You'll catch the sun. A lady should not be freckled.'

And here I am. Still a lady. It's the only decent thing left to call myself.

From below comes the dogged slap of good leather boots on cold stone slabs. Through the small square of bars at the top of the door I watch my advocate, Mr Dalhousie, take off his hat. His beard is unkempt from the way he ruffled and pulled at it as he bumbled and stammered over his sprawling notes in the courtroom. He puts his hands on the bars. I walk over to him.

'There's nothing more we can do,' he says. 'I will speak to the prison minister. He will pray with you.' His voice slips in his throat.

'Mr Dalhousie,' I whisper, pressing my hands over his fists so tightly my knuckles go white, and tasting my own sour mouth, 'of course there is something we can do.'

'I fear not,' he says. 'Your defence has not been believed.' He picks his words carefully. I wonder if he even believes me, for his furrowed brow has always seemed to have a question hidden behind it. 'The prison minister has counselled other condemned parties, my lady. He is a reassuring presence.'

'I don't want you to fetch me a minister.' I say it slowly, so Mr Dalhousie understands. I have come to realize, too late, that he is not the shrewdest of men, despite the piles of books and papers that threatened to topple his assistants in the courtroom. 'Go to my husband and tell him that I still love him, no matter what's happened. And if he has any love left for me at all, then please can he do one last thing? Or does he want to suffer the public humiliation of his wife on a block?'

Mr Dalhousie has likely never heard a lady speak in such crude terms. His Adam's apple bulges as he swallows. I imagine the excrement stench that boils from the jail's central pit does not sit well on his palate.

'I cannot see that there is anything your husband can do now,' he whispers. 'Mr Nimmo has already spent a fortune on your legal case, a fortune that he did not have any obligation to spend. And the cost of keeping you in here – well fed and kept safe from these criminals: that has been quite a bill, my lady. I'm afraid it's time to accept your fate.'

I squeeze his thin fingers with mine and whisper back, 'Tell my husband that I want to offer my guard a bribe to help me escape.'


Mr Dalhousie never stays long. Long enough, I'm sure, to be able to recount the daily details of my fragile state to his fellow advocates in the taverns. Or to tell Mother and Johanna, 'She is bearing up courageously. Her headstrong nature has its advantages.'

When I am alone again, I feel my breathing coming back to something close to normal. My mind wills Mr Dalhousie to get to my husband's front door as soon as he can; pushes him past the glovers and the hatters in the Luckenbooths and into a hackney coach.

All I can do now is wait.

I hear the high street getting busier now: the late-afternoon rush through the horse shit and the bird shit and the human shit to the apothecaries and wigmakers, before it gives itself over to the evening whorehouse trade. The oyster bars and the coffee houses will be steaming with gossip, the gentlemen and guild brethren poring over the broadsides, picking them up at a penny a time: *what's the scandal?* And choking on the court reports printed in all their glorious detail.

*Mrs Christian Nimmo DENIES murdering Lord James Forrester, the man who was her lover and also her uncle!*

Who would have thought? The merchant Nimmo's wife. With Lord Forrester – shame on them both. Shame on the family. And guilty. Yes, just this morning, did you not see the scuffle? Those constables looked bitten and kicked to bits.

*O God, have mercy on her soul.*

Gossip runs through Edinburgh like its fleet-footed urchins. It starts in the coffee-house broadsides. Then rumours weave up the narrow closes to the firesides and bedchambers and out into the countryside and its grand homes. To parlours; across backgammon boards; and into the bottom of teacups.

But gossip, like urchins, steals valuables as it goes. Treasures like the truth and reputations.

I close my eyes and remember who I am, for they cannot take that from me. I hold my story fast, reaching backwards to remember when things started. I think it was an autumn day in Roseburn, a year ago. Hardly any time at all.

## *THE CALEDONIA BROADSIDE*

### EDINBURGH, 26th September

### PROCEEDINGS OF THE TRIAL OF MRS CHRISTIAN NIMMO BEFORE SHERIFF JOHN MACDONALD

The sole witness, Miss Violet Blyth, maid to the murder victim Lord James Forrester: 'I saw it clear as day, sir. Because I was right there, sir. It all happened under the sycamore tree at the bottom of the castle avenue. It was her, sir.'

(Here the witness points to the Pannell, Mrs Nimmo.)

'No, I hadn't taken any drink, sir, hardly a drop in my life and just sweetmeats that day. Well, candied cherries, if I recall, sir.

'Oh, they shouted, sir. I told the constables, sir. She ran his sword right through him. She might be a lady, but she can certainly fight like a man.

'Yes, you can, my lady. There's no use you saying it was me who killed him. No one believes that nonsense. I wouldn't know the first thing to do with a sword, sir.'

Mrs Rita Fiddes, an acquaintance of Miss Violet Blyth: 'Oh, Violet knew fine well what to do with a gentleman's sword, if you understand my meaning, sir. She was very experienced in those matters indeed. A very experienced girl.'

(There was sniggering and gasping from the public benches before the case adjourned at four o'clock, as Sheriff MacDonald had an early dinner engagement.)

Chapter Two

# CHRISTIAN

*Roseburn House, near Edinburgh*
*October 1678*

Exercise keeps the thoughts pure, so they say. Each morning, after making sure we ate all our porridge and drank all our milk, Mother sent Johanna and me out for fresh air. We would circle the garden, always in the same direction. Left from the main door, past the box hedges. Down to the woodlands, then up the avenue again. Stop to admire the roses, but never pick the blooms. Don't leave the grounds. Don't go near the stable boys.

It took around forty-five minutes, although Mother called it our exercise hour and would often watch from her window to make sure we did not skip any corners. When we returned, she would insist on being entertained with what we had spotted, taking much greater care to ask me than she ever did Johanna. *Oh, the crows were so fussy at their nest-gathering today*, I would say, or, *Look, conkers!* And she would touch her chin with her perfumed-gloved fingers and nod and say, *Fascinating, Christian*, and smile at us before departing in the carriage for one of her social visits.

It's important to be fascinating. It means you can make an entertaining story out of barely anything at all. And that's vital, if you're to hold a gentleman's attention at a dinner and you do not have the benefit of rosebud lips or golden curls like Johanna.

Which I did not.

And that was why I was spending that autumn morning trudging the grounds again, not-yet-betrothed. Instead, as had been my duty in recent weeks, I was helping my younger sister prepare for her imminent marriage, from the floral wreath she would carry at kirk, to the layout of the afternoon tea-table in her new home.

'And light curtains for the bedroom, or something dark, like navy?' she asked. 'It's just so nerve-racking making all of these decisions.'

'Navy for the bedroom,' I said, swerving a fallen branch on the pathway. We'd had to let some of the groundsmen go, when the money started running out. 'A dark curtain is the most practical; it will stop your chamber upholstery from fading in the sunshine. And for privacy, of course.'

I did not envy my sister her nerve-racking decisions, and I did not envy her for marrying first, although all of Edinburgh were no doubt talking about it, and how her beauty entirely outshone mine. Despite the lyrical love-notes that had passed between her and Robert Gregor these past six months, their marriage was really about his wealth.

'Navy indeed.' Johanna gave the prettiest of nods.

We had wandered to the north corner. The trees hid it from Mother's view, which meant it ran wild. Thistles rioted across the borders, and brambles clambered up the walls. I have always preferred this part of the garden for, like me, it always seemed to want to escape. Roseburn House was the grandest home for miles, its chimneys and attic rooms towering over the Water of Leith and the wives washing their sheets and their feet in its dark rush. The lintel on our doorway had a carving that read 'Hope Lies Within', and that was never truer than on the days I spent at my window, following the river with my gaze.

Now we were hidden, I knew what Johanna would ask.

'Did you bring the book again?'

I had. A small, thin book with a burgundy cover and fine black print: *Instructions on the Benefits of Marriage*. Right on the top shelf of the library, where the most interesting books were kept. The ones we were not supposed to read. Her cheeks were already pinking up nicely. It was too easy to get Johanna to blush.

'Nothing dreadful this time, Christian,' she whispered.

I opened it at the part I'd found the night before and had read by flickering candlelight in bed, my eyes growing wide at the illustrations:

*'A husband should creep in, little by little, and tempt his wife with kisses and gentleness and wanton words before he attempts to put his hands on her secret parts. And when he does this, she should submit.'*

'Oh, Christian.' She shuddered, all her talk of navy curtains quite abandoned now.

'Oh, Johanna,' I whispered. 'Robert Gregor will be doing this to you soon. Look at this illustration; you can see how you'll be expected to lie for him when you submit.'

'Please no more,' she said, refusing to look at the open page.

'Oh, but we must,' I said. I still couldn't take my eyes off it. How long must a lady lie there like that? He would see everything! Would it hurt? 'Otherwise you'll not learn how to be a proper wife.'

'Of course I will be a proper wife,' Johanna hissed. 'I have met Mr Gregor a dozen times and he has grown more and more enamoured of me. It is you who should be worried. You are almost eighteen, with absolutely no sign of a suitor yet.'

Well, that was enough to silence me. I would poke her in the ribs for that, but she was right. The elder sister should always go first. But who would have me? Mr Gregor was so rich he was undeterred by our money problems and was paying for every stitch of those curtains and the teacups, and more besides. Mother called Johanna *bonnie lass* and fussed when she came downstairs, all gleaming and hairpinned. Robert had persuaded Mother to give him Johanna's hand over two of the Hardie brothers, and there were even whispers about London gentlemen being interested. Not yet sixteen and her life assured.

But not with me. I imagine the word they used to describe me, behind my back, would be *plain*. Eyes the muddy grey of the Nor Loch fog. Hair that escaped from ribbons. For social calls Mother gave me her pearls, to brighten my complexion. *Such a shame that no one has proposed to poor Lady Christian yet, for she is fascinating in company and is a wonderful hand at painting and embroidery. Perhaps once Johanna is out of the way.*

But even when Johanna was married next month, I would still be the same girl who secretly hated dancing and dreamed of travelling the world. Although I read avidly and wrote with flair, far exceeding the direction of the tutor who came to Roseburn, these assets were not considered to be as attractive as obedience or serenity or silence. In short, although Mother and Johanna would have publicly denied it, none of my strongest qualities were desirable in an Edinburgh lady.

I had been pushed towards eligible young men all over town

and, for my part, found none of them dazzling enough to keep me fascinated, for there was nothing duller than watching men drink whisky and brag about how smoothly their fathers' new carriages could go, or slur about the great architecture they'd seen on journeys to Glasgow or London – places I would never be allowed to visit. And nothing more intrusive than having them eye me up and down. On these occasions I made it clear I was bored, by stifling yawns and letting my eyes wander the room, and breathed a sigh of relief when there was no follow-up invitation the next day.

Father, when he was in his best health, would sometimes regard Mother with a look of sheer love. Not at her pearls or puffed sleeves or hairpieces, but at Mother herself, as though he would do anything to please her, and it was that kind of affection I wished for myself, even though that felt so daring I would not utter it out loud to anyone, not even to Johanna.

And now she was marching ahead, as usual.

'Come on, Christian. I can't be doing with you dragging yourself this morning. I have letters to write. And don't pick the rosehips. You know the rules.'

I watched her stride away, the frills of her dress bouncing over her heels. How confident she looked, despite her fears about her wedding night. How would I feel on mine, should it ever come? Would I lie like that? What if I didn't want to? I tucked the book back into the pocket under my petticoats.

When we returned to the house, there was an unfamiliar coach in the driveway, a great luxurious thing, enclosed with glass, and Mother was waiting for us at the foot of the stairs, all jittery.

'Come inside, the haberdashery merchant is here with his

suggestions for your new home, Johanna,' she called. Then she took me by the wrist, squeezing it so hard it pinched. Before I could say, 'Ouch, Mother!' she warned me, 'He has come in person, so we are very honoured. The renowned Mr Andrew Nimmo, who has the most sumptuous samples with him, and an entertaining tale of a recent trip to Calais and back on a ship. You will find it charming, Christian. Freshen yourself up.'

Another gentleman with tall tales. But what else was Mother to do? You can tell everything about a family's wealth by the way the lady of the home conducts herself. In society, is she talking of her new glasshouse and parading an Italian gown? Or is she discreetly enquiring about the marital status of the male guests, from behind the feathers of her drooping fan?

My mother, Lady Hamilton of Roseburn, was the latter. Father, two years deceased, had let the family's wealth slip at the gaming tables. When he died, his title went to his younger brother, but when all the money problems came out, we were pitied and given permission to remain at Roseburn. Mother lacked money, but she knew everyone in Edinburgh.

My wrist was still pink. Andrew Nimmo must be a rich bachelor. How tedious. I had wanted to get on with my painting. I knew Johanna had said not to pick the rosehips, but how else could I get an accurate study? They fitted perfectly into the pocket under my petticoat, beside the marriage manual. I slipped everything into my desk drawer before going downstairs.

Mr Nimmo was seated in the parlour with Mother and Johanna, a hint of fading on the top of his head. I could not help but suspect a bald patch was coming and he was too drab to consider a wig. He leapt up as soon as I entered, his assistant scurrying around the room, placing fabric swatches in elaborate arrangements, like peacock tails.

And what he lacked in hair, Mr Nimmo made up for in stature and broadness of shoulder. His suit fitted him perfectly and was matched with a gold-embroidered waistcoat. He had sharp blue eyes and even sharper manners as he bowed and helped me to my seat. And, oh, the samples! They were already spread out across the table: swatches of crimson silk and light ripples of chiffon and swathes of deep, rich velvet. They hung from the edges of chairs. They even had a scent of spice. Tea was served by Fiona, the only housemaid we could keep, on the walnut table by the window, but no one paid attention and, instead, we stared at the displays.

'The trading in London and overseas is good,' he said. 'They are keen for our wool. The ladies of Edinburgh are falling over themselves for these materials, and we all know how demanding they are. Let me advise you on the choices the most fashionable families are making, for your upcoming marriage, Lady Johanna.'

I knew none of it was for me, but I couldn't help myself. I stood and made my way around the room. I traced my fingers over the soft swatches. The velvet ran from rabbit-fur smooth to prickly on the turn of its grain. My fingertips itched. The chiffon was stiff with dye, the silks regal and rich. They bristled with foreignness.

'I see you are quite an admirer of fine fabrics.' Mr Nimmo was watching me. Mother twitched, not touching her tea. Johanna was oblivious, deep in the folds of a navy swatch. 'These fabrics are from China,' he added.

'China.' As I uttered it, the word felt like a gust of wind in the sails of a ship. 'Have you been there?' I asked.

Mr Nimmo's eyes creased into a smile. He looked most

pleasant when he smiled. He walked over to where I stood and lowered his voice.

'Not quite,' he said. 'But I have had the fortune to sail to Norway and Denmark and have had some thrilling voyages. It is all silver out at sea, and the sky stretches over you. You can gaze into the waves beneath and imagine you are seeing mermaids or whales.'

Well, that was fanciful talk if ever I heard it, and he was only a trader. Still, it sounded far more idyllic than the architecture of London.

'And have you ever seen mermaids, dancing in the waves and luring you to your death?' I asked. I could not help but smile, for this Mr Nimmo looked far too sophisticated ever to fall prey to a mermaid's call.

'I confess I have not,' he whispered. 'But perhaps they are easier company than some of the ladies of Edinburgh.'

I stifled a laugh at that. I couldn't help it.

'And many of the gentlemen too,' I said.

Mr Nimmo looked into my eyes for longer than is polite, until we were interrupted.

'Mr Nimmo, would you advise me on curtain swagging? We don't want to take up your entire day.' Johanna poked at a pile of velvets, scowling at me in a most surly way for a bride-to-be.

'Indeed, Lady Johanna, indeed.' And with that, Mr Nimmo turned his attentions to her, whilst I continued to admire the swatches.

My sister chose fabric that would make handsome navy bedroom curtains and bed hangings to match. As the morning went on, her new home filled, with Mother saying over and over again, 'She must have the *very best*.'

I lingered over a silvery silk so long that Mr Nimmo joined me again.

'So elegant,' I said, running my finger over it. 'I imagine this is the colour of the sea.'

'Indeed,' he agreed. 'You've identified it accurately without ever being in its midst. You have quite an artistic eye.' And then he took the swatch from me, produced his knife and cut off a section.

'A keepsake,' he said, 'for a lady who appreciates the finer things in life.'

After he left, when Mother had overseen Fiona serving us chicken pie and had made sure we did not overindulge on barley pudding, I went upstairs for my rest. I did not look at the marriage manual. That would wait till night-time. Instead I brushed my hair at the mirror, sprinkling the brush with water to tame the stray strands. Afterwards I took out Mr Nimmo's piece of silk and let the slice of sea ripple in my fingers. I thought of fantastical things: wide horizons, deep creatures, starry skies. Was I foolish to think of these things?

I did not know.

I did not even want to speak about it with Mother and Johanna, in case they said Mr Nimmo probably handed out silk swatches to every lady he visited.

Roseburn House, like many grand homes filled with widows and unwed daughters, did not go many days without gentlemen callers.

The following day we received another visitor.

My uncle by marriage, Lord James Forrester, came to see Mother about a particularly delicate business matter that would have had the kirk pews tittle-tattling behind their prayer books, had they caught word of it.

He came just after our exercise hour when I'd read to Johanna:

'*A wife should ensure her husband is satisfied and not refuse him when he approaches her, so that he is not tempted by the lure of wantonness elsewhere, for there is plenty!*'

He arrived in a rush of horses' hooves, stirring up the crows that had settled into their day. Making the wind crack with their wings.

### *THE CALEDONIA BROADSIDE*

EDINBURGH, 29th September

Sheriff John MacDonald: 'Before we commence this morning's hearing, gentlemen, I would like to reassure you all that although I have seen the content of those vulgar ballads on the coffee-shop walls detailing the circumstances of this despicable murder and the relationship between the victim and the accused, I am not in any way prejudiced by them. Not in any way at all.'

# Chapter Three

# CHRISTIAN

*Roseburn House, near Edinburgh*
*October 1678*

James had always been a regular visitor to Roseburn. And since Father's death he had taken to visiting us more and more.

Every time he departed, leaving a scent of cloves from his pomander that would linger for hours, something valuable from the house would follow. One day it was the French tapestry of Adam and Eve from the dining room. Another time, an engraved oak trunk from the hall. They disappeared in coaches that he sent. And then we got the best cuts of meat, for a while. Steak-and-kidney pie. Lamb chops. New dresses. I had worked out what was happening. He was selling our belongings, on Mother's behalf – and taking a commission, I was sure. But I couldn't ask Mother about it. Questions of that nature were not tolerated. And, anyway, we needed the gowns.

I was upstairs, beginning a sketch of the rosehips I'd picked from the garden, when his carriage clattered up the driveway, setting the household into a flurry of doors thrown open and aprons straightened, perfume dabbed and skirts swishing and *Lord James! How wonderful!*

My uncle had that effect on ladies, even the ladies in his own family. Even the servants.

There was no point trying to sketch now. I would be called downstairs soon and my hair always took exactly eight minutes to tame, never mind the fact that my dress was already crumpled. I took a deep breath at the mirror, tucking the loose strands as neatly as I could into my ribbons, and pinching my cheeks to make them look rosy. I would hate for my uncle to see me looking unkempt.

He always stayed to eat, entertaining us with tales of the fairs and fights at Corstorphine, the village three miles west of Roseburn where he was laird, whilst I took small bites and minded my elbows, to seem as composed as possible. He knew himself to be handsome, you could see it in every furrow of his brows and every pout of his lips, but I did not want him to think I was affected by his looks.

We would talk of his wife Lillias, Mother's sister, such a beauty once but latterly mostly bedridden at Corstorphine Castle with some sickness that had spread through her body and made her thin as a pin, and yellow in the eyes.

'But she was once the toast of Edinburgh, do you remember?' he always reminisced to Mother. 'We were such a splendid pair – remember the dances? Her illness is a tragedy.'

Mother would say, 'God bless my dear sister. She is in the best hands, with you at her side.' And he would nod and sip his wine. But there was always something unsettled about my uncle. He had the air of a pressing engagement elsewhere. As if he was a little too important to stay very long. And whenever he glanced at me, I was nervous to pick up my fork or glass, in case he found me somehow lacking in grace.

Sure enough, as I was beginning to admit defeat with my

ribbons, the dining bell rang. I took a deep breath and went downstairs.

He was at the head of the table where Father used to sit, and Mother was being curt with Johanna, saying, 'Hands off the butter until James is served.' Fiona brought sliced leg of mutton, which he tucked into as though he had not eaten in days. Mother eyed every forkful. James eyed the silver candelabra. Johanna spoke at length of the floral arrangements being grown in the garden for her wedding day, but obviously she made no mention of *Instructions on the Benefits of Marriage*.

James found the topic of Johanna's wedding frivolous, I could tell by the way he played with his wine glass, but I didn't want to be caught looking at him, so I focused my gaze on the window, with its view of the avenue.

'Christian,' James said, 'are you not listening to Johanna? She was asking whether you thought there will be enough heather for the altar?'

'Of course,' I said. 'I was just watching the crows outside.'

He grinned. 'Crows, indeed. If you're so taken with birds, you'll be interested to hear we've finished building the dovecote at Corstorphine Castle.'

Well, that set Mother off. 'A dovecote! A wonderful asset that will be,' she said, signalling to Fiona to pour him more wine.

'Indeed.' Lord James nodded. 'Now we'll never go short of pigeon pies or poached pigeon eggs. An abundance. I shall bring some at my next visit, if you would like that. What do you think, Christian? The meat is good for a lady's complexion, I believe – not that you ever need any assistance.'

I felt the dreadful rush of my face flushing. He was only being kind, but Johanna would tease me to death about it later.

'Perhaps Johanna and Mr Gregor could build a dovecote,' I said, hoping that would change the subject.

'Well, the Gregors could certainly afford one,' said James. 'What an excellent match you've made there, my dear niece.'

We all nodded and chewed our mutton. It was dry and needed a sauce. I wondered if James loved Lillias or simply thought her an excellent match.

'The fabric merchant called yesterday, and Johanna was spoiled for choice,' said Mother.

I had thought of Mr Nimmo constantly. I wondered if he would take another voyage soon and whether he was lonely at sea, and whether he was engaged to anyone, which surely Mother would have known. The thoughts rattled. It was most unlike me.

'Johanna will be spoiled for choice for the rest of her days,' observed my uncle. 'But Robert Gregor is the lucky one, for there are no two finer ladies in Scotland than my nieces.'

Johanna and I looked at each other and she rolled her eyes at me. She was so used to compliments. They simply washed over her.

I admit it. I relished mine.


After we had eaten, Mother sent us away so that she and James could continue their discussions. I stood at my easel for several minutes looking at the sketch of the rosehips, which I now hated, and picked up my chalk with renewed determination. I could not control the sale of my family's furniture or stop myself wondering what my uncle was doing. But I could shade and highlight these red fruits, if I concentrated hard enough.

And that is what I did, for thirty minutes or so, until there was a rap at the door.

It was him.

'Dear niece,' he said, striding in and putting his hands on his hips. 'I wonder if you would be so kind as to show me your latest paintings? Your mama tells me your technique is quite improved.'

'Where are Mother and Johanna?' I asked.

'I excused myself momentarily; they are downstairs gathering up some silverware,' he said. 'There is no use in it hanging around your cupboards when it can be sold and keep you all at Roseburn for as long as possible.' He spoke with quite a gentle tone, despite the harshness of his words.

He came further into the room until he was close to me. He made my armpits prickle like the morning heat of the garden. I could feel my hair ribbons tickle my neck and I felt ridiculously girlish.

'Don't you ever bore of this room?' He smiled, with all the privilege of someone who never has to tolerate boredom. 'Does it not make you feel trapped to spend your days here?'

Well, I bored of it every day, but I would never let him know how tedious my life was.

'Quite the opposite,' I said. 'The view of the garden is excellent. Squirrels and deer. And the Water of Leith beyond. Always something changing with the seasons. Blossom or berries or roses or snow.' I was trying to be *fascinating*, but of course Uncle James was so worldly he would find talk of squirrels dull, so I bit my lip to stop myself from rambling further.

After he'd looked at the view, which at that moment unfortunately offered nothing more than the mild-mannered nod of the apple trees, he picked up one of my paintbrushes and fiddled with it. Then he sat down and looked at my sketches. His dark curls shone, and not a hair was out of place. Pomade, I supposed.

'You certainly have improved,' he said, leafing through the drawings as I hovered nervously. 'Some of these are quite sophisticated.' Well, this was the second time in as many days that a gentleman had praised my artistic skills and I was beginning to feel quite the talent, when he put the drawings down.

'Christian,' he said, 'Lillias sketches when she is well enough to sit in her chair. I wonder if you would bring your chalks to Corstorphine Castle. Stay for a day or so and keep your aunt company. We have such superb views of the Pentland Hills. It will be good for you to have a change of scene and get away from all this frivolous wedding talk. It must be getting you down.'

'Oh, we are far too busy with Johanna's wedding plans,' I said immediately.

'Well, afterwards,' he said. 'Lillias would love to have some young company. And you'd enjoy it. You could make a study of the new dovecote. Or the trees. They are magnificent this year, particularly the sycamore at the castle gates.'

My heart pounded. I felt dizzy. A visit to Corstorphine Castle alone, with no one to keep the conversation going but me? How would I ever provide entertaining company on my own? I was so dull and he so worldly. I would simply die of mortification.

'I couldn't leave Mother,' I said. 'And I enjoy my painting room here.'

'A pity,' he said. 'But let me know if you change your mind. You will be lonely when Johanna is gone. I do feel a responsibility, now your father has passed away.'

I said nothing, for talk of Father still sometimes brought tears to my eyes, as grief does, and I did not want that to happen.

'For now, I will leave you to your art,' he said. 'And these wonderful views of your garden.' He glanced at the window, nodded to me and went back downstairs.

I stood in the middle of the room for several minutes, heart still pounding, wondering whether I should have said yes.

When finally he departed, taking some of our silverware with him, I went to my bedroom and opened my top drawer. I couldn't look at the marriage book.

But the furl of silk from Mr Nimmo was there. Pale. Soft. Flawless. I wondered if he believed in mermaids. I wondered if he had thought of me today. I remembered Johanna, bracing herself for a husband chosen by Mother. Mr Nimmo was only a merchant, but he intrigued me more than any of the aristocratic young men I had met. I took out my writing set:

*Dear Mr Nimmo,*

*How kind of you to gift me this fabric at your visit to my home yesterday.*

*I imagine myself sailing on the high seas when I look at it, captain of a ship. Yesterday I took it to the window and the sun shimmered off its surface so brightly I saw the froth of tides!*

*I am curious. Do you have anything the colour of the midnight sky over the Orient?*

*Yours respectfully, and in anticipation,*
*Lady Christian*

*Dear Lady Christian,*

*I found your colourful description of the seas so vivid I*

can hardly believe you have never been on the ocean! I sat sipping my Burgundy wine, reading your poetic line over and over again, and what handsome script!

It was my delight to have met you and I trust the arrangements are going well for your sister's wedding. I have found a swatch of black velvet. They call it Deepest Noir, but I found, when I took it to my window, that there are shimmers of navy and even green in the threads.

I do believe it could be the same shade as the sky over the Orient on a winter's night.

I am passing Roseburn House Tuesday next, as it happens, and will call in with it, unless that is terribly inconvenient. I will also bring a bottle of this wine for your mother. It is too fine a vintage not to share, and I have an entire case gathering dust.

Yours humbly, and in anticipation,
Mr A. Nimmo

# Chapter Four

# CHRISTIAN

*The Tolbooth Jail, Edinburgh*
*October 1679*

And what shade is the sky over the high street of Edinburgh, as the wind whistles down it at seven o'clock on an autumn evening, almost whipping St Giles' chimes away?

If I had composed this night at my easel, it would have been all the pinks and yellows of a girl's oil paintbrushes, but this is no work of my imagination. Tonight is the colour of blood. My own blood thumps through my body to the rhythm of the clangs and thuds outside the Tolbooth as they make sure the Maiden is in working order. They have been doing this all afternoon. Its cranks and weights are lifted and dropped, and each time it happens a roar rises from a restless-sounding crowd. I am sure it is mainly for the show of it, for a sharp, weighted blade is a sharp, weighted blade. A seller has taken a prime spot selling *mutton pies, best mutton pies*. My stomach has congealed with dread, like the top of a best mutton pie. What will it feel like when the blade drops? Will they really do it? Can I drink enough ale to knock me senseless? How long will I remain aware, once my head is severed?

I have been waiting a full day since my plea to my husband via Mr Dalhousie. Time stands still.

And then the scuff of boots on the stairs again, a light scuff. Unfamiliar. My eyes dart in the gloom. I have grown smart as a rat for noises and disturbances.

A face appears at the cell bars. I have not seen this man before. He lights the wall lamp beside him, with a trembling hand. He has a shock of white hair. Dark veins spread in cobwebs across his nose. He closes his eyes when he talks.

'Lady Christian, I have come to pray with you.' His eyelashes flutter on his closed lids. His hands rise to his chin in prayer. His lips part. His anticipation could not be more obvious if he was licking his thin little lips.

I do not speak. He opens his eyes. Grey irises glide down and rest on me, flat and cold as a seagull's wings.

'I am Reverend Raeburn,' he says. 'Join me in prayer.'

The last time I prayed was in summer, in the stone silence of Corstorphine Kirk. The bruises on my shoulders had faded to almost nothing.

'Lord, we pray for the soul of this woman who has received the heaviest sentence under Scotland's laws. We ask that You forgive her deadly sin, and You take her into Your kingdom when she is delivered to You, two days from now.'

His eyes remain closed, eyelashes flickering. I should close my eyes and pray. I should close my eyes and ask God to deliver me from this fate, but my eyes are stuck open, my throat is sealed shut. My hands are frozen to my sides. I cannot even perform the motions of prayer.

Reverend Raeburn's breath whistles down his nose. When his eyes reopen, the movement startles me. We regard each other.

'I shall return in the morning, after my kirk service,' he says. 'You will be in my prayers. The Lord is with you tonight.'

I do not feel Him. I do not think I ever have. Johanna would say He is everywhere. In the snowy blossoms of Roseburn and in the hues of a February rainbow. But Johanna did not know about the darkness that could fall sometimes, that could cast shadows over our childhood home, leaving no room for blossoms or rainbows or God.

As Reverend Raeburn gathers himself, I hear another set of footsteps on the stairs. My advocate Mr Dalhousie and the reverend greet each other in the shadows, in a whirl of cloaks and hats and awkward nods. The reverend disappears and I am left with Mr Dalhousie. He is Saturday-evening ruddy. He has the air of roast beef and rich sauce. Of red wine and pipe smoke and a win at cards. I remember Andrew like that. His pleasures always came from the finer things in life. I remember the way I would touch my forearms and elbows in the evenings as we sat opposite each other in the candlelight, watching him ignore me, the bittersweet feel of my fingertips on my skin where his ought to be.

'Good news,' he says. 'Very good news.'

I catch my heart before it soars. Mr Dalhousie has so far failed to deliver anything good.

'I have arrived this evening with payment for the guard. Your husband has arranged your safe passage. Your instructions are here.' He passes me a slip of parchment. 'You are to head directly south to the English border and go nowhere near Leith Port. That is the first place they'll look. When the constables call on Mr Nimmo, he'll say he's no idea where you are, but the only place you might flee would be on a ship. He will show them your paintings of Italy.'

The parchment is thin and curled tightly in my palm. I imagine my husband hunched over his desk, scratching his instructions carefully onto it. Mr Dalhousie sniffs. He will be wanting to get back to his alehouse or his wife. Perhaps he has daughters, and he has been going home from my trial each night, telling them cautionary tales.

'The guard will let you out in an hour or so,' he says. 'You are fortunate to have married Mr Nimmo. He wishes that you survive, despite everything.'

And with that, he slips back into the Edinburgh night. The commotion at the Maiden has subsided. There are no more *good mutton pies*. I did not doubt Andrew would help me. He knows, deep down, that were it not for him, I would not be here in this jail.

I wait again with a half-soared heart. An hour or so is an eternal night when you are waiting to see if a guard fancies making good on a bribe and letting you free.

Eventually he unlocks the door, a scrape so metallic I can taste it.

This time he does not stand in his menacing way, but strides straight into the cell.

'My advocate has made payment.' I step back towards the wall, though it is of little use to cower in the corner.

'That part of the deal is settled,' he says. In his hands is a bundle of clothes. He dumps them down on the hay bale. 'You will put these clothes on and disguise yourself as a man.'

He does not make to leave. Instead he watches me as I reach for the bundle.

'But first I'll need a decent goodbye,' he says, 'so I forget to check on you till morning.'

I knew it would come to this.

Slowly, he loosens his breeches.

If I can get it done with quick, he won't have the time to try much more than grope at me. I walk the three steps to him. I take him in my hand. He shivers with the horror and the thrill of it.

His beard scratches my ear as he whispers insults at me. *Whore. Murderess.* I have heard them all before, but not in such filthy proximity. I bite my lip so hard I taste my blood. 'Whore,' he says again.

I whisper back to him, 'Aye, sir, that I am.' It works. *I am nearly out.*

Afterwards, he fumbles over his breeches far longer than it took him to untie them, but what can I do but put on the men's clothes he has brought and hope he does not want anything more? A plain coat. Breeches that scratch my legs. A black ribbon for my hair. Finest velvet. Oh, Andrew. *I am nearly out.* The guard turns his back. I follow him down the steps into a corridor I have not seen before. We spiral through the jail until it spits me out into a courtyard. I think he will call me a whore again, but instead he looks me up and down as though he owns me, before he shuts the door in my face. *I am out.*

I want to bolt, but I can't. I have never been more relieved to set foot in these miserable streets, with tenements leaning towards one another, looking braced for battle. The closes are in shadow, and I turn down to the Grassmarket, then on to Greyfriars Kirk. I am walking faster than an innocent man ought, and lighter on my feet too, and it's fortunate that everything is quiet, save for those too drunk or useless to realize. At the kirk a man is waiting with a horse, as Andrew's letter had said, and I mount it, despite losing my footing twice because my legs tremble after these weeks in captivity. I sit astride it, a position I have not taken since I was a child learning to ride, but I cannot be seen sitting side-saddle. The man disappears back into the shadows. I take the south road, leaving the jail behind me. Leaving the trial behind me and the witness account of that bitch Violet Blyth, deceitful as her own paste jewels.

I can still taste the metal bars of the Tolbooth Jail.

I can still see James on the ground, bathed in his own blood. Violet holding his sword and gasping.

## *THE CALEDONIA BROADSIDE*

### EDINBURGH, 29th September

David Wilson, High Constable of Edinburgh: 'We found the deceased in a most grisly state, Your Honour. Stabbed with some almighty force. One of my men near fainted. Oh, I'll never forget the way the blood was spreading across the ground. Thick and oozing, it was. As though he'd been attacked by an animal. I can hardly believe that degree of violence could have been the work of such a delicate young woman as Lady Christian.'

## Chapter Five

# CHRISTIAN

*Roseburn House, near Edinburgh*
*October 1678*

For Andrew Nimmo's visit, Mother suggested I wear a white dress of Johanna's, cut low at the front. I agreed. She wore her wig with the high topknot from Mr Adam Scott's emporium.

He brought the black velvet swatch, *Deepest Noir*, and as Mother busied herself bossing Fiona, about the way she had set out the cups, he beckoned me to the window. I was quite exposed in the light, and he looked everywhere but at my décolletage and I was glad of that, because it had become quite goose-pimpled, which I am sure was unbecoming.

He cleared his throat and held the swatch to the light.

'This is from Italy, of course. The craftsmanship is exquisite. But what do you see?' he said.

I was not sure what to say, realizing that there was most probably a right answer and a wrong answer to this question. I studied the swatch and fiddled with my hair, which Mother always said was the sign of a nincompoop, and hated myself, but could not stop.

I would never, ever be the perfect Edinburgh lady.

'Go on,' he said, 'you are not really looking at it, you are too busy fussing over your ribbons, which are perfect, I assure you.' He smiled. My stomach did something of a jump and I wanted to reach for my hair again, but of course I did not dare, so I put my hands behind me. I examined the material again. And then I saw it. Shimmering on the fibres in the afternoon light was a green like the algae on the pond in our woodlands, and there was also a sheen of blue. I looked at Mr Nimmo.

Blue like Mr Nimmo's eyes.

'It is captivating, Mr Nimmo,' I said. 'I can see turquoise hues.'

'Indeed!' he answered, quickly. 'This shade is utterly daring, and it will be on all the ladies next season, and some of them will suit it and some won't. But it matches your skin perfectly. I will see to it that you are given a bolt. And do, please, call me Andrew.'

He was charming at dinner, declaring the roast chicken as good as any he had eaten, which I am sure could not possibly be true, what with him having dined with the noblemen of France and Italy. He confided that most foreign ports were not worth the trip, for they were crammed with thieves. Then he asked me about my painting and my embroidery and how often we all dared visit town, for despite its wonderful dressmakers, Edinburgh was not a place where ladies dared tread unchaperoned.

'But I do wish, sometimes, that we ladies could wander freely in town without a guardian,' I said. 'Just as some do on horseback around the countryside, so long as they do not stray too far from their homes.' Mother stiffened and Johanna shot me a warning glance, for they disapproved of declarations like this. Andrew looked intrigued.

'You are right,' he said earnestly. 'It is not fashionable to say so, but sometimes I do sympathize with the limitations placed on the fairer sex.'

'And until we ladies are able to wander free, the thought of foreign ports remains merely a dream,' I said.

Mother clutched at her ringlets so hard I feared she would set her wig askew.

But Andrew beamed.

'Dear Christian,' he said, 'you are both insightful and wistful, and these are intriguing traits.'

*Dear Christian!* My heart swelled in my chest. The looks on Mother and Johanna's faces! And when Fiona brought the apple pie, I could barely eat it, even though it is my favourite.

I did not feel the urge to yawn or let my eyes wander the room once. We learned all there is to know about Andrew, which is not much, he said, modestly. A fabric merchant, son of a fabric merchant, with both parents deceased.

But Mother had thoroughly researched him, and we already knew that, as well as the fact that he had recently built the splendid Carrick House on the outskirts of Corstorphine, which would have cost a fortune, and even had a glasshouse, Mother said.

I think Andrew would have stayed the week if Mother had not tipped him out after the last of the Burgundy, saying, 'Forgive us, the girls need their beauty sleep, but we must have you again.'

'He well admires you,' said Johanna as soon as the door was shut and Andrew's carriage was retreating from Roseburn's gates. 'Despite having his pick of ladies.'

'Johanna, that is unnecessary,' warned Mother. 'Christian is highly accomplished and held herself remarkably well in his company, despite her views.'

'I am sure he was just being polite,' I said, running my fingers over the *Deepest Noir*.

'He is entirely smitten, and so are you,' said Mother, grasping it from me and poring over it. 'This is excellent quality. Do not be at all surprised if we are not invited to tea with him by the end of tomorrow.'

And we were. To Carrick House itself, which was as grand as its reputation, with acres of land. 'I should have built something nearer Leith Port, but I prefer these woodlands, and I am too fussy for my own good,' Andrew said, showing us the dense oaks and the view of Tyler's Acre. And then there were teas at his, with rose biscuits from France; and teas at ours, with Fiona's gingerbread, until tea was coming out of our ears; and gifts sent.

First, hair bows: 'No fiddling, Lady Christian, these are Italian silk!' And then larger gifts. A silver locket to wear at Johanna's wedding. Swagging for the parlour. 'Remnants, clogging up the storeroom,' he'd said, and Mother wrote back, 'I cannot possibly accept' whilst directing Fiona, who was pinning them up.

It was like a dream. I could not stop thinking about him.

'You would not be poor, as Andrew Nimmo's wife,' Johanna said, admiring the new parlour swagging.

I would be blissfully happy too. Or so I believed.

Johanna and I took our last walk on the morning of her November wedding, when the heather had been stripped for the kirk.

'Let me read from the marriage manual one last time,' I said. I conjured the book from my petticoats. I could hide anything there.

'*Relations between husband and wife should be frequent although not too vigorous and take place around one or two times each week.*

'*On entering marriage, a woman should expect that her husband will be enthusiastic, and she shall spend the first months providing as much encouragement as he requires, for that is part of the role of being a wife and is as important an element of household duties as overseeing staff and meals.*'

I stopped because Johanna was getting quite flushed. It suited her. She would be such a bonnie bride.

'Sister, this is terrifying,' she said.

But when it came to it, Johanna glided down the aisle of St Giles' as though she had never read a vulgar word in her life. I was in her wake, as I had always been, in a modest white gown trimmed with lace that paled beside her rippling silk skirts, both of us in embroidered velvet capes. Andrew, who occupied a pew at the back, caught my eyes and beamed at me.

And so did my Uncle James, second from front and quite apparent by his scarlet cloak, and, if it is not boastful to say so, I felt more beautiful in those minutes, having two men openly admire me, than I had ever felt in my life.

Outside, on the freezing high street, the carriages lined up and caused a commotion, and beggars swarmed for coins. I lost Mother in the sea of guests and grew nervous. Edinburgh has a darkness, even in broad daylight. Despite the biting weather, young women stood in bright, revealing silks, dazzling as gems, with rouge smeared across their cheeks and elaborate bows in their ringlets; and I knew what sort of women they were, for the marriage manual had said that the act of intimacy was something occasionally purchased, *as one might purchase a fine-looking dinner of pork chops at an alehouse. But that is a dangerous transaction, for you know not who has prepared those pork chops or sampled them before you.*

James found me before I could see Andrew. He looked splendid in that cloak, and I suspected he knew it.

'White suits you,' he said. 'You are changed since we last met, and I can't quite put my finger on it.'

'It must be all the painting,' I said, blushing with embarrassment, and I was about to excuse myself, but Andrew found me and said, 'Lady Christian, I am delighted to see you wearing the locket.'

The two men nodded to each other. Andrew smiled. James did not.

'Have you gentlemen met?' I asked, although I could not imagine them having anything in common.

'Indeed, I supply Lady Forrester with her shawls,' said Andrew. 'How is her health?'

'As well as can be expected, given all that ails her,' said Lord James. His face clouded, as it always did when he talked of his wife, but he was also eyeing my locket. My throat constricted and I swallowed. I could not help it and I hoped he did not think me unsettled in his presence, because I was most certainly and absolutely not.

'And are you also supplying my niece?' he asked, looking at my throat. 'I was not aware she was in a position to buy expensive trinkets.'

'Mr Nimmo gave me this locket as a gift,' I said.

Andrew nodded confidently. Lord James sniffed. There was a catch in my voice, and it sounded as though I was nervous.

'How generous, Mr Nimmo,' he said.

'Lady Christian deserves nothing but the best,' said Andrew.

Both men squared their shoulders. I racked my brains for something sensible to say, but fortunately Andrew was accosted by friends of the Gregors, who had decided to use the occasion of my sister's wedding to bother him about a delayed shipment. He excused himself, and I thought he must spend so much time appeasing the fur-trimmed ladies of Edinburgh who have nothing better to do than look magnificent; he wasn't simply well travelled and handsome, he was also quite the most patient man.

'How generous of Mr Nimmo,' repeated Lord James when Andrew's back was turned. 'Did he supply the dress fabric as well? I only ask because he cannot take his eyes off you.'

'I hadn't noticed. Mr Nimmo is a perfect gentleman,' I said.

'I have noticed. He is taken with you. Do we have a suitor on our hands?'

This was excruciating. His eyes kept flickering up and down my body in a way Andrew's certainly would not have done. It was unsettling. I was not sure whether ladies were supposed to feel so affected by such stares. He bent conspiratorially low.

'He is an excellent prospect. But you would think,' he whispered, 'that with all his trading connections in the fabric world, Mr Nimmo might have obtained a wig by now. It is very unfashionable to be balding. The way his hat-brim is pinned up at the side reveals far too much.'

'I had hardly noticed,' I said. 'Mr Nimmo is simply not as vain as other men.'

It was true. He was not like James, pomaded and preening, although James's hair was thick and lustrous under his hat, and showed no signs of falling out or even going grey.

And Andrew was well travelled.

I should not be comparing them.

'I only want what's best for you, Christian,' my uncle insisted. 'And the offer of a trip to Corstorphine Castle still stands. Why won't you come?'

'I haven't the time,' I said. 'I have been busy with Mr Nimmo.'

My uncle looked most put out.

'Excuse me,' I added. 'I must make sure Mother is not getting too tired.'

'But first,' he said, regaining his composure, 'you must allow me to give you something. Your sister is getting all the attention today, but I haven't forgotten you.'

He produced a parcel from his cloak.

'As soon as I saw this, I thought of you. As Mr Nimmo says, you deserve nothing but the best.'

What could I do? Mother was shuffling towards us in a ripple of cream feathers and flounces and frills. She should stop dressing with the curtains half closed in her bedchamber, I thought. The light in that room overly flatters. Whatever was Andrew thinking of her? I would need to speak to Fiona.

I tucked the parcel into my purse. James's eyes did not leave mine.

'My dear brother-in-law,' cooed Mother, putting her arms around James and kissing him on his cheek. 'You are resplendent in that red cloak.'

'Congratulations on such a magnificent wedding,' my uncle replied.

'And we are hoping,' said Mother, puffing her feathers around her as a hen might after laying a particularly decent egg, 'that there may be another wedding in the not-too-distant future. We have been keeping company with the esteemed Andrew Nimmo, no less.'

'So I have been hearing. Well, that would be a magnificent match,' he said, looking most unamused.

My chest filled with satisfaction. I knew pride to be a sin, but there was such pleasure in seeing people's reactions.

'Ladies, excuse me.' His air of having better things to do was back. We let him drift away, although he did not seem to join any of the little groups, but rather stood near the edge of the roadside and regarded the comings and goings of the town. How lonely my uncle looked. I felt a little sorry for him.

I fought the urge to wonder what was in the parcel all the way through bidding everyone farewell and getting settled in the carriage with Mother, and the two of us coming home without Johanna for the first time. The stairs of Roseburn were bare and echoey without the murmur of my sister's laughter and her sweet, rosewater scent. I would be next, I hoped. After Mother had been tucked up with a cup of hot chocolate and I was finally alone, I opened the parcel.

It was the most beautiful silver hair comb, set with pearls.

## THE CALEDONIA BROADSIDE

### EDINBURGH, 30th September

Lady May Hamilton, mother of the accused: 'My late husband was a great collector of books, and of course our library is extensive, but I have no recollection of this so-called "marriage instruction manual" your constables claim to have found in my daughter's bedside drawers. I simply have never seen it before. I object in the *strongest* terms to being questioned on such a *vulgar* matter. A man knows what to do in the marriage bed and there is no need for any woman, my daughter included, to be seeking an education in the matter. Lady Christian would simply not have had such a notion. And the chaos they left her chamber in was *an abomination.*'

Mr Harold Dalhousie, advocate representing the accused: 'Despite his high standing in society, it was a well-known fact that Lord James Forrester had certain habits that took him directly into the company of some of Edinburgh's most undesirable characters. People of the loosest morals.'

# Chapter Six

# VIOLET

*Mrs Fiddes's House of Pleasure, Bell's Close, Edinburgh*
*November 1678*

Beauties of all shapes and sizes. Pleasures to suit every taste. And as long as you keep your head down and your arse up, you've a roof over your head. Just remember to stay in Mrs Fiddes's good books. And she takes a daily note, I can tell you. Now come, let me pour you a whisky and I'll tell you a tale that's taller than these high tenements, and quite as reeky and debauched.

Once I was merely a morsel in rags, sitting with these hands outstretched at the foot of this very close and waiting for the rattling cough that took the rest of them. Thinking, *Any day now and that'll be me a goner*. Sit all day, I would, in the freezing fug that comes seeping up the closes from the Nor Loch, bringing the stink of the flesh of its drowned witches. And then, by chance! The beefiest wifey you'd ever seen rolled by, stately as a coach. And she stopped and bent down with a wheeze that rasped so deep I thought it would be her last and then we would have a calamity.

But instead of keeling over dead, she gripped my face and said, 'Poor wee lamb!' Close enough to see the individual black bristles on her chin. And then, peering into my eyes as if she were inspecting my soul, she opened her mouth again, teeth rotting to the gums, and said, 'Sitting on the street'll get you murdered, girl. I'm Rita Fiddes and I'd like to be a friend, if you'd allow.'

Well, what else could I say? Ma and Da and my baby sister all gone. That's right. And so long ago their faces have clouded over, making it hard to remember them. Already the bairn is barely there, just a whisper of milk and a wet mouth, sucking away at Ma whilst she whispered, *Princess, princess*.

So, with Edinburgh Castle glowering down at me, a whore I did become. One day off a week, to spend my coins at the oyster bars or the confectioner. Or wandering the narrow lane, admiring the silks and stockings for sale in the Luckenbooths. Mrs Fiddes dresses me in frocks in every shade from emerald green to shimmering rose from Miss Marigold's Emporium. And a maid who does the laundry and the gardyloo, so I never have to chuck my own shit out of the window. What a glorious life! Luckier than most round here.

Excuse me if I blether. Some of them like a bit of chatter. Some of them not so much. Mr Rathen. He calls on Sundays after kirk. He likes it a bit too much, if you ask me. *Tell me what you were up to last night, ye bad wee lassie, and don't spare the details*. He hates the touch of flesh and prefers to sit and pleasure himself, listening to me tell him about whoever-it-was givin' it laldy and saying, *Did you like that, did you, lassie? Bet you loved it, dirty wee bitch*, and gawping away, slavering like a dog at meat scraps.

But most of them just want you to shut your mouth and open your legs and, aye, I'll do that, so long as I can think my nice thoughts of one day having a grand home and a warm fireplace. Servants all around. I even help out in the kitchen sometimes. I can pull a hen's neck, pluck and gut it in the time it takes our rotten old cook to find the carving knife. No fear of blood with me. But Mrs Fiddes won't get rid of her stinking cook. And there she is now, Mrs Fiddes, that same wifey who saved me from the streets but made me pay the price with my flesh. Watch how magnificently she hands out the sweetmeats and tobacco. White-wigged and so plump she barely needs those padded rolls under her skirts. One of the grandest dames in all of Edinburgh town. God bless her.

Well, my story starts one cold autumn afternoon, as the sun is bouncing off the crown spire of St Giles'. Opposite, taking up the entire top floor at Bell's Close, Mrs Fiddes's Pleasure House is the closest thing to heaven that many will get. The kitchen fires in the tenements below have made the parlour stifling, and the reek from the poultry market rises up to greet us.

One of the girls by the name of Ginger is playing the piano in the corner, her wee freckled face shiny in the glare of the window, and her thin fingers splayed carefully across the keys, as instructed by Mrs Fiddes. Oh, Ginger is squeaking out some of Mr John Dowland's finest songs as the gentlemen begin to arrive for the start of the day's trade and take their pick. From all corners they come, from Parliament House and the Incorporation of Surgeons and Barbers. From the alehouses and the flesh market. Each man an equal under Mrs Fiddes's roof, so long as he has a shiny coin in his purse and a stiff prick in his breeches.

Some of the girls are whisked off quick, but I'm often the last book on the shelf, so to speak, down to me being a bit long in the chin. Even Ginger sometimes gets picked before me, leaving me sitting until the late crowd arrives, and Mrs Fiddes bustles them in and pours them a whisky and hoots, *Violet is sleekit and agile and extremely eager to please.*

So that is why Mrs Fiddes often sends me out for her afternoon treat. A sugar cake here, a lump of cheese there. Whatever takes her fancy, and today I am shooed down the stairs for a bottle of Mr Saltoun's damson wine, which she takes to cure her creaky knees. Well, just as I make my way back from the grocer with the tonic, I am distracted by the gaudiest crowd spilling out of St Giles', grasping their fur coats and their feather hats, lest they be tugged by the wind or the beggars. That will be a wedding or a christening of the upper-most, and well worth hanging about for, in case they chuck coins at us as they depart.

As they chatter and look nervously for their coaches, one of them detaches from the crowd and paces up and down, looking most dejected. He is a very well-turned-out gent, too, all ruffles and bows and wearing the most conspicuous red cloak. A more handsome devil I have rarely seen, so there I stand, trying to look ladylike and impoverished at the same time, which is always the trick with these sorts. Lucky I am fairly conspicuous myself, in a pink silk gown with red frills at the bosom that catch this gent's attention, and I am hoping he will throw a coin for me, for he stares long enough, quite ignoring the hustle of horses and carts and the wifies queuing at the water fountain.

I venture my coyest of smiles.

He nods his head in return.

I wait, hoping to see a purse produced from under that cloak, for there is nothing luckier at a wedding than throwing a coin or two. I smile again, bobbing my head low.

No purse. Just the lewdest of grins until the bride and groom emerge from the crowd and jump into a grand black coach.

Well, I can't stand here all day and smile for free, and no sign of coins from any of the rest of the congregation, who are dispersing now and ignoring us poor buggers. Some of the gentry is like that, and may God have mercy on them for their selfishness. Glancing over my shoulder with a wink to the gent, I make my way back to Bell's Close.

'Nearly half an hour for a bottle of plum tonic,' mutters Mrs Fiddes when I find her in the parlour, snatching the drink from me and pulling out the stopper with gusto. 'You are lucky no gents arrived in your absence.'

There is no point arguing with Mrs Fiddes when she gets like this. After the first glass she will have mellowed, so I take to the couch and try not to scratch at my nits or get weepy again about Ma and Da and the bairn, whilst the beds rattle with delights all up the corridor.

I can feel I am about to go into one of my depressive moods when the door knocker goes and, moments later, in comes that very same gent. He bows so deeply at the door he could oil the floor with the grease off his hair pomade, and he clutches a great silver pomander to his nose as his whisky is brought.

I would say I was surprised to see him, but truth be told, I dawdled back to Bell's Close on the chance this gent might follow, for if he has as much coin as that lavish cloak suggests, he will be a worthwhile customer.

'You'll have no need for perfume in here, sir. My girls are clean and wash with rosewater between each caller,' Mrs Fiddes assures him, setting his drink and a saucer of prunes on the table next to the armchair and sweeping his hat onto the stand. 'And a physician visits monthly and checks them over himself, prescribing any vapour baths or ointments as is needed. We are the most modern establishment in Edinburgh. And the cleanest.'

'That is reassuring,' he says, looking at me. 'Just a shame about the poor devils begging outside in the high street.'

'Poor devils indeed, and we consider ourselves most fortunate, don't we, Violet, that we live so well,' says Mrs Fiddes. 'Violet here is one of our more experienced girls. And there is also Ginger in the corner, if you like a younger beauty.'

Well, this gent has no eyes for our young pianist, of course. It is me he has come for, which he makes clear with a nod in my direction.

And Mrs Fiddes says, 'As you can see, Violet here is sleekit and agile. And she is extremely eager to please.'

'And free of any pox?' asks the man, raising a dark eyebrow at me.

'Clean as a babe,' says Mrs Fiddes.

'And what age?' asks the man, narrowing his eyes as though he already disbelieves the answer.

'Nineteen, sir,' I whisper.

'Hmm. That seems about right,' he says. 'I will take her.' Then he drinks his whisky in one big swallow and bangs his cup down on the table. Well, that is a warning, because sorts like that can get rough.

'Violet, take the man to your chamber,' says Mrs Fiddes, rising to stoke the fire as it has fair died down and she hates the chill. And she hisses in my ear, 'This one here is gentry. Show him every trick in the book.'

'No,' says the man. 'I will take her home with me. I will take her off your hands for the month. Now what is her price?'

Well! I go suddenly cold, for that is not something I have done before. And it stops Ginger in her tracks, halfway through 'Fine Knacks for Ladies'. But Mrs Fiddes pays no heed, because now this chap is dangling a purse. Black velvet it is, with a long rope cord. I knew he had one.

'Oh, I have never released one of my girls for a longer period,' she says, all eyes on the purse as Ginger boggles away at me in the corner, her wee hands hovering over the keys as if wondering whether she should resume. 'I would say this is a most unorthodox offer, sir. And Violet here often helps out in our kitchen too.'

'There are ten pounds Scots in this purse. You can count it,' he says. And Mrs Fiddes bloody fuckin' does! Tips it into her meaty hands. Ginger's face is a big 'Oh' and now I start to shake, because surely not; because how would this happen, and what about tomorrow, and who will go for Mrs Fiddes's afternoon treat? The damson wine or the tobacco or the whatsits from the confectioner's — funny name, can never remember it.

'But I can make twenty pounds Scots from Violet in a good month,' says Mrs Fiddes.

Twenty! I had never even thought.

Ginger is fair blinking now, her fingers still in mid-air. We are not going to hear the end of 'Fine Knacks'.

'Twenty it is, then,' says the man.

Marzipans. Those are Mrs Fiddes's confections. Marzipans. He turns to me.

'Now there is no need to be alarmed,' he says. 'My home is very well appointed. In fact it is a real castle, in the village of Corstorphine, just west of Edinburgh and not far from here.'

'Twenty for the girl for the month,' says Mrs Fiddes, rising to face the man, hands on hips now, her great shoulders swelling up and her bodice fit to pop, 'and an extra five for my utmost discretion.'

The man produces another purse and I wonder if his cloak is full of them. More coins pour out. And then they vanish. Mrs Fiddes has the art of palming coins into nowhere.

He stands up and fetches his hat.

'Violet, I have some business to attend to, but I will be

waiting outside for you in my carriage at six o'clock this evening. Don't disappoint me by being late.'

He goes, and now it is only me, Ginger and Mrs Fiddes, with the occasional sigh and squeak from the corridor.

'Twenty-five pounds!' says Ginger.

'Ginger, you can be quiet. Think of the cost of the roof over your heads, the piano lessons, the meat on Sundays and the fish on Fridays. Miss Marigold's bills for the frocks!'

'What does he want with me for a month?' I say, knowing the answer and feeling weak.

'Ginger, go and start putting some things together for Violet,' says Mrs Fiddes, collapsing on the couch as if it has all been too much for her.

But I am the one shaking. I am the one who's just been sold for a month.

'He wants what they all want,' she says. 'He wants a bit of fun with a lady and then he wants his own freedom. Some of them want it for the night, some for longer, and he has the finances to do as he pleases.'

'But I can't leave, Mrs Fiddes, this is my home now,' I say. And it's true. I have my own room and a place at the dinner table, top left. Suddenly my dreams of a grand home of my own fade. I am taken care of here, despite the rats and the rot. Despite the men.

'He will not mistreat you, Violet. If it is Corstorphine Castle, as he says, then he is laird there, and fortune has come calling. Now if you do as I say, you can have half of this money for yourself. If you had a head for numbers, you'd know I don't make more than ten pounds a month from you; aside from Mr Rathen, you'd have been getting the heave-ho long ago. If he enjoys your company, he will come back for more. And word of it will raise your price around here too. *Violetta* – exotic companion to a nobleman.' She sucks on a prune, which she never does, as they are delicacies reserved for the gents, and her face screws up into the shape of an arsehole.

Ginger has put everything I own onto the bed. It amounts to one pot of rouge, three dresses, three petticoats and three pairs of stockings, all in shades of crimson, green and yellow. Hairbrush, pins and ribbons. Beside all that, a box of things from Ma and Da and the bairn, which I take out from time to time to remember feeling proper loved again.

She stands next to the bed, hands flitting between her head and her hips, face translucent with shock.

'This is a fearsome turn. What if he's a bad one?' Her voice quavers. 'I'll miss you terrible.'

'I'll be back in a month, you dafty,' I say. It's best to be brave with Ginger. She's only a young lassie. But I have no idea.

She shakes her head, casting her eyes to the bed where my worldly possessions lie folded and neat. I think Ginger's talents are wasted in a bawdy house when she could be a maid. I stop a minute, looking at the box, thinking whether to leave it here, but consider it best to take it with me, even if I don't want to go. And I sit on the bed and wait for six o'clock.

It comes soon enough. It comes in a darkening of the afternoon and a chill rising from the close below. Even the chickens in the poultry market downstairs seem to know something is in the air, for they are uncharacteristically quiet. When I hear St Giles' chimes, I slip out of my room. Mrs Fiddes is drinking a whisky in the parlour and sooking on her pipe. Two of the girls are on the couch, fluffing their hair and chewing mint leaves, and there is a hullaballoo at the door with more callers arriving. 'See to them, Ginger,' she cackles.

She heaves herself to her feet, her knees creaking so noisily under the weight of her belly that I am convinced damson wine is no cure. She takes my hand and peers at me, like she did that very first time we met on the street, only this time I have the slight height advantage. Her pipe reeks away in her fist.

'Now remember, Violet,' she says. 'This customer, more than any other, show him every trick in the book.'

# Chapter Seven

# VIOLET

*Corstorphine Castle*
*November 1678*

I've never been on wheels before, and I don't know what's worse: the fact that I'm now jolting in and out of potholes fast enough to make me retch or being at the mercy of a stranger. What if Ginger is right and he's a bad one? Oh Lord, I could weep for myself. I should never have winked on the street at this chap. Nothing good ever comes of such coquetry. I have never felt colder, and I can't stop the shakes.

'Do forgive my manners. I am Lord James Forrester,' he says, nodding down to me as if I should have heard of him.

And he is such a broad gent in all that finery of cloak and hat, taking up three-quarters of the carriage, it feels; and me squashed into a damp corner, lurching out of my seat. He lurks behind his own pursed lips, despite the swaying and the bouncing. He is the sort of chap who knows how to arrange his features best to show them off.

'Look,' he says pointing out of the carriage window, 'a grand view of Edinburgh Castle.'

I have never seen it from anywhere but the high street itself, but it looms above us now, perched on its black rock, and we are headed into the unknown, for anything beyond the high street is foreign country to me.

My parcel of clothes, and the box of Ma and Da and the bairn's things, is on my lap. I have one hand on that and the other grasping the carriage side to steady myself. I drape the box with my palm, to cover their eyes and ears to this unholy turn.

'Are you sure I can't take that?' he says, eyeing it. 'It can be stored safely.'

Well, that is asking for trouble. I can just see the bairn's bonnet flying off into the night and then I would have nothing left of her, poor soul.

'No, thank you, sir,' I say. 'These things are very precious to me.'

He smiles at that, and his eyes flick between them and me.

'All your worldly possessions, I suppose.'

'Aye, sir,' I say. 'They are.'

His face slackens, or it might be the shadow of a passing tree in the moonlight – it is hard to tell.

He leans forward an inch.

'I suppose you'll be wondering what's happening to you, and I'd like to assure you nothing dreadful,' he says. 'I am simply in need of some honest female company.'

He makes to touch my knee, but we jolt again, the wheels careening over another hole in the road that has us bouncing around the carriage together, as if we were doing the deed already.

'I don't usually require the company of a harlot,' he adds. 'In fact, there was only one other occasion and that was in London, and let me tell you this.' He reaches for a flask in his pocket and opens the lid. 'I found her in Covent Garden and took her to an inn, and my company was so enjoyable she halved her normal price. So I can't be all that bad, eh?'

He gives out a great wheeze, then knocks back a gulp from his flask as if it had been quite the most hilarious turn, but that is a sorry story. I have never heard of a girl who would half her price for anything other than desperation. Happens on the street all the time, Mrs Fiddes says. Sometimes they'll do it for a bottle of ale. *So be warned.*

'How impressive, sir,' I say, giving my eyelashes a flutter, like Mrs Fiddes tells us to. 'You must have fair swept her off her feet.'

'Perhaps,' he says, inhaling deep on his pomander; not that he needs to, for it has already filled the carriage with a scent like spiced plum pudding. 'It was a most satisfactory night for both parties.'

'How long might this journey be?' I ask, with the last of the tenements disappearing behind us.

'Oh, an hour, give or take,' he says. 'Time enough for us to get to know each other.'

He points the flask at me.

'A whisky, Violet? I believe whisky is quite the aphrodisiac. Do you know what that word means?'

I have lived in a whorehouse five years. I take the flask off him and take a good glug.

I am relieved when we get to Corstorphine. It looms up on us – lamps in the darkness, and the outline of a kirk spire. The air is even colder here, but what fresh pleasure compared to my own dirty streets.

'This is the inn,' he booms, as we whirl past it. My belly is a spinning wheel of whisky and horses' hooves, and stories about his wife's imbalanced humours. 'Now you're not to worry about Lady Forrester,' he'd said. 'She is more or less bed-bound, and the maids answer to me, not her. Your quarters will be at some considerable distance from her chamber, and we are arriving under cover of darkness when she will be unconscious from wine. Quite safe.'

But I do not like the sound of the Lady Forrester. Not one bit. How will he get away with having a harlot in his house? What if she discovers me?

We stop just short of the entrance to the castle, which is up an avenue of trees, and it is all torchlit and grand, with a moat and four towers, and I wonder what Ginger would make of it.

'The rest of our journey will be on foot, for discretion,' Lord James says, 'so take care.'

He takes up a lamp from the carriage and helps me down. He strides smartly, so I scamper behind him over the moat to the courtyard. But instead of going straight to the main building, he turns right into a corner tower. I would have missed it altogether as we are fair shrouded in darkness in this part of the grounds. Inside is a curved hall and we go up stone steps. I'm wondering if he's going to keep me a prisoner, and if all his talk of aphrodisiacs and the tots of whisky were simply a ruse to keep me from jumping out of the coach. I clutch my wee box tight, because he might be thinking of taking it from me, and I whisper, *Ma*, in case it's our last time together. Frightened, I was. See the goosebumps on my bare arms, even talking about it.

And then we are in a room in the shape of a circle, with a big four-poster bed and sheepskins everywhere, and small candle lanterns that he lights as we go. But my eyes just about pop out of my head at two great oil paintings. I have seen a fair few things in my time, such as that night I had to take on two French traders because Lisbeth and Flora were getting wabbit with the men's demands, and that was a long night, I can tell you; but these two pictures are all buttocks and bosoms, and I even see a mound of Venus in all its hairy glory. Skirts up, bodices ripped open, faces in ecstasy, men's parts all charged and ready, and some of them hung like bulls. I have never seen the like on a wall. Even Mrs Fiddes, for all the high jinks that happen in our chambers, would not have allowed such vulgarity on display.

'This turret room is where I entertain ladies from time to time. What do you think of the art?' he asks. 'It's my little eccentricity.'

'It is quite the eye-opener, my lord,' I say, and he laughs and gives a most ungentlemanly snort.

'I bet you and your whorehouse girls could learn a few tricks from these paintings,' he states with a great grin. 'Quite outrageous.'

I survey the paintings. Coitus in all its manners and positions. But nothing on these walls I haven't done before a hundred times or more. Oh no. And soon we shall see what tricks he has learned from his Covent Garden harlots, if any.

'I shall make a study of these, sir,' I say, sweet as a cherry, and he blushes like a lassie for a moment before he gathers his wits again.

'Come, Violet, make yourself comfortable, and we shall converse and get to know each other a little better,' he says. 'I do enjoy the company of a woman in all regards.'

Aha! This is a gent who likes to feel that he is with a mistress, not a whore. The commonest sort.

He removes his great feathery hat, and I can see beads of sweat on his forehead, and that means he is not as confident as he likes to make himself out to be. He rattles around in a cupboard and produces a bottle of whisky and pours two generous splashes. I put my box on the table and I sit on the bed, for there is only one chair and he has taken it; and anyway, I believe the bed is my place for the duration. Well, as soon as I take the weight off my feet, I realize this bed is the comfiest I have ever put my arse on. I almost begin to relax.

'My wife,' he says, with a wave of his ringed hand at the feast of nipples and cocks on the walls, 'would never understand all of this. She has a sickness that prevents her living a full life. Her physicians have tried every poultice and leech. But I believe she doesn't just have a sickness of the body. She has a feebleness of the brain.'

He looks anything but miserable when he tells this tale.

'It leaves me quite at liberty to pursue my own interests. This turret has been my sanctuary over the years. Already, Violet, I can see that you are a worldly girl. I saw it in the way you carried yourself outside St Giles'.'

Some do flatter and that is a trial, when all you want is to get them seen to, so you can lie in bed alone and fart and pick your nose to your heart's content. But I am casting my eyes around this luxurious room and thinking it will be a splendid place to do these things when he's off being lairdly, and no queue of filthy gents to service.

'It seemed quite the occasion at the kirk today,' I say.

'A wedding. My younger niece to one of the Gregor boys.' He says this as though I should know who the Gregor boys are. 'And soon, I believe, my older niece will also be wed to a most distinguished merchant. Which is excellent news, as the fortunes on that side of the family have fallen into some diffi-culties.' He does not look pleased, though. In fact, he looks troubled. 'Tis bad news when a gent gets melancholy, and a poor reflection on the harlot, so I turn the subject away from his family.

'And you, sir,' I say, for gents love nothing more than to talk about themselves. 'Tell me all about the Laird of Corstorphine.'

'Oh, the cursed life of a laird,' he sighs. 'The problems never end. The peasants are always tugging at my collars and cuffs, Violet. They come to me with their trifles: the price of ale rising, or asking when the tooth-puller will next visit. Always a hag needing to be punished for gossip or casting curses. You cannot imagine the burden. And how stupid they are. Always breaking rules and having to be reminded how to live decently. I am quite exhausted by it.'

'It must be a terrible duty upon you, sir,' I say, supping away at the whisky, though it sounds a sight easier than working a night in a whorehouse.

'And Lady Forrester is quite unable perform her wifely duties,' he adds, lowering his voice to a whisper, although I am sure no one is lurking to overhear him. 'Quite incapable. Her brain and her body are simply not up to the task. Most likely the imbalance in her humours. I need someone – an earthy girl like yourself, who can devote herself to my relaxation.' His eyes go that dark, glittering way men's eyes do when they broach the subject of intercourse.

'I am sure I can try,' I say. And he seems to take great relief in that, although I have heard it all now: earthy girl indeed. And why he can't just say he likes a good ride I don't know, but perhaps if we both pretend it's his wife's fault, he can live with the guilt.

He gets up from the chair. 'We shall relax on this fine bed together, then, Violet.'

He takes off his cloak. I see the black slash of a sword belt and watch him unbuckle it and place the weapon against the chair.

'A fine instrument you have there,' I say with a wink, but I shiver. I cannot help it.

'Do not alarm yourself with that,' he nods at the sword, 'I'll have no need for it, unless you misbehave.'

I don't know him well enough to tell whether he is jesting or not. 'Come on,' he says. 'Petticoats up. And afterwards a fine meal of roasted marrow bones, and syllabub, if you have a sweet tooth. I intend to treat you finely. I am a pleasure-seeker in every way.'

Syllabub in a castle turret! I wager that will put Mrs Fiddes's plum pudding to shame.

I hitch up my petticoats and brace myself.

### THE CALEDONIA BROADSIDE

#### EDINBURGH, 29th September

Mrs Christian Nimmo: 'I beg of you, sir, do not take the word of a common harlot over mine. She seduced Lord James and had him eating out of her hand, and she has the wiles to do that to every man who puts eyes on her.'

Mrs Rita Fiddes: 'Are you suggesting I run a brothel, sir? I beg your pardon. I simply rent out rooms at a fair price to young women with nowhere else to go; decent meals and sweet desserts to build them up and nourish their tender flesh. But ho! I was not sorry to see Miss Blyth depart, for she was trouble from the get-go. If she had men in her room, it was nothing to do with me; I am so troubled by my wheezes, I am asleep most of the day. Have you a comfy chair, sir? I think I can feel one of my funny turns coming on.'

# Chapter Eight

# CHRISTIAN

*Roseburn House, near Edinburgh*
*November 1678*

A ndrew asked Mother for my hand on his return from a short trip to Fife. I'd hoped and prayed he might. The proposal came after he had taken us on a marvellous outing to Fisherrow Harbour for the freshest of herrings and a taste of the sea he knew so well, saying we needed cheering up now that Johanna was gone.

'And when he asked me for your hand, he flushed pink as a rosebud,' Mother announced, slicing into an orange that Andrew had brought for us to try, and which had travelled all the way from Spain. 'You have done well to secure this offer, Christian, you will want for nothing now.'

No, I would want for absolutely nothing now. But more importantly, I was in love. I thought of Andrew when I fell asleep at night, and he was my first thought when I woke up. I swept my hair confidently into its ribbons and wore jewels in the daytime. I tamed my curls within six or seven minutes on some days, so self-assured did I become. He stroked my hand in the parlour when Mother was not looking, although he did not dare to kiss me anywhere other than on the cheek.

I did not wear the hair comb that my uncle had gifted me, though. That was far too extravagant.

Andrew said we should marry as soon as we could, to give us time together before he travelled again.

The date was set for a December wedding at Corstorphine Kirk.

The oranges sat in a crate in the kitchen. Fiona didn't know what to do with them and consulted a cook she knew from her old days at the house of a trader, and they made their way onto the breakfast table and into stews. It was a most agreeable change. Mother quartered them and we shared the pieces, and discussed who would attend the nuptials.

There were no visits from James. Perhaps Mother had no need of him and his trading connections, now that I was engaged to be married to the notable Mr Nimmo.

The oranges diminished. The days until my wedding passed, like candles being blown out, one by one.

'And now it is my turn to instruct *you* on the benefits of marriage, Sister.'

Johanna was paying a visit. Married life suited her. She walked with higher shoulders and was haughty all through the house in a new emerald-green frock, sweeping up the staircase and looking superb, now that she had a maid to dress her and do her ringlets. Perhaps I would have one too; I would ask Andrew. Perhaps he would take me on a journey one day, on a sailing ship.

We were in Johanna's old bedroom to escape Mother, on the pretext of packing the last of her trinkets. We were at the dressing table, putting hair pins and ribbons into a box, and a tarnished hairbrush that Johanna would never use, but insisted on taking because she wanted all her memories with her. The mirror had a haze of dust across it, like light snow. Behind it, our heads bobbed in a blur: her blonde twirls and my white ribbons. She smelled foreign, of the musk of sharing a bed with a man. I missed her.

'Fetch the marriage book,' she whispered, 'and I will explain in detail what it all means.'

'But I don't have the book,' I said. That wasn't true. It was still in my drawer, but its illustrations were off-putting, now my own wedding night loomed. 'I am sorry I teased you with it.'

She winked and the old Johanna was back. 'No need, Sister. The marriage bed is quite unlike the sketches in that pamphlet.'

'Really? Tell me, so I can prepare myself.' I took the hairbrush and ran my fingers over the soft little bristles.

'Well, there is much more of a preamble,' she said. 'Robert takes his time with me. It was quite strange at first, but has become . . .' She stopped and caught a glimpse of herself in the mirror and smiled, coyly. 'Most *passionate*.'

'Enough, Sister, I am having disturbing visions of the two of you.'

She laughed – the throaty laugh I have missed. I imagined Robert Gregor hearing it as he touched her skin.

'It is my favourite pastime now,' she whispered, 'and in two days' time on your wedding night, it will be yours.'

I give her a smack with the hairbrush.

It was all very well for her to say the act was enjoyable, for she had crossed the threshold. My wedding night would be just me and Andrew Nimmo: no guidebook, no soft reassurance from my sister, no going back.

*

My wedding was smaller than Johanna's, but all the better for the addition of Christmas holly prickling at the ends of the pews and the absence of Lord James Forrester, for despite the fact that Corstorphine Kirk was their own parish, he sent apologies that Lady Forrester was too unwell to leave and he had another commitment. I wondered if that was true.

The kirk, which sat beyond the clatter and chicken-sellers of the broad main street, was alight with candles. It was also lit up with the ogling eyes of the peasants crammed into the back rows, but that is the prying nature of a village, and I was its most fascinating new neighbour.

Johanna had dragged me and a bale of Andrew's best Lyon silk to a seamstress in Edinburgh, squashed between a goldsmith and a confectioner. Robert chaperoned us and took the opportunity to visit a coffee house, to read the scandals in the broadsides. As well as the dress, I received a blue garter, at Johanna's insistence. When we'd left the shop, even though Robert was waiting and the horses were impatient, Johanna pushed me into the confectioner, fussing over the apricot pastes and quince cakes and settling on a grand marzipan decorated with candied fruits. 'To celebrate,' she said, sharing it out all the way home, her cheeks rising with the flush of the sugar.

The garter rustled secretly on my thigh, squeezing the flesh, all the way through the ceremony, and made me think of wanton kisses and secret parts even when I was making my vows to my new husband. I had never felt the press of a garter before, never been so aware of the sensitive tops of my own legs. They shivered beneath my thin gown. I could feel the goosebumps. But even with candles and holly, my wedding was more modest than Johanna's had been, as the minister of Corstorphine Kirk disapproved of indulgence.

Reverend Ian Brodie would be my new pastor, now I was moving from Roseburn. I had not met him until today at the altar. Andrew had warned that he was quite authoritarian, keeping the village in order with gruelling weekly sermons. Any wrongdoing reported to the Kirk would be preached back at them and examples made of the sinners. Its repentance stool was often occupied, Andrew said, and my eyes had widened, for Roseburn had been a gentle parish, more concerned with collecting outgrown clothes for the poor than with punishing the wrongdoings of its wayward congregation.

Reverend Brodie seemed personable enough, as he read slowly and steadily from the Bible, but I barely noticed him, as I was so taken with how handsome and serious Andrew looked, uttering his vows.

I glanced at him, at the confident smile of him, and wondered how he would look when he was on top of me. Would he creep in slowly or would he take me by surprise? Would it hurt? I thought of it even when I was admiring the small holly wreaths with Mother. Even when I was thanking Reverend Brodie. And especially when I was saying goodbye to Johanna, her hand clutching mine tighter than ever, as though neither of us wanted to let the other go. Knowing this would be the last embrace where one of us was truly innocent.

In the coach, on the ten-minute ride back to Carrick House, through the woodlands of his estate, Andrew turned to me and smiled.

'This is all yours now, Christian. I am looking forward to walks in the woods with you when I am not away on business.' The carriage creaked over the frost.

'I will enjoy sketching it, and the flowers in the glasshouse,' I said. 'That is how I will pass the time whenever you are away.'

'Indeed! Indeed! I'm fortunate to have found a wife who will not be cross that I am gone half the year, and who will be able to keep herself occupied rather than sigh and waste away.'

'I do not plan on sighing or wasting away,' I said.

'You are far too wise for that. Wise beyond your years,' he said, smiling indulgently.

We arrived to a small feast of calf's head with oysters, a trifle made with cream and rosewater, and Burgundy wine. The table was strewn with hothoused purple pansies. But I could barely eat, for I was not used to rich food like that, and for thinking that this was my life now and how blessed I was, watching the candles shimmer and the moon rise over the black oaks. And despite our sporadic chatter, about how fortunate a day it had been, the dining table was heavy with silences, for we both knew what was to come. One by one, the servants slipped away with cleared plates and empty glasses.

And then it was time.

My belongings, sent ahead, were already arranged in a large room that was to be my bedchamber, adjoining his. I stood beside the fire, warming myself as a maid brought a jug of water.

'Shall I help you undress, Lady Christian?' she asked.

It was the first time I had heard myself called by my husband's name. I had not been undressed by a maid since I was a girl.

'I prefer to see to it myself,' I said. I was about to experience one unfamiliar pair of hands upon my flesh. I did not want another.

Despite the fire, my bedchamber was cold. Frost had crept

over the windowpanes. It was colder than Roseburn because the ceilings were even higher and the room so vast, with the poster bed its centrepiece, with damask curtains the same shade as Andrew's fine wine. Even so, I undressed before a large mirror, the wedding dress dropping to the floor, revealing the other gift Johanna had given me, a white petticoat trimmed in French lace. *He will adore this, Sister.*

I was wearing nothing but the petticoat when Andrew knocked lightly at the adjoining door. A moment later he came in, attending to his buttons and cuffs. He took ten full minutes to remove his clothes. I avoided watching him and crawled under the bedclothes shivering at their heavy chill, so much that my body went into tremors. Then he drew back the sheets and got into bed beside me.

He turned to me, bringing me into his arms.

'You are freezing, my love,' he whispered.

I huddled into him and lay there, feeling awkward, until my shaking subsided and I began to notice the warmth of his skin comforting me, but still I could not relax, and I felt my heart beating so loudly he must surely have heard it pulsing at his side.

'It has been such a momentous day,' he whispered.

'I will never forget it.' I lay against his chest, unfamiliar and strange. *I am a wife now.*

'I feel quite overcome with it all. Not to mention the feast,' he said, patting his stomach. 'I wonder if you would be agreeable that we both get our rest?'

My mind reached into the marriage manual. But there was nothing about a husband needing his rest or feeling full of his dinner.

'I am very happy, my love,' he whispered, kissing the top of my head.

And then he grew still and gently began to snore.

And that is how my wedding night went.

Why did he not try to kiss me? Or touch me? Was there something wrong with the petticoat? Perhaps I should have removed it, as a signal of sorts? Was that how these things were done?

Or was there something wrong with me?

Was it because I was not beautiful, like Johanna?

Perhaps it was too good to be true, after all.

I remained on his chest, consoled that I had escaped the dreaded marital act, but also wondering about the book, whether its intimate subjects were even true, and whether Johanna had played a cruel trick on me with all her talk of passion.

I wondered for hours, until the silence of Carrick House eventually lulled me to an uneasy sleep.

## *THE CALEDONIA BROADSIDE*

### EDINBURGH, 30th September

Mr Andrew Nimmo, husband of the accused: 'Marital relations between myself and my wife were perfectly normal.'

# Chapter Nine

# VIOLET

*Corstorphine Castle*
*December 1678*

Mistress Violetta, exotic companion to the Laird of Corstorphine. Well, what of it? Far worse things that a dafty like me could end up being.

I have made an enormous list of all the things I'll tell Ginger and the lassies about what it's like to almost be a princess. He's given me a load of fine silk nightgowns that he likes me to dress in, lusty devil. And there's a maid who brings me three meals a day. And hot water and lavender soap. And a scent that I still wear now. If you put your nose to my wrist, does it not smell of the headiest roses? And the maid takes away my chamber pot each morning and looks with horror at the rouge on the dressing table. A rouged cheek is the envy of many a lady, no matter that they turn their noses up at it, and do you know why? For it mimics the flush of pleasure, that's why. No need to be embarrassed about that.

This maid is set in a holy way and mutters prayers, as if she thinks herself too godly to handle a whore's piss. But she is not sour enough to spoil my glory days. And the views are most pleasant of the snowy humps of the Pentland Hills.

Not a beggar to be seen. Nor any sign of Lady Forrester. The surly maid is silent on that topic when I ask. All I manage to prise from her is her own name. Oriana. She offers it high and thin, like a psalm. Her skin is so greyish-white she looks like she has never sat in the sunshine of an afternoon, nor laughed so much her cheeks flushed.

I am lolling on the bed in nothing but scarlet stockings and a matching petticoat one afternoon when she comes in with a plate of roast-chicken legs. She clatters the plate on the dressing table, face in a grump.

'You look the perfect trollop,' she scolds.

'Don't fret. My sinful ways will not corrupt you,' I say.

'There is no danger of that. But your whoring will stop you getting into heaven.'

'So be it,' I say. 'But I'd have been dead a long time ago if I hadn't taken up whoring.'

She blinks. She would make a good owl, this wide-eyed, beaky thing.

'And how does a godly sort like you cope in this castle of immorality?'

She blinks again and opens her pale lips as if to say something profound. Instead she says she must go back to the kitchen to do proper work.

Proper work, as though whoring is not proper work.

Has its perks, though.

I wake each morning, toss back the covers and look forward to another day of roast goose and wine, of candied cherries and barley sugars. Oh, what a dumpling I was, to fear leaving Mrs Fiddes! A life as Lord James's turret-whore might be the best I could ever hope for. Sad as I would be, never to see

Ginger and the girls again, the days pass far more gloriously here.

If I want to stay, I will have to make him adore me. Depend on me.

'Oh, Laird, I cannot help but worship your marvellous manhood,' I murmur as we embrace after the deed and, by Jove, he believes me.

'Tell me, Violet, is it not among the finest you have ever seen?' he says.

'Truly the most magnificent. And my exquisite honeypot is the most desired in all of Edinburgh town,' I remind him, 'and you, my lucky laird, have it all to yourself.'

'A laird's luck is not all it is made out to be,' Lord James says, looking grave. 'This morning we had a sombre meeting of the Kirk Session. The fornicators have been busy with each other's husbands and wives this month and we have several to put on the repentance stool.'

The repentance stool. We lassies of Mrs Fiddes's are not welcome at any kirk in Edinburgh and, as such, we have the good fortune to avoid these humiliations. But I have seen one, when Ma and Da took me to St Giles'. High and hard it was, in a corner of the kirk, creaking with shame, waiting for the next sorry arse to sit upon it.

'And does that stop them?'

'Sometimes,' he says.

'And have you ever done your own penance?' I ask, tapping his belly. 'Or shall I march you up to Corstorphine Kirk myself?'

'I can fair see that happening,' he whispers. 'The hags would be lining the streets for a gawp, and Corstorphine would talk of nothing else.'

'It is one rule for them and quite another rule for you,' I whisper back. 'Even your own kitchen maid Oriana has a purer soul.'

'Indeed,' he ponders, scratching his chin. 'But I shall never be publicly shamed. No one would dare.'

And that is why he lives as he does, without a care in the world.

Look at him. Lying there, satisfied again and again by his hard-working harlot. There is not a place in my body he has not plunged himself.

'Now come and worship me again,' he says, drawing himself higher in the bed and pushing my head down to his lap.

Perhaps he does believe I worship him, but that is the singular talent of a good whore, to disguise her disgust as lust.

One evening as we are lying drowsy and my teeth are furred from barley sugars, he announces that he must return me to Mrs Fiddes the next morning, as it is nearing Christmas.

'That was my deal with your mistress, and I have feasting and family matters to attend to. Anyway, I cannot have you languishing here. What if Oriana forgot you?'

'But why?' I ask. 'You can make anything happen, if you want it to. It is no trouble for you to keep me here.' I feel panic rising in my throat. I am not going back to that squalor and danger if I can help it.

'It is your home,' he says. 'I have an obligation.'

'It is no home, and you know it,' I say.

He takes my head in his hands, a habit he has got into, and looks into my eyes. 'We have grown fond of each other, Violet. This will not be the last of it.'

'You will be back for more of me – you will not be able to stay away,' I coo, artily. But I feel my voice crack in my throat.

'I will, Violet,' he says. 'I have a special fondness for you, I cannot deny it. You are not like the other women in my life.

Your laughter is medicine to me. Your hands have healing powers. Magnificent. Look!' He nods up to one of his erotic oil paintings, the ladies sprawled eating grapes, with their legs in the air and arses bare. 'You are finer than these Venuses!'

'I am indeed,' I reply. 'You would be a fool to discard me. Your life would never be as pleasurable again.'

He looks at me solemnly. His fingers brush my hair. I sigh, to make it seem I am in bliss with his touch.

'Indeed,' he says. 'Now goodnight, Violet, and don't fret, I will look after you, my tasty treat.'

But I don't know if that's true and I barely sleep at all that night, tossing and turning under the sheets and dreading my return to the filth. For a tasty treat is something you might fancy one minute, but push away another time.

In the morning Oriana brings porridge that I have no appetite for.

'I am off soon,' I tell her, thinking she will be pleased. Instead her face falls.

'I will miss your company,' she says. 'I was just getting to know you.'

What a funny sort she is, standing there all grey-faced and miserable. I have a good mind to tell her how lucky she is, but folk never understand.

'It is not my choice to leave,' I say. 'And I don't have the stomach for this porridge.'

'Try a little,' she says. 'For it will be a long day for you.'

But I cannot.


The laird takes me back to Edinburgh himself, wrapping me in a fine wool shawl in that juddering carriage. I have rouged myself and washed my hair and let the shawl fall open at the cleavage, so that I look too desirable to say goodbye to, but he is too busy pointing out sights and telling me their stories to even notice, the great selfish shit.

His stories become a wall of noise, filling up the carriage like his pomander scent. Corstorphine Hill, where the witches gather under the light of the full moon for their devil worship. Sometimes you can see them flit across the sky. Arthur's Seat, which he says is a lump of an old volcano that I now wish would erupt and wash us all away with its boiling lava. Heriot's Hospital, where he says the sickly orphans are looked after, and I wonder what my fortunes would be if I had gone there instead of begging on the street. But it is all words, words. Out they tumble. He is frightened of what a silence might bring. It might give me the chance to beg, or accuse him of abandoning me, or start to sob.

And so I am returned to the high street on Christmas Eve. To vapours of chimney smoke and the gristle of street mince pies. To the clatter of carts and the knobbly ribs of knackered horses. To fine feathered hats, and shit and snow stuck fast to the bottoms of petticoat frills. To the eternal rotten-egg stench of the Nor Loch.

'I will accompany you upstairs myself,' Lord James says, when the carriage finally halts. He looks perturbed at the shivering vagrants and the chickens pecking the wheels and is no doubt worried I might run away, given the chance. When my feet touch the earth again, it all floods back. I'd forgot how much Bell's Close stinks of decaying vegetables and how the ground slips with the gardyloo slops.

The door at the top of the stair flies open. Mrs Fiddes is so surprised to see me again her eyeballs bulge. The besom must have suspected she'd seen the last of me and didn't give a hoot if I'd end up a laird's fancy piece or dead in his moat.

Her skirts have the whiff of something sour, high as mutton on the turn, and I believe it was always there for it smells familiar – the smell of rot and greed, and the threat of something nasty if you don't do as you are told. We are ushered in and follow the trail of her pipe down the damp hallway into the parlour.

'I trust you have had a pleasurable month,' she asks Lord James with a low curtsey and her knees creak as she totters her way back up. Her gown is new, and she has a new brooch at her throat, round and gold. 'Violet, what a handsome shawl – is this a gift from the laird?' she fusses, whipping it off and hanging it on the peg so fast he doesn't have the chance to say no. I will not see that again.

'Violet has been the most delightful company,' he says, clearing his throat and having the decency to blush. 'I am grateful for her services, and once again I trust your discretion.'

Mrs Fiddes bats her eyelashes as though she had provided the very services herself.

'We have a vast array of ladies here,' she says, glancing at me with sweet threat. 'Violet is but one of them, and hardly our most dazzling or entertaining, my lord.'

And with that, it feels I have never been away.

'I found her most dazzling and entertaining,' he says. As he makes for the door he gives us one last glance. 'I may be back for more of her. It is quite the sport to watch her wallow in luxury for a while.'

And then he is gone, leaving nothing but the flick of his cape and the soft memory of furs.

Mrs Fiddes rests her gnarled knuckles on each hip.

'Well, pardon me if this is no castle,' she says. 'But we have missed you enough and your chamber still happens to be empty, if you've a notion to stay. We have also missed your talents in the kitchen, as that cook has been spooning up tasteless slop.'

'I'll take my money first,' I say. 'God knows I earned it.'

'You certainly did,' she says, reaching for the purse she keeps under her petticoats, a flash of her lumpy thigh purpling beneath. 'I hope you did not get too attached to him.'

# Chapter Ten

# VIOLET

*Bell's Close, Edinburgh*
*December 1678*

I slink back to the damp grey chamber at the end of the hall, where the reek of the kitchen fire lingers. A window with a view of a wall across the close, which is only a few steps away. Always too hot or too cold. Ever the threat of a customer's boots making their way up the corridor. With nothing to entertain me but the parlour view of the high street and the fortunate bastards who wander up and down it, visiting confectioners and haberdashers. I put the money away safely.

Corstorphine Castle. Who would ever have thought I would roll grand words like that over my tongue, pining?

'You've not missed much,' says Ginger, sticking her head round my chamber door before the evening rush, almost lifting me from my glum mood.

A pretty, pale face and curls the colour of carrots. She is not every gentleman's choice, on account of her flat titties and sticky-outy teeth, but those that like her, like her plenty.

'Mrs Fiddes bashed me for playing bad, but that tuneless

piano's the problem, not me. And anyway, I am right pleased
to see you again.'

'Me too, Ginger,' I say, and it's true. Despite my mourning
for all the luxury I have lost, I have the softest spot for wee
Ginger.

'But it must have been grand,' she whispers. 'Up at a big
castle. We talked of nothing else, imagining it. Were there
turrets?'

'Oh, it was grand. I often thought of you when I was wearing
a fancy gown, or eating a rich cream pudding, or looking out
at the hills,' I say.

Her eyes look fit to pop. 'You were a princess,' she says.

'For a while,' I say with a sigh.

'One day I would like a life like that,' Ginger says. 'Even
just to be a maid sweeping floors.'

'Well, work hard here and who knows what chances may
come? You are the finest piano player I have ever heard.' What
else could I say? If Ginger went knocking on the doors of the
gentry, she would have them slammed in her freckled face,
with no letter of reference, poor soul. But she has time yet;
she cannot be any older than thirteen. I change the subject
and start unpacking my things.

'How's business?' I ask.

'Busy,' she says. 'Too busy. I am only getting to bed these
nights in the early hours. But Mrs Fiddes says that's 'cause
I'm getting popular at last.'

Ginger looks wabbit. There are silver shadows under her
eyes. If my wee sister had lived, perhaps we would have sat
like this on the bed, sharing stories.

She sees my box of memories and reaches for it. I don't
stop her, for there's something gentle about Ginger and you
know she wouldn't harm a flea.

'Go on,' I say, and she opens it.

The bairn's bonnet is on top; she places it on her lap and strokes it.

'Elizabeth,' I say, 'hardly six months in this world.'

I have never told a soul about my baby sister before.

'Sweet Elizabeth,' coos Ginger, tracing her fingers over the wool. 'Sleep tight and know your sister is safe with me.'

Poor Ginger, what could she ever do in a fix, but she means well. She lifts out the other keepsakes. Ma's ring. A sketch of them the tattie-seller did for their wedding day. A leaf from the first autumn I remember, when Ma said, *Keep this safe to remember the way nature always turns.*

Oh, Ma. Sometimes it feels as though nature has turned a hundred times since she last held my hand. Sometimes it feels as though it hasn't turned at all. And if she was here beside me now, how could I explain all that has happened to me since she departed this earth? Tears spring at the thought. And that is how a girl truly knows just how much she misses her dear ma.

I know I can be all bluster at times, but a girl needs her ma.

'I wish I remembered mine,' says Ginger. 'I was put in the orphan house as a baby.'

She looks up at me, her eyes all watery too, and I feel sorrier for her than I do for myself, for at least I had a family, when it sounds as though Ginger never even had one in the first place. And then I notice something. Dark purple spots at the base of her throat.

'What are those?'

She puts her hands to her neck.

'Don't tell Mrs Fiddes. The fellow gave me extra money for myself after it happened, and I've spent it already on a fancy hair pin and marzipans.'

'Which bastard did this?'

'Violet, you mustn't.' But she is desperate to tell someone, to be rid of the story, and she says a gent took her rough two nights ago.

'Rougher than anyone. He pulled clumps of my hair out, and called me every dirty name under the sun and more. He had his hands at my neck, fit to choke me, and then the next minute after he'd spent himself he was good as gold, saying he was sorry. Resting his head on my breast. I even found myself stroking his hair.'

'Oh, Ginger,' I say. Poor soul.

'Not seen him before, so I don't know his name, but he didn't look rough. He looked smart. But never mind that. See this.' She shows me a pretty hair pin, the kind the pedlars sell that is paste made to look like real jewels, and it is tucked into her red locks so that only someone with the sharpest eyes, or who gave any kind of a toss for Ginger, would notice. 'My wee secret.'

'Tell me if he comes back,' I say.

She slips out, for Ginger is always nervous to be found anywhere she ought not to be, and I carry on sweeping and tidying up my chamber. For I am back now, in the horrors and the grime, and I might as well keep my room as decent as I can. You have to take pride in something.

Well, don't I become the most popular turn at the pleasure parlour! And that is a poisoned chalice. After the lull of Christmas, when gents are back with their families, that wily bawd Mrs Fiddes makes sure every man who arrives at our door is told I've recently returned from a special assignment of *a most secretive nature*, and soon they all want their turn with a laird's mistress.

Lord James's name is never mentioned – just as well. If her exaggerations got back to him, I'd never see him again. I'd told her little, as I am also of the utmost discretion, unless I absolutely have to betray secrets. I merely said that he kept me in a turret and visited twice a day, for conversation with a satisfactory ending. She elaborates the scene, with me all dressed in fancy gowns and picking up tricks he'd taught me from the courtesans of Paris. *Violet is well versed in pleasing noblemen and will only service our most esteemed customers, and there is a queue.*

I barely have time to take a breath between them. I grow to dread the knock at the door, for I know it will likely be for me. Gone are my days of picking my nits and waiting in the parlour, or running out for Mrs Fiddes's afternoon treat. Instead I am so busy I need to be treated by the physician for a dose of something nasty down below, and a few days later I need my menses brought on with herbs.

Oh, the entire month of January is a vile time.

I make sure to tell Mrs Fiddes I am taking a wage rise, thank you very much, and she does not object, which says it all.


February arrives. Drizzle and mist. It is late Sunday morning, our quietest hour, when most gentlemen are between kirk and lunch, when the man who beat poor wee Ginger returns.

I have just finished chopping some potatoes, for the cook is in no fit state again and I am back in the parlour. Must be eleven of us girls, none occupied with entertaining, leaving us restless, picking fault with each other's hair and habits, and the squabbling causing Mrs Fiddes to threaten us with the flogger that she keeps for the deviants. She is always in bad fettle in the mornings, on account of the drink. She remains unwigged and that ages her a decade, with the look of a plucked chicken about her, and she keeps the parlour curtains closed, which is a shame for it is a big window. It affords a grand view of the high street, from the Mercat Cross up to St Giles', all busy with the smartly dressed on an Edinburgh Sunday. But we would be whipped to hell if we tried to press our faces to the glass and watch them scurrying in their finery from their humble prayers.

I realize something is up because Ginger stops playing 'Weep You No More, Sad Fountains', and at first I think Lord James has returned and I feel myself go dizzy; but it isn't Lord James, it is a smart-dressed man in a pea-green coat with silvery, thinning hair and a ruddy nose and cheeks. I am disappointed. Ginger has fallen silent, fingers drooped on the keys.

'You're an early bird, sir. You have the choice of all our young ladies at this particular hour,' croaks Mrs Fiddes, cheery enough, but not mustering her usual enthusiasm, which only comes after her lunchtime nip and a sook on her pipe.

He stands at the door, surveying us restless kittens. He holds himself stiffly, in a confident way, and Ginger is as still as a statue, and that is how I know.

His eyes dart from one to the next, as the girls quietly murmur and flutter, but not with much gusto at this hour. I sit still, just like Ginger.

His eyes lock on mine, piercing blue under wild brows, and I dare not look at Ginger, but I can feel she is looking at me. Then he addresses her.

'I have a specific girl in mind,' he says, and she sinks into the piano stool as if it could save her.

'Up, Miss Ginger,' says Mrs Fiddes. 'You have an admirer here.'

Ginger stands and pushes the piano stool in, all nice and tidy, like she's been taught. Her eyes grip mine, before she takes the man's arm and leads him out of the room, the baldy patch at the back of his head as round as an oatcake.

I follow Mrs Fiddes to the kitchen, where she is looking on the shelves for a nip of whisky.

'That man with Ginger. Keep an ear out for her,' I say.

Mrs Fiddes turns round and rolls her eyes.

'If he was trouble, Ginger should have said.' Her hands are on her hips as though we are nothing but bothersome children to her.

'She's too scared. But he's not the sort we should be encouraging,' I tell her.

'I shall put a description of him on the bad list,' she sighs. 'Now come and have first lunch shift, and I will keep my ears out for Ginger.'

I gobble down my ham and potatoes and no sooner am I done than I'm summoned, for a regular arrives, asking for Mistress Violetta, and off I am taken to my own chamber.

I am scunnered with it all, and when I feel that way I get even worse about having a dead ma, who cannot comfort me or at the very least drag me away from it all with a skelped arse. When the gentleman is finally near finishing up his business after a lot of rutting and grunting, I brace myself and truly wonder if I might be better taking my chances on the streets again.

But what if Lord James came back for me, to whisk me off for a life of syllabub, and I had gone?

Just then there is an almighty commotion of squawking and screaming down the corridor, which fair brings this customer back into the present with a *whatinthenameo'Christisthisplace?* and he jumps up and pulls his breeks back on and I pull on my dress quick, for commotions in corridors never bode well. Quite right too, for there is a burst of knocks at the door and it is one of the girls looking frightful as a banshee, saying, 'You're to come as soon as you can. There's been a calamity.'

Well, this chap can't take his leave quick enough. I make my way back up the corridor to where the girls are gathering at the doorway of Ginger's wee room. And I suppose, on account of me being most acquainted with Ginger, they make way for me. Mrs Fiddes is in there, crouched at the bed. Crouched at Ginger, all bashed with blood everywhere, and her wee skinny white legs and arms hunched around herself as though she spent her last moments curled up trying to save herself, but that did not work.

## THE CALEDONIA BROADSIDE

### EDINBURGH, 29th September

Mrs Rita Fiddes: 'I do believe the death of Miss Ginger McKenzie, who was another of my lodging girls, had a most profound effect on Violet and she was never the same since. Close as two peas in a pod, they was. I took care of the entire burial of poor Ginger myself, and the headstone, not that I am seeking any reimbursement, or any thanks from anyone, for it all comes from the heart.

'But after that incident, a murder in cold blood, my lord, Violet looked like she was out for vengeance of any sort.'

## Chapter Eleven

# CHRISTIAN

*Carrick House, Corstorphine*
*February 1679*

I never felt uglier than in the early days of my marriage. In the first weeks Andrew did not reach for me once. I kept expecting that he would, and then wondering if I might have missed a passage of the book and whether I ought to reach for him, and that it was my fault. I wore all my new shifts, with low necklines and high sleeves, but nothing stirred him. He slept facing away from me in bed, so one night I curled myself around him and gave him gentle strokes on his arm, mimicking what I had read a man ought to do for his wife, and he grew tense but said nothing to deter me, so I continued a while.

'Mmm,' he murmured. 'This is very soothing.'

'I am glad you enjoy it,' I said.

'I am so exhausted from all my work today,' he whispered. 'Let us just lie close for a while.' And he fell asleep again.

The next night I stripped to nothing, despite the fact it was freezing outside and snow was falling. When he pulled back the sheet, I ensured my breasts were exposed and he saw them, but said nothing.

He got in beside me and pulled me towards him and we kissed for a while and it was quite pleasurable, but I was a little fraught, so I could not enjoy the kissing in full and, in any case, it did not develop into anything, but instead slowed to a halt.

'Let us take our time,' he said. 'We have all the time in the world.'

Was I even a real wife yet?

Mother visited to admire the hothoused pansies and grape-vines. We visited Johanna, who had conceived within weeks of her marriage. I found myself thinking about how the baby had got there and whether Robert Gregor had ever avoided relations with my glorious sister. I thought not. He had embraced married life wholeheartedly.

I become bold enough to reach down to Andrew and, when I did this, he would also reach down to me, but always at my instigation. Never at his. And we did not once manage the deed. I came to dread night-time. All in all, the marriage bed was a disaster. Some nights he pleaded he was too full up from roast dinner or too tired, or there was an order to deliver first thing, or I had approached him too delicately or not delicately enough. He enjoyed his dinners and his sauces and his pastimes. His fine wines. Card games and writing. Every pleasure except his wife.

It was not a subject he was willing to discuss. We carried on as if all were perfectly well. He even left love-notes around the house. Swatches from his workshop. *Darling Christian, I saw this silk and thought of you.* But truly that was my darkest winter, when I felt grotesque to the core, for my husband clearly had no desire for me whatsoever. And were it not for the mindless tasks of running Carrick House, and its diligent staff and its endless meals, and the errand boys calling at all times, I would have ripped at my legs and arms with my nails and pulled out my own hair and screamed at the candelabras – all at the horror and shame of the sheer ugliness of my own self.

And in the deepest hours, when he was either asleep beside me or in his own chamber, I lay with my tears streaming, uttering the words 'What's wrong with me?' Over and over and over again.

When March came, and the weather improved and the days were lighter, Andrew finally set off again for Calais. I was utterly relieved.

Mother and I visited Johanna again at her home in Warriston. She was in slightly looser clothes and wore an embroidered house-jacket, with bows closing up the front. It was hard to see if she had started to show yet but I could not help staring at her belly, wondering if mine could ever be filled with a baby.

'All is wonderful,' she insisted, when tea was served and the door was closed, sitting back on her chair. She had ordered another marzipan from the confectioner and offered us generous pieces.

'You must guard your figure,' warned Mother, downing her tea in a few gulps. 'Oh, the carriage ride parched me.'

'Of course I am guarding my figure.' Johanna patted her belly. 'Well, I am trying my best.'

We nibbled on the marzipan, but it was rich, and Mother laid hers back on her plate.

'And is Robert thrilled?' asked Mother.

'Robert is beside himself with joy,' Johanna assured her, and Mother took her leave to use the chamberpot, saying tea ran through her like a waterfall.

Johanna took her own cup and spooned sugar into it. 'I find sugar keeps my strength up,' she said. 'Don't tell Mother. Robert simply wants things to remain as normal in the marriage bed, if you understand my meaning, and all I want to do is sleep.

The pregnancy exhausts me and has brought out a new tender-
ness in my breasts that make his touch feel almost painful.'

I tutted sympathetically, but I felt myself tense.

'Understandable,' I said, sucking the inside of my cheeks.

'I knew you would understand. I can't talk to anyone else
about it. Men are insatiable, are they not? What do you find
to be a solution, Christian, when Andrew is overly amorous
and you are just exhausted from the day?'

I found myself reaching for the sugar, although I never take
it. I stirred a spoonful into my tea and realized I would have
to drink it now.

'Well, it can be an issue,' I said, 'but husband and wife must
simply find a way of negotiating a compromise. Understanding
each other's needs, I believe, is vital to a happy union.'

'Oh, you are such a lucky duck!' exclaimed Johanna. 'You
two are so happy, of course. And the marriage book certainly
gave us ample instruction, did it not?' Johanna grinned, taking
another nibble of the marzipan.

The tea was vile. *He doesn't want to fuck me,* I screamed
silently into the teacup, white porcelain with blue flowers and
leaves. *He hates touching me. He would rather sleep. What's
wrong with me?* Tea and sugar drained into me. The cup
emptied.

*Corstorphine Castle*
*March 1679*

*Dear Niece,*

*Your new husband is at sea! To Calais, I believe (how
industrious). Lady Forrester and I request the pleasure of
your company at our home. You cannot possibly languish
alone. Lady Forrester is feeling somewhat more robust,
although she still spends much of her time in her chamber.*

*Nonetheless, this is an excellent opportunity for you to join*
*her in some painting.*
   *Lord James Forrester*
   *P.S. Did you like the hair comb?*


The hair comb had been swept up in the great transfer of
my belongings from Roseburn to Carrick House and it took
me an hour or so to locate it, in a trunk of trinkets that I had
not touched since becoming a wife.

It looked marvellously expensive. But why give something
so precious to me on my sister's wedding day?

I sat on my cold marriage bed and ran my fingers over its
sharp teeth.

The letter lay on the top of my dressing table beside my
scents and powders. All gifts from Andrew. None savoured by
him. I lifted it and read it again. I put the comb to my head
and watched the pearls catch the light. I tucked it into the
side of my hair. It looked sophisticated. My hair, always a chore
to tame, curled around it. I smiled.

It was the first time I had smiled in days.

I put the letter down. I picked up a bottle of rose-oil scent
and dabbed it onto my throat. It smelled as a woman ought.
Heady and sweet.


*Dear Lord and Lady Forrester,*

   *I am agreeable to your offer of spending some time at*
*your home. The first weekend in April suits. I will bring all*
*my painting materials with me, as I am sure Lady Forrester*
*would like to see my latest colours.*

   *Your loving niece.*

# Chapter Twelve

# VIOLET

*Bell's Close, Edinburgh*
*March 1679*

G inger lies in the earth at Greyfriars cemetery.
The High Constables had been called, and they'd asked about the man who killed her. What had he looked like and how many times had he visited? And there was even talk of them putting out a broadsheet. But that never happened. Nothing happened. In the end everyone was keen to sweep the poor soul under the rug, so to speak. No one wanted a fuss.

Ginger was buried at Greyfriars instead of being buried in the mass grave at Burgh Muir or chucked in the Nor Loch because Mrs Fiddes, now in a black veil each morning until the first customers arrived, wanted to do something right by her. I'd made poor Ginger look as decent as I could, and washed her face and brushed her fine hair before we wrapped her in a white shroud. Four men in black hats took her. We followed. A procession of gaudy whores, with the neighbours tutting and judging. Up to the Landmarket, then turning left before the castle hill. Down into the Grassmarket, where they sell horses that she would never ride and cattle for beef she would never eat.

I'd found the wee hair pin nestled in amongst her ringlets

and taken it, for Ginger would not want a grave-robber to find it. Now it is in the box with my other mementos. My box of the dead.

There is an absence of piano tunes, and Mrs Fiddes takes to weeping. A crusty kerchief never far from her leaking nose, her smoking pipe never far from her lips. I am surprised, for I thought she was just an old boot, but perhaps it is sorrow, or perhaps it is the guilt. As for me, I have a mixture of feelings, which are mostly loneliness and sadness and anger, and a feeling that if I were ever to see that murdering bastard again, I would rip him apart.

Mrs Fiddes summons a meeting with the other bawds, for there are half a dozen in this town, all broad-shouldered madams who rustle into the parlour and out again, leaving oily lip-stains on the whisky glasses and the scent of mint. Descriptions of the man are shared, but no one knows who he was, and he has truly disappeared into the night. But I turn cold as a winter bed when I remember how he looked straight at me and decided whether he would take me or Ginger that day, for the only thing that saved me was that he already had a taste for her blood.

If I ever see him again, it will be me or him left standing.


And then just as I am settling on the couch for another night and wondering how much longer I can do it, getting an elbow in each rib from Flossie and Bess, finding myself humming 'Fine Knacks', Lord James returns.

I look up at the doorway to find him standing there, bigger and bolder than ever, with his hair even curlier and shinier than I had remembered and his eyes darker and lustier, and his coat buttons and ruffles an undoubtable triumph of fashion.

It is like a punch in the guts.

I quake in my thin silk gown, my hair still untidy from the last gentleman. A poor version of Venus if ever there was one.

Mrs Fiddes can't pour his whisky fast or large enough, and the girls in the parlour fair hoick up their titties, for who wouldn't want a month in a castle after all they have heard me bleat on about it? But I know he has come back for me, 'cause his face flushes pink when he sees me.

'I have come with a proposal,' he says to me and Mrs Fiddes when, at his request, we have retired to the kitchen with a whisky.

The kitchen is a damp, hot, windowless room that reeks of mutton fat and I wonder whether he has been anywhere so grim.

He takes a great whiff of his silver pomander and clears his throat. 'I would like Violet to come and live with me for some time. I will pay you again and, Violet, I will also pay you a weekly wage,' he says.

'To live with you?' squawks Mrs Fiddes through the blue-grey smoke.

'To live with me,' he confirms.

A shiver runs through me. It is not terror, though, but a thrill of excitement.

Mrs Fiddes sets down her whisky glass.

'I know you are a laird, sir, with all the respectability that comes with that,' she says in a warning tone. 'But I have just had one of my girls murdered by a gent who looked like butter would not melt, and I am not inclined see another one killed.'

He looks most shocked.

'I would not harm a hair on her head,' he says.

'So what is your intention? Surely a gent like you could have his pick of women – harlots and ladies alike?'

'Oh, indeed,' he sniffs, looking most immodest. 'In fact I have some experience in this and I am hoping to take a married mistress soon, but a situation like that comes down to opportunity. Regardless, I am in a position to be able to afford a kept woman, long-term. Violet will be well looked after, and every need attended to.'

His eyes begin to water, what with the smoke and whatever unholy herbs are in that silver device. I feel the flush of pleasure you get when you have won a long-fought hand of cards.

'I have many other girls,' Mrs Fiddes barters, 'and you can take a few with you. Your own harem, as you are clearly that way inclined.'

Well, I could have slapped the bitch for that suggestion, right on her wobbly chowks, for I have no desire to share that turret with anyone.

The wanton devil even seems to consider this, swallowing his whisky hard with his eyes closed. Then he opens them.

'Just Violet. For now.'


And so that is how I come to be returned to my turret, with my box of the dead at peace in a dressing-table drawer. My laird is mighty eager to reacquaint himself with me, slobbering and slavering all over my head as he humps himself into his blissful place.

'The arrangement is exactly as before,' he says, settling himself into the pillows afterwards. 'Keep yourself to yourself and never wander about the castle. Visitors may come and go, but that is no concern of yours. The maid, Oriana, will make sure you are well fed and watered. And she will take you for a daily walk, for I am not wanting you to run to fat.'

I agree to it all.

What choice do I have?

He takes his leave after a few minutes and, good as his word, the sour and dour Oriana turns up with a spare cloak and stout boots.

'I'm to take you for a walk in the village,' she says. 'And we are to talk to no one.'

'I'll wager you thought you'd seen the last of me,' I say.

She peers at me as I lace up the boots. She wears a tight, white frilled cap from which no hair is allowed to escape. Her eyebrows and eyelashes are almost translucent. She looks like an angry egg.

'I am quite pleased you are back,' she whispers, when my boots are laced. 'Despite the fact you are a hoor and destined for hell, unless you start praying, there are not many girls my age in this place. Now wipe that rouge off, for Corstorphine has never seen the like.'

I do as she says, wondering what will we ever talk about to keep each other decent company on these walks? When all she knows is laundry and table-setting and pouring tea. What could we ever have in common – a pious thing like this, and me?

We walk down the long castle avenue, past its high trees with their barren branches filled with solemn-looking pigeons that peer down curiously, as if they know I am not from around these parts. Oriana is fast on her feet. Must be all the marching from the kitchen to the turret. I have to put in the effort to keep up.

'You have the wheeze of sooty chimneys about you,' she says. 'What is Edinburgh like?'

'A good place to make your fortune, if you have the right sort of luck. Traders in every spare inch. And every type of trade too, from cattle-sellers to entertainers and musicians, and pie-men claiming horsemeat and rat meat is best beef.'

Oriana baulks. She would have no stomach for the town. I have a pang for Ginger. She gathered treasures found in the dirt, like buttons and bottle-stoppers, and said she would sell them one day on a stall. Kept them under her bed. I wonder if Mrs Fiddes has chucked them all out. Wee Ginger, swallowed up by the town, nothing of her left.

'Well, it sounds an unholy place.'

'They say the Devil himself rides the streets on horseback.'

'You are wicked,' Oriana scolds.

'I am sure Corstorphine has its evils too,' I murmur.

'We are a God-fearing village. Nothing much ever happens here.'

'And the laird watching over it all,' I say.

'He does,' she says, pursing her lips and striding forth. 'We are at his mercy and, if not him, we would be at the mercy of another laird. They are much the same, and we are better with the Devil we know.'

Oriana, I realize, is more worldly-wise than she pretends to be.


Winter turns to spring. I watch it from my turret, where I am warm and cosy with furs and roast beef and hot chocolate, and I thank my lucky stars for the turn my life has taken. I barely mind the humpings.

Then one morning at the beginning of April, as the grounds are starting to green up, the laird says he will not be coming for a while, because he has a visitor arriving. A few days to myself. What bliss. That is what I think at first.

I spend the morning tidying and sweeping and airing the

room, for it has got dusty and it has the smell of human bodies about it. Then Oriana brings breakfast, and it is a half-bowl of pottage gone cold.

'I hope lunch is better than this,' I say to her retreating arse, and she turns round and folds her arms on her chest, wearily.

'It will be a feast,' she says. 'Me and the cook are rushed off our feet getting it all prepared. You are lucky you can just sit here and do nothing. And I am sure there will be plenty of leftovers, for it is only one visitor coming – a fine lady that I suspect he has a particular fondness for, with all the demands he is making for polishing and pastry.'

A fine lady. A particular fondness. Oriana looks fit to burst with her own importance in these preparations and launches herself out of the door, brushing the dust off her apron. But I pause, ignoring the pottage. He'd said he hoped to take a mistress. That did not bother me back at Mrs Fiddes's, such was my desperation to escape.

But now that I am here I do not fancy the prospect of competition, for a kept woman is always at the mercy of her keeper.

And that gives me something to do for the rest of the afternoon. Brood.

I watch for the visitor, for there are four wee windows in the turret: facing north, south, east and west.

This supposed fine lady arrives with a maid, who scurries around righting skirts and taking bags, and I get a right good keek. She is wearing a thick fur cape over a grey gown that is most extravagant-looking, but she has a long nose, and her forehead is too high, with her hair on the frizzy side of curly, swept back harsh with a fancy comb.

But then I am no rare beauty myself – oh, don't try and argue. What you see is what you get, with me. Bit of rouge, of course, but not enough to upset any members of the kirk. No padding in this gown, and look – my hair's real, from top to bottom. And my jewels: why, look how they gleam in the morning light. Each of them proper gems.

Perhaps my honesty is why Lord James can't keep his hands off me, which goes to show that beauty matters not, in the end. It's all about whether you can make them laugh, and tease them good enough with a promise of exquisite pleasure, and I wonder if she can.

For if she can, what's the point in me being held in his castle turret? What use paying a pleasure girl if there is pleasure for free elsewhere? I can almost feel the fingers of the whore-house scratching on my spine and smell the reek of Mrs Fiddes's kitchen.

I will not go back there.

## Chapter Thirteen

# CHRISTIAN

*Corstorphine Castle*
*April 1679*

Corstorphine Castle: grandiose, like its occupants. I had visited before, when the Forresters hosted dinners and Mother and Father took us. I had always felt intimidated.

I felt intimidated again. I had diligently packed paints and brushes, and gingerbread and six bottles of Andrew's Burgundy wine, all the time thinking, *I should not go.*

My uncle had sent his own carriage for me, on Friday mid-morning, piled with furs and filled with his scent of lavender and cloves, which made me almost dizzy, whilst the silver-and-pearl hair comb pinched my scalp. And he'd also told Mother that her sister wished me to visit, prompting letters galore. *You must keep Aunt L entertained, Christian. Tell her Johanna is blooming. Tell her all about Andrew's glasshouse.*

A maid swung open the carriage door.

'Good afternoon, Lady Christian,' she said, curtseying with the pomp I remembered of James's staff. 'Your hosts will receive you in the dining room.'

I stood in the courtyard, surrounded by windows that looked like black eyes, and suddenly I thought of Carrick House, and

Andrew, and felt a pining that started in my belly and rose into my throat.

I should not be here. But here I was. I had brought one of the Carrick House maids with me, so that everything was seemly. But I'd chosen one of the duller girls, who would pay more attention to the castle furnishings than to the hosts and their guest. Who loved playing cards for coins far more than she enjoyed gossiping.

I went inside.

The dining room was so imposing it even put Andrew's to shame. Gold-framed oils hung side-by-side on the walls. Gleaming side-tables spilled over with silver candlesticks and tall china vases.

I was admiring the symmetry of the decor when I was interrupted by a clattering so cacophonous that I went to the doorway to see what was causing it. Two servants were bringing Aunt Lillias downstairs, on a chair contraption that clanked and banged on every step, heralding her arrival, with her cries croaking above it all: 'Go more gently, you fools, I can feel every bump in my bones.'

Lillias's descent into ill health had been legendary. But it was another thing entirely to see her so dependent on assistance. She had indeed been dazzling, once. When I was around twelve, Mother and Father had a trio of fiddlers come to play at Roseburn; Lillias and James were among the guests. I remembered her rich auburn hair, curled and topped with jewels, and a black gown with a high, creamy ruff, and the pointed toe of her black shoes, embroidered with red roses, tapping the tune to 'Katie Beardie'. I remembered the shoes whirling before my eyes, for Johanna and I spun in circles to this song, with everyone clapping and Mother sitting next to Lillias. Both of them watching us with different sorts of smiles. Mother's warm and beamy; Lillias's thin and closed.

I remembered James taking his wife's wine glass from her hand and whispering something in her ear that shut the smile down.

And here I was now, in their dining room.

I was so nervous I feared I might not manage to eat.

James strode over the stone floor with great thuds of his high boots. What an ill-matched pair they had become. And how assured he was, in his stance and in the firm lock of his chin. I blinked and tried not to remember Andrew, struggling to remove his boots quietly at the bedside and glancing at me to see if I was asleep yet.

'Come back inside the dining room,' James said, gripping my arm and swerving me firmly away from the commotion on the steps. Lillias would not wish you to see her looking so unladylike.'

He put me in a dining chair and stood on ceremony whilst the servants brought his wife in and set her down.

'Dearest niece,' she croaked across the vast table, as skirts were righted and her water and wine poured for her. 'You are quite changed since we last met. Not a young girl.' She screwed her eyes at me. 'But your hair is still unruly.'

My hands flew up to pat it down. I felt twelve again.

Her husband coughed and that must have been a signal she was becoming impolite, for she reached for her wine and beckoned the maid to serve up.

'Come, Oriana, you are slow today. We have a guest.'

A more awkward luncheon I have never sat through.

Lillias remained sour and stiff like a stick of rhubarb, florid-faced, and her words unpeeled from her, fibrous. If I cut into her with my knife, she would be just as stringy. She may once have been a beauty, but she had gone to rot. The meal was pigeon from their dovecote, baked into a pie with a rich sauce and heavy crust. The kind of feast that would sit in the belly all day.

'Are you enjoying your meal?' Lillias asked, peering at me over her glass of red wine. Its level never seemed to drop below one-third full, and the maid topped her up and righted her silverware when her arms knocked it, looking as anxious as I felt.

Lillias drank copiously but remained thin because she barely ate, I realized. Above her placing at the left side of the table, on the wall, was the head of a stag. From where I sat directly opposite her, its antlers framed her tight little skull, so she had the appearance of a horned beast.

The maid set about making sure I wanted for nothing, peering at me from under her white frilled cap and looking away whenever I caught her eye.

The pigeon was spiced and peppery, with a curious fire that mingled with its gamey flesh. Mother had always fed us plain food at home to stop us becoming over-excitable, and Andrew let me deal directly with his cook, so we were a household of beef broths and oatmeal puddings and trout, as that was what I tolerated best.

'Mr Nimmo is a prosperous merchant,' Lillias probed. 'Although he is rarely seen at kirk, I hear, for he is always on business.'

James swilled his wine around his mouth, watching me.

'He is extremely industrious,' I said.

'I do hope he will make time for you. For that is the key to a successful marriage,' said Lillias.

I wondered if she thought her own marriage successful.

There had been no children. And now they seemed to lead separate lives.

We ate until James's plate was empty and we two ladies had picked our way over our pie. The same happened with a whipped-cream pudding served in glasses. When James was finished, he put down his cutlery with a clatter and motioned the maid to clear the table.

He addressed his wife. 'Now if we are all finished, I will take our guest for a walk around the grounds before it gets dark and the pigeons have roosted. A pity you cannot join us, but it would be unhealthy to have her cooped up all day.'

I waited for Lillias to say she too would like to come and be pushed around the grounds on her wheeled chair. But all she did was sip her wine and look at me.

She would not be joining us.

I found my cape – for my own maid had disappeared into the kitchen with the other staff – and joined her husband on a walk.


James took me through the long avenue of sycamore trees. I knew this route. I had walked it before when we had visited, when Father was alive.

It was a fine evening. The sun's last cold rays cast pale hues across the grounds. James's face was rough and weathered where Andrew's was smooth. It added texture.

I was comparing them again.

'Lady Forrester seemed in good spirits,' I offered, for he was too silent for comfort, just the clip of his feet on the dried earth.

'She always improves with wine,' he said. 'She will have time tomorrow to have you sketch in her room, for she will be wanting all the news you have. Then she will be ill for the remainder of the weekend, and by Monday the physician will be out again.'

'I hardly have any news,' I said. 'I have been more or less isolated at Carrick House, unless you count the news of my mother's latest hat.'

'Another gift from Mr Nimmo?'

I nodded but didn't meet his eye.

We were at the end of the avenue. The largest of the syca-more trees rose above us, its tiny new leaves the lightest shade of green. Sycamores whisper in their own particular way. They shimmer, as though passing the most shocking of gossip from branch to branch, desperate to spread it.

Nearby was the new dovecote, a three-tiered stone structure that stuck out oddly.

'The villagers complain it's quite the eyesore, but there is room for a thousand birds in there,' he said. 'Not as novel as Mr Nimmo's glasshouse at Carrick House, I imagine.'

I knew he would bring up the subject of my new husband.

'Andrew adores his glasshouse,' I said.

'And what do you grow in it? Citrus fruits? Vines?'

'It is Andrew's passion, not mine,' I said. 'There is something unnatural about watching oranges grow when it is snowing outside.'

'You are unenthusiastic,' he said. 'I would have thought you would be glowing with happiness, but you are not. Is he away on business too much for your liking?'

I knew, then, that I had a choice.

I could say that Andrew and I were *perfectly matched*, with Andrew sailing and me sewing. That I was planning on hothousing some palms or feeling broody, now that Johanna was with child.

I said none of these things. The pent-up humiliation of my failing marriage was banging against my chest.

'Unfortunately, my husband is so preoccupied with his fabrics and his sailings that he quite forgets his wife at times,' I said, choosing my words with great care. 'I wonder what I should do.'

James frowned, and appeared to consider the matter.

'You know, the gossip on Mr Nimmo is that he was barely interested in taking a wife,' he said. He looked at me, as if wondering if he should go on.

I nodded.

'His acquaintances were quite surprised to see him settle down,' James continued. 'I know this because I made some enquiries. Oh, don't look so surprised, Christian; with your dear father deceased, someone had to. And there were no surprises. No lovers – male or female – or offspring that anyone knows about, which is quite miraculous for a handsome thirty-year-old bachelor. My conclusion is that he married because he felt he ought to, rather than because he wanted to. It is not uncommon.'

My heart sank utterly. I should have realized my marriage was too good to be true.

'I am a fool,' I whispered. Tears sprang, stinging my eyes.

'You are nothing of the sort,' James said. But I felt awful. I did not doubt that Andrew had *affection* for me. But he had no *passion* for me, and never would. He had simply decided that he needed a wife to match his splendid new home, as he might have decided he needed a water-fountain. He had picked me, but he could happily have picked anyone.

The trees rustled overhead as the last of the pigeons gathered themselves together. I tried to breathe slowly to maintain my composure.

James cleared his throat as if considering what to say next.

'A woman in your position has options,' he said.

I blinked, to disperse the tears.

He regarded me for a moment. 'You are beautiful tonight, Christian. This silver gown and silver hair comb suit your complexion so magnificently. Has Mr Nimmo ever said you are beautiful?'

My face burned. 'I cannot recall,' I said.

He was earnest. 'It is a matter of the utmost importance in a marriage. Has your husband ever made you feel that you are beautiful?'

I raced through my memories. Had Andrew ever made me feel beautiful? Interesting, yes. Clever. Entertaining. He had admired my artistic eye and poetic script. But he had never looked at me the way that Father had looked at Mother. He had never told me I was beautiful. My own husband had never made love to me. The realization lodged in the pit of my stomach, exquisitely humiliating.

'You are beautiful,' whispered James.

'Lillias will be thinking we are gone too long,' I said.

'You saw her yourself tonight. Imagine having all this, with no love or affection within these castle walls.'

We were facing each other and slowly he lowered his face, until it was almost touching mine. I was no more in control of myself than a sycamore seed controls its destination, whirling on a summer wind. I tilted my face up and kissed him and when I did, I heard a sigh escape from me. A light gasp, the like of which I had never made before. And that urged him on to kiss me back and this time our mouths opened, and that kiss was like nothing I had felt before. Like me, it was beautiful.

*They are kissing, they are kissing.* I heard the sycamore leaves sing and dance with it, shocked and jiggling, spiralling and horrified, startling the pigeons, sending the last of them skittering into the dovecote, and even through that commotion James did not stop; I did not stop.

## THE CALEDONIA BROADSIDE

### EDINBURGH, 30th September

The Maiden has been in use since 1564, based on the concept of the Halifax Gibbet, replacing Scotland's executioner's sword. Its parts are stored at Blackfriars and taken to the execution sites of Castlehill, the Grassmarket and the Tolbooth and assembled as required.

It is largely used for executions of nobility and enemies of the Crown. The Maiden's block stands four feet tall, requiring the condemned to stand and bend over, placing their head on a crossbar, rather than lying prone. This act has come to be known as *Kissing the Maiden*.

Chapter Fourteen

# CHRISTIAN

*Corstorphine Castle*
*April 1679*

I did not take my leave the next morning.

In hindsight, I should have.

When I woke, and the memories of the previous evening hit, gathering my belongings and fleeing was my first impulse. But the thought of returning to Carrick House filled me with utter despair. There was a knock on the door from the maid, bringing hot water, and before I could think straight, I was dragged into a cheerful yellow silk gown and the fanfare of breakfast and jam and cream, and my aunt's clattering wheeled chair.

I don't know how long James and I had spent under the sycamore tree. Long enough for me to feel drained of my senses and engulfed by him. Then he had walked me back to my chamber, leaving me there. *I will think of you all night,* he'd said. I had lain awake for hours, almost falling asleep, then jerking awake with the shock of it. Now I buzzed with anxiety as we sat waiting for him, and I tried to drink a cup of thick-tasting coffee.

'We cannot paint the hills in this dreary weather,' Lillias said, looking out of the window at the dull sky. 'But it might clear by the afternoon.'

'Then I should like to walk the grounds,' I said. 'I am still in the habit of a morning exercise hour.' I was desperate for time alone. I could not process my thoughts whilst chitter-chattering. Inside my skull, the truth screamed. But when my lips moved, niceties flew out. *Such delicious jam – pass on my compliments to Cook.*

James joined the table looking as polished as he always had, as though nothing at all had happened between us. Not a curl out of place. Not a shadow of guilt. The maid rushed to serve him a plate of runny-looking eggs. How could he stomach them?

'How delightful to breakfast with two beauties this morning,' he said, beaming at us both. *Oh God, James*, my head seethed. *Don't use such words.*

'It's refreshing to have young company,' Lillias said. 'Your niece will walk the grounds this morning if you are free to accompany her?'

'Oh, no need,' I insisted, trying to sound bright. 'I am sure you have business to attend to in the castle.'

'As a matter of fact, I do,' he said, tucking into his eggs and barely concealing a grin. 'Enjoy your walk and take as long as you like. Exercise keeps the thoughts pure.'


It was sheer relief to be alone. I walked as far as I could, along a trail pungent with wild garlic, the hem of my skirts gathering damp.

What on God's earth had I got myself into?

I pictured Johanna and her perfect marriage, and the ladies in our circle who seemed content enough in their various marriages and their afternoon socials, playing cards and chattering about fans and hats. Heaven only knew what the gentlemen did, whether any took mistresses, but that is a gentleman's prerogative.

I was entirely on my own in this matter.

But my husband and I had not consummated our marriage in three months, and it was not my fault.

The earthy scent of the dewy wild garlic filled my nose.

What if Andrew never made love to me? What if he could not? Was I to spend the rest of my days untouched? I would die. I would wither. Now that I had experienced desire, I knew it to be a natural part of me.

The path drew into line with a shallow stream.

I wanted to sit somewhere but dreaded getting the yellow dress dirty, for the maids would sigh and everyone would pass comment, so I stood, watching the water trickle a slow, brown path.

I could do this.

And still be a decent wife to Andrew.

It was sinful. But it was not me who had broken the marriage vow, it was him – failing to love me as a husband ought.

And James was the right man. Older and more experienced. He was lonely. He was loving and kind. He was a perfect gentleman. I felt passion for him.

# Chapter Fifteen

# VIOLET

*Corstorphine Castle*
*April 1679*

I am surprised when the laird turns up, not to mention flustered, as I have spent most of yesterday and this morning battering around, furious and helpless as a hot wasp.

'I thought you had a visitor,' I say.

'She is out on a walk,' he says.

'Then you are taking a risk coming here,' I say. 'For she could see you.'

He laughs. 'She is too caught up in her own thoughts to notice anything,' he replies. 'And anyway, I enjoy taking risks.'

I turn from him and dab on my rouge in a slow and careful way. I watch him in the mirror. His eyes are as bright as his polished coat buttons, and he peers over my shoulder to catch a look at his marvellous self.

Well, no good comes from holding in your piss, so I say, 'Who is she?'

And he flops on the bed like a dizzy girl and fans his brow with his meaty hand and says she is the delightful Lady Christian, a niece by marriage but not blood, recently married to a merchant who sells fabrics but cannot bear the touch of his own wife's flesh.

'And are you fucking her?' I ask. I have applied too much rouge. My cheeks look alight.

And he laughs and says, 'You sound like my wife. Not yet,' he adds. 'But I've been considering seducing her for a while. I gave her my utmost charms last night under the sycamore tree, whilst Lillias settled to bed. And I intend on fully seducing her tonight.'

He talks as if I am nothing to him. He brags as though I would be interested, and I hear myself laugh along with his jokes. *You sound like my wife.*

As if that would ever be possible. How ridiculous, Violet.

How low must he think me, if he is able to talk of fucking other women with such merriment. He sits up and catches my eye in the mirror.

'Far too much of that rouge, my dear,' he says, studying me. I take a cloth and dab at my cheeks, but it only serves to make them redder. He loses interest and pours himself a wine and one for me – a mean glass too.

I do not sip. I need my head straight. Wine is a poison, and those who think it a simple pleasure are deluded. His problem is he drinks far too much of it. It is barely eleven o'clock. I let him sip away for a minute or two.

'Tell me more about Lady Christian,' I say, coming to the bed. 'Tell me everything about her, for I am quite curious.'

Some, mostly the French, say a woman should never enquire about a gentleman's other lovers, but I have said this already and I will say it again. I have worked in a whorehouse five years. There are tricks of the bedroom, and I know them all. Learned them from Mrs Fiddes and the other girls. Learned how to smother a lover in kisses and act shameless and tickle him in his favourite places.

But in this harsh life a girl must also survive. So I let him drone on about this grand lady, until I have learned everything I need to know. For she is my rival, and I have far too much to lose.

'Damn, the time is ticking on,' he says, after he has rambled on for half an hour or so. I had been stroking his chest whilst he spoke, and I take my hand lower, thinking he will be wanting a quick roll-about.

Instead he pushes my hand away.

'Not today, my dear,' he says. 'I am saving myself.' And with that he lets out a wicked chuckle. But the bastard means it, and the next minute he hops out of the door, bidding me a relaxing afternoon.

And relax I do not, for he has never turned me down before. What need will Lord James have of me if this lady lets him have his wicked way? I might be sent back to Mrs Fiddes and condemned to a life of servicing the hairy-arsed pedlars and pie-sellers who creep into her pleasure house, chomping at the bit. The horrors of it all seem far worse, now that I have tasted a better life.


I spend the day mostly fretting, until Oriana brings dinner. He was set to impress this lady, for Oriana tells me it is yesterday's leftover pigeon pie cooked delicious and tender, and a pastry tart with a dark, spiced filling. I poke at it with my knife and in the end give in to temptation and gorge down the whole plateful. And then, with pastry sprayed across my bosom, I feel most disappointed in myself.

Oriana is no more tolerable, as she thinks herself crucial to the success of the visit, blethering about how she has put crocuses in vases in the lady's chamber and a sprig of dried lavender by her bed.

All through my dinner I am thinking of nothing but Lord James watching this lady's lips as she swallows down her prune tart, and getting merrier by the minute on his wine. She will no doubt have a canny way of stopping the crumbs from spilling on her lap. I should push it all from my mind and go to bed, but I cannot. I am sitting in the chair and the cold air has oozed through my body.

I open and close my fingers into fists to get the heat into them again. A draught is drifting in through the doorway, which is not something I remember happening before. Then I hear a gentle rattle coming from downstairs. I must go and investigate it, for I don't want to spend the night lying in my bed being disturbed by taps and rattles. I tread gently down the spiral staircase and, when I get to the bottom, I realize why I am so cold.

Oriana has not closed the door.

# Chapter Sixteen

# CHRISTIAN

*Corstorphine Castle*
*April 1679*

Lady Lillias invited me to spend Saturday afternoon sketching in her chamber, saying it had the best views. It was a dark room with navy curtains, which made me think of Johanna, but these curtains were dusty, and I wondered if this chamber had ever been filled with laugher or soft sighs. I decided not to think about that, for it was not my fault if it had not.

'See, the tips of the Pentlands are majestic,' she said, her sketching paper laid out on a table beneath her trembling hand. 'Look at those mauves and greens and blues.' It was the most enthusiastic I had seen her about anything.

I had betrayed my aunt.

I drew lines with my chalk.

Women are burned for less.

But no one would ever suspect that anything had happened with James and me, would they?

I would rather burn than die unloved.

'Your sketch is strong – look at those powerful lines,' my aunt observed.

She wore herself out after an hour or so and only joined us

for a few bites of food at dinner, before being taken back up
in her chair with her wine. I pretended to be disappointed
when she left, but in truth I was thrilled.

'She really has no stamina at all these days,' James sighed.

'I can see how difficult it is for you,' I said.

He looked at me mournfully as the maid refilled his glass.

'I am the loneliest man alive,' he whispered.

I told him I was feeling tired myself and he did not persuade
me to stay up, but after a few minutes in my chamber I heard
a knock at my door.

I'd known he would come to me.

The click as the handle turned was so sharp that I flinched.

'I will leave if you wish,' he whispered, just a shadow in the
feeble candlelight.

'You will stay,' I said in a voice I had not heard before. Low,
like Johanna's throaty laugh.

But nothing that happened next was like anything Andrew
and I had done together in our chamber. It was of a different
texture. And when I try to judge myself on my behaviour, I
also recall, quite vividly, the pain of sharing a bed with a
husband who detested my body. The way Andrew turned away
from me. The way he blamed his heavy meals or my indelicate
approaches.

And so that night I felt I deserved a man who did not despise
me. And he did not. James adored me. He delved for all the
parts of me Andrew avoided, lingering so long and giving me
so much pleasure that I know the marriage book was right and
Andrew wrong.

'I have wanted this for so long,' James kept whispering, and
he insisted on looking at my face, so that he could see my

pleasure for himself, and any embarrassment left me. I watched his eyes too, and he wrapped me so close I could not imagine two human bodies being closer. And I made all sorts of noises that I was not aware I was capable of. I couldn't help myself and I clasped my hand over my mouth, and he took it off to hear me better, and it was all so much more intense than I realized. Our skin and the sheer strength of him. Everything warm and sweet and lavender-scented, and Johanna was right and it was also very unladylike, but what did I care? For that night, for the first time, I was not a lady. I was a woman.

# Chapter Seventeen

# VIOLET

*Corstorphine Castle*
*April 1679*

Oh, there is nothing finer than a good, honest humping, is there?

It's the friendliest way to say *goodnight* and the finest way to say *good morning*. Some of us girls are night-time girls, and some gentlemen are at their best first thing in the morning, if you catch my drift. But that night all I want to know is whether that fine lady is allowing the laird a visit to her pleasure garden.

For my fate rests on this detestable bastard's whims.

I know I shouldn't, but this place is near deserted. Oriana will be sitting at a dying stove with the lady's maid, the two of them warming their skinny buttocks and sneaking leftover prune tart, and no one will give two hoots.

Do real ladies let lairds hump them if they are not wed? Or will she tease him half to death and send him to his chamber? I follow the wall towards the keep, in full shadow now, my blood thumping in my ears. It is strange to be out in the dark air and I take great lungfuls of the night. The first door I try is locked and I think maybe they will all be, and this journey just a waste of my nerves, but when I turn the handle on the next door, it opens. From what he's pointed out to me, I am standing in a hallway underneath the chambers, with the laird's room on the left and Lillias's on the right at the top of the stairs. The house is silent. If he were entertaining this lady innocently, surely there would be loud clatters of conversation and laughing; I'd hear him guffaw at his own jokes.

But with Lady Forrester sickly, as he says, the only folks likely to find me are Oriana or the laird himself, and I can always say I had a funny turn. I creep up the stairs, a wide staircase hung with tapestries of battles and knights, but no tits and cocks, the cheeky devil. Imagine this being your home. If it were mine, I would not be wasting my time fornicating with whores. I would lie on couches, eating marzipans until my belly blew up and I popped.

I turn left, past animal heads staring at me eerily with beady eyes and spiky horns, and I am just about thinking, *Violet, this is far enough now, you daft cow,* when I hear something: the faintest of sighs, and that is a sound I am all too familiar with. Coming from behind the first door. I stay very still and wait. There is another sigh and a creak of a bed, and another sigh and then the creaks get faster and so do the sighs.

Oh, without doubt Lord James Forrester is humping away at this fine lady and she is fair enjoying the ride.

*Oh, oh, oh!*

My heart sinks so low into my belly I fear it will knock to the floor with a thud.

I should be used to this. Happens every night at Mrs Fiddes's when a man you've teased and tempted chooses a different girl and you think, *What was wrong with me?*

Those times, you dab on a bit more rouge and bat your eyelashes fast as bees' wings at the next one that walks in the door.

But this time I want to open the door and shout at the crack of his thrusting arse. *What is wrong with me?*

When I am right under his roof, in his turret of lust and pleasure, and he ditches his Mistress Violetta for this plain scone.

And his sickly wife up the corridor, the bastard.

Lord forgive me for what I do next. For it is truly done in a moment of spite.

I unclick the door and open it and see that these two are quite in flagrante, with bodices and petticoats and breeches cast across the floor. I edge the door open and flee down the corridor, with the creaks and gasps fair haunting me. Then I do the same at the grand double doors that must be those of Lady Lillias's own chamber: open them a crack, just wide enough for her to be roused, should she be a light sleeper. Then I scamper back to the south turret, their moans and groans following me all the way down the stairs like stabs in the back.

# Chapter Eighteen

# CHRISTIAN

*Corstorphine Castle*
*April 1679*

James yawned and dozed as soon as he was spent, but I could not, for I was wide awake and in need of mulling it over. To gather my thoughts.

I wrapped myself in a blanket and stood at the window looking down into the castle courtyard, where all was still, under a fat moon.

There was nothing wrong with me.

It was not me that had the problem.

The worry dropped from me like a heavy bag that I had been carrying since my wedding day.

Tonight was an exotic place, so near and yet so far from Carrick House, and its plain soups and boiled hams and acres of solitude and stiff, expensive fabrics.

What did my future hold?

I would not think on it.

Then something caught my eye.

A shape moving towards the south turret. I was sure of it. I watched, but it disappeared, and it was too dark to tell. Perhaps it was a fox. Or perhaps he had servants in there. Nothing to worry me. None of my business. I slipped back into bed beside my new lover. Before I closed my eyes I surveyed the room, now that I was accustomed to the dark. Tapestry wall hangings and sweeping curtains. In the far corner of the room was the door through which James had entered not one or two hours before. It hung slightly ajar. I felt the blood drain from my face. He should have been more careful to close it.

The next day, a Sunday morning, I once again ate breakfast whilst trying to appear perfectly normal. I accepted porridge and coffee and jam from the maid, with nods of my head, and Lillias must have thought me quite hungry, although I was anything but. He'd slipped away in the small hours, back to his chamber.

'Did you sleep soundly?' Lillias asked, as the maid poured her third coffee.

The woman was largely composed of dark and potent liquids. It was no wonder her humours were melancholic.

'Indeed, thank you,' I said. My heart hammered in my chest. I could not mouth the porridge. I could not look at her directly.

'You have dark circles under your eyes,' she said.

'Just my complexion,' I said. 'I assure you I had a most peaceful rest.'

'I am not so sure,' she said. 'I could swear I thought I heard you cry out in the night.'

James shifted a little in his chair and cleared his throat.

'More jam,' he said to the maid. 'There is barely a scrape in the damned pot.'

His spoon clattered onto the floor, and he and the maid went to pick it up and there was a fussing whilst Lillias watched me.

She knew.

I fought the urge to leave the table and splash my face with cold water. I could do that later. Instead I played with my porridge spoon and sipped coffee and said how much I was looking forward to sketching with her again.

But first, she sent James and me to Corstorphine Kirk together. I usually made the trip with Andrew, or with my maid when he was away. Reverend Brodie was in the habit of calling on the Forresters instead of expecting them at his sermon, as Lillias could not manage to travel around the corner and across the road. Instead she said it would do James good to sit in God's house for a change.

'Pray under His roof, James,' she said. 'We have much to ask the Lord this year. For my ailing health, and the new marriage of Christian and Andrew. The spire will help your prayers get to heaven.' She did not look at me.

We walked with the castle staff dawdling beside us, making the most of their day out, and villagers taking the opportunity to question their laird on matters from the plans for the Lammas Fair to the rogues gathering nightly outside the Corstorphine Inn. And that meant we couldn't speak of what had happened the previous night, but instead made niceties with all and sundry about the displays of primroses at the edges of the road, and how the gorse on Corstorphine Hill was blooming bright as fire, and where Andrew was and when he would return.

James was dressed smartly as usual. A black wool cape and black feathered hat and his sword hanging at his side. The other elders joined us as we approached the kirk and soon their conversation turned to the subject of the man and woman who admitted fornication this week, who were to be set upon the repentance stool this morning as their punishment.

"'Tis a pity, but it must be done,' agreed the elders, my own lover among them, in shakes of the head, and no man meeting the eyes of any other.

The repentance stool.

I felt sick. It would be like watching another version of myself. I entered the kirk behind James and felt as though everyone could see my own guilt.

They had both been put at the front of the kirk on two high stools.

The woman repentant was defiant and met the looks of the congregation. She was around my own age, bonnie with pink cheeks and blonde curls that escaped from her cap, and around half the age of the husband who sat four pews in front of us, being clapped on the shoulder by those around him as if we were at his wife's funeral.

The man stared at the floor and fidgeted with his hat.

I and the rest of the two hundred of the congregation opened our prayer books and imagined them together.

Lillias must have known the dread I would feel, watching this pair sit aside from the rest of the flock, with the fear of repentance dancing like a demon between the words in front of me.

But regardless of the sermon Reverend Brodie delivered in his monotone, about the importance of being faithful to one's spouse, for God watches us in all that we do, I spent the service thinking about what happened the previous night, and the way James made me feel such pleasures.

I wondered what the fornicators did.

Whether it was under the moon, like me, or in the spring sunshine down a lane where they thought they would never be seen. I wondered what the woman was thinking. Soon she would have to ask forgiveness for her sins. I wondered if it was worth it for her, for the thrill of having a man enjoy her body and her, his. I wondered if she enjoyed thinking on it, as I do: these secrets we hold.

I closed my eyes, like everyone else, and said 'Our Father'. James stood beside me the whole time. Afterwards he would join in the continued shaming of the fornicators, and would posture in his feathered hat in the kirkyard, saying, 'I hope that was a lesson to everyone.' As we stood there in our pew, though, our knuckles grazed each other's. When there was enough of a stir in the standing up and sitting down, he murmured, 'Forgive me for saying this under God's roof, but I will have you again before lunch.'

'Lady Lillias has guessed,' I said.

'And yet she has not sent you home,' he said. 'She knows of her own shortcomings as a wife.'

I did not know what I was doing.

I prayed to God for forgiveness, but I knew I would let James have me again because it was so exquisite.

And what price would I pay for my sins of the flesh? For even then I knew I must, one day. Would I sit on a stool, or be cast out by Andrew?

Yet nothing would have stopped me from opening my chamber door again to James Forrester.


Dear God, have mercy on my soul, for I let him into my room again and he slipped inside me easily, as my body had been waiting for this all day – had been waiting ever since my wedding night – and he knew it. I could tell by the way James groaned that my pleasure was something he gained pleasure from. Everything flashed before me as he took me: his hair dark and thyme-and-lavender scented; the trail of cloves from his pomander; the woman on the repentance stool; the birds scattering to the dovecote. And then it was all a blur, for he put his head between my legs, like one of the most outrageous illustrations in the marriage book. At first, I tried to cross them, because this was far too much of an intimacy, but he kept going and I could not believe what he was doing: it was outrageous; it was delightful.

Lady Lillias took luncheon in her chamber, and I was summoned there to sketch again, just as the maid was clearing her tray and empty wine bottle.

Her ink pen scratched on her parchment.

I attempted to carry on with my chalk strokes.

'How was kirk?' she asked.

I told her the sermon was illuminating – a lesson against greed and giving what we can to the poorest – and she clucked and said the poorest are the poorest for a reason, and giving them handouts was simply indulging them and not helping them better themselves with honest work.

'And the butcher's wife and the man from the inn did their penance?' she asked.

Indeed, I said. My hills looked lumpy, like a woman's breasts and belly.

'They will be back fornicating within the week,' she said. 'They are better put in the branks – that would stop them. Men cannot help themselves, but women should know better.'

I shuddered. I had seen the branks nailed to the kirk wall, a harsh iron contraption idly threatening its inhabitants: either remain obedient or be restrained by the head, with a spike in the mouth that could cause the tongue to bleed if you so much as moved an inch. They did not have branks in Roseburn. Its repentance stool was hardly used.

She continued to sketch. Her image of the Pentlands was far more artful than mine, and she had detailed the dark clouds hanging over them so heavily I could almost hear them rumble.

'Lord James is immune to such punishments, for he is an elder and pays a great donation to the kirk and has a hand in the running of this village. And I am well aware that he takes women from time to time,' she said. 'But I am Lady Forrester, his wife and mistress of this castle, and you will do well to remember that.'

I reached for my paints. She glanced at my work and frowned.

'This is not as good as I thought it was yesterday,' she said. 'You still have much to learn.'

## THE CALEDONIA BROADSIDE

### EDINBURGH, 2nd October

Reverend Ian Brodie, Minister of Corstorphine Kirk: 'My Lord James Forrester was a most highly regarded member of our Kirk Session. An upstanding character. He gave generously to the kirk. He was a source of personal advice to me on how to deal with the comings and goings of the parishioners. Not an easy flock, Sheriff MacDonald. Forever stealing and fornicating, if you will pardon my language.

'Yes, I do recall one occasion when he was sitting in very close proximity at kirk to Lady Christian. I do remember thinking at the time that it was unusual, for an uncle and niece to be quite so close together on a pew.

'My lord did seem most subdued around that time, which I now come to believe is because he was under the influence of Lady Christian. And I am sorry to say this, Sheriff MacDonald, but that woman is most likely under the influence of the Devil himself.'

(Reverend Brodie's remarks cause such excitement in the public gallery that Sheriff MacDonald is forced to call for a five-minute break.)

# Chapter Nineteen

# CHRISTIAN

*October 1679*
*Near Fala, south-eastern Scotland*

The river rushes over the rocks and the sunlight flashes over the water. I am somewhere close to Fala, if I am following Andrew's map correctly, but this world is greener and lusher than the woods of Roseburn. It feels like a place I would once have loved to escape to, in the time before, when I felt trapped by my own iron gates. How little did I realize. They weren't just keeping me in; they were keeping out the wickedness of the world. Some of it.

I slow and then eventually stop. I must spend time by the river. There is something in the fresh splash of it that fills my soul with comfort. I feel the dappled woods close over me and keep me safe. I stand at the riverbank. I count back to the last time I was near a river and it was mid-August, two months ago, at the stream that runs near Carrick House, and I was thinking and fretting over it all.

Two months that feels like two minutes.

And that is when I realize. I put my hand to my belly.

I have not bled for two months.

## Chapter Twenty

# CHRISTIAN

*Carrick House, Corstorphine*
*April 1679*

I returned to Carrick House after my painting session with my aunt. It was lucky we had not planned another night's stay. My nerves were in shreds.

Thank God Andrew was still away. I asked for dinner and wine on a tray in my chamber because I could not bear the prying of servants as I ruminated.

James had made it clear that he saw our liaison continuing. He had come into my chamber as I gathered my belongings together.

'I have wanted this, my sweet,' he had whispered.

'We are no better than the adulterers on the repentance stool,' I said.

'Our situation is different,' he said. 'Neither of us had the luxury of marrying for love.'

I had believed myself to be in love with Andrew. Now I realized it was nothing of the sort. Love between a man and a woman is more than wedding vows and gentle conversation and gifts. It needs intimacy, to keep the bond strong.

*

Andrew returned. He insisted on coffee in the glasshouse, beside an arrangement of topiary, and the windows steamed up with tales of rocky sailings and inns with lumpy beds. I felt queasy listening to him and wished he would go and rest. I had not realized how he could drone on, without ever stopping to ask what I had been busying myself doing. My thoughts churned whilst I toyed with my fingers and pretended my nervousness was just down to worrying over Mother, who had become lonely now that she was rattling about Roseburn without either of her daughters to keep her company.

James had said he would call for me again when Andrew was next gone. There were no question marks in his parting speech; simply, *I will see you as soon as I can.*

I kept having vivid recollections of sex with him. I wanted it again.

'Christian, you seem miles away.' Andrew was stock-still, staring at me as though he didn't quite know what to make of me. We were surrounded by young trees. Oranges and lemons and figs. He was weary and unshaven from travelling and smelled of musty linen.

'It's nothing,' I said, 'it was just that I missed you when you were gone.'

'And I you,' he said. 'I hope you were not bored.'

'Sometimes. But I had the pleasure of my trip to Lady Forrester to paint with her.'

'That was kind of you,' he said, patting my hand. 'She's a troubled woman with her ailments, and her marriage seems to have brought her no joy. I hope Lord James did not make a nuisance of himself and left you ladies in peace. He thinks himself far better company than he actually is, and I think he has more than a passing interest in you, however indelicate that may sound. I saw him stare at you quite openly at your sister's wedding.'

'We hardly saw him,' I said. 'He had no interest whatsoever in our frivolous pursuits.'

'You should visit her again,' he said. 'I will give you a plaid shawl for her. And this time sketch me the dovecote: a detailed one, for I have a fancy to have one built here.'

He began inspecting the leaves of one of the baby trees. God knows whether it was an orange or a lemon – I had enough to fret about without tending a citrus grove. There was so much innocence in his pose. I felt a lurch of guilt. *He cannot find out.*

'I think Lillias would prefer the crate of Burgundy,' I said, as sweetly as I could. 'She spent most of the visit in her cups. Goodness knows if she can even remember what we did together, and her sketching was erratic. She gossiped a lot, but I am not sure how much truth was in any of it.'

'I suspected that,' he said earnestly, standing up and straightening his back. 'The countryside is full of idle gossips, even in its castles. Do not feel you must go to the Forresters if you were uncomfortable.'

'It was pleasant enough,' I said. 'Pleasant enough for a return trip.'


I had promised myself I would wholeheartedly arouse my husband upon his return, for I had learned something of the arts of the marital chamber and, without attracting his suspicion, I wanted to touch him in certain ways.

But when we retired, my heart filled with dread. He drew me into his arms and kissed the top of my head. A month or so ago this would have brought me joy, for it might be a signal that he was keen on taking things further. Instead I found it unsettling. I froze. I could not raise my head to kiss him on the lips. And when, after a moment or two, he moved away and said, 'Goodnight, Christian', I felt nothing but relief.

## *THE CALEDONIA BROADSIDE*

### EDINBURGH, 5th October

The Murderess Christian Nimmo has made a defiant escape from the Tolbooth Jail. A reward of One Hundred Pounds Scots for anyone bringing her back to the High Constables alive.

# Chapter Twenty-One

# VIOLET

*Corstorphine Castle*
*May 1679*

I need a cunning woman.

Mrs Fiddes kept notes of our menses in her head and she also made us learn our own cycles. Mine were every twenty-eight days, except for the times when they were not.

The cunning women visit the whorehouses weekly and give us girls an appointment, if needed, and a bottle of something is passed and the bill taken from our earnings; and if you ever want to spend two days shitting and boaking and bleeding into your slops bucket, thinking your belly is being squeezed by the hands of a monster, that will do it. Pardon my crude words, for it is early in the day, with breakfast still being digested, and some people cannot stomach such talk. But there is interest enough in my story, and you'll have to pick around the gristle if you want the flesh.

Mrs Fiddes insists that we make a man interrupt the coitus and spend himself on the bed, or anywhere else for that matter. Usually works. But alas, Lord James did get the better of me from time to time.

You've not to wait too long, else the herbs won't work. I must attend to it now for it has been a week since my blood was due, and I have spent a week thinking, *Any moment now*, and that moment has not arrived with its familiar drag.

I don't know who to tell. The laird himself or the God-fearing Oriana, who has likely never needed her menses brought on. But Lord James might haul me back to Mrs Fiddes to be fixed, and never return for me again. Or maybe he would stick me and his unborn bastard with his sword and bury me in his castle grounds.

I seize Oriana, after she scuffs up the steps with my porridge and jam, in no great hurry as usual.

'I do not feel like a walk today. I have been feeling quite out of sorts this morning,' I say. 'I think I am in need of a physician.'

'Then you need some fresh air and exercise,' she says. 'You spend too much time in that bed.'

'The activities in that bed are likely the cause of my ills,' I say, rubbing my belly.

She stops and gawps.

'You are nothing but trouble,' she hisses. 'Do not tell me you have managed to get pregnant with the laird's bastard.'

'It was not entirely my doing,' I tell her.

I think she will get all godly on me, and prepare myself for a lecture and some choice Bible words on sinners, but none are forthcoming. Instead she continues to stare at me in her pale way.

'I cannot have a baby,' I say. 'Is there a herbalist? A physician who deals in such matters?'

'There is a herbalist who lives on the outskirts of the village,' she whispers, ashen-grey.

'Well, can you go to her for me? I am desperate, Oriana. Don't fret, 'tis not sorcery, nor ungodly,' I say. 'Just a potion to bring on my menses.'

'I know what it is,' she says.

'Please. I am begging you. Just a trip to the herbalist. You would do the same if I had a headache or a pox.'

She sighs. 'Let me tell you something, Violet Blyth. You are not the first girl to need the herbalist because of Laird Forrester. You are not the first he has had in this turret.'

I close my eyes. Of course I knew this. How many others? I wonder. And where are they now?

'The herbalist will need payment,' Oriana says, bringing me back to my current plight. 'She does not give away her tonics for free.'

I scan the room for what I might use as payment. A painting of titties and cocks would stick out like a sore thumb in the village, I have no doubt, as would some of these fine furs.

'You cannot take anything from here, you daft hoor,' she chastises, 'I will be whipped for stealing if I am caught.'

All I have with me is my box.

*Dear Ginger, please forgive me for what I am about to do, but I am fair up against the wall and I am sure you would not want to see me bring a bairn into this world, as that would ensure my stay in this decent place is brought to an end.*

I give the maid Ginger's pretty hair pin.

'That is worth a bottle of herbs at least,' I say, 'and enough for you to buy whatever you fancy.'

'I will do this for you *once*,' she hisses. 'In future, take better care. If you stay around that long.'

She slips the pin into her fist. Then she leaves, throwing a scowl at me from the door.

The questions keep repeating themselves in my head.

How many women has he kept in this turret? How many have needed the herbalist?

For all her piousness, Oriana knew how to help me.

I go to the window and watch her sneak back to the kitchen, still clutching the pin. Likely the first paste she has ever owned. She takes the same route I did, keeping in the shadows, so as not to be seen by Lady Forrester, should she take to surveying the courtyard.

I see how small and unnoticeable she keeps herself.

It is better to be unnoticeable, I think.

I would even hear Ginger whisper in the trees, *Hush now, Violet, don't worry about that daft pin, I am looking after you now. Weep You No More, Sad Fountains,* were I fanciful like that. But of course I am not.

Lord James is late coming. I spend the afternoon flitting between the bed and the window. My mind feels encased in iron bars, for I cannot think of anything but this fix I am in. Reliant upon strangers to assist me in the passing of a potion from hand to hand.

It will not always be like this.

One day I will be queen of my own affairs.

I put my palm to my belly, where the wee unborn soul swims, feeling notions I have not felt before, when I was desperate for the cunning woman to rid me of the offspring of whatever beast had implanted his seed. This time is different. I imagine this bairn, his scrap of dark hair, a pink rosebud of a mouth.

If I were lady here, I would be put to bed-rest and fed milk and honey for the confinement. I would grow plump and bonnie and, in no time, I would hold my wee laird in my arms. James would be proud.

But I am not the lady here. I am nothing here. I slip onto

the bed. Inside me the wee soul swims against a tide that will drown him after the herbalist's bitter dram meets my lips. My wee laird.

James enters my room in the gloaming. I feel the click of the door in the back of my throat, silvery-tasting. The way my tongue gets when my blood is late. He joins me on the bed, curling into me. He touches my breasts and I shrink away, for they have become so sensitive I can hardly stand it.

'What's wrong, lass?' he says, making as if to have another tweak on them, but I put my hands up against my chest.

'Just sensitive,' I say.

'Women are peculiar,' he mutters, 'changeable as the wind.'

I turn over to meet his eye, but I make no move to touch him. I cannot bear to turn this quiet moment into yet another bout of sex. I am tired.

'Are you not fancying me today?' He blinks with the surprise of it.

'My body is a wee bit tender.'

'Is it a woman's thing?' He looks uneasy.

'No, I am just tired,' I say.

'But I am not paying you to be tired,' he says, and his fingers move back to my breasts.

I let him touch them, bracing myself against the pain.

'They are swollen today,' he says. 'The puddings are working their magic on you.'

He turns me over and clambers on top of me, all elbows and fingers.

'You are a very good whore for me, Violet, you know that, don't you?'

And this is what I am for the next few minutes, a very good whore for my master as he heaves away at me until he is happy enough.

'Nothing so tranquil as the aftermath of a humping,' he says, when his breathing is back to normal. 'You can rest a while. This coming week or so I might be busy with some urgent matters, so may not be able to visit you.'

I am relieved he does not mention her name.

He drifts in and out of sleep. It has the air of a tender afternoon, lit by candles, with tendrils of fog drifting in through the windows. I feel the heaviness in his hands, of a life bound by bloodlines and rightful heirs. And the privilege, too, of choosing whatever he wants for dinner or sex. My wee soul rests in the black waters between us. Waiting unawares for eternal silence, the spawn that never leaves the pond.

# Chapter Twenty-Two

# CHRISTIAN

*Fala, south-eastern Scotland*
*October 1679*

I taste Fala before I reach it, in the black damp of a burn that unfurls from thick conifers and licks the side of the road. The hamlet is just a smattering of dwellings and I feel the eyes of each of them bore into me as I ride in, grateful again for the cap and coat disguising me. This is a place where strangers stop daily, drifting between England and Scotland. They will glance at me and think nothing more of me. I hope.

It is the seventh house that I am to knock upon. An inn. Bigger than the others, two-storeyed and half-timbered with a thatched roof and orange flickers of hens pecking in the mud, but there is a silver birch outside and that is the sign I was to look for.

As I dismount from the horse, clumsy and stiff, the door opens and a woman hugging herself into a shawl the shade of cold ash watches me. Her eyes glower from under the shawl's peaked hood.

'Put the horse in the stables. Don't take all day about it,' she says. 'They notice everything here.'

My fingers fumble with the rope. It was always the stable boys who did things like this.

'William's out,' she says. 'You'll need to wait in the kitchen with me.' And she retreats, leaving the door ajar.

The kitchen smells of wood-smoke and unwashed bodies. The inn owners eat and sleep in the same room, by the looks of it, a fire billowing in the middle and lit only by a narrow window that has never been cleaned, for it is laced with cobwebs and dust. There are low wooden stools beside the fire and a small table. By the wall, a bed piled with blankets.

'Sit yourself down – it must have been some journey,' she says, handing me a cup of water. I make to take off the hat, but she stops me, stretching out her hand and nodding at the door. 'You never know who might call,' she whispers.

'I'm very grateful.' I don't know what else I should say.

'Don't bother me with your sorry tale, whatever it is,' she says. 'But it must be some grand trouble you're running from. William said he's getting plenty coin for helping you. He's my brother,' she adds.

I sip the water. It tastes like the bottom of a well, but is fresher and colder than the Tolbooth water. I wonder when the jail guard will raise the alarm. What path they will take in their search. When they will hear the rumours that I am gone to Leith Port and what they will do when they don't find me there. A ship was to set sail at eight, Andrew's note said, with traders bribed to say they saw me heading for it. Will they send word to Flanders – men checking everyone who disembarks?

'You are quiet,' she says. 'Best to forget your past, if you're running from it.'

But I can't, of course.

'Are you a good hand at sewing?' she asks. 'I have a basket of mending here and I have bad eyes, and you have idle hands. William will not be back from market before lunchtime.'

'I'm good at needlework,' I say. 'It's the least I can do.'

We spend the next hour or so together at our tasks. She scrapes potatoes and carrots and I patch the clothes of a man I have never met.

She tells me her name is Mags and she hates carrots and can't understand why people eat them, and I tell her I hate needlework and only ever did it to please my mother and my husband. I ask her about herself, and she says there is nothing much to tell, except that she was born in Fala and has lived here all her days and runs the inn with her brother.

'Go on,' she says, 'I'm curious. What's your connection to my brother?'

'I don't know him.' I sew a steady seam across a ripped tunic. 'But he must be connected to my husband, Andrew Nimmo.'

'I have never heard of a Nimmo.' Her hands are covered in dirt and peelings. She peers at me. 'You have fine skin. You must have led a comfortable life.'

I finish off the seam. I would once have judged myself quite unfortunate. In Johanna's shade, and bothered by my forehead being too high. Now, mending a threadbare garment that is fit for nothing but use as a cleaning cloth, I realize what a life it was.

'My husband is a fabric merchant,' I say. 'He often travels up and down the country, and beyond.'

'That makes sense,' she says. 'The traders often rest a night here in the winter when it gets too dark to ride further up the road.'

So, Andrew has stayed here. Snoring in an upstairs chamber, on a mattress stuffed with straw. Was it a night when I was with James? What journey was he on? Did he sigh in his sleep, restless on the thin bed with the scent of damp straw seeping into his hair as I poured myself wine and dreaded his return? Did he ever wonder why I was growing increasingly restless in our marriage?

We talked about it, once.

'We should discuss the marital chamber,' I said to Andrew, not long after that first time with James, when he seemed at ease because he had rested well from his trip and he was so much enjoying his supper of trout and tomatoes.

He stopped chewing. Swallowed. Stared at me, surprised.

'Why ever should we? Is there something the matter with it? Is it the curtains?'

'It's not the curtains,' I said, gulping my white wine. 'It's not the furnishings.'

He went back to forking at his trout and seemed taken with inspecting it. I picked at the flesh, avoiding the scales and the eyes.

'Then what?' he said, his voice down to a whisper.

'I think the problem is you,' I said. I should not have worded it like that.

He scraped at the last of his meal.

'There is no *problem*. The purpose of the union is to achieve a child and there is time yet. I am not quite ready for fatherhood. The noise of children would spoil the peace and tranquillity we enjoy here, and we are only just wed.'

'But are you not tempted by the pleasures of the marriage bed? I have heard, from conversations with my sister, that it can be most enjoyable. If husband and wife are relaxed.'

Andrew regarded me, appalled.

'You have discussed our marriage with your sister?'

'Of course not,' I assured him. 'I am merely describing something she herself has said.'

Dear God, it was excruciating. And it would not be long before one of the servants interrupted us and the conversation would be swept away like the fish bones, and there would not be another chance because he would be on his guard against it.

'I am not sure such affairs are enjoyable,' he said. 'That is the talk of taverns and coffee houses, and I hear enough of that on my travels. I find this talk unseemly. Nature will take its course when the time is right.' He looked disgusted. 'I suggest you put your attentions to needlework or your sketching; they offer more pleasure than carnal lust. I shall order you some bright new colours. If you continue to feel these yearn- ings, then we can always ask a physician to give you a tonic.'

I did not raise the matter again.

And I felt no further yearnings for my husband.

A week after our conversation a set of bright threads arrived from the haberdashery shop. Dazzling golds and reds. In the evenings we sat opposite each other by the fire. He sipped his wine and read his books. I sewed.


'Your needlework is good.' Mags runs her fingers over the mended shirt. 'So, what are you escaping from?'

Ha. That didn't take her long, despite her apparent disinterest.

'People who want to harm me,' I say, and she nods, leaning closer for the juice of the gossip.

'Aye, folk can be cruel right enough. But what did you do to deserve it?'

A movement catches my eye and I look up. A man stands in the doorway surveying us. I don't know how long he has been there.

'You'll be the lucky lady whose neck's just been saved from the Maiden,' he says, coming into the room and throwing his hat on the table.

'William Watson,' says Mags, 'hat on the peg.' But she's not even looked at him; she is so agog now that I can see the pink veins in her eyes and the white spittle at the sides of her gawped-open mouth.

## *THE CALEDONIA BROADSIDE*

### EDINBURGH, 29th September

David Wilson, High Constable of Edinburgh: 'Extensive searches were made of Lady Christian's chambers, both at the family home, Roseburn House, and at her marital home, Carrick House, and a number of items were found proving beyond any doubt her relationship with Lord James Forrester. They included letters and gifts, Sheriff MacDonald. A number of them. It must have been a long-standing relationship both before and after her marriage to Mr Nimmo. And, of course, there was also the book with instructions on how to perform the act of sexual intercourse in the most satisfactory manner.'

# Chapter Twenty-Three

# VIOLET

*Corstorphine Castle*
*May 1679*

This herb potion comes in a clay pot with a cloth over the top, and that is different from what I'm used to. At Mrs Fiddes's we are handed a bottle with a glass stopper. As though it were a fancy drink.

Oriana brings it on the breakfast tray with bread and a jug of water.

'Drink it all,' she says, 'and if you boak, I'm to go back for another one – so don't. I've a busy day, for Lady F is off to the healing waters and the laird must be having that special lady back, for Cook says the food order is extravagant.'

He will be warming his arse by the fire right now, waiting on the lady in grey. But I am in no position to care about that now. Caring can wait.

The potion is the colour of sludge, the colour of the ground on a winter morning in Bell's Close when the slops buckets have been emptied, and it smells the same too.

I take the potion, drink it back in gulps, each more vile than the last, then take the water from the tray and wash it down, fighting the bile.

She stares.

'I will need plenty of rags,' I say, and she scurries out of the door, her face blanched white.

I wait.

## Chapter Twenty-Four

# CHRISTIAN

*Corstorphine Castle*
*May 1679*

Andrew was off again to Calais before long, and of course nothing of note had happened in the marital bed.

But that did not matter. For I was beautiful now. And my desires were not unnatural.

James had written to me, a perfectly polite note enquiring about my health, with the news that Lillias would be visiting the healing waters at Willow Springs, some twenty miles away, and would be gone for a while with two hired nurses, as the treatment recommended by her physician was for a full week. Perhaps he even bribed the physician. I did not care.

The morning after Andrew left, I took an age to decide what scent to dab and which earrings to wear, before I rode the few minutes to the castle. I could not stay away. I would have preferred the comfort of the carriage, but travelling alone would be more discreet. On horse I could move swiftly through the fields across Tyler's Acre, under the spring sky, wild as the gorse on Corstorphine Hill.

He was waiting for me at the dovecote. He looked magnificent, dressed in a dark-brown coat with a white knotted silk scarf at his throat, his curls at his shoulders.

'Come, my beauty,' he said. 'Let's take a stroll.'

I tied up the horse and we walked slowly round the dovecote. He could not take his eyes off me and kept moving closer, his arm brushing mine. I wore a green velvet gown that dipped low at the front, which I'd hoped was neither too dressy for daytime nor too sensible for the Venus I now was. I lifted the hem suggestively high, stepping over the rough ground, and he watched me. The pigeons swooped in and out of their nest-boxes, landing on trees and searching the earth for insects and seeds.

'Coming by horse was a sensible choice,' he said, 'But I don't like you travelling alone.'

'I am perfectly safe in Corstorphine,' I insisted.

'I'll give you something for your protection,' he said. 'I have a ladies' sword in the collection. Lillias has never even been interested in it.'

We fetched the horse and walked it back up to his stables, before going inside. I wondered if he would serve me luncheon. He did not. Instead he took me upstairs to his chamber.

He drew the curtains and lit candles.

He took great care over my gown and petticoat. His hands were broad and heavy, but his fingers were expert at handling delicate lace, and I did not care to wonder how he had become so good at it.

He breathed words into my neck. *How could anyone resist you?*

It went on all afternoon. He fetched food on a tray. Cold white wine and cheese and honey, and apples and fresh bread. I returned to Carrick House at dinner time, with the sword under my skirts. It was light and nimble, two feet in length, with an elaborate basket hilt. James advised me to hide it from Andrew and, in case of any trouble when travelling, to aim it at an attacker's chest and strike hard. I said there would be no trouble.

I should have been more afraid of that sword.

I returned the next day, and the day after that, spending my whole days there. I told the maids at Carrick House that I was out with the horse or up at the village. I told them anything I could think of. Sometimes we stayed in his chamber. Other times we would walk or ride to Corstorphine Hill and he would even take me under the skies.

It was a velvety time, apart from when he would let sharp words out of his mouth, like *damned bitch* at the maid, for not setting the fire right. Andrew never spoke to anyone like that. Every so often I felt the pull of Carrick House and it startled me. The fear of what would happen if I was caught.

But I would not get caught. We were too careful.


We had three days of bliss until a hullabaloo set James in a mood that I had never witnessed before.

The groundsman had not closed the dovecote door and a fox got in, killing half a dozen or so birds in a frenzy. James must have had a thousand pigeons in there, for they were forever pecking at the nearby fields and making the neighbours irate, he said; and it would not surprise me if the groundsman had been bribed by some farmer to leave the door open. But when James learned of the incident, he set about shouting at the groundsman and calling him all manner of names, and he would not be calmed, even when the mess was cleaned up.

'He is a useless bastard. I should get rid of him,' James growled. We were alone, in the dining room. He was pacing up and down by the fireplace, obsessing over the incident.

'Perhaps I should go home,' I said. 'You are not in the mood for company.' Each thud of his boots jangled my nerves.

'You will stay here,' he said. 'I have already arranged food.'

'Is it pigeon?' I offered, thinking he might see the humorous side, but that only set him off again.

'This is not a laughing matter. It is all very well for you, who have nothing to fret about.'

'I am not laughing,' I said. 'But your pacing is irritating me, and there is no point worrying after a handful of dead birds.'

He stopped pacing right at the spot where I was sitting. He put his hands on my shoulders, gripping them so tightly I tried to shrug him off, but he wouldn't let go. His face was an inch from my face, his eyes locked onto mine.

'Stop,' I said, utterly shocked. 'That hurts.'

'Then mind your tongue,' he whispered. 'Or I will drag you to the branks and leave you there, for your inadequate husband to find when he returns.'

He let go, but I could still feel his fingers burning into my skin. I would bruise, I was sure. I hunched forward, letting my hair fall into my eyes, blinking back tears by following the swirls in the oak table, minding my tongue whilst James paced to the door and slammed it on his way out.

I could not believe what had just happened.

How could he be so cruel? I had no idea what to do, so I sat in the dining room and let the maid lay the table as I lingered there, not caring a toss what she must have thought of it all.


His temper softened once he had eaten. Fortunately it wasn't pigeon, for that would not have helped the mood. It was pheasant, gamey and metallic, and I dared not leave a scrap on the plate. The red wine was robust. I drank more than usual, but James said nothing, for he was generous with wine. As he ate, my eyes wandered to the mirror on the opposite wall. I caught myself, glass in hand, and thought for a moment I was not unlike Lady Forrester and wondered if he had driven her to drink. The mood of the entire castle was dependent upon him, I realized. His temper hung in the flickers of the candle lanterns and in the glances of the servants, and in the rolling, dark skies of his oil paintings.

'Food is a pleasure, is it not?' James said, warming up in the simmer of the meat and wine.

'One of life's few,' I said, pushing this morning's events behind my smile. I felt my shoulders relax, finally, and realized how prettily the candelabra shone on the table.

When the maid came to tidy away the pudding bowls, I offered her a small nod. She did not return it. She disapproved of me.

And he was sorry, in bed. 'I did not mean to hold you so roughly, it was just the sheer frustration,' he whispered. 'The damned groundsman.'

'You are forgiven,' I said, and his hands were so gentle again, seeking forgiveness, almost as though the row had not happened at all.


I rode home discreetly, in the slope of the late-afternoon sun, sword tucked into sheath. Over my shoulder sat the spire of Corstorphine Kirk, filled with repentance stools and studded with branks. I remembered how the stools rose, hard and harsh and waiting for soft, sorry sinners. I remembered how the branks hung, their jaws slack and empty, waiting for their next soft mouth and reminding me to watch my tongue.

# Chapter Twenty-Five

# VIOLET

*Corstorphine Castle*
*May 1679*

Nothing.

Oriana returns with her boggly eyes and a lunch tray piled with sweet treats stolen from the kitchen.

'Fancy something nice to take your mind off it?' she offers. But I know better than to eat. She disappears and says she will keep an eye on the window, and I am to wave if I get into difficulties.

But still nothing.

She returns with a dinner tray and says I must have a bread roll, and she even butters it and watches me force it down. I wonder if the bub is still somersaulting or lies motionless.

Nothing.

I tell her to go, and that I have done this before and this is just the other side of Mother Nature, and she leaves, the dinner plates trembling on the tray.

I go to bed.

As the moon kisses the edge of the window, the cramps begin.

I watch the moon rise, crouched over the chamber pot. A low life under a high moon.

It comes in waves, spilling over the chamber pot sides, seizing me with its burning pains.

I am there till dawn, when I crawl under the bedclothes, leaving trails of blood across the floor.

Oriana returns in the middle of the morning. She scrubs the blood and takes away the chamber pot for me. She returns with a supply of clean rags and menstrual girdles.

She does not mention God or sinners and I am grateful to her for that.

Despite her piety, she has cared for me gently and with dignity in my darkest hour.

But I vow I will never suffer this bloody hell again.

## Chapter Twenty-Six

# CHRISTIAN

*Carrick House, Corstorphine*
*June 1679*

Two letters arrived, the first as crumpled as an old silk
kerchief, the second as stiff as confectioner's icing. The
first was from Andrew, who was delayed until a week next
Tuesday; he'd been asked to stay at a merchant's house in
Calais and could not turn down the opportunity for making
connections. The family was throwing a social dance. I put
the letter to my face to detect whether there were any untruths
in it: whether there was anyone in his other life, as there was
in mine. All I could detect was the powdery scent of parchment.

The second letter was from Johanna:

SISTER,
 *Come immediately. I have heard the most hideously*
*horrible talk about you. I absolutely must speak to you about*
*it myself. And do not even think about ignoring this, for if*
*you do not come AS SOON AS YOU CAN, I will be forced*
*to come to Carrick House.*
 *You would not wish that journey upon me, would you?*
*It would be perilous for me to travel alone in my condition.*

It was four miles to Johanna's grand home in Warriston, past villages with roaming sheep and grey kirk spires, and I spent the journey thinking up lies as to why I had been spending long hours at Corstorphine Castle, for that was surely the *hideously horrible talk*. I wondered if it was servants or peasants. We should have been more careful.

Johanna looked captivating, blooming in a billowy pastel gown. But she was not amused to see me.

'Look at you,' she said when I entered her parlour. 'You are *thin*, Sister.' She did not stand up to greet me.

She had the maid bring us chocolate in two porcelain teacups and a plate of almond cake. Johanna sat under a wall tapestry of stiff-looking trees, resting her feet on a stool, and I sat opposite, the tea-table between us, a cabinet of Robert Gregor's whiskies to my left.

Her parlour was enormous – even bigger than the parlour at Carrick House. She rested in a walnut armchair, all belly and bosom and curls and lady-of-the-house.

'So, Sister. What is this horrid talk of me?' I asked. Neither of us touched the almond cake, although I knew it to be Johanna's favourite.

'I sincerely hope there is nothing in it,' she said, looking grave. 'But Robert heard from one of the burgesses that you have been spending your days at Corstorphine Castle.

'Indeed,' I said. 'Painting with Aunt Lillias.'

'But how could you paint with her when she is not there? Apparently she has been at the healing waters, which means you have been alone with our uncle.'

She watched me.

I said nothing.

'You have always had a thing for him, haven't you?' She glinted. 'You would go red whenever he spoke your name.'

My chocolate was congealing, a skin of milk wrinkling on the top.

'You won't deny it, then. How could you do it to Andrew?' she said.

'Pour me a whisky instead of this, Sister,' I said. 'And I will tell you.'


Johanna was so aghast at the details of my marriage that her bonnie face fell ashen-grey. It was beyond her safe world of afternoon teas and Robert Gregor's contentment.

'Are you saying Andrew is *uncurious* about you? What are you possibly doing wrong?'

She had poured me a whisky, but it was on the mean side. I finished it, then went to the cabinet and poured another.

'You are not unattractive, Christian. Perhaps you could do more with your hair. Or tempt him with nice nightgowns. I have some that I have not even worn.'

'He just has no appetite for me,' I said.

'But the solution is not to run to the bed of Lord Forrester,' she said. 'What if you are found out by the Kirk and both of you made to repent? Imagine the shame on all of us.'

'We will not,' I said. 'He is a member of the Kirk Session. He will see to it that never happens.'

'How can you be so sure?' she said. 'And on the matter of producing a child? What if you conceive and give birth to one that is the spit of Lord James?'

'He is careful,' I said.

But that was not the truth, for I had no idea if he had been as careful as he might, and the notion was worrying me.

'Ugh! You have become a *hoor*,' she said.

I finished the whisky. I never touched the vile stuff in ordinary circumstances.

'I will not be called names. I have explained my predicament. How would you feel if Robert were reluctant to touch you?'

I did not tell her how I really felt about James. That he was the only man to have called me beautiful. She would not know how that even felt.

I did not tell her I was constantly desperate for him.

Johanna slackened. Her shoulders dropped and she put her hands to her face.

'I am sorry, Sister. But you must stop this dalliance. I can assure Robert this is nothing but idle gossip, but there can't be any more of it.'

'And what of Andrew?' I said. 'He's gone half the year and I have no idea what he gets up to when he is away. He could have another wife and child, for all I know, or a string of lovers.'

'That's not for you to worry about. You are Mrs Nimmo now and you must behave as a wife. Do you not remember what it said in the marriage book?'

'I have it etched into my head, Sister. And that is why I know there's something wrong with my husband.'

'It is a wife's duty to serve her husband's needs. It does not really matter what they are,' she said. 'That is the very essence of the marriage instructions. He keeps you in fine gowns, fed on meat from his estate and wines from his travels. You even have a glasshouse, Christian.'

Johanna was right.

'Promise me,' she said. 'No good will come of breaking your marriage vows or causing Lord James to break his. If the two of you weren't married, perhaps it would be a different story altogether.'

'You are right, Sister,' I said.

She pointed at my belly. 'Get yourself with Andrew's child. That is your obligation, even if you must degrade yourself in the process, or act the hoor with him. Then all these theatrics will fade to insignificance. You will be too busy with your swollen ankles and hands, like me, to worry about anything else.'

I would not let Johanna see how terrified I was at the thought of getting caught. But it slapped me in the face all the way home, each carriage-window flash of kirk spire giving me the horrors I no doubt deserved. We had been seen. To stop it now would put an end to the gossip.

When I got home I went straight to my chamber and I wrote him a letter:

*Dear Uncle James,*

*I am grateful for the hospitality both you and my aunt have shown me, but I am indisposed for the foreseeable future as I prepare for the return of my beloved and much-missed husband.*

I gave the letter to the errand boy and watched him run out of the estate. Then I sat on my bed and sobbed as though my heart would break.

What was wrong with me?

I should have realized James felt as passionately as I did.

The next day his carriage flew into the driveway of Carrick House and it was fortunate indeed that I was able to have the servants show him into the glasshouse, on the pretence of him being interested in its structure and heating system.

'Andrew will hear of your visit on his return,' I said, when we were alone beside the citrus plants. They were not thriving. Not a fruit on them, and the leaves wilting.

'You have no real wish to try to end our affair,' he said, picking up a fallen leaf and inspecting it. 'You are just frightened of the gossips. This hothouse is a nonsense. Why is Mr Nimmo intent on replicating the continent in Corstorphine? What will he bring back next? A sea monster?'

'We will tell him you were keen to see the plants in here,' I continued, ignoring his comments.

James threw the leaf away and it fluttered to the ground, dark and curled, with brown mottling. 'Come with me,' he said.

I followed him through the grounds, winding away from the main buildings into the woodlands. 'Where are you taking me?' I kept asking, but he ignored me, and I could not have let him wander alone, without alerting the servants that something odd was happening. And in truth I could not stop myself from following him, for I had thought of him every waking hour. I could not think of anything else.

And here he was. Fighting for me. I confess, it felt exhilarating. Being in his presence, I felt whole again and realized how horribly I had missed him.

He finally stopped by a large fallen tree on the bank of the shallow river that ran through the bottom of the woodlands. I never usually came this far.

'I will take you here and now, at this tree, and you will know who your lover is,' he said.

And he did. I let him take me in the grounds of my husband's home and it was fierce and furious and thrilling, and I realized I could never stop, not even if I tried. And I loved it and I hated myself, feeling pleasure and shame, and relief and delight, all at the same time.

## *THE CALEDONIA BROADSIDE*

### EDINBURGH, 6th October

The Murderess Christian Nimmo remains alive
and at large on the very day she was due to be
executed, to the embarrassment of the custodians
at the Tolbooth Jail and the High Constables of
Edinburgh. Whilst crowds swarm at the coffee
houses, awaiting news, rumours abound that there
are even celebrations in honour of her escape,
with officers urging the public not to attend an
unauthorized gathering planned at the Maiden's
platform tonight, or risk spending the night in
the jail themselves.

## Chapter Twenty-Seven

# CHRISTIAN

*Fala, south-eastern Scotland*
*October 1679*

Mags and William Watson are staring at me in the smoky gloom of their kitchen. He is dressed in an unkempt way, tattered coat and bristled chin, but there is a strength to his shoulders and a lift to his head that tell me he is a proud man.

I swallow and rub my hands together. They feel papery from sewing.

'A lucky escape from the Maiden indeed,' he says.

'You said nothing about a murderess,' hisses Mags. 'She could have killed me stone-dead as I sat in my chair.'

'Shh, she would have done no such thing. And you are still here, are you not?' He sits between us, refusing to take his eyes off me. There is a light scarring to the skin on his face where he would have had blemishes as a lad. Mags hauls herself to her feet and goes to the fire where the pottage is simmering and declares it ready. It has only been boiling a few minutes, but she is no doubt desperate to be rid of me.

'You've a long road ahead of you, so eat as much as you can,' she says, handing me a bowl filled to the brim and a thick piece of bread.

'How do you know my husband?' I ask William. I want to be sure I can trust this stranger.

'I know everyone who passes through,' he says. 'Including Mr Nimmo. He sent a messenger late Friday night with this request.'

Oh God. I get a flash of him. Hunched and conjuring panicky plans. A purse full of coin. Saving his unfaithful wife's wicked neck.

Over a meal that I can barely eat for trembling, William tells me the plan. He dishes it out to me in instructions that I must not deviate from. I am to remain dressed in men's clothing and we will ride south to London, where I will board a boat to Calais. He will remain with me, and we will pose as trader and apprentice, taking a trip to buy the fine wines of Burgundy. I am to say nothing to anyone and act a simpleton. I am not to take off my hat. We will leave as soon as our meal is finished, because he thinks soldiers will be sent south looking for me.

'As soon as they have searched the ships docked at Leith Port and found you are not on them, they will scour the countryside,' he says. 'And I am not in any mood to be found aiding a convict, so let's make haste.'


The road stretches ahead of us, a dirt trail leaning heavily into sheep-scattered hills that climb to meet low clouds. I remember the times as a girl when I had longed for a view like this. The kind of view the well-travelled Edinburgh gentlemen would brag of, and I would roll my eyes, but secretly envy them. Little did I realize then that the view ahead might be full of hidden dangers. And that I might be running for my life.

With a jolt we are off, and the village disappears.

'You're not afraid of me,' I say, keeping my eyes on the horizon.

'Not one bit,' he says, doing the same.

'Why not?' I am curious.

'Because I cannot imagine a lass like you murdering anyone,' he says.

I pick at the seams of my coat. Fine threads. I had not realized how rough my hands had become. They do not even feel like a lady's hands any more.

'That's not what everyone else believes,' I say.


We ride for six or seven hours, then stop for the night in a copse of woodland. I had thought we would stop at a tavern, but William says that is foolish and we must keep away from prying eyes.

'You might be dressed as a man, but you don't look like one,' he says. It is dark and I can't see his face, but he sounds as though he is smiling. 'Come here and bed down beside me. Take these blankets. You'll need the warmth. I trust you'll not stab me in the night.'

By now I have come too far to be intimidated by such an offer. I need the warmth or I will spend the night freezing. We lie next to each other on the hard earth, wrapped in blankets, and William reaches for a flask of whisky, offering some to me.

I wonder if I will ever get any rest, being so close. He has a heavy scent, not of pomade or spice but of the deep musk of a man.

But I have never truly been alone, have I? There have always been maids or guards. I wonder what I am like when I am alone, and whether I would be content in my own company.

'Would your wife not be furious to see you now? Lying next to a woman,' I ask.

'There is no wife for me yet,' he says. 'Mags keeps chasing them away.'

'There's still time,' I say, although he does not seem young. Perhaps in his thirties already.

'And how much trouble might a wife cause? I have enough work with my sister breathing down my neck, and my inn barely bringing in enough coin to keep us in pottage.' His breathing is heavy, the way a man breathes in his own bed.

He has money troubles, and they must be serious. No wonder he is prepared to risk escorting me. I wonder how much Andrew has given him.

Overhead, an owl screeches. Then nothing but the rustle of the trees. The black night. A wash of stars.

'I used to dream of nights like this,' I say. 'I used to paint nights like this, but now I realize you cannot capture this kind of beauty.'

'Is it the fear of death? Makes you appreciate the world?'

I should flinch at that. But I know he means it genuinely.

'I have been frightened for so long I have become used to fear.'

'I know. I could see it in your eyes the minute we met,' he says. 'You looked hunted.'

Hunted. Like an animal. But what do animals know of betrayal or lies or broken hearts?

He drinks from the flask and hands it to me again. My mind searches for something to say. I could tell him what adventures I once imagined. Or I could say something about the horses or the itchy blanket, or the slip of the moon or what happened that night under the sycamore tree. I can choose it, like a story from the library at Roseburn, and it will make the shape of tonight. This could be the first night we are together for a week. Or the only night we spend together. I feel the pulse of it in my neck. In the wind.

I cannot speak of it yet.

He can tell. Instead he holds me, all night long. Over autumn earth, hard and full of sleeping seeds. I pray that I will still be alive when they burst into life in the spring.

# Chapter Twenty-Eight

# VIOLET

*Corstorphine Castle*
*June 1679*

When will he bore of me?

It will only be a matter of time.

He kept away for several days whilst Lillias was at some magical waters, and Lady Christian came back and forth, thinking no one would notice her stamping through the fields on her horse, cloak flying in the wind, horse snorting and whinnying.

She will get caught.

I loll alone under the paintings of pricks and honeypots, thinking of ways to get rid of the bitch before Lord James gets rid of me. Lillias returns, most obviously unhealed, as she still needs that chair on wheels. I watch her arrive back in the courtyard, assisted by Oriana. Head to toe in black. A crow.

And then the laird returns to me in my turret. When I hear his footsteps on the stairs I whip off my comfy gown and pull on a petticoat, teasing my hair with my hands, so that he finds me in the way he likes me best.

'Most agreeable,' he nods when he strides in the door. His hands wander up my petticoat, but not with the urgency they once did. I still bleed, so I am forced to make up a tale that I am bothered by a bad dose of the monthlies, and take his cock in my hand as masterfully as I can whilst he rubs and squeezes my thighs. That's a task that can tire a girl out, and though he gets there in the end, it was with less exuberance than usual, as if talk of my monthlies made me more of an earthy girl than he really imagined.

Or perhaps Lady Christian is proving more interesting than I.

I catch myself in the mirror and see myself as I truly am. Messy-haired. Soiled. Puffy about the face.

He stays barely half an hour.

When he dresses, he puts his hand on the sheath of his sword and I swear it lingers there longer than it needs to.

'I will send Oriana for you,' he says. 'This time, walk to the top of the hill and back. Your thighs are getting wobblier than I like. 'Tis a pity you cannot ride a horse, for that would firm you up.'

Like his lady on her fine horse, he means.

I try to be excused, reminding him of my monthlies, but he says that is no reason to avoid a walk and leaves.

He doesn't even say when he will be back.

Oriana looks fed up, and doubly so when I send her for extra clouts to stem the blood, since I know the walk will worsen it. 'I have been on my feet since five this morning and now this carry-on,' she says, throwing me a clean belted girdle. 'And it is boiling hot out there.'

I am livid at Lord James sizing me up like that, grabbing parts of my flesh and finding it wanting. The woods are alive with singing birds and bursting with buttercups, yet I sweat each step of the way, the belted menstrual girdle thick and moist between my legs.

'He is an arrogant bastard,' I mutter.

'All masters are,' she says. 'There is nothing you can do.'

'I cannot stand it,' I say.

'Promise me you won't do something daft,' she pleads. 'You don't know how angry he can get. You don't know the laird.'

I say nothing. Just drag myself back, arriving in the turret in a hot, sweltering temper that quickly turns to tears.

The mood does not lift. In fact, as the day rolls on, it gets worse. Eventually I see him head out in his carriage. Perhaps I should take the opportunity to walk around the castle again. It will do me good. It might calm the anger that is raging at the unfairness of it all.

But I will wait for the dark, for I am not wanting to be caught.

Oriana never locks the door at night. Does she leave it like that deliberately, to tempt trouble? There's no moon, merely the tail end of the sunset's glow. I slip like a shadow to the top of the tree-lined road and breathe in the heady scent of night.

Country nights are so different from those in the town. They are soft and ripe as low-hanging fruits that you can pluck and taste. To the left, the birdies in the bird-house sleep nestled in their wee pairs, beaks tucked tightly under wings. Down in the village, the fornicators turn and sigh and smack their gums in their sleep and dream of their next tussle with their neebors' wives.

The last tree is a black giant. So much bigger than the others, it must have been planted with some form of magic. I stop just shy of it, fearing its sorcery. I stand and listen to it shush under the stars. A chill runs up my spine from my backside to my neck. I shiver, breaking out in goosebumps, and realize the sky has got dark as death now and it would be better for me to creep back inside.

As I cross the moat bridge again and come back into the safety of the lanterns, I can't help but think about paying another visit into the keep, for Lord James is nowhere to be seen, his coach still away.

I only want a look about his room. Just to see what trinkets and treasures he has.

My belly sings with the thrill of my night wander. It has been a long time since I did anything for the lark of it. Me and Ginger might have gone squealing up the closes from time to time, and she would shout *fatty* or *boot-face* as we passed gents and ladies dressed in finery. Or we would squabble over Mrs Fiddes's spare pennies in the confectioner's shop. What a hoot! Daft lassies risking a whipping for sheer laughs. But there's not much fun to be had when you've nothing. And I am too smart and quick to get caught. Sleek as a whisper.


The keep is silent. I steal up the stone steps and slip into the hall. The doors to the laird's room are closed, but one wee push and I am in. It is dark and I take a few moments to become accustomed, but the room smells of him and that pomander scent I have come to feel is the very essence of sex.

The lanterns outside give a faint glow into the room. There are so many drawers and dressers. But I keep my own secrets within reach of my sleeping head, so I go to the drawers closest to the bed and even more of the trail of him seeps out. It must be where he keeps his scents. Inside are letters in writing that is so thin and shaky it could be a spider's footprints, but I have no use for letters, so I tuck them back.

Further in the drawer is a large box with all manner of rings and pendants inside it. Heavy and gold, crammed in a heap as if they are little more than junk. They clink against each other as I touch them. I think of Ginger's hair pin, worth nothing more than an abortion. Of the money the laird promised to pay me each week, of which I have seen nothing yet.

Would he miss a ring or a chain if I took it?

Would he guess it was me?

One of the trinkets catches my eye, for it twinkles even in the dark. I bring it out for a good look. It is a decent size, long as my palm, a sharp pin decorated with a wee sword. It glitters. I think it is made out of diamonds.

The night is marching on, and there is no way of knowing when he will come rocketing back in his coach, waking up the servants and demanding a late supper. I slip out of his room, closing the drawer and the door as if I had been nothing but a passing cloud.

The door to Lady Lillias's bedroom is only three steps away. As I grow close, I hear the squeak of her snores reaching a high crescendo.

Emboldened by my good luck so far, I turn the handle and the heavy door swings ajar. She snorts, as if sensing me, and I hold still. When the snores resume, I peer round the door and see the pitiful lump she makes in the bed, a wheeled chair contraption next to it. There is a rattle in her breath. I listen carefully to it for a few moments. I know that sound. I have heard it before in my own ma and da. It comes in the days before death.

I have heard enough to know the fortunes of this house are changing. I scuttle back to the turret, the night folding back on itself in my wake.

The diamond sword pin warms my closed palm.

It will fetch a good price if I ever need it.

I have enjoyed my wee wander, and profitable it was too. I might do it again, another night, see what else I might find.

# Chapter Twenty-Nine

# CHRISTIAN

*Corstorphine Castle*
*June 1679*

I cannot believe the risks I took. I must have gone mad with lust. I lost my appetite. I thought of nothing but sex. Another note arrived: *Come on Wednesday for an hour. After lunch. Lillias ails, and will be in her chamber.*

I left at two, thinking that would be time enough. How wrong I was.

The groundsman tied the horse in the stables behind the castle and I slipped in a back door, but there was no sign of anyone.

I was in a maze of dark corridors – the working quarters, which house the kitchen and storerooms – barely lit by small lanterns. I followed the most obvious route, turning corner after corner, with nothing but the echo of my own footsteps. I did not dare call out.

I decided to make my way to the kitchen and tell a servant to go and fetch James, rather than try to creep around further. It was unbecoming.

As I walked along the corridor I noticed one door was half open and, as I drew past it, I could have sworn I heard something from behind it. I froze. What was that noise? It sounded like a muffled cry. Half of me wanted to bolt as far away from the door as I could, but the other half of me was rooted to the spot. Then I heard it again.

It was the noise of someone gasping.

Fear crept over me like shivers do. Was someone in trouble? Then I heard James's voice.

'Having a wander around, were you?'

And then a woman's voice. A young woman, with no airs and graces about her.

'I was just stretching my legs, Laird.'

He laughed at that. 'Do I not keep you busy enough?'

Then there was a muffled noise as though one or both of them were moving. The noise of skirts and rough hands. And then I thought I heard something muttered and low, like, 'Keep still, lass.'

I pushed the door.

Two faces looked straight at me. Both shocked. He had her bent over a table, next to a small window.

'Oh,' she cried out, "tis the lady.'

I looked up from her into the face of my lover. And then back to the girl, for I realized at once who she was. The saintly dining-room maid, Oriana.

I ordered her out of the room, a tide of nausea almost gagging me. She fled, righting her cap, brushing past me in a harsh flick of woollen skirt.

'Pray to the Lord for forgiveness,' I stammered after her, not caring who might hear, for what did it matter now?

'Christian, I know you are furious,' he began.

'What were you thinking?' I was utterly shocked. 'How long has this been going on?'

His face was gaunt in the weak light. 'She has tempted me from time to time. She behaves in a pious way, but she has carnal lusts like any woman,' he said, looking sorry for himself. 'And I spent so many years being denied by Lillias.'

'But a serving girl,' I said. 'A maid. How could you stoop so low? You repulse me.'

I marched out and told the groundsman to get me organized to ride again. He said nothing, but shook his head in puzzlement. I cared not what the bloody groundsman thought, for I was buzzing with fury. I rode home faster than I have ever ridden before, determined I would not cross the threshold of Corstorphine Castle again, no matter how many damned notes the bastard sent.

# Chapter Thirty

# VIOLET

*Corstorphine Castle*
*June 1679*

Oriana is late bringing my lunch and I am fair starved, and when she does arrive, she looks like death and the soup is stone-cold.

'That looks inedible,' I complain. There is a skin of grease over the top.

'It is not my fault,' she says. And then she says it again, this time shouting, 'It is not my fault.'

'Calm yourself down,' I say. 'No need for hysterics. Come and sit on the bed, take off that cap. You are shivering.'

She does as she is told, like a puppy, and it reminds me of poor Ginger.

'You will be angry with me,' she says.

That sends a warning shot.

'I promise I will not,' I say, for that is the best way to get things out of folk, even if it might not be true and you might want to slap them in the face five minutes later.

'It is the laird. He took advantage.' She starts sobbing, a horrible sort of blubbering, like a bairn. 'At first I tried to stop him, but he never takes no for an answer.'

This I can barely believe. A plain and godly thing like

her? What possible attraction could the laird feel towards Oriana?

'Are you sure?' I ask. 'What does he do?' For sometimes, you see, girls do not quite understand the ins and outs of it all and need a bit of explaining. Happens at the whorehouse all the time when new ones arrive. Happened to me, when I arrived.

Through the tears, she explains exactly what Lord James has done. What he does. And for how long he has been doing it.

'I was relieved when you came here,' she heaves. 'For it stopped then.'

But I can barely hear her, for my ears are filled with a ringing noise as I sit, agog.


Eventually Oriana drags herself back to the kitchen. I tell her to say to Cook that she is poorly, and to go to bed. Lady Christian walking in on them like that means only one thing. Oriana is doomed.

I did not tell her that.

Some men will take advantage even when the girl is most reluctant. One week to the day after I joined the whorehouse, Mrs Fiddes auctioned off my maidenhood for a big purse of coins and a box of tobacco. She had put word out for the whole week and messages were sent to and fro, from all manner of gents. She offered me a puff of her own tobacco afterwards, but I was already close to retching, as I had been throughout the ordeal. Not that the old gent gave a toss. In fact I think he enjoyed the way I trembled, and Mrs Fiddes said this was his special eccentricity.

'Hurts a bit now, but by morning you will come to realize

this is better than sleeping on the streets,' she said, tucking me into my bed and leaving some meat pie for supper on the side.

He had not been rough. Just firmly in charge. Strong arms and a chest that sagged and wobbled. Long white hairs on his nipples, and I remember the shock of seeing them. The girls had talked me through it and given me a tot of whisky. Much is a blur, but I remember weeping and turning my face to the side so that he would not see my tears, for I knew he would have enjoyed that even more.

Mrs Fiddes came to me again, in the morning, to check how I was. Supper plate untouched.

'The main door to my apartments is not a prison gate,' she said. 'You are free to leave. But if you stay, you will eat. A girl cannot go all day on thin air.'

I lay there, remembering the night. It had been disgusting. Repulsive. But it had been over and done with soon enough. And now I was snug and warm. What would Ma have wished for me if not for me to be snug and warm? I sat up, weakly, and ate the stale pie.

# Chapter Thirty-One

# CHRISTIAN

*Carrick House, Corstorphine*
*July 1679*

I spent several days bringing myself to my senses.

It stung. I kept seeing them. Flashes of white cap and the sheer look of lust on his face. The very same look I had watched in his eyes in our moments of intimacy. How on earth had she tempted him? Surely he had been the one to tempt her?

It was impossible to continue our affair. Lillias would be bound to put a stop to it soon anyway. I slept badly, startled awake by my own miserable dreams. I drank bottles of wine and woke up groggy and thirsty. I rode the fields, keeping away from the castle. I waited for Andrew to return.

Nightfall brought him rattling home in a horse and cart from Leith Port with the sticky salt of the sea in his hair and clothes. I was relieved to have the distraction of his presence and said we should host a dinner. Desperate to keep myself occupied.

I pleaded for dancing, as everyone knew social dances were happening all the time in Edinburgh, behind the closed doors of the grandest homes, despite what the Kirk says about them being a wanton opportunity for drunkenness. Mother and Father had even hosted them. But Andrew said we did not want to be seen as those sorts of people, allowing men and women to jig together and risking the wrath of the Kirk and accusations of encouraging promiscuity.

Instead he promised me a lute player in the corner and a peacock pie as a centrepiece, served at the table with its head and tail, which he talked of seeing in Calais, and I supposed I would have to amuse myself with the sight of that. It was better than ruminating over Lord James Forrester. Wondering if he was with Oriana again. Obsessing over why I had not been enough.

On the day of the dinner I oversaw the maids decorate the dining room with purple thistles to echo the hue of the peacock's feathers, and the candelabra were alight with silver flames. It looked marvellous. *How fortunate I am.*

It would always be like this, now, I realized. I would drift from one wholesome task to the next, occupying myself. Keeping my hands busy and my mind distracted.

But I would settle for it.

It was better than being a mistress.

At seven, as I had shooed the jittery maids out and was rearranging the flowers myself, the lute player stalked into the room in a black cape and took his place, his silver buckled shoes gleaming. Soon the room filled with sweet plucked chords that cried out in such a melancholy ache that I hoped he would gather his tempo before I wept and spoiled my face-powder.

But at a quarter past seven the guests arrived and there was so much kissing and admiring of gowns and hats that I swallowed down the lump in my throat and put on my most engaging smile. When we were seated and I surveyed the well-groomed heads of our guests nodding at each other in polite conversation down the table, I couldn't help but feel a twinge of satisfaction at how splendidly we hosted. I really did have an eye for it, and I was pleased with my dress, which was from the bolt of *Deepest Noir* velvet, the same bolt Andrew had gifted me not long after we met. I was handsome in it. It set off my skin and my hair magnificently. The windows were ajar onto a warm summer's evening and the fragrant scent of the honeysuckle and river trickled into the room.

It was definitely all for the best.

Finding James with his maid was a lucky escape.

Mother was late, but the first course of scrambled eggs with anchovies would spoil if we did not get on with it, so we had to begin without her. The couples were of Andrew's trade, much older than me, with the exception of Robert and the heavily pregnant Johanna, attending her last social outing before her confinement. I smiled and nodded at Mr James Keith, an esteemed tailor on my left, as he confessed that his favourite midday pastime was a wander through Edinburgh to see whether any mischief-maker had been caught lately and was having his ear nailed to the Mercat Cross by way of punishment.

'A sight to behold. Makes you grimace, but you're rooted to the spot as you're wondering how long the poor fellow will last before he faints,' Mr Keith observed, waving his knife in the air. 'Some of the fellows run wagers on it. And then I usually take luncheon in a decent wee tavern called Nell's on the corner. Has Andrew been there? Tell him they do a fine mutton stew. But not half as tasty as these eggs, of course.'

I thought he was a nasty little man, and I was cross with Andrew for making me sit next to him whilst his wife painstakingly picked out all her anchovies, leaving a trail of them at the side of her plate. I was tempted to do the same, for anchovies are the best way to spoil a dish of scrambled egg, but I had better manners.

Where was Mother? She was three-quarters of an hour late. I hoped she had not come to some mishap in that old carriage of hers. Johanna caught my eye and frowned, shrugging her shoulders. It was not like Mother to miss a minute of something fancy.

But she arrived just before the peacock, in the same shade of blue and quite as showy in an elaborate ruffled gown that could only have come from my generous husband.

'How incredibly brave,' said Mr Keith under his breath, as we all stood and let her make her way up to me.

'My utmost apologies, my dear,' Mother rattled, as we all sat down again and the hubbub of chatter around the table resumed, 'but we have had a shock at Roseburn this afternoon.'

'Be calm, Mother, and catch your breath.' She was entirely blue from collar to shoe. I waved the servant over to get Mother served her wine and her eggs.

'A terrible afternoon,' she went on, 'and I shouldn't even have come, but decided it best, as I could not be on my own.'

Then we were interrupted by the arrival of the peacock in all its baked glory. A golden pie-crust covered the creature, and I knew that underneath the bird was baked in butter and bacon, with an onion studded with cloves. But at one end was its head – beak and all – and at the other a great plume of feathers from its tail. They would talk of this for weeks!

'What do you think?' I asked, knowing she would be proud of me for producing such a fine dinner table.

'Oh, splendid, but I can hardly think,' she said. She had not touched her first course. 'A letter came this afternoon from Corstorphine Castle. From James.'

The sound of his name out loud at my dinner table was like a pinch in my shoulder blades. It chilled my back, tingling all the way down my spine.

'What did he say?'

Down at the bottom of the table there was an explosion of laughter. The crockery rattled. The lute soared to a crescendo.

'He said that Lillias had returned from taking the waters and seemed in good spirits. But last night she took a turn for the worse and despite a physician being called out to attend her, there was nothing he could do, God rest her soul.'

I felt that I was going to faint. I had to breathe slowly.

'It was the drinking, I fear,' Mother said, weeping now. 'But we will not speak of that further and will ask God to forgive her weaknesses.'

The servants filled my plate with peacock meat, potatoes and cabbage. I had envisaged it looking far more appetizing than this. It looked like nothing more than a plain chicken dinner. Mr Keith asked the servant if there was any sauce. I wondered if James was grieving or relieved. I wondered if I might vomit, and I gripped the cool wooden tabletop for comfort.

'The pity is, she was such a promising bride,' Mother went on. 'A beauty on her wedding day. And he was the most eligible bachelor in the south-east of Scotland. Well, now he is its most eligible widower, for he comes with that castle and that title. If the family ties had been different, I might have fancied him as a husband for you, Christian, but of course there would never have been a way of making that work.'

I finally got to Johanna after the almond cream, when the men retired to smoke and the ladies were seated in the glasshouse with coffee, warning my sister of the perils of childbirth and chewing over the news of Lillias's passing. Johanna radiated in a pink gown beside the hothoused French roses.

'I feel hideous about Lillias,' I said. Johanna nibbled on a marzipan.

'I am sure there will be a stampede of ladies offering a shoulder for James to weep on,' she said. 'And you are to stay out of it. You have a husband, and that matter is settled.'

The thought of James with another wife chilled my blood. A young bride.

I realized then just how deep my feelings for him ran.

What if I was free of Andrew? If James and I were free to wed and I was always at his side, he would have no need for dalliances with his serving girls.

'Men have divorced their wives,' I told Johanna. 'For adultery. And desertion. It was in the marriage book.'

'You are scandalous,' Johanna said. 'What has become of you? We know of no one who is divorced. Imagine the shame! And does James love you? I doubt it. I have heard he has women all over the place.'

We were interrupted by Mrs Keith, who wanted the recipe for the peacock pie and insisted on sitting beside us, for she had trouble with her hip and needed a firm chair. She was soon engaged in chatter with Johanna about her aches and clicking bones. Mother was in the corner being comforted by the other ladies. I had already said she should remain here overnight.

I felt such emptiness in my own glasshouse at that moment, with the bold July moon luminating my polished silver coffee pots, as I have ever felt.

# Chapter Thirty-Two

# CHRISTIAN

*Corstorphine Castle*
*July 1679*

Lady Lillias was buried to the peals of the dead bell, ringing away the evil spirits that gather at the bodies of the dying. The Forresters had their own corner of Corstorphine Kirkyard with views up to Corstorphine Hill. Grey rain hammered down in cold nails, despite the fact it was summer, sealing her into the ground along with the secrets she kept about her husband.

Her funeral was like her life: stiff and black and reeking of alcoholic fumes. The ladies attended Corstorphine Kirk for the sermon. I prayed for Lillias's soul, trying to push away the memories of her husband's hands on my skin. His intimate touches. I ached for him, despite Oriana. Despite the fading bruises on my shoulders from where he had gripped me in temper. Without him, my life was empty.

But we ladies were spared the graveyard and the raw elements, for a burial site was not the place for us. Instead we sipped wine in the castle dining room – conspiratorial ravens picking at the flesh of Lady Lillias's life. The beauty she once was. The fall into ruin. Lord James bravely enduring her moods.

I was elated to be at my own aunt's funeral.

What kind of woman did that make me?

The men returned from the burial soaked to the bone and we ate platters of mutton, and the men drank whiskies and toasted all their dead, whilst the bell-man continued with his unearthly cries in the courtyard.

James looked as sombre as I had ever seen him. But not distressed. He was as handsomely groomed as ever, and head to toe in black. But as I scoured the room I realized there were far more young ladies at this funeral than was seemly. They had sprung from all corners of Edinburgh and beyond, with the tightest of corsets and the loosest of connections to the deceased. Lady this and Lady that. A Miss Mariota Blair from Fife, weeping behind an ornate black fan, and a Lady Jane Stewart peeping at James from behind her mourning veil. Cousins-once-removed and families-once-visited. Bosoms heaving with black opal necklaces. He kissed hands and performed deep bows and I slipped invisibly to the back of the room and watched the bell-ringer from the window. I did not want to watch James eyeing his next bride.

Even in the thump of the summer rain, which made its walls all the more desolate, this place had more draw than my own home because it was where I had felt beautiful, and in those moments I had even desired my own self, so captivated had I become with the softness of my flesh.

It was true, the thing I said to Johanna. The marriage manual said there were circumstances in which a man may annul his marriage. What would Andrew do if he knew of my secret life? I put my fingers on the windowpane, its chill numbing my skin. The bell-ringer was soaked. He threw his last swings and wiped his face with his free hand. A servant scurried out and passed him his payment and then he slipped away.

I felt James's breath on the back of my neck before he even spoke.

'You were good to come,' he murmured. 'My behaviour with Oriana was wicked.'

I did not move my body, but tilted my head sideways to him, and that forced him to lean in closer.

'You have many distractions today. Every unwed woman in Scotland has arrived.'

He laughed, low and hoarse. 'Now you see how popular I am! But look at them, for God's sake, Christian. Fools and idiots. I need a real woman. One I truly desire. Not one of these simpering bitches. No more serving girls. When is Andrew next away?'

The words I had longed to hear. I gripped the windowsill.

'He has two trips planned in August,' I said.

'Then visit the day he is gone. I can't stand another moment without you. Lillias's death changes everything, Christian.'

In that moment, I knew I had him. But he needed to understand that I was willing to assert myself as his wife.

'I will not return to this castle unless Oriana is gone,' I said.

The rain streamed down the windowpane.

'I will dismiss her,' he said. 'I have my suspicions about her anyway, as I cannot locate a diamond cape pin I am sure was in my bedside drawer, and she is the only servant with access to my chamber.'

'Then dismiss her immediately,' I said. 'We cannot have untrustworthy staff.'

I only knew he was gone when I heard him greeting a group of mourners at the edge of the room.

I put my forehead to the windowpane, feeling my pulse cooling against the cold glass. Everything could change. James had said so himself. I grasped the thought like a slippery fish.

The rain was easing. Something caught my eye in the window of the south turret. Pale as a face, fleeting away just as I tried to focus on it. Perhaps it was the reflection of the clouds in the glass. Perhaps it was the ghost of Lady Lillias. I shivered. It would not serve me well to be afraid of ghosts in this castle if I was to be its queen.

## Chapter Thirty-Three

# VIOLET

*Corstorphine Castle*
*July 1679*

Time for another whisky! And if anyone is peckish there's a grand spread about to be laid out. A Parmesan cheese all the way from Italy, stinking to high heaven. Anchovies, capers and pastries. As you pick over the *quelquechoses* I'll tell you one of my philosophies on whoring. Pay heed – a brain as well as a pretty face. And if someone fancies bringing me a plate, I'll try a little of everything. Oh, don't all rush at once; we don't need a stampede, gentlemen.

Men, I do declare, turn to whores for all sorts of reasons. Some come for the deed itself, in which case it is over in a heartbeat. Some for the desperate ripping of clothes before, others for the velvet stillness afterwards, when they can lay their heads upon a breast and feel like bairns again. Some come because they love women. Others come because they hate women.

I think Lord James Forrester takes mistresses and whores and maids because he likes to think of himself as always having a choice of women to fuck, whatever the hour of the day.

He thinks each brings out a different side in him. Laird James the Lover. The Rescuer. The Conqueror. He sees himself more handsome in his mirror because of it. If he had seven turrets, he'd have seven whores and even more ladies in his bedrooms. He thinks nothing of their reasons for spreading their legs to him, be it money or fear or, in that grey-gowned lady's case, the desperate yearning to be loved. I heard her loneliness in the ache of her moans and quivers that night I listened at his chamber door.

She sounded as though she'd never been touched before. But all he would have heard was *James, James* – the echo of his name.

And Oriana, who he took, from time to time, from the age of fourteen, so she says. She did not want his paws on her, but how could she ever say no? He was paying her a wage. A castle servant. One of the best positions in Corstorphine for a girl like her. She was his to fuck. Was that why she became so meek and pious? Was she trying to dampen his lust? What was she like, under that cap and shapeless sack of a gown? Did she despise her natural beauty for what it had brought upon her?

What betrayal must she feel when her own God never answers her prayers? Without the fear of hell and black marks on the soul, how vengeful might she become?


I am not surprised when Oriana comes, shocked, and says Lady Lillias has died in the night, for apart from the death-rattle there had been a parade of physician-looking men in spectacles with black leather cases shaking their heads in the courtyard. But I am surprised when James comes to me the day after that miserable-looking funeral party, for I thought he would be in mourning and would leave me be, not striding in the door fresh as a daisy.

'I am sorry about your wife,' I say.

'It was not unexpected, but it is still a shock,' he says, sitting down on the bed and not taking off his coat.

'Are you not staying?' He looks fit to leave at any minute, his eyes wandering the room.

'I am preparing for Lady Christian. She may come for an hour or so, here and there, when her husband is away. I must organize a chamber for her, and the servants are not making a decent job of things.'

And his wife's deathbed not yet cold.

'Which brings me to the reason for my visit.' He puts his hand on my leg, giving it a measured squeeze as if it were a sausage on a stall. 'Business, not pleasure, this afternoon, I am sorry to say. It may be a little unseemly to have you in this turret whilst Lady Christian is visiting. There is a risk she will find out that I have put you here. She is far more inquisitive than Lillias was. I have a vacancy.'

'A vacancy?' I do not like the sound of this.

'A vacancy for a maid,' he says. 'You shall fill it, and with extra pay on top of the wages I have already put aside for you. You will come into the main house and live in the maids' quarters and help Cook in the kitchen, and assist Lady Christian with anything she needs. You are my maid, but at her disposal. She cannot bring her maid from Carrick House. Servants gossip, and our private business is none of theirs. Now don't gawp, Violet, it gives you the air of a fishwife.'

I have never heard the like. What is he thinking? Does this mean I am to work? This feels like a most terrible idea.

'But what about Oriana? Should she not assist, rather than me?'

James frowns.

'Oriana is leaving in the morning. She has not been the best of maids. She has got herself into somewhat of a fix and we cannot have her in the castle any longer.'

Something – a deep instinct – tells me not to ask any more questions. Not to appear interested. Play stupid. So I ask nothing. I will see Oriana at dinner time and get her to tell me everything.

'A lady's maid,' I say.

'There is nothing to it; just flatter and assist,' he says. 'And you will move to the servants' quarters where the company is better, but we will both retire back to this turret for an hour or so when it is convenient.'

He squeezes my leg again and then he strides off, flicking his curls behind him and giving himself a nod of approval in the mirror on his way out.

Risen up from the slums to powder cheeks and lace corsets and brush hair. I should be pleased. But I am not. I am Mistress Violetta now. I have no inclination to bow and scrape to the laird's other whores.

Or to live in the servants' quarters.

How dare he do this to me?


Oriana tells me she is dismissed, whimpering and quivering, her face red and bloated with tears.

First caught acting the harlot, now suspected of stealing his jewellery.

'The shame of it,' she whispers. 'I did nothing wrong. It was the beast himself making me, and that whore of a lady getting rid of me.' I do not think I have seen anyone look so distraught. 'One rule for them, and another for the rest of us. It's not right, Violet, is it?'

I know this girl is neither a whore nor a thief, but what can I say? I cannot say anything about the sword pin. I have hidden it under the bed for now and I dare not look in its direction. The laird has given her the full month's wages to keep her mouth shut, but what of her then? Who will employ a dismissed maid?

I know what happens to girls like that.

I do the only thing I can. Give her Mrs Fiddes's address and say she'll find lodgings there, should it ever come to it. It is the least I can do for Oriana.

'Lord James Forrester is a cruel bastard,' I say. 'Where is the justice in this world?'

She nods, looking at me, then her eyes dart away to the turret door. I can already feel him standing there.

He has heard me.

'A cruel bastard indeed,' he says.


He makes Oriana watch as he whips me with his belt.

'The problem with whores is that they forget their place in the world and think they can speak ill of their masters,' he says.

He makes me strip. Oriana tries to look away, but he tells her if she does not watch, then he will whip her too, and she pleads and cries fit to wake the dead.

He gives me ten lashes of his belt across my arse and my back. She sobs in the corner. I try to hold in the tears, but I cannot help it, the whipping is too painful. He is calm. He is enjoying it. I have never been whipped before, not even by customers, for Mrs Fiddes does not allow it. 'They can go elsewhere for that sort of cruelty,' she says. 'My floggers are for the gents' arses alone.'

'And do not think about trying to escape,' he says, when it is over and Oriana is sent fleeing out of the room, and I am lying on the bed curled into myself. 'For if you are caught, I will have you put in the branks.'

# Chapter Thirty-Four

# CHRISTIAN

*Corstorphine Castle*
*August 1679*

The grander Carrick House became, the more Andrew and I became like strangers again. He got the gardener to scatter the grounds with seedlings from the continent in the sunniest spots and he imported French and Italian furniture in walnut and oak. I wanted for nothing. There was no silk he could not procure, and he had a modern eye for my gowns, and his coats. But he was most content at his papers, balancing his books with a bottle of Burgundy at his side, and if I ever knew what it meant to be invisible it was on those afternoons when I was setting out to visit Mother or Johanna, after being powdered and pinned by the maid, and he waved me goodbye without lifting his eyes from his books.

But what did I care now?

James was free to remarry.

A divorce, even if it was successful, would take a long time. Years. James would have to help. And I went straight to him once more, as he had asked, as soon as Andrew departed again. God knows how Andrew expected a wife to suffer his absences and not tire of the situation.

James had a room prepared. Not Lillias's chamber, the door to which remained closed. But a room near his.

'To give you some privacy during your days here,' he said, swinging the door open to reveal a large, bright room swathed in white curtains. 'You should make yourself comfortable. I have organized a maid and she will be in here shortly. She is at your beck and call. She's also very discreet and not from this village and will have no idea who you are.'

He meant to keep me well here. The bed had a feather mattress and was curtained in white. There was a bowl for washing on the dressing table. A walnut armoire in the corner, which I knew contained dinner dresses he had had sent from Edinburgh. The floor had been swept and there was not a speck of dust anywhere.

It could be my new home. This could be my chance at a real marriage. James watched me take it all in. There was a carefulness about him now. I imagined that he did not want to put a foot wrong. I allowed myself an emotion I had not let myself feel for a long time.

I allowed my heart to soar with hope.

James was looking at me in the ravenous way he looks before he kisses me, when the door interrupted us with a long creak, heavy as an accusation. I jumped. A maid I had not seen before stalked in and put her hands on her hips. Underneath her apron was a swish of damson-plum skirt. Not the dark garments that staff usually wear to hide the grime of their moppings and sweepings and the wipes of their hands. But my greatest astonishment was that she appeared rouged, with two pink specks on her cheeks like the ladies on the high street of Edinburgh who'd mingled with the traders and the beggars outside Johanna's wedding, pulling up their skirts to show their ankles.

James took a step back from me and surveyed his maid carefully.

'Violet, perhaps you will knock the next time. But I am glad you are here. Please see that Lady Christian is comfortable.'

The girl said nothing, but lifted her chin in a way I might describe as defiant and, ignoring him, assessed me slowly, running her eyes down my body like a cold finger.

He turned to me with a half-smile.

'Forgive Violet. She is new. And perhaps a little shy. Violet does not have much experience as a maid, but it was hard to find a replacement for Oriana at such short notice.' His eyes flickered between the two of us. I imagined he was hoping I would approve of her, but I did not. Not yet. Not with that rouge, and his reputation.

'Violet. Please fetch rosewater for me to freshen up before dinner,' I said, attempting to be bright.

'Yes, my lady,' she said and disappeared, sneaking a scowl before her back was fully turned.

I looked to James, but he had not even noticed her scowl. Instead he was catching his own eye in the mirror, adjusting his head so as to get his best angle in the light.

'You will keep your hands off this one,' I told him.

He dragged his gaze from the mirror.

'I will not betray you again, my love. I would not even dare contemplate it. And certainly not with that one. You can see for yourself that she is nothing to look at.'


Violet took her time, and James was long gone from the room when she returned, clattering and sighing.

'There are dresses of mine in the armoire,' I said. I was

distracted by the way she proceeded to open it, stealing glances at me from under her cap as though she was trying to make a study of me. I was covered in sweat from the ride.

'Tonight I'll wear the navy one. But I will need your assistance.'

She blinked, as though this was a surprise to her, and I was on the cusp of tutting, but Violet managed to understand the task and laid out the dress on the bed, then stood behind me, unhooking the stiff buttons all the way down the dress I was wearing. When it dropped to the floor and I was left in nothing but my shift, I stretched my arms and neck and closed my eyes, feeling the sweet shivers of freedom cascade down the bones of my back.

'It's always a relief, eh?' she said softly.

I opened my eyes. I did not usually make it a habit to chit-chat to staff about intimate matters of the body, even when they were assisting me in them.

'It's always a relief when you take off your dress,' she said, nodding to the heap of fabric on the floor. 'I'm never happier than in my nightgown.'

'Indeed.' I managed a small smile and made to begin to wash. 'One of the trials of the fairer sex.' I could smell my own stale sweat. I stood in my shift, my pale arms and legs sticking out and my hair a dry-looking frizz. It was absurd that I felt awkward when she was the underling.

'Let me,' she whispered. 'I'm told I have a good touch.' And before I could object, for this was a task I always did myself, she took the cloth and dipped it into the bowl. 'Your shift,' she said, and instead of saying that I would manage myself perfectly well, I found that I lifted it over my head obediently.

She was the third person to see me naked in as many weeks. I would have felt like a child, but a child has fewer blemishes to hide. She began to wash me. She was careful and, despite her rough accent, she had the gentlest manner. Healing hands, I thought, as though she had much experience of human skin.

'Where were you maid before?' I asked.

She lifted my arm and applied the cloth to my armpit, her fingers light on my wrist.

'To a mistress in Edinburgh town,' she said, her eyes shifting away from mine in the mirror.

'Which family?' I expected to hear it was people like the Cuthberts or the Strangs, for the ladies of those households were forever employing staff and losing them in petty squabbles.

'It was a Mistress Fiddes,' the girl said, still not meeting my eye and concentrating on the washing instead. I had never heard of the Fiddes family, but I didn't know everyone in Edinburgh. How could I? I had barely been the mistress of my own household five minutes and if this girl was to know that sour detail, she might gossip.

'I don't think I am acquainted with her,' I said, closing my eyes and letting her cloth work its way down my skin.

'She keeps herself to herself,' said Violet and I swear she sounded as though she was smirking.

She started to hum softly as she carried on washing me, various ditties I have heard at social dinners, so her Mistress Fiddes must have entertained often. Then her washcloth came to my stomach, stroking the skin there so firmly I couldn't stop my mind drifting to Lord James.

'Shall I continue, my lady?' Her voice was a husk. I knew she was watching me, even my private parts, but there was something gentle in the light of Corstorphine Castle, the sunshine softened by its pink sandstone walls, that made me feel unashamed.

James had made me feel unashamed.

'Yes, thank you.' I shifted my legs so that they were parted slightly, and I heard her dip the cloth into the water. It was lukewarm by now, but the scent of rosewater drifted from my skin. It would please my lover.

'You're smiling,' she whispered. 'Must be something awful nice you're thinking of.'

But it was not a question, so I didn't answer it, just let her carry on stroking the cloth between my legs, the heat of my body warming it up; and with the way she hummed gently, it felt as though this was something very normal, as if some maids washed their ladies all the time. Perhaps some did. I have never sought Johanna's advice on the matter.

'I think you are clean now, my lady.' She stopped, although I would not have wished her to. I opened my eyes, but she was already rinsing out the cloth. 'I will have a mountain of chores piling up downstairs.'

'Will you assist me to dress? I have the most complicated evening gown you can imagine.'

She folded up the flannel and set it aside on the tray.

'As you wish,' she said and bobbed down so meekly she could be curtseying to me.

The dress was navy with cream point-lace roses down the skirts. It was low at the front, showing the top of my shoulders and the hint of my breasts, which was a fashion I was becoming bold in, and the sleeves were finished with cream lace. As Violet helped me step into the hoops, I realized her humming had stopped.

As the last button loop was hooked, I studied the magnificent shape it made of me: a low, tight corset and wide skirts.

'That is some frock,' she whispered.

I saw envy in the gleam of her eye, the purse of her lips. You get that with maids sometimes, and it is a trait that can lead to trouble. I felt I'd had enough time in her company. 'You're dismissed for now, girl,' I said. 'You may go back to your tasks and apologize, on my behalf, if you have been kept longer from them than necessary.'

She slipped out of the room, taking the wash tray with her. The air in the chamber eased. She was the kind of person who filled a space strangely.

# Chapter Thirty-Five

# VIOLET

*Corstorphine Castle*
*August 1679*

I am scunnered. She is a fine sight, bare naked, ripe in all the right places from rich puddings and jams, but with a waist narrow as a wasp's sting. She barely needs the fussy hoops and contraptions that she buckles herself into. Face like a skelped arse, though. Red and furious.

I bet the laird would never dare whip her.

My skin still stings from the whipping he gave me, even though the red marks have faded. I think it always will sting, that whipping.

I wonder what he will do next time he is displeased. For it always gets worse with whippings. Not that I had ever had one myself, before that day. But from what I heard from girls who'd had them from their pa or their sweetheart, before ending up at Mrs Fiddes from it all.

It starts with a smack and ends up with a bruised face or a broken nose. And look at what happened to poor Ginger. I am uneasy now the lady is here. I feel like I am drifting in the here-and-now, waiting for something to change for the worse. The laird is dangerous. And I am his prisoner, stuck in a grey apron stained with the blood of skinned rabbits and sooty fingerprints.

I am glad I sneaked the whisky and wine to my dismal new quarters in the maids' room. I would not get through the night without it. I would not sleep well.


I am dragged up with the sunrise by Cook and set to work making up a soup for everyone's lunch whilst she prepares pastry. The brothel had a soup that I know the recipe for, so I make that, with carrot and lentils and leek and ham and a sprinkling of parsley. If Cook knows I was once a whore, she says nothing of it, nor does the boy who scampers in and out, bringing pigeon eggs and pails of milk.

But although my hands are far from idle, my mind whirs. Cooking is a damned sight better than my other occupation. The warmth of a kitchen fire and the hustle of staff coming and going.

When Cook is next to me, slicing bread from a loaf and taking as much for herself as she puts on the plate, I heave a great sigh and inspect the soup spoon. 'I hope this is decent enough for the lady,' I say. 'I think she might be quite particular.'

'Particular,' sniffs Cook, falling into my trap. 'Not if her habits are anything to go by. She has her own home and a husband just across the fields on Carrick House, but they say he is never there, forever gallivanting at sea.'

'She has a husband,' I gasp, as though I had never heard the like.

'And that is none of your business. Now, that soup is going to stick to the pan if you don't get it off the heat.'

She takes the pot and places it on the table so that I can't spoil it. When everyone upstairs is served, we sit and have our soup. Cook takes a second bowl and declares it as tasty a lentil soup as she has ever eaten. I don't tell her it was declared just as tasty by hungry whores coming off their afternoon shifts.

The lady's husband is within walking distance, when he is not at sea. I slip the nugget of information into my pocket.

Lord James grasps me by the arm as I am finishing getting Lady Christian trussed up ready for a walk in the woods with him, in her buckle boots and leather gloves. We are outside her door and she is only a few feet away, dressed up like the window of Miss Marigold's gown emporium for her two-minute turn under the trees.

'I am missing your amusing company, Violet,' he says. 'She'll be gone at dusk. Meet me in the turret.' His mouth brushes my ear. The rich stench of his breath makes me gag. I can smell her on his skin.

I am late getting to the turret, as I have to pluck a chicken. I arrive with feathers in my hair. But that is his fault for putting me in his kitchen.

'What do you make of Lady Christian, then?' He parades up and down with his hands behind his back, as though she is something he is considering purchasing and my opinion matters. He does not mention the whipping. It is as though it never happened.

'She's a fine lady indeed,' I say.

'I am thinking of marrying her,' he says.

I brush feathers from my apron. Look at the mess of me, with half a farmyard on my skirts!

'And what of my fate then?' I ask, feeling despondent. 'Am I to be released or to continue as your maid?'

'Come now, Violet, you know you are not really my maid,' he says, patting his knee for me to go and sit upon. When I refuse to move, he reaches over and grabs me and forces me upon it, like a bad infant.

'Then what am I?' I sound like a whining child, detesting myself, but detesting him more – far more – for how he always gets his own way.

'Well, Violet. A gentleman such as myself is not expected to have just one woman in his life,' he whispers, running his finger up my thigh. 'As you knew when Lillias was alive, God rest her soul.'

'But you and Lady Christian are passionate lovers,' I say. 'It is evident by the way you look at each other.' I hope, even now, that he will say they are not.

'Very passionate,' he crows. 'She absolutely trembles at my touch. Whereas you, Violet, you are quite another story. Dare I say your years of experience have made you quite the most skilled lady I have ever taken? I can't imagine a future without you.'

'So you mean to have both of us here, in this castle,' I whisper. 'That is your proposal?'

'Indeed. And a decent proposal it is for both of you. Now let me take you, Violet, as all this talk is stirring me up.'

I let him take me; I let him turn me onto my front and let him take me rough as he likes, grabbing my hair, all the while whispering in my ear, *My whore, my whore*. And as my blood pounds in my head, I am wishing that he would drop down dead. *Drop down dead.*


He sends me back to the kitchen, still sore from his handling.

'There you are, girl,' says Cook. 'I need you for a delicate platter. Oriana never had the skill for it, but you will, with those nimble fingers, I can tell.'

I slice ham and eggs and kidneys and tomatoes. I garnish
the platter with some herbs growing in a pot on the kitchen
windowsill. And fine it looks too.

'Well, fancy that,' says Cook. 'You are worth two of that
Oriana. She pulls me closer, chewing on a slice of the ham as
she does so. 'This is a household in turmoil,' she whispers,
although there is no one near to eavesdrop. 'Lady Forrester
not dead five minutes, and he is courting trouble upstairs.
Would not surprise me if that woman becomes lady of this
castle, and who knows if we'll be in a job this time next month,
or if she might bring her own servants with her. But I should
like you to stick with me, whatever happens. I can always use
an assistant in whatever kitchen I work in.'

She hands me a piece of ham, nicely darkened at the edges,
salty and sweet. I look at it and turn it over in my hand.

Perhaps all is not lost, after all.


I am shocked when Cook says I am to come to kirk on Sunday.
Of course I remember worship, when Ma and Da took me.
But Mrs Fiddes and her girls are not considered part of
Edinburgh's congregation as such, and so I have not crossed
the threshold of a kirk in five years.

Oh, the Devil has got me firm in his grasp.

I do not tell Cook about my absence, for she would likely
suspect me a witch and blame me the next time the milk goes
sour and, before we know it, I would be a burnt pile of bones
at the village cross. These country sorts are the worst for poking
fingers of accusation. Instead, off we both trot to kirk. She has
given me a fine clean cap and I match the wild roses at the
side of the road, just as bonnie and just as thorny, for I can
think of a hundred better things to do on a Sunday than sit

and listen to some wrinkled old minister bleat from the holy book.

'I am so glad to be praying to the Lord on this fine morning. Heavenly Father, bless us all and amen, so help me God,' I say to Cook, by way of conversation, thinking this is the kind of thing the holy sorts say to one another on their walks to kirk.

'You do not need to overdo it, Violet; piousness does not suit you,' she retorts, and I keep my mouth shut after that.

When we arrive in the kirkyard I see that Lady Christian is mingling quite the thing, arm-in-arm with a gentleman I do not recognize, who must be her husband. I have never seen him before, which means that he has never visited my whore-house, which likely means he is a decent sort.

So why is she risking everything?

She ignores us, of course. I watch to see if she even gives myself or Cook a sly look, but she does not. Oh, she is a canny one, that lady. Butter would not melt in her mouth, and I bet she knows all the prayers in the holy book.

Then James arrives.

'My lord.' Cook curtseys and that means I am obliged to do the same, lowering my head and feeling my blood boil.

'A fine summer's day – I hope you ladies enjoy it.' He nods. 'Take your time coming back, for it is only a light dinner tonight, is it not?'

'Kind of you, Laird,' says Cook, beaming away.

'Mercifully kind,' I add, and he looks at me with a very obvious frown.

'Ladies,' he says. 'Before we go in, there is something you might want to know.' But we are not told what it is, for at that moment he is accosted by a bustling man in a long cloak, obviously the minister, who sweeps him into the kirk, followed by a flock of men who look as friendly as crows.

'Well, bless my soul. I wonder what all that was about,' puzzles Cook, scratching her cap where it is rubbing against her hairline.

Well, bless my soul, we soon find out.

We find out as soon as we enter the kirk.

Oriana is on the repentance stool.

# Chapter Thirty-Six

# CHRISTIAN

*Corstorphine*
*August 1679*

I t was Oriana's own fault.

Shortly after James dismissed her, she was caught stealing from Tyler's Acre Farm. She admitted the sin, sitting there upon the repentance stool, her voice thin and nasal, 'I tried to steal a chicken. God forgive me.'

'A miserable state of affairs,' whispered Andrew.

The morning's fried bacon lingered on my clothes. Mr Tyler, the farmer, shook his head from his pew.

I grew hot. The kirk stank and we were three rows back from the front. I knew James was somewhere nearby, but dared not look round. I had taken to wearing a lavender pomander for kirk and I clutched it to my nose now, hoping the silver chain would not catch the light and look decadent. Oriana was a pale slip, balanced on the high stool beside the pulpit, her skirts dangling and dirty.

'Thou shalt not steal,' said Reverend Brodie, addressing his congregation.

Oriana was told to explain her sins. She had a mother who was blind and a father who was a drunk, and a brood of brothers and sisters. Her wages had been going back to them each week until they stopped when she lost her job.

I held the pomander to my nose, dreading her describing the circumstances of her dismissal.

'Perhaps we should hire her. Give her a second chance,' whispered Andrew.

'We shall not,' I hissed.

The pews jostled with mockery. Elbows nudged bellies, and hats shook with mirth. Oriana's fear of God; her praying ways. Now look at her!

Thankfully, Reverend Brodie cut Oriana's confession short and made us all close our eyes in prayer. We prayed for forgiveness for our own sins.

We prayed for the soul of Lillias Forrester.

I wondered what would become of Oriana. Was it my fault she had lost her job?

Of course it was not.

After the service I told Andrew I could not linger as the oppressive air of the kirk had made me feel faint and I did not want to stand beside him in the pews making idle chitchat. I dreaded to think of making conversation with him and James. I walked to the carriage, passing Reverend Brodie on the kirk steps.

'A sombre service today,' he said, a glisten of sweat on his nose and upper lip. 'But a necessary one.' His breath had the dry rankness of a mouth that has spoken too long without thirst being quenched.

'For the sake of a stolen chicken,' I said. 'I hope the girl has learned her lesson.'

'The value of the stolen item is irrelevant,' he said.

'All the same, it is not easy to watch such a humiliating act,' I said.

'My child,' Reverend Brodie's face took on a furrowed, condescending air, 'I hope you are not questioning the way we serve the Lord in Corstorphine? You are new to the parish and your husband rarely here, always on business. Perhaps you should meet with the wives of the Kirk Session and let them take you under their guardianship.'

I could not think of anything less appealing. Praying and drinking weak tea and being scrutinized. Fortunately, Andrew came to my rescue. 'Come, Wife,' he said, 'let's get you home and into the sanctity of the garden. Forgive us, Reverend, but Lady Christian's nerves got the better of her this morning.'

We departed swiftly, the carriage leaping away from the dour minister. But he watched us – I saw him. He watched us all the way to the turn in the road.

When Andrew departed for France again on Monday morning, I rode out to James. I had not been able to stop thinking about Oriana.

He was in his dining room, reading a letter, with the new maid Violet tidying the table. He had not been expecting me so early. He got to his feet, shooing the girl away. She was as rouged as ever.

'Why did you not use your influence in the Kirk Session to spare the poor maid that horrific ordeal?'

He was finishing a plate of porridge, in no hurry. He put the letter down on the table. I could tell by the looping script it was a lady's handwriting.

'I could not speak in her defence, you fool – it would have drawn attention,' he said.

'Do not call me a fool,' I said. 'I was not the one fucking her.'

'You were the one who told me to dismiss her. What did you think would happen? She has a family to feed.'

Truthfully, I had not even thought. I had assumed Oriana would find a job or would have a family willing to support her. I was dismayed at myself.

'You're a hypocrite,' I hissed.

He walked towards me and grasped me by the arm, his fingers squeezing my skin.

'Do not call me names,' he said. 'Do not blame me for your behaviour.'

'Do not grab at me,' I said, shaking him off.

I walked away and I was almost at the door before something hit me square between the shoulder blades, knocking the wind out of me. I turned round and his porridge bowl was rolling away from me across the floor.

'You are fortunate you did not break that,' I gasped. I left him standing at the table, as furious as I have ever seen anyone.


I was still shaken and was at the stables, getting ready to leave, when James came out.

'I will not stay and be shouted at and attacked,' I said.

'My temper is my downfall,' he said, not meeting my eye.

'Is that why Lillias kept to her room and drank? Your temper and your adultery?'

'Most likely,' he said. 'But I could live with that. I can't live without you.'

'There is no hope, unless you stop being vicious,' I said.

'If there's any love between you and Andrew Nimmo,' he whispered, 'then tell me now. Mariota Blair is writing to me, asking how I am faring after Lillias's death. All it would take from me is an invitation to this castle and I could be betrothed to her by the end of the month.'

He left a silence for me to fill, but the only sound was the soft buzz of flies around the horses. Mariota Blair. A fraction of his age.

'I will meet Andrew,' James went on. 'I will ask him to divorce you. It will be expensive, and you will lose friends and family, but I have always wanted you, Christian. Even Lillias knew that.'

I understood that he was offering me a thread and, if I pulled it, my entire world would unravel. Mother would never live it down. Johanna might never see me again. And if I left the thread where it was, refused to touch it – what then? James would eventually remarry. Mariota Blair or one of the other glittering mourners at his wife's funeral. Andrew would continue to work away as much as he did, and I would be left at Carrick House to stain my fingers with my oil paints and oversee peacocks being stuffed into pies.

I looked up to Corstorphine Hill, shimmering with oak and birch.

No one I knew had ever, ever divorced. The hiss of the word's syllables rang with shame.

'Be bold with me, Christian,' James whispered, taking my hands. 'What a future we could have.'

'Do not meet him,' I said. There would be nothing worse, in Andrew's eyes, than hearing this news from James himself. 'I will tell him myself on his return from France.'

That night I lay alone in my bed at Carrick House, cold as it always was. I could still feel the thud of the bowl in my shoulder blades. But James would not do something like that again. He promised this as he kissed me; said that his temper was caused by the uncertainty and, if we were safely wed, he would be calm. Perhaps when we were married we could go somewhere like France, or Italy. The places I'd dreamed Andrew would take me. I would ask James tomorrow, at the Lammas Fair.

# Chapter Thirty-Seven

# CHRISTIAN

*Corstorphine*
*Lammas Fair, 26th August 1679*

I had always loved Lammas Fairs, with their fresh offerings of loaves and sheep-chasing games and ribbons and races.

Corstorphine's Lammas Fair was held late in the month, right at the end of August. The day dawned gold and warm, and I dressed in a light-blue gown and simple silver necklace and flew out of Carrick House with Nellie, one of the maids, as soon as I could. The sun sang down on our coifs and I told her that, in the absence of my husband, Lord James would chaperone us, but she looked dismayed and said she was keen to meet a friend at the inn. I could tell from her flushed cheeks it was a sweetheart. I secretly hoped she would spend the entire day adoring his company, for it would be a long three months till the next quarter-day fair, and there was something in the togetherness of us, as we rode out onto a blank page of a morning, towards candied fruits and stolen kisses, that diminished the divide between lady and servant.

My spirits were in full flight as we entered the village. Already stalls were towering with brown loaves and fruit pies and a hog was roasting on a spit. Pigeons and chickens rattled in cages. But the greatest hubbub occurred at the entrance to the kirk, where a crowd hung.

'Look, someone's in the branks,' called Nellie.

Dread crept up my spine, sending a chill into the warmth of the day. I handed the horses over to Nellie and she was glad to be away, for standing on a platform by the kirk door was an old woman, a short, squat thing, shackled by her own head in a way that forced her entire body upright against the wall and her neck to strain upwards. She had her eyes closed to the crowd, but its jeers would be jangling in her ears.

I had known Reverend Brodie would not be far away. Sure enough, he drifted over, his dark robes sweeping over the dirt, a frown hanging over his face.

'You will be thinking this village is full of sinners. Perhaps this is not a sight for you to see,' he said, taking my arm and turning me away.

'Who is she?' I asked.

'Calls herself a cunning woman. Meddles with plants and sells potions that claim to cure all ills, but are more likely sorcery or poison. She's a constant trouble to the parish, picking at the hedgerows and terrorizing anyone who crosses her path. She'll be in the branks till evening, and she'll be lucky if she's not pelted black and blue with sour apples before then.'

At that, I recognized her. The woman was nothing but an old herbalist. I had seen her myself, when I was out riding between Carrick House and Corstorphine Castle. She spent her mornings picking leaves and her afternoons sleeping in the sun. The reverend still had his hand on my arm. I let it rest there, although I wanted to withdraw it.

'But I hope she is not harmed, Reverend,' I said. 'She is old.'

'If she is harmed, she will have brought it on herself,' he said. He pulled me away from the crowd and I had no choice but to let him lead me, for what could I say: that I wanted to watch over her? He surveyed the street in front of us and then his gaze settled back on me, his eyes narrowing to little beads.

'I see your maid has disappeared. No doubt gone to the inn. But where is your husband?'

'Andrew is in France again, unfortunately. My uncle is due to arrive any moment and chaperone me,' I said.

'Lord James,' he repeated, nodding for slightly too long. 'He seems to have become a regular companion for you in your husband's absence.' He cleared his throat. He was still nodding.

'He is a trusted companion indeed. And a noble one,' I said.

Over the reverend's shoulder the woman was a dark silhouette stretched against the cold kirk stones.

'It is decent of him to keep you company, particularly through his mourning.'

I wondered if the reverend was guessing at our secret. And if he would like to see me in the branks and would enjoy pacing up and down, watching me suffer.

'Indeed, and Lord James often reports on his time at the Kirk Session,' I said sweetly, putting my hand over his.

'You should really make an effort with the Kirk Session wives,' Reverend Brodie said. 'Your late Aunt Lillias was once a highly valued member of their group. It would be a fitting legacy if you were to come to the meetings.'

'I am quite busy with my own family,' I said. I felt his dry hand stiffen underneath mine. He withdrew it.

'The meetings are held every Tuesday,' he said. 'There are Bible readings and prayers for the sick, and Mrs Fowler always brings a cake.'

'I will make every effort,' I assured him. There would be no way of avoiding it. This officious man clearly thought himself my moral guardian.

'Being an active member of Corstorphine Kirk is obligatory for the more fortunate members of our congregation,' he said. 'Your husband ought to have told you all of this by now, Mrs Nimmo.'

I felt a fury rise at that. *Mrs Nimmo*. I could not help it. It was a deliberate disregard of my family title.

'Reverend Brodie, I will do what I can. But please call me Lady Christian. I do not want the parishioners to mistakenly think I lost my title on marriage.'

He blinked and looked stunned. He opened and closed his mouth. I had overstepped the mark. Quickly I made a peace offering. 'But please, as *Mrs Nimmo*,' I said, 'I'd like you to let Andrew and me know if there is any more money we can donate towards the repairs that we hear are needed on the pews.'

He regained his composure.

'A donation would be much appreciated,' he said. 'The back pews are quite kicked to pieces. It's the peasants and their boots.'

'Then I will see it is done,' I said.

'And I am grateful, Lady Christian,' he said, each syllable of my name simmering on his resentful tongue.

He detested me.

Would I be next on that damned repentance stool?

'Excuse me, Reverend, but I will make my way over to the castle now,' I said. 'My uncle will have forgotten the time and will need to be dragged from that dovecote of his.'

I slipped away. The branked woman stayed in my mind, like a shadow following me. I could taste the spike on her tongue.

# Chapter Thirty-Eight

# VIOLET

*Corstorphine*
*Lammas Fair, 26th August 1679*

O h, what bliss is this Lammas Day Fair! I have never been this free. In Edinburgh you are always watched with suspicion by constables or soldiers. Or with wet lips by the fleshers' boys and the wigmakers' assistants. Mrs Fiddes's girls are known.

Here I am nothing but a simple country maid. Well, not quite. Tucked beneath my petticoats, pinned tight, is the laird's diamond sword pin, and that's worth far more than a maid's yearly wage, I suspect. I cannot risk leaving it with my things in the servants' quarters. Nothing nosier than servants. So now it stays with me. Except when I have an appointment with the laird in the turret, of course.

We stop at the first stall and Cook buys us a candied cherry to sook. She wants to accompany me around the stalls and tucks her hand into my arm, and there is something in the light touch of her that reminds me of having a chum – and of Ginger. I think of how wee Ginger might have loved a day like this, cramming her pockets with heather posies, and I blink back a tear and hope she is looking down on me with heather sprigs tucked into her bonnie hair.

Next, we see the men throw a hammer. I stop to watch a wee baldy man, who looks like an egg on legs, chuck the hammer so far it skims over the kirkyard wall, and his pals pat him on the back, crying, *Fair play, Master Bathgate.* Cook says he is the strongest man in the village and does this every year, before chasing after the Lammas Queen whilst Mistress Bathgate downs ales. Oh, to be part of all of this.

I see the branked woman too late to steer away from her, Cook stopping in her tracks. 'That's the herbalist,' she whispers. 'Caught at last. Can't feel sorry for her. Meddling in the unholy.' We stay where we are, for I have no desire to get any closer. I feel Cook's breath heaving. Quick, thrilled gasps. So this is the cunning woman. She does not look like she could cause any harm, for she is tiny and weathered as a prune. But she is nailed to the wall by a contraption containing her head, and that is one of the ghastliest sights you will see.

And in these bloody times that we live in – days of war and plague and fire and execution – there are sights to turn your stomach everywhere you look, are there not? Why, I have seen beggars with rotten legs and bairns begging for scraps, but the sight of a woman dragged to public punishment is the worst terror you will witness. Like the awful thing they did to Oriana, with everyone muttering prayers around her, the worst fate that could happen to a pious girl like that.

I warn Cook, 'There are far worse punishments up the road in Edinburgh town.' I watch her flinch. And I am quite getting into the spirit and thinking I will have some sport with this cook, when I reach into my skirts and realize I forgot to put my coins into the pocket. I have left them in the drawers in my room. 'You carry on,' I tell her, and I make my way back, the song and dance of the fair all whirling in the breeze behind me.

Just as I approach the castle gates, I see the laird is on his way out. Newly scrubbed and buttoned up smart. His curls tumble over his shoulders and his boots look as though they have never seen a splash of mud. He is directly ahead of me and his face breaks into a most wicked grin.

'Are you not out enjoying the fair, Violet?'

'Oh, very much, my laird. But I have left my coins in my room, like the forgetful fool I am,' I say, not wanting to get caught up in his nonsense. He is running his eyes up and down me. We are facing each other. He is looking every inch the master of the castle, hair all shiny and oiled, sword hanging at his side.

'Is that a new dress?' he asks.

It is. Cook passed it to me, a smart grey dress, because she said I ought to be looking more a member of the household. I think it was one of her very own, for it bags out a little at the shoulders and, as you can see, I am a slight-built girl. She is a little sturdy, is Cook.

'I'd like to pull up those skirts and give you a seeing-to,' he says.

I think of the sword pin and feel faint with terror.

'But then you would miss the fair,' I say, hoping he gets the hint. 'And I have a taste for those candied cherries, and I am frightened they will sell out.'

'I'll buy you a whole bag if you give me something,' he says. He takes my hand and drags me behind the biggest sycamore tree, into a copse of bushes scattered beneath it, and runs his hands up and down my chest. My other hand grasps my skirts for the pin. I will have to do some artful arranging of my underclothes to keep it hidden, for there is no way out of it now. My heart beats so fast I believe he will be sure to notice it and think something is wrong.

But he doesn't. He whispers and talks to me, telling me all kinds of dirty things and saying he is sorry for the whipping, and how only I understand him and how we are one. I agree and agree. Wishing it over. My hand stays on the pin, my palm damp with sweat.

'Dear Violet, you are beautiful, and hiding it under this drab old dress,' he says.

His groping moves downwards.

His hand brushes mine.

I think that if I hitch up my skirts and grasp onto them, that might keep the pin buried, but he gets himself into a frenzy and pushes my hand out of the way.

There is nothing for it now but to hope he does not find it. Then his kissing stops.

'What was that?' he says. 'Something jabbed my hand.' A look of puzzlement comes over his face as he fusses about my skirts.

I try to stop him. I try to get the kissing going again. 'Never mind that, Laird,' I say. But he is far too strong for me.

'I must see what the matter is,' he says. 'That just about jabbed me to the bone.' And now my skirts and petticoats are up, his head is tilted almost upside down, and his hands are buried in frills and ribbons.

He finds it.

He gazes at me as if he cannot believe what he is seeing. Then he bends his head and whispers in my ear. 'Well, Miss Blyth. A thief as well as a whore.' And then he looks at me and smiles – an evil smile that would jab you to your bones, for he knows he can truly do whatever he likes with me now.

I am about to think of my excuses. That Oriana gave it to me. That I found it in the servants' quarters. Anything. But he puts his finger to his lips and drops my skirts.

'Shh,' he says. 'Listen.'

At first I hear nothing but my own palpitating heart. Then I hear the scuff of tight boots on dried earth. The rustle of a gown. Fast, low breathing. I hear the clink of a necklace against the swallow of a throat. Then Lady Christian stalks out from the other side of the sycamore tree, eyes blazing, looking fit to murder the both of us.

## THE CALEDONIA BROADSIDE

### EDINBURGH, 28th August

### MURDER IN BROAD DAYLIGHT!

Lord James Forrester of Corstorphine was found dead by his own sword, in the grounds of Corstorphine Castle on Saturday shortly before noon.

Two women were apprehended at the scene of the crime. One is his own niece, Lady Christian, wife of merchant Andrew Nimmo. The other is his maid, a Miss Violet Blyth, background unknown.

*The Caledonia Broadside* will report every detail of this gruesome murder as it unfolds.

# Chapter Thirty-Nine

# CHRISTIAN

*Corstorphine Castle*
*Lammas Fair, 26th August 1679*

There was blood everywhere. Violet was grasping his sword, and she was panting, panic in her eyes, and poised as though she was going to come for me. James was lying on the ground, blood spreading through his shirt.

'Look what you have done,' she screeched.

'It was you,' I screamed back at her.

She looked fit to plunge the sword into me and she made a step towards me, eyes wild and hair flying into her mouth.

'Run for help,' she shouted, 'before I stick this into your belly.' She knelt at him and pressed her hands over his chest, to try to stop the flow.

I whipped away from her. I ran up the castle avenue, flying past the sycamores, leaping over the moat bridge and into the courtyard. I ran into the keep shouting for help, scrambling from room to room screaming for servants, clambering up the three flights of steps to their attic rooms, but no one was there. I screamed into empty hallways. They were all at the fair. I stopped at the end of a long corridor, at a window that looked down across the grounds, gasping for air, my heart about to explode out of my chest.

Violet was down there. She was marching up the avenue, with men following her. I could not hear what she was saying, but I could see her mouth going, opening and closing, filling the air. *He has women all over the place*, that's what Johanna had said. *All over the place.*

I ran back down the steps and out into the courtyard. She was there already with the men. One of them was Reverend Brodie.

'There she is,' Violet cried, pointing at me. 'She tried to run away.'

'I did no such thing,' I shouted, 'I was looking for help.'

'Lady Christian, stop immediately.' Reverend Brodie's face was ashen. 'Do not take another step. What has happened here?' He stood, staring at me. The other men did too – faceless men whom I had never seen before. The entire group was staring at me, Violet in their midst, a queen dominating a chess board.

'Is he dead?' I asked this of Reverend Brodie, as I would not believe any word coming out of Violet's mouth. 'She has caused this.'

'She came for help, child,' he said. He spoke gently. He never usually spoke gently. His eyes were saucers, as though he was witnessing some unholy terror. 'She said there was an accident. Someone is with him now, and the physician has been sent for. Tell me what happened.'

'I must go to him,' I said. I made to move through them, but instead of allowing me to pass – which is what I am accustomed to, from strangers and anyone who knows me – these men obstructed me. Faceless men, in brown country clothes, stood in my path.

'Move out of my way,' I demanded.

'And why are you so close with your uncle?' asked the reverend in a low voice, heavy with threat. 'Why are you always here instead of being at Carrick House?'

'That is none of your concern,' I said. 'Let me see him.'

They could not keep their stares off me. I folded my arms across my chest and made to stand my ground, and that was when I saw the blood. Streaks of it, down my arms and the front of my gown. His blood across me like red slaps.

Reverend Brodie placed his hand on my arm. 'You will go nowhere for now. We will go inside the castle and sit down and wait for the constables.

'I must go and help attend to the laird,' Violet said.

'You will remain with me,' the reverend said, and Violet stopped in her tracks. She regarded him long and slow, her eyes dark pools and her face without flicker, for so long that he was forced to break the silence with a shake of his head and a series of blinks, before ushering me forth.


He walked me into the dining room as though the castle were his. The pressure of his fingers on my arm felt like teeth. Behind us, the men followed in a scuffle of threadbare shoes and consternation. Violet took a place at the top of the table and arranged her elbows on the wood, her chin balanced on her hands.

'That is the top of the table,' I warned, trying to keep my voice steady. 'And you are a serving girl.'

'No matter,' said Reverend Brodie. 'We are hardly having a dinner.'

I sat at the place where I was usually seated. There were crumbs on the table from yesterday's meal.

'Will someone fetch me news of the laird,' I insisted. 'You.' I pointed to one of the men. He looked to the reverend for instruction. 'I will not suffer this,' I cried. 'My husband will be furious to hear of the way you are treating me.'

Reverend Brodie raised his head to the man.

'Go and see what is happening,' he told him.

I crumpled into my seat. The blood had soaked into my gown. I had left streaks of it on the table. Then Reverend Brodie addressed me.

'Lady Christian, we are aware of your status,' he said. 'And no one more aware than me, for you reminded me not an hour or so ago when I made the error of calling you Mrs Nimmo. But I must warn you that if you speak out of turn to these good men here, then Corstorphine has a way of silencing women who nag and needle and whine.'

He lifted his gaze and met Violet's eyes.

'And that goes for you as well, Miss Blyth. You are only a maid, and you will do well to remember that. Now tell me what happened.'

Violet placed her hands on the table and fixed her eyes on the minister. 'I can hardly speak,' she choked. 'The whole thing was so horrible, Mister Reverend.'

'You must, my dear,' he said.

One of the men brought whiskies from the bottle on the side-table. Violet sipped hers and winced.

'Too strong for me, gentlemen,' she whispered, her voice hoarse.

Reverend Brodie fixed his gaze upon her. The curls tumbled from her ribbons, her cheeks pink rosebuds. Her lips wet and full. It was no surprise my lover wanted to kiss them.

'Will he live?' she asked.

'I am sure the physicians are doing everything they can,' he replied, pouring himself another whisky. 'Now tell me what happened, and then Lady Christian will tell me what happened.' He paused. 'Gentlemen, we shall separate these two women into two rooms and hear their stories. Lady Lillias would often receive me in the front parlour. I shall take Miss Blyth in there.'

## *THE CALEDONIA BROADSIDE*

### EDINBURGH, 26th September

Proceedings of the trial of Mrs Christian Nimmo
before Sheriff John MacDonald.

Sheriff MacDonald: 'Miss Blyth, you were a maid
at Corstorphine Castle, is that correct?'

Miss Blyth: 'Yes, that's right, sir, an assistant with
the laundry and in the kitchens, on account of my
skills with cooking and so on, and also a lady's
maid.'

Sheriff MacDonald: 'A maid to Lady Lillias
Forrester?'

Miss Blyth: 'Oh no, sir. I was Lady Christian's
maid. The laird employed me to take care of her
during her visits. She made plenty visits, sir. Plenty.
She was as regular as clockwork coming to the
castle.'

Sheriff MacDonald: 'Gentlemen, may I remind
you to remain silent when a witness is speaking?
Continue, Miss Blyth. Were these visits with her
husband, Mr Andrew Nimmo?'

Miss Blyth: 'Oh no, all alone, sir. Never knew
she had a husband, sir, never saw hide nor hair of
him – now what a shock that is to me. I think I
need a drink of water, sir. That has taken my breath
away, you see, because she had *her own chamber.*
I kept the room all nice and warm, for I did not
want to get on her wrong side. She and the laird
were forever fighting. Oh, regular fights.'

Sheriff MacDonald: 'Silence in court, please! I

will not have this courtroom descend into a rabble. Miss Blyth, now I want you to move on to the afternoon of the twenty-sixth of August. Your memory of that is clear, is it?'

Miss Blyth: 'Yes, clear as if it was yesterday, sir. I was at the fair and realized I had forgot my purse, what with all the excitement. I turned back and only got as far as the sycamore tree at the castle gates when I bumped into the laird and—'

Sheriff MacDonald: 'Do go on, Miss Blyth. I'm afraid we need to hear everything.'

Miss Blyth: 'Well, he put his hands on me. In a most vulgar way, I am sorry to say. His hands, well, he put them just here, look: on my breasts like this and down here, see, on my behind, saying it was such a lovely one. Oh, you are blushing, sir; no need to blush, I am simply telling you what happened. And the rest is a bit of a blur, but I remember Lady Christian pouncing on us – furious as the Devil she was – and the pair of them started shouting at each other, all kinds of names, and he drew his sword. Huge beast of a thing. I will never forget the sight of it. I stepped back, but Lady Christian drew her own sword, whipped it from her skirts, like this, sir, lifting her dress right up like this. Next thing I know there is a scuffle and her sword was on the ground, but she had his in both her hands and she went at him, stabbed at his arm and then drove it right into his chest. Right into him, sir. Right here: see where my breast is, sir, right here. And then she stood over him and said all manner of things, all manner of accusations of terrible deeds he had done. So terrible it would make your hair turn silver overnight.'

Sheriff MacDonald: 'Court, if you cannot keep a respectful silence when witnesses speak, then I shall move this entire hearing into private session. Wolf-whistling and cheering indeed!'

# Chapter Forty

# CHRISTIAN

*Corstorphine Castle*
*Lammas Fair, 26th August 1679*

A physician was found, drinking in the Corstorphine Inn, and he was rushed to the scene, but pronounced James dead of blood loss as soon as he saw him, they said. They told me this as I sat in the dining room.

Dead.

I heard Violet's howls as they told her, loud and mournful as if she was truly devastated.

I could not even manage a sob. I saw Reverend Brodie watch my eyes for tears, but they did not come. I was too stunned.

Then there was much consultation.

Reverend Brodie and the men discussed me outside the room. I could hear muttering and murmuring, and the deep burr of them rumbling over what to do.

All the while I stared at the oak chest under the window. Carved with his family crest. I had never noticed that before. Three hunting horns.

Were they sure he was dead? What if the physician was drunk? Perhaps we could save him yet. I rose and made for the door. But Reverend Brodie came back in.

'Sit down,' he said. 'In case your nerves cause you to faint.'

'Are you sure he is dead? He is strong. I must see him.' I realized, when I spoke, how wild I sounded. Mad.

'The laird is dead,' said Reverend Brodie.

I heard a humming noise in my ear. A whistling that I knew was coming from inside my own head. Perhaps the shock would kill me too.

'Two swords were found at the scene,' Reverend Brodie said. 'One that killed the laird and another – a ladies' sword – on the grass. Was that yours? I doubt it was the property of the maid, for it had jewels in the hilt.'

I nodded. No point denying it.

'And what need have you of a sword?' He was beginning to tremble. I realized it was excitement.

'Simply for my own protection,' I whispered. The whistling was still there. I sipped the whisky.

'Your protection,' he repeated. 'What possible need do you have for protection, my lady, when you have a husband and servants to accompany you everywhere and keep you perfectly safe?'

'Against highwaymen,' I whispered.

'Highwaymen,' he whispered back. 'In the rolling fields of Tyler's Acre. Well, I never.'

There was a stillness in the room then. The whistling in my ears subsided. I realized the castle was now bereft of both its owners. Lillias gone, and now James.

'We must take you women into Edinburgh,' Reverend Brodie said. 'And deliver you both into custody. This is a matter for the highest powers in the land.'

'Send for my husband,' I said. I began shaking. I did not want the reverend to see my fear, but I couldn't stop it. 'Andrew's in France, but he can be reached with a messenger. I know his route.'

'We are going to the Tolbooth Jail,' Reverend Brodie said. 'It's the safest place for both of you whilst we get to the truth of what has happened.

A prison. 'I have done nothing wrong,' I shouted. 'Are we to believe what a common maid has to say? I am Lady Christian.'

'You keep reminding me of your position,' he snarled. 'So I will remind you of mine. I am a servant of God, sent to protect this parish.'

'Take me into Edinburgh, then,' I said. I needed to find some sensible men to deal with these village idiots. 'When we reach the Tolbooth I want a sheriff sent for and my husband sent for. A real sheriff, not a village constable. And an advocate. We need proper men to deal with this matter. That maid needs to be charged with Lord Forrester's murder immediately.'

Coaches were called for and found within the hour, the drivers hauled from the Corstorphine Inn. I was put into the first one.

The minister disappeared from my eyeline as we cracked away. He shrank to the size of a raven. I hoped I would never see him again. A crowd had gathered at the entrance of the castle, the Lammas crowd, leaving the apple pies and the cunning woman to rot. Now they swirled around fresh death, their laird's blood spattered on the fallen sycamore leaves, as my thoughts swirled and I tried to catch onto them.

Where was James now? What had they done with his body? Was it at the kirk or in his own chamber? This must be a nightmare and I would wake up from it, to a bowl of porridge and honey, with Andrew sitting sipping his coffee.

Two men were guarding me in the carriage. I thought about jumping out, but they would grab me. And anyway how would that have looked? Where would I even go?

They glanced at each other, two men who could not be any older than me, with scratches of beards and wary eyes. They watched me spy the door handle. They shifted and said nothing, all the way into Edinburgh. And that was a hellish journey. Through the burning end of summer, from Corstorphine's deep-green farms and fields and woods. Edinburgh. Where Andrew would never have let me go unaccompanied. Now I was thrust into its hostile heart.

# Chapter Forty-One

# VIOLET

*The Tolbooth Jail, Edinburgh*
*26th August 1679*

I follow hot on the heels of the lady, in a carriage with one of the constables of Corstorphine and Reverend Brodie, who spends the journey looking as though he wants to put his hand upon my knee.

The laird gone. The sight of him. The blood. I can't breathe properly. My chest keeps heaving. He was fine and dandy not three hours ago. Full of himself and bursting with his own gloriousness.

Oh dear God, have mercy. Now I know why folks pray.

What will become of me? What about my box of things? And the money the laird said he was setting aside for me? What if they search me at the Tolbooth and find this pin in my skirts?

Did Reverend Brodie believe me?

They will never believe me in Edinburgh.

When we arrive there is much ado, with more men in cloaks but fortunately no searching, and I am shoved into a cell. Oh, have you ever had the misfortune? To be thrown into a basement dungeon and left there to rot? The Tolbooth Jail, of all the hellholes in this town, the place you stride by in your polished boots, giving no regard for the unfortunates within.

Hurled in, I am, by the constables and a great giant of a jailer with jangly keys and eyes on stalks, to appear before a sheriff in the morning, who will decide what to do with me and whether my story is to be believed.

'Make yourself comfortable,' the jailer grunts, throwing me a thin blanket crusted with shards of hay, 'for it will be a long, cold night.'

'Sir,' I say, scrabbling at the door bars and his disappearing back-side, 'I can promise you two coins if you fetch someone to me.'

He turns.

'I doubt you even have one single coin upon your person,' he spits, 'you have the look of a common criminal.'

'Oh, nothing common about me,' I coo shakily, pointing up towards where I imagine Bell's Close is situated, not five minutes' walk away from the jail door. 'I am one of Mrs Rita Fiddes's pleasure girls from the apartments just beyond, and if you fetch her, she will pay you with two coins she has of mine, and I dare say treat you to a night in one of her rooms.'

I do not like the sound of my voice in this cell. Muffled. Weak. Begging.

The jailer strides slowly back to the cell door.

'You don't look like much of a pleasure girl,' he says, and I silently agree. I still have on the plain grey dress Cook put me in this morning. My hair is a greasy mess, and my face must be red raw from the blubbering and shock of it all.

Seeing the laird lying there like that, blood pissing out of him. Such a violent end. And to have been born with so much gold in the family coffers and the promise of a good life. The shame of it! I keep seeing it. The blood and the look of shock on his face. I swallow back a shudder.

'Tell Mrs Fiddes her Violet needs her,' I say.

*

The bawd takes her own good time coming. I am shivering under the stinking blanket having all but given up hope, and staring up at the dimly lit ceiling, by the time I hear footsteps descend from overhead, scuffing and heavy as thunder, so I know it is her before she even reaches the barred door, wrapped in a dark fur cloak with a new white wig towering above her head, studded with pink bows. The jailer is with her, and lights a lantern by the door. Mrs Fiddes looks like one of the laird's trifles. She takes a coin from the depths of her skirts and passes it into the shadows.

'This will be a private discussion,' she tells him. Then she comes to the door. 'What calamity now, girl? I cannot stay out long, for it's the usual Saturday-night carnage in the parlour, a randy lot waiting in there and the girls only half ready, squabbling over lost stockings and stolen rouge.'

'Have you not heard? Lord James Forrester murdered this morning by his mistress, Lady Christian,' I say.

'Murdered.' The wig wobbles. Her lip quivers. She reaches for her pipe. 'No. I cannot believe that could be true.'

'True as I live and breathe. I was there. I saw the whole ghastly thing,' I say.

'You were there?' Her eyes bulge.

'Right in the middle of it,' I say. 'A fight between the laird and his lady mistress.'

'Oh, Violet. You are in trouble,' she says. She taps her pipe on a bar of the door.

'But I did nothing, except try to stop it.'

'I doubt that,' she hoots. 'And it will not be long before you are blamed. A lady mistress will scream her own innocence and blame you. She will have advocates and lords and family connections, and no one will want to see her in trouble. Think of the scandal. They will be cooking up a story on you as we speak. Oh, you are in some shit, girl.'

A chill slices through my bones like nothing I have felt before. Not in the coldest ice of winter. I can feel my own end looming up at me. I see my own ghost in the gloom of the room.

'Mrs Fiddes, stop this,' I hiss. 'The minister at Corstorphine believed me. I am before a sheriff tomorrow to tell of what I saw.'

The old bitch slaps her thigh. Like she is listening to a tavern tale. She grasps her sides. I think her wig will hop clean off her head.

'By the end of tomorrow a murder will be pinned on you,' she says. 'It's the way of the world, Violet. Who would believe a common whore? Grisly, was it?' she narrows her eyes. 'A strangling? A stabbing? Poison?'

'Mrs Fiddes, you must help me,' I say, panicking. 'You know every man in Edinburgh. Sheriffs. Constables. Advocates. Men of the Kirk. You even know the executioners. You are owed favours up and down the whole town. Can you put a word in for me, so that I am believed?'

Mrs Fiddes heaves her solid frame to the candle lantern by the door, producing a thin paper from her hand and using it to take a flame with which to light her pipe. Mrs Fiddes never goes without her comforts. She never fails at anything. She survived the plagues of coughing and boils that hit this town thirty-odd years ago and escaped with nothing worse than a scar on her cheek where the plague-doctor lanced her and cured her. The Four Horsemen of the Apocalypse could be storming up the high street and she would most likely sell the beasts for pie meat when their masters' backs were turned.

I wait, heart in mouth, to hear her decision.

It is a long wait.

'And what if I do you this favour?' she says, taking a long, languid draw on that filthy pipe of hers. 'For this is no small favour you ask.' She blinks as the smoke disappears into her wig.

'Then I am in your debt most substantially,' I say. 'And you are better to have me in your debt than hanged or burned, for I can do far more for you alive than I can dead.'

'Violet Blyth. The day I first clapped eyes on you when you were begging at the foot of Bell's Close I knew you were a survivor like me,' she says. 'I recognized myself in that determined face. Not a bonnie one, but it shows such strong character.'

'You are like a mother to me, Mrs Fiddes,' I say, and I almost mean it.

'And you are like a daughter to me,' she says. I know she doesn't mean it at all, and I wonder what fate will befall me if she should save my arse, but that is another worry for another day.

'I know the sheriffs in the High Court of Edinburgh, of course,' she sniffs. 'They are constant visitors to Flora and Mollie in the flogging room and they insist on best-quality raw beef steaks applied to soothe their red arses afterwards, as though we are an inn. Ho! It is a devil to keep the beef from going rancid in the summer. I have to store it under my bed.'

She rouses from her reverie and smiles, pointing the chewed end of her pipe directly at me.

'I will help you, Violet – how could I refuse? How could I watch you hang? Dangling and pissing yourself as you twitch and choke to death. Lord, no. Not my Violet. And when you are back in my pleasure house we will both rule Edinburgh town with your tales of witnessing this ghastly murder.' She stops there. The pipe quivers. She lowers her voice. 'And I will never ask if the laird died at the hand of his mistress or his whore, Violet Blyth. For I know when to keep my nose out of another woman's business.'

'In that case,' I whisper, 'Take this jewelled pin and hide it somewhere in your apartments.' I push the cursed ornament through the bars and she looks at me with narrowed eyes.

'This looks like an expensive little trinket. Laird give you it, did he? Or did you steal it? Oh, you are trouble, girl, but I suppose you are my responsibility now.'

And with that, the newly philanthropic Mrs Fiddes excuses herself and returns to her apartments, because randy men and squabbling whores will not soothe themselves.

I cover my face and ears with my hands. The room is better without her loud wig and galloping mouth, but I know she will see me right. I hunch myself into a ball under the blanket, thinking that only just this morning I was striding out for a country fair, thinking how I had left these horrors behind me for the joys of apple pies and lute players and dancing dogs.

I cannot believe he is dead.

That's when the tears come. Big, horrible tears that sting my eyes and gag my throat. My bones ache with the aftershocks of it. Worse than the whipping Lord James gave me.

Of all the horrors I have seen, death is the worst.

Oh, is it not a shocker, how the fortunes of life can turn in a flash?

## Chapter Forty-Two

# CHRISTIAN

*The North of England*
*October 1679*

The further from Edinburgh we ride, the more I dare to believe I am free. I know they will be searching every corner for me. Are they interrogating Andrew? Or, God forbid, Mother? She is no match for the High Constables. She would faint.

William Watson does not overcrowd me or demand idle chit-chat. He lets me sit in silence. He concentrates on the road. We pass hamlets and farms and I wonder at the lives there. I have never spent time with working folk.

I never even noticed them much.

Now I am fallen, they have caught me.

My legs ache. I am not used to riding for hours without stopping, or riding astride the horse like a man. The breeches I am wearing itch and there is an uncomfortable heaviness and chafing from the fabric between my legs. How can men abide it? Stripped of petticoats and gowns, what remains of me?

I carry cloths with me, stuffed into my coat pocket by Mags Watson, but I still have not bled. I wonder if it is the shock of everything, and from not eating or drinking properly in weeks, or if I am with child. The marriage manual had much to say on the subject of carrying and birthing safely. But bed rest and sweet wine are not in abundance on this journey. I cannot think of it. I cannot take responsibility for a child until I am safe myself.

We reach a village.

'I'll get fresh bread,' he says. 'You stay here.'

The village has a baker's, a butcher shop, a kirk and a tavern, all set in a row along the curve of its road. It reminds me of Corstorphine. It reminds me of Roseburn. I will never return there, will I? To Roseburn House, where *Hope Lies Within*.

Children run and chase each other in a patch of dirt in front of the tavern. They tire of their game and begin to stare at me. I pull my hat lower over my eyes. I wish William would be quick, but he has disappeared into the baker's shop. I used to love the taste of fresh bread. The smell of it rising through Roseburn House each morning as we put on our walking boots.

I cannot remember the last time I savoured food.

The children approach.

One girl at the front is taller and bolder than the rest, in a filthy apron and her hair hanging in wisps from beneath her coif.

'Spare a penny, Mister,' she calls. Her accent is not Scottish but has an unfamiliar twang. We must be over the border.

I shake my head.

'Come on, sir, we've not eaten all day, have we?' This she says to the other children, who are now drawing close alongside her. I dare not say anything in case they realize I do not have the voice of a man. The horses twitch nervously, and I grow afraid they may bolt.

I dip my head and hope that if I ignore them, they will drift off.

The next thing I know is that the girl is right beside me, a look of curiosity on her face.

'Why you ignoring me, sir? What's your horses called?'

I fear this is going to go on interminably, when they are called away by a shout from a man at the tavern door. I watch them skip back to where they had been playing and stand with the man. They are clearly talking about me because they all look in my direction, with no discretion about it.

William returns, packing the provisions into his bag and mounting his horse swiftly.

'We should leave before we attract more attention,' I urge him, nodding at the group, who are all staring.

He looks troubled.

'We should not have stopped so near the village,' he mutters, urging the horses on. 'Folk have nothing better to do than gawp at passers-by.'

But what else could we do?

It will always be like this, I realize. I will always be at the mercy of others.

The group of children and the man continue to watch as we ride away.

And I will always rely on the protection of others. Today it is William Watson. Next week it will be a trusted acquaintance of Andrew's in Calais, a man I have never met, who will take over my safekeeping and escort me to Paris, to an apartment in a place called Faubourg Saint-Germain, where I can live anonymously and in some degree of comfort.

Scratches of this new life were inked out to me on the parchment from Andrew which Mr Dalhousie passed to me at the Tolbooth. I try to join the dots of them.

I speak some words of French. The tutor who came to Roseburn insisted that we learn it, to give us an air of sophistication. Now, instead of using it in the drawing rooms of Edinburgh, I will rely on it. He told us of the elegant French, their literature salons and palaces. Johanna and I half listened, counting down the minutes to luncheon when he would bid us *au revoir, mademoiselles,* and we would giggle at how ludicrous the accent sounded in the thin mist of a Scottish morning.

We have been on the road for hours and it will be dark soon. William thinks we are in England and that the High Constables won't come this far. We have passed several carriages on our route, nodding at their occupants, but people keep to themselves, in a hurry to avoid highwaymen.

'You are the easiest company I've kept in a while,' William says. 'I'd have thought you'd complain about the potholes and the wind, but you've not said a word.'

'I'm thinking about Paris,' I say.

'Terrible place, so they say. Worse than London for cattle and beggars roaming the streets.'

'That is not encouraging,' I tell him.

'You'd be better off in the countryside. A lady like you would suit a cottage beside a lavender field. No one to bother you,' he says, half smiling.

'You hardly know me, or what I might want,' I say, but he is right. The minute the words leave his lips, I imagine it. France has sunshine and mountains and valleys and beaches, the tutor said. But how could I survive alone in the French countryside?

'Come to think of it, I fancy the idea myself,' says William, pulling his horse to a halt at a stretch of woodland. 'Come, let's bed down here for the night.'

I am getting used to sleeping under the stars. It lets the nightmares escape, instead of them rattling around my cell.

He makes a fire, and we eat a cold meat pie and drink ale.

The pie is flavoursome. I eat more than my fair share and he watches me with amusement.

'Got your appetite back,' he says. 'You can taste the freedom.'

It is true, I can. And how can I be with child if I am so hungry? For all Johanna wrote to me about during the first weeks of her pregnancy with little Robert was how nauseous she was, and the only thing she could stomach was fresh bread and butter and the physicians were pleased as that suggested a strong boy.

We lie down again together. The fire crackles gently. He reaches for my hand.

I had known he would.

'I can't sleep,' I say.

'What keeps you awake?' he asks. There is no tiredness in his voice, either. I feel that the night is open.

I tell him.

I tell him everything about my uncle. And everything that happened that day under the sycamore tree, and everything that happened afterwards.

# Chapter Forty-Three

# CHRISTIAN

*The Tolbooth Jail, Edinburgh*
*26th August 1679*

When we arrived at the Tolbooth, they took me to a small, low-ceilinged room. I did not argue. I paid heed to what the reverend had said and went obediently. It would not look favourable if I began to screech and howl. Everything was dark, even though it was still bright outside. But it was not the darkness that frightened me. It was the stink of men. The oppressive musk of them. Unwashed. Dangerous. I could not see them, but I could smell them. I could hear them swearing and growling behind their bars. Soon the news of my arrival would be all round the jail. All round the town. What was happening at Corstorphine? Were letters being sent to James's next of kin? I could not even remember their names. Were constables arriving at Roseburn? Were they finding Andrew?

At first there were too many constables and guards to count. Then there was just one.

'I will be watching you all night,' the guard said. 'You are my only charge. So don't try anything.'

'All I want is my husband,' I said.

'Not my problem,' he replied, approaching me. 'Now I'll be

checking through these fine threads you're wearing, to check for any more swords.'

'Don't lay your hands on me,' I said, stepping back.

'Don't make an enemy of me,' he whispered, his mouth grazing my ear.

He said nothing as he stripped me. He merely watched me as he tossed my garments to the floor. My coif on the hay bale. My cape in a damp patch on the stones. My gown took the longest to unbutton and untie. His breathing became shorter and shallower. When it fell at my feet he stood back and nodded at me to untie my petticoat and unhook my necklace.

Finally, when I was shivering before him, he picked my clothes up, one by one, and inspected them, then took my necklace.

'You can have your gown and cape back,' he said. 'But I will be taking these.'

He had my necklace and petticoat in his hands. I was merely relieved he was no longer touching me. I had been terrified he would force himself upon me.

I never saw the necklace or the petticoat again. I wonder if he sold them or kept them.

If they execute me, I wonder what they will do with my body when I am dead. Will they hand me over to Andrew, or will they hold on to me and defile me?

Andrew. Why did he never want me? What did he find so undesirable?

What did James find desirable? When he was kissing my neck and seeming so rapt, what was he thinking? Was I merely another of his women?

Oh God, I think I was.

And what seemed exquisite to me, so joyous that it was not even of this earth, was just another conquest. His maids. His damned maids. Girls who swept the floors and boiled soups. He was undiscerning.

No one came with food or drink. I spent the time pacing the pathetic square of misery, a few feet away from the guard, surrounded by the wall scratchings of previous inhabitants and rat droppings, trying to rid my thoughts of James and to concentrate on how to get out.

Why were they listening to Violet? What spell was she casting? I recalled how she had behaved around me when she was helping me wash and dress that day. Confident. *Seductive*. It was in her nature. She was wilier than me. I needed Andrew. I needed all the help I could get.

Finally, as the bells of St Giles' tolled eleven o'clock, I received a visitor. Robert Gregor. In the absence of my husband, who was not due back for several days, the constables had located my sister and her husband. Caped and bewigged, in quite an ostentatious fashion given our surroundings, my brother-in-law pushed his way past the guard.

'What in God's name has happened, Christian?' he said. 'Open this door, sir.'

'You cannot enter the cell,' the guard barked from behind him.

'Open it now, sir,' Robert told him. 'I am making sure my sister-in-law has not been harmed.'

'You will step back or you will be spending the night in the next cell,' shouted the guard, spittle and fury flying from his mouth. Robert backed away and joined the brute in the corridor.

'I am fine, Robert,' I said, although I felt anything but. *James's face, the shock in his eyes when he realized the sword was sticking out of his chest, looking to me and pleading, 'Get help.'*

'They are accusing me of murdering my uncle,' I said, as calmly as I could. I would not have my mother and sister rattled by tales of my unravelling. 'It is nonsense. But we must let justice take its course.'

'My sister-in-law would not harm a flea,' Robert told the guard, as though the man was the sheriff himself.

The guard shrugged. 'Heard it all before,' he said. 'But not often we get a murderess in here.' He nodded at me as though I was a rare treat.

'Fetch me food, and ale and blankets for the night,' I told Robert. 'And in the morning, fetch me an advocate. Tell Mother and Johanna there has been a terrible misunderstanding, but we can remedy the situation when I have spoken to an advocate and a sheriff. And send word to Andrew that he must return immediately.'

The two men stared, as though my organization and planning skills were some unnatural tendency, given my dire circumstances, and I would be better served by taking to weeping, like an innocent woman might.

'I'll be back with provisions tonight,' Robert said. He almost made to bow to me, and I wondered if being accused of a heinous crime had elevated me somewhat in his views, when previously he had regarded me as nothing but an uglier version of his wife. Perhaps he thought I might murder him too.

I braced myself for his return, for a well-meaning basket of good ale and cold sliced meat and one of my sister's best blankets, scented with lavender. I braced myself for more questions. I braced myself for the return of my husband. I could not admit my affair, to him or anyone. If I was guilty of adultery, I would be judged guilty of murder.

Adulteress. Murderess. How similar they sound.

## *THE CALEDONIA BROADSIDE*

### EDINBURGH, 2nd October

Miss Mariota Blair, cousin once removed to Laird Forrester: 'I saw them together when I attended the funeral of dear Lillias. I had been very fond of James, and he fond of me, and I was hoping to pay my respects, but hardly got the opportunity. Lady Christian was most inappropriate. She embraced him at the window. She was the absolute talk of the wake. His wife not cold in her grave.'

Reverend Ian Brodie, Minister of Corstorphine Kirk: 'Lady Christian had more reverence for her own title than for the word of God.'

# Chapter Forty-Four

# VIOLET

*The Tolbooth Jail, Edinburgh*
*August 1679*

Monday morning, first thing. I know it, for I can smell its fresh bread rolls mingled with the dewy rotten-egg fug rising from the bowels of the Nor Loch. I can hear the flap of tenement pigeons and the banging of shop doors as the candle-makers and grocers and stationers begin their trade with a chorus of yawns. At Mrs Fiddes's I would lie in bed, awoken by the squawks of the Bell's Close wifies, tipping their bairns out into the street to roam amongst the chicken-sellers and rolling out their high lines of dripping, grey washing. Today I have nothing to do but wait to be called to see the sheriff. Wait and fret. Will Mrs Fiddes be true to her word or will I hang from the Tolbooth gallows like a common criminal? Will I be next Monday morning's crow fodder, swinging from a noose to the horror-struck gawps of all the gentlemen who have humped me?

The jailer brings a bowl of clean water for washing and a cloot for drying, as well as bread with cold, creamy butter. These are promising. The telltale signs of Mrs Fiddes's bribery and connections. I wash, and piss and wipe and eat, and scrape my hair neat into its ribbon and pack my titties as high as I can in my bodice.

And how do I look? Bosum bulging and cheekbones sharp as knives, from a weekend spent fretting and off the syllabub. Sheriff John MacDonald – for that is this fellow's name – peers at me through round spectacles and I am certain I have seen his baldy head before, sitting sweetly as a babe in Mrs Fiddes's parlour, waiting patiently for his turn under the flogger, like the good boy he is.

But this morning he is perched on a grand wooden chair, engraved like a throne, and I am before him, feeling most lowly and near shitting myself in fright. We are in a courtroom with high ceilings and wooden panelling all around. I have been escorted in by men in shiny buttons, and our little parade caught the attention of the market sellers and pie boys in Parliament Square, who have stopped for a good old stare. The men in the shiny buttons have told me I must stand for the sheriff and only sit if he tells me and, even then, to sit attentively and listen to every word he says and to stand when he leaves. It is a whole new world, this court business.

'Miss Blyth, you are before me today on a very grave matter,' the sheriff says. 'Do you understand the consequences of your testimony?'

'Indeed, sir, and enthusiastic to help in any way I can,' I say, hearing the quiver in my voice and giving a nervous wee curtsey.

Sheriff MacDonald scowls.

'You can leave your enthusiasm at the door, Miss Blyth. And your bowing and scraping.'

He asks me what I saw, and by the end of the morning I am heartily sick of going over it again. He is less than impressed that I was kissing my laird, but I explain that the lusty devil grabbed me, despite my protests, and that I was only going back to the castle for pennies. And the sheriff takes notes with a great feathery quill.

'Now, when this case goes to trial, you will be asked to promise you are telling the truth,' he says. 'Do you understand the consequences of lying in court?'

'Indeed, sir,' I say. 'I would burn eternally in the fires of hell, with black marks all over my soul.'

The sheriff blinks.

'Indeed you would,' he says. 'But more importantly, you would be sending an innocent woman of high standing to her death.'

'Oh, I would never do that,' I say.

He nods and beckons the men in shiny buttons over and a great amount of whispering takes place.

I am allowed out of that shithole of a jail and put into a safe house, as I am now Sole Witness. Together with the blood across her dress and hands, the absolute disgrace of her affair with the laird and her habit of carrying a sword on her illicit journeys from her husband's home to her lover's castle, Lady Christian is well and truly done for, Mrs Fiddes thinks.

The old bawd joins me for tea and cake that afternoon at the safe house, which is a plush apartment near the courthouse, with painted ceilings and a four-poster bed and an ornate fireplace.

'You have fallen in shit and come up smelling of roses again,' she observes, sooking at her tea in a noisy way that makes me want to put my fingers round her throat and squeeze it tight.

'Hardly,' I say. 'I was very fond of my laird and now he is dead. He was the only man who ever cared for me.'

'Pff, he did not care for you,' Mrs Fiddes says, with a raw cackle. 'He was knobbing half of Scotland.'

'That did not matter to me,' I retort. 'Men are ruled by their cocks. They cannot help it. He treated me finely during our times together. I miss him.'

'You are an idiot,' she says.

'Will they hang Lady Christian or burn her?' I am not tempted by the honey cake. Trials and executions do not whet my appetite.

'Far bloodier.' Mrs Fiddes takes a great slice, running her finger over the knife and licking the crumbs. 'She is of the upper classes. She will suffer at the Maiden.'

## THE CALEDONIA BROADSIDE

### EDINBURGH, 2nd October

Learned scholars of Edinburgh's aristocracies will already know this. But the ordinary reader will be most fascinated to know that Christian Nimmo is a descendant of the notorious Jean Livingston, Lady Warriston, executed at the Maiden in 1600 for getting her servant to murder her husband John Kincaid, Laird of Warriston.

# Chapter Forty-Five

# CHRISTIAN

*The Tolbooth Jail, Edinburgh*
*August 1679*

Mr Harold Dalhousie is a venerable advocate, according to Robert. Mr Dalhousie has represented a number of unfortunate people in *similar circumstances*. He and the advocate refrained from saying *accused of murder,* with the same air of civility as the manner in which they shuffled next to each other and avoided looking at the chamberpot brimming with my bodily functions in the corner of the cell.

Monday. No one had taken the chamberpot away and I had been sick to my stomach with fear all weekend, the horror of Saturday emptying from me in waves. My ears had buzzed, my head throbbed, and I had vomited and emptied my bowels until there was nothing left inside me. I had covered the chamberpot with hay from the hay-bale bed they gave me, but yet it reeked, filling the room with the stench of my terror.

Robert excused himself and left me with Mr Dalhousie, who proceeded to open a leather bag and bring out a wooden writing box. He sat on the hay bale, looking as though he would rather be anywhere else in the world, opened the box and produced a quill and ink.

'From the beginning, please,' he said.

'There has been a terrible misunderstanding, and no one is paying heed to me,' I said. 'I paid a call on the Lord James Forrester as I was in the vicinity, at the Lammas Fair, and when I turned the corner to his property—' I stopped. I could not go on.

'My lady, you must describe the events. You will be required to do this before a sheriff.'

I gave myself a few moments. 'When I turned the corner to his property, he was with his maid Violet. So I confronted them.'

'Why did you confront them?' He regarded me warily. 'Why not just walk past and avert your eyes?'

My mind was racing. It was the terror and the lack of sleep.

'I did not think,' I said. 'I supposed I wanted to make sure the girl was not being compromised. Being taken advantage of. Her bare legs were exposed.'

'And was she being taken advantage of?'

'I don't think so. When I challenged them, she seemed complicit.'

I would have expected Mr Dalhousie to squirm at the topic, as I did. But he was clearly made of sterner stuff.

'But Lord James was furious at being caught. I suppose it put him at risk of gossip. With his wife so recently deceased, and Violet being a maid. He became aggressive towards us both and that is why I drew my sword.'

The venerable Mr Dalhousie scratched notes down on a parchment that rested on the lid of the writing box, dipping into the ink and leaving blots on his trouser leg.

'And then there was an altercation,' I said, watching him record it. 'And he drew his sword, but Violet grabbed it and stabbed him with it before I could do anything to stop her. Why would I stab him with his sword, if I had my own?'

'Indeed,' muttered Mr Dalhousie, the ink blot on his trouser leg blooming to the shape of an overblown rose. He repeated what I said as he wrote it down: '*Why would I stab him with his sword if I had my own?*'

'Mr Dalhousie,' I said, steeling myself for his answer, 'what penalty might I face if no one believes me?'

He continued to scratch away with his writing set. But he detested the question, because he frowned and took a deep breath before looking me straight in the eye.

'The penalty for murder is execution,' he said. 'You know that, do you not?'

I knew that. 'But are there alternatives? If the sheriff is minded towards leniency?'

Mr Dalhousie kept his gaze on me. 'Execution is sometimes commuted to banishment,' he said. 'But not if a murder victim is a person of high standing.' He blinked. 'Lord Forrester was a man of quality. The sheriff will see to it that justice is served.'


I was brought before the sheriff that afternoon. Johanna had sent Robert with a clean gown, in mourning black to show my respects for my deceased uncle, and I saved it for the last minute, to stop strands of hay and muck from soiling it. She had also sent a black felted hat with an ornate gold band, which was dignified, for I could plait my greasy hair and hide it underneath the brim. I did not want the sheriff to think me filthy; I wanted him to understand I was too clean and neat to be a murderess. One of his own kind. The sort of lady who would sip tea in his parlour and exchange pleasantries with his wife, behind our fans. Not like the witches he would send to be dooked at the Nor Loch, or burned up at Castlehill, or the filthy robbers he would send to have their ears nailed at the Mercat Cross.

Not like my great-great-aunt, Lady Warriston.

Her husband had beat her, they said. Repeatedly. She plotted with her servants and had him killed. The servant who carried out the murder was executed on a breaking-wheel. I do not know this from a pamphlet or book. I know it from whispered stories at night-time with Johanna.

I knew how Lady Warriston had felt. The moment when the man you love turns furious. The fear that rises in your throat. The panic and the desperate desire for it all to stop.

I stood upright in the cell in the clean, black gown. Underneath the linen skirts, my legs shook.

Shortly after St Giles' struck two o'clock I was marched from the cell across the square to the High Court of Justiciary, in Parliament House. A crowd hung by the door and at first I thought they were other people with business at the court. But when we drew close, all heads turned and the chants began. 'Here she is, the murderess!' The constables bustled me straight through the group and into the doorway as hands grabbed and spit flew, until we were into the safety of the entrance hall.

'You are famous, my lady,' said one of the constables, catching his breath. 'Word has spread. I think one of them was even sketching your likeness.'

'You're in the broadsides,' warned another. 'They will write ballads about you, my dear. Just like Lady Warriston.'

Ballads. Sketches. Printed tales. The kinds of tales we were forbidden from reading at Roseburn. All I could think of was Mother and Fiona, no doubt opening the door to curious visitors, acquaintances not seen for years. Suddenly rolling up in carriages. Sitting for tea and asking questions.

Of Johanna and Robert, disinvited from every foreseeable social dinner.

Of Andrew receiving a hurried letter, and his look of utter incomprehension under the Calais clouds.

'I have done nothing wrong,' I said, tears springing, with that hideous, helpless feeling that kept engulfing me, but the constables gritted their teeth and hoisted me up the steps to the courtroom.

The entire hearing was over within a matter of minutes, and I was not even allowed to give explanations. I had thought I would have the chance to plead with the sheriff. To beg. Or that Mr Dalhousie would make a persuasive argument, for he had arrived, with thick sheaves of parchment tied with black ribbons tucked under his arms. But none of this occurred.

Instead Sheriff MacDonald made me stand and told me I would face a formal trial for the murder of Lord James Forrester.

### *THE CALEDONIA BROADSIDE*

#### EDINBURGH, 2nd October

And who, exactly is the Sole Witness to the murder? Miss Violet Blyth, a low-born obscurity, has been thrust into the centre of the trial of the century. Little is known about her early life, but her lodgings until recently were the infamous Bell's Close, an address of ill repute that no person of good morals would wish to visit. From there, she apparently moved straight into a comfortable position as the deceased's own maid.

Can we trust her word above that of an aristocrat? Has the word of a maid ever been taken above that of a lady? Let us hope, for Miss Blyth's sake, that she is not hiding anything.

# Chapter Forty-Six

# VIOLET

*A Safe House, Edinburgh*
*August 1679*

For the second time in my life I am kept in luxurious confinement. I am to remain in this apartment until the trial, for it would not be safe anywhere else. The sheriff said I might flee, or that associates of Lady Christian might silence me in the way she silenced her lover, with a puncture to the heart.

Truthfully, both are possibilities. This apartment is grand, on the first floor of a stately looking building. It has a four-poster bed hung with curtains and a white china piss pot with a gold brim. But I see shadows everywhere. I see faces in the wood-knots of the ceiling beams. There are not enough candle lanterns to keep me from getting the shudders. The walls are hung with prints of figures and creatures that seem to jump and dart at me from the corner of my eye. Even the fire in the fireplace is restless, as though the air in the room is constantly shifting. The only place I feel safe is leaning out of the window, watching up and down the high street, for it has a decent enough view of any potential trouble.

The sheriff has stationed a rotation of men at the door below, which is at the bottom of a flight of turnpike stairs. They mind their business and I mind mine. Theirs is the business of watching the street, eyes a-twitch. Mine is the business of a grand rehearsal. The trial of the century, they are calling it. I receive Mrs Fiddes daily, for she is registered in a great book of the court as the only living soul with an interest in my welfare, and she brings French wine and gowns to try on, so that I shall look my best on the witness stand. She also brings smatterings of the gossip that is brewing, as well as her own tall tales.

'They are calling you the star witness,' she booms. 'Some think you are the real murderess and will trip yourself up on the witness stand and land in a noose.'

'I am innocent as the day I was born,' I insist. I am trying on a pale-pink dress that froths with ruffles and lace. 'Christian Nimmo was an adulteress with a sword in her skirts. Too gaudy?' I swallow down my fear. I am in dangerous waters, I know it, but if I give in to the fear, I will become a nervous wreck.

Every day is a fight against the vision of him, lying there, on the ground. At night, I see red in the darkness.

What if I am not believed at the trial? What if Lady Christian's advocate blows holes in my story and accuses me? After all, it is the word of a harlot against that of a lady, before all of Edinburgh town. Mrs Fiddes's influence can only stretch so far.

She regards me with her head at a tilt. ''Tis difficult to stop you looking like a whore, no matter what we put you in,' she murmurs. 'It's the way your eyelids sag – and one more than the other. You have a look of easy fornication about you, even dressed in silk.'

'This dress has suffered years of service in your apartments,' I snap, irritated with her. 'So it's no wonder. Fetch me something

new, and some decent jewels for my neck and my fingers. I
will not be taken with any credibility otherwise.'

It is all right for her. This is the most entertained Mrs Fiddes
has been for years. She is loving every minute of my predicament. But her face sours.

'I do not like that tone, Violet Blyth. You might have lived
in a castle, but you are no better than me, and you had best
remember that. Why, I can think of one very particular piece
of jewellery that the court would be most interested in seeing.'

The laird's sword pin. The old hag still has it in her possession. She sees me flinch.

'He gave that to me as a gift,' I lie.

''Tis a beauty. I might wear it to the trial myself,' she says.
'Unless you can give me reason not to.'

She has me exactly where she wants me.

'Are you threatening me? After what I've been through?' I
act surprised, but of course I am not. Nothing Mrs Fiddes
does should come as a surprise.

'All I am saying is that you are best to do as I say, girl,' she
continues. 'And then no harm will come to you. Remember
what we stand to gain from your notoriety. I already have gents
asking when you might return.'

I sit back in my chair and let her refresh our wine glasses.
One day I will be free of Mrs Fiddes, mark my words. For
now, I have no choice but to do everything she says.

'Now,' she goes on, innocent as a lamb. 'I do have a few
bits and pieces of jewellery here. She reaches into a sack at
her side and tips handfuls of junk onto the table. Paste and
pins. Scarves and hair ribbons. And after all of that, out clatters a small, sheathed knife.

'Dear Christ, this is the last thing we need in here,' I cry,
throwing a kerchief over the damned thing.

'Calm down. I brought it for your protection,' Mrs Fiddes hisses. 'Do you honestly think those dafties at the door can save you if someone wants you dead? They are too busy swigging whisky and watching the flower sellers' arses. Hide it under your bed.'

I take a mouthful of the French wine she has brought. It is lukewarm and sharp and tastes of cellars, but I need it for my nerves. Mrs Fiddes lifts the kerchief, slowly, and unsheathes the knife. It gleams in her fingers, in the light of the candle lanterns.

'Now look, Violet. It has lived under my bed safe enough for years and given me many a peaceful night's rest. If it is discovered, just deny all knowledge. This is not your house, and you cannot be held responsible for the clutter that is in it.'

She is right. That bawd is never wrong. I do not fancy waking up in the night and being faced with an intruder and no means to defend myself. It will do no harm to slip it away. It is only small.

Mrs Fiddes sighs and lumbers back to her feet.

'That's me away back up the road,' she says. 'Mr Rathen is due and, though he did pine for you a bit, he's taken a fancy to one of the new girls.'

'New girls?' I had not thought, but I suppose she must have filled my space by now.

'Two,' she says. 'One in your room and one in poor wee Ginger's.'

Our eyes meet. Mine saggy, apparently. Hers wet with rheum.

'To Ginger,' she says, raising her wine glass to mine and finishing the last of her dregs.

'To Ginger,' I say. 'We have not forgotten you.'

*

After Mrs Fiddes has taken her leave, knees cracking as she goes, I finish my own wine and study the knife. It is so pointed at the tip it would pierce anything. It is a knife made for trouble.

# Chapter Forty-Seven

# CHRISTIAN

*The Tolbooth Jail, Edinburgh*
*September 1679*

Andrew had barely slept or eaten. I could see it in the sunken hollows of his face. Unlike my brother-in-law, he made no attempt to persuade the guard to let him join me in my cell. Instead he stood a foot back from the grille.

'I am so relieved to see you,' I said, hovering before him, not knowing where to put my feet or my hands.

His grim expression did not change. His eyes roamed up and down the length of me, taking in the creased dirty gown and the strands of hay in my hair. I hoped he could not detect my new, foul scent.

Eventually he spoke.

'I had a feeling,' he said, 'that there was something amiss. It was the way you changed. When we first met, you were timid. Exquisite. But then you became quite bold.'

His voice had an edge.

I had never heard it like that.

'You seemed to daydream,' he went on. 'You would sit at dinner, after your first glass of wine, and look into the distance and smile, as if you were remembering something. I sometimes watched you, and you never even realized I was doing it.'

The observation came like a blow to the stomach. But he continued.

'You never minded me going away. When any other wife might have complained. But you did not. Recently it was as though you were glad to see me gone.'

'I was not glad to see you gone,' I lied. He ignored me.

'And at your sister's wedding. The way James looked at you, and you at him. You have never looked at me like that. I never trusted him, of course. But I trusted you. When you said you were spending time with Lillias, I assumed that even if the bastard tried anything, at least you would remember your marriage vows. At least you would remember our love. And all that I have done for you, and provided for you and your mother. But it seems not.'

'Of course I love you,' I protested. But we both knew that was not true.

'So how did it happen, Christian? How did you end up sticking him with a sword?' My husband blazed at me. 'The bastard deserved it,' he whispered. 'I dare say if I had found out about you two, I would have murdered him myself.'

'Please listen,' I said. 'No one believes me, but you must. I did not kill him – it was Violet.'

'Nonsense,' he said. 'I spoke with Reverend Brodie this morning. You were seen, many times, coming in and out of the castle these past weeks. On horseback through the fields. Avoiding the main village. And a sword under your skirts? I have been married to a savage.'

'I am no savage,' I said, my blood rising. 'I trusted you to be a proper husband to me and you denied me physical love and affection. I craved it. My needs were natural.'

He exhaled, the breath leaving his body in a way that caused him to sink.

'Why did you avoid making love to me?' I pushed, the tears coming now. 'What was wrong with me?'

'There was nothing wrong with you. You are being melodramatic.' He blinked two or three times. 'I did not want a child yet, and you put too much emphasis on physical relations.'

'But I needed you,' I said. 'You made me feel unwanted. Ugly. And you were never home, always out on business. You paid more attention to your fabrics than to your own wife.'

He shrugged, avoiding eye contact. 'You are too caught up in the notions of romance. For me, these were never priorities.'

'Then you should not have married me,' I said.

He sighed. Brushed his beard with his hand and pulled at his chin.

'Perhaps I should not have married you,' he said. 'But I needed a wife, even though I did not truly desire one.'

'And I needed a husband,' I said quietly. 'But I also desired one.'

'But of all people – him?' Andrew shook his head. 'Did you not think of the shame if you were caught? Did you not even try to resist?'

'Oh,' I said. 'If only. If only you knew how many times I had resisted him.'


We were interrupted by the clink and shuffle of the guard. Visits to the Tolbooth were paid for by the hour. He coughed, to signal we were out of time.

'Do not abandon me, Husband,' I pleaded.

'I will not abandon you,' Andrew replied. 'You and your mother are still my responsibility.'

'But will you help me?' In the gloom, which was setting in now that the sun was lowering, he could have been anyone. I barely recognized his features.

'I will do what I can for you,' he said. And with that he nodded and disappeared, following the guard down the steps, back to Carrick House, where he would open a bottle of Burgundy wine and sit at his desk as his candles burned. Perhaps he would write to every one of his connections, begging them to come to the aid of his fallen wife with the best of advocates and most persuasive pleadings to the sheriff. Perhaps, having signed these letters, he would sweep me to one side and write out his invoices, until he reached the dregs of the bottle and the candles flickered to nothing. Either way, he would go to his bed tonight, and every night until his last, utterly failing to understand me and all that I had needed from him.

I could not stop thinking of James. What had they had done with his body? When would they hold a funeral and place him in the ground with the cold bones of his poor wife? Who would attend? Mother? Or would that be unseemly? I thought of Violet and wondered if she was locked somewhere in this prison too, and who she might be bribing for meat and ale, for no doubt she would have found someone. I could tell that, in the short hours I had spent in her company. She had the survival instincts of a tenement rat.

I wondered where she had come from.

But mostly I thought of my own plight. I bit my lips raw and rubbed my cheeks until they roughened, going over and over what had happened, hoping that my testimony would give the sheriff the chance to finally see sense.

## *THE CALEDONIA BROADSIDE*

### EDINBURGH, 1st October

Donations are sought for a permanent memorial to the late Laird Forrester, taken too soon. It is thought a statue could be erected at or near the kirkyard in Corstorphine, where he rests in eternity with his loyal wife. Much has been said about the manner of his life and death but, when all is said and done, Laird Forrester was a person of quality who did much to enhance the life of the village.

It is hoped that placing this appeal in *The Caledonia Broadside* will bring it to the attention of the great and good of Edinburgh, who may find it in their hearts to contribute a financial token, however small.

*Remember this: Whoever sows sparingly will also reap sparingly, and whoever sows generously will also reap generously.*

Reverend Ian Brodie, Minister of Corstorphine Kirk

# Chapter Forty-Eight

# VIOLET

*A Safe House, Edinburgh*
*September 1679*

There is always a kerfuffle when the men at the door change their shift. I can watch them if I wish, for the main window of this apartment is on a wall that sits at a right angle and overlooks the doorway. They greet each other with shivers and grumbles, as though standing on the street doing nothing is a real chore. The departing man lumbers off towards the alehouse on the corner, and the new arrival rubs his hands and blows on them for heat and stamps his feet and reaches for a pipe. Sometimes they glance up for a glimpse of me at the window. Sometimes I let them have one. The toss of a curl. The slip of a hand over a curtain. They will go home and tell their wives what they saw. I feel my notoriety blossom. I feel myself gossiped about over oysters and ale.

Tonight the high street hangs in a brief, dead lull. It has the first bite of autumn about it: a purple sky settling over the tenement tops. A sky the colour of violets and leaves turning gold. Edinburgh town is a cold, beguiling witch. With wind about her cloak and spells in her hair. The market stalls are long packed away, and the gents tucked into taverns. Stray dogs and cats roam. I lick my lips. They still taste of rich wine. A tide of goosebumps swells over my bare arms. I am still in the pale-pink dress.

I have got to know the men who guard the door these past few days. There are three shifts: the morning, the evening and the night. There is a fellow with dark-red hair who does the mornings, and one with silver hair who takes over from him. Then in the evening comes the rougher sort, with small, sharp ears and wide shoulders and a scar on his forehead.

But tonight it is a different man who takes over for the night shift. I pause, half in and half out of the window, thinking I should tidy away the honey cake before bed, when I am struck by the look of this new man as he comes up the road and stops just underneath me, waving off the previous one. It is the bold way he carries himself and the faint baldy patch on the back of his head that looks like an oatcake.

He stands only a few feet below me, looking up and down the empty street and settling himself into his shift.

My breath catches in my chest.

That's the man who murdered Ginger.

The knife glints in my hand.

Did I lock the door after Mrs Fiddes left? That is my first thought. For he could easily stride in, this brute, and knife me like he did my dear friend, Lord rest her soul. Perhaps this gives him his kicks. Perhaps he has sought me out. There is a likeness of me in the broadside Mrs Fiddes left, though I can't read the words, and neither could she, so we cackled over the sketch and propped it on the table beside the door. I pick my way there now, over the red patterned rug, and touch the key. It is locked. The creature will no doubt have a key, and a key to the main door downstairs, for they are guards after all, but at least I will hear it rattle. There is a heavy-looking chair near the door. I push it across, so at least he would have an obstacle, and sit in the chair and think.

*Dear Ginger. Fate has dealt us a funny hand tonight. He has either come to finish me off too or he has no idea that the witness he is protecting is the same lassie as the one he glanced over, the night he took you.*

I stand up slowly after my think. The knife has not left my hand, and will not leave my hand the whole time that bastard is in my vicinity. I walk back over to the window and peer down, just far enough to see the top of his oatcake head. Oh, it is him. The stance of him, stiff-necked and broad-shouldered. The same pea-green coat. He is leaning against the doorway, a pipe in his hand.

I watch him until St Giles' chimes midnight and the taverns empty of men like rats scattering to their burrows. He smokes his pipe on and off, and changes position from leaning on one leg to leaning on the other, but that is the sum of his activities in those high hours. How can the bastard stand so confidently? If I had ripped wee Ginger apart like he did, I would forever be a-twitch with the guilt of it, spooked by her red-headed ghost and seeing her pale face illuminate each dark close.

In these hours I concoct my plan.

Oh, it is a daring one.

But I am full of vengeance. It oozes from me, like blood from an old wound that cannot heal.

I will slip downstairs and open the door with a sly little smile, the pink ruffle of my dress peeking out from the door frame. He will turn and ask me what I am doing, and I will say I fancy some male company. He will look me up and down and sook on his pipe. I will offer him a swig of whisky. He will ask to come upstairs, perhaps with a nod of his oatcake head. And then I will slip it to him – the knife will cut his throat. And he will clutch at his neck and bleed to death on the doorstep. I will take any coin from his pocket and even his pipe, to make it seem like a robbery, and I will pass them to Mrs Fiddes for safe disposal. I will leave the knife in his neck. In the morning there will be a commotion and I will arrive at the window in a white nightgown, hair in a tumble, and look as shocked as everyone else, as they blame the rogues of the high street and cart him off to the kirkyard. And the ladies of the high street can sleep easy in their beds, for that is another horror dispatched.

And Ginger can take one last sigh, then sleep easy with the angels.

I pour myself a whisky for courage. I dab my cheeks with rouge. I say a prayer to Ginger: *Dear pal, I am sending this bastard to hell.*

I walk to the door and place my hand on the key.

I turn the key and it clicks sharp in the lock.

I open the door and the night breeze drifts upwards, settling under my skirts. And that is when I realize. I cannot do it. I cannot kill a man. Even for all this bastard has done. Oh, Ginger, I am sorry. But a murderess I am not. I have seen a man bleed out on the ground before – that devil of a laird – as Lady Christian stood agog, sword in hand, and I had to prise it from her to stop her from doing any more damage, whispering to her as though she were a babe, *Come now, that is enough, leave him now*, and she screamed as his mouth frothed with blood, terrible cursing for such a fine lady, *You had this coming a long time, you have no one to blame but yourself*, and I knew there was more to their fight that day than a lovers' tiff. That it was an act of revenge that had been a long time brewing.

# Chapter Forty-Nine

# CHRISTIAN

*The Tolbooth Jail, Edinburgh*
*September 1679*

The prison guard arrived with deliveries. The first was a note from Johanna saying she had given birth to a baby boy, named Robert after his father. He was healthy and suckling well at the wet nurse. My sister planned to cut short her confinement to attend my trial.

The second was a basket of pale-green apples with a letter. The apples were sour.

*Dear Daughter.*

*I still call you that, despite what I am hearing. Is it true? I wish I could look you in the eye and ask you, but Andrew says the Tolbooth Jail is no place for me and that he hopes the advocate will have you cleared, and soon returned to me at Roseburn. I have tried telling myself it is all lies. But I find instead that it slots into place. Were you really visiting James? After everything Andrew did, including that spectacular wedding and the wonderful home he provided for you? I am fortunate he still sees me as his mother-in-law, despite this horrific turn of events. I wake up every morning, seized by dread, fearing for you and what may become of us.*

*Oh, Christian, what was it about your uncle that had
you blush every time he entered the room? When you visited
Lillias to paint, did you tempt him?*

*Did you not foresee that there would be only tragedy?
Did you not see how Lillias suffered?*

*Did your common sense not tell you to stay away?*

*Your loving mother*


I foresaw nothing.

I remember the night of the fiddlers when Lillias watched
me with a tight, cold smile.

I remember Christmas Eve a few months later, when I was
thirteen. I had helped Fiona put up the paper garlands.

I was in a pale-blue silk gown and Johanna was in one that
matched but, oh, she was more beautiful than me and I bobbed
in her wake. I was a paper flower, like those on the Christmas
garlands that we had pinned above the tapestry of Adam and
Eve. She was bright winter heather. Everyone watched her,
except James and his wife.

I remember the nod of his curls following my steps as I
moved around the parlour. The fire flickered and we had been
given chestnuts, and Johanna had passed me hers because she
hated their sweet musk. There were shell fragments in my
closed fists.

When it was time for me to curtsey goodnight to my aunt
and uncle I felt Lillias's eyes follow the dip of my head. I'd
had thirteen years of being judged by women who had guided
me in how to be appealing. *Smile. Cross your legs. Pull up your
stockings. Take up less room.* But her gaze had an ice to it, like
the December frosts we had been waking to, fit to crack the
fallen leaves.

Johanna had gone to bed first, disappearing into the rustle

of her dress until she was nothing but the shadow of my own sister on the stairs. I was slow. The shells pierced my palms. I walked into my chamber and stood there a while.

My uncle admired me. My aunt felt threatened by me.

It was a powerful feeling.

I did not sleep well that night. Instead I tossed and turned and wondered why this was happening, knowing it was something I could never speak of.

One month later, he sent his first gift.

It arrived with a parcel for Mother and Father, and she unwrapped it and handed it to me, saying nothing. It was officially from Lillias, a plaid shawl. *This should keep you warm,* her crooked script read. But I knew it was from him. And Mother insisted I write a thank-you note and that I wear it to the Strathearn–Aitken wedding at St Giles', which was the social event of that winter, and let Lillias see me in it.

'You are quite the favourite of our aunt,' whispered Johanna on the way to the wedding, touching the shawl's soft weave. The carriage was so fine in those days. Polished and oiled. And Johanna and I gazed out of its windows, huddled under rugs, mesmerized by the sights we saw on the road from Roseburn House into town. Glimpses of Edinburgh Castle. Beggars, missing eyes and limbs, scraping their way through the frost.

I could never say the gift was really from James.

But as we sat in St Giles' – too near the back for Mother's liking, watching her crane her neck forward as if to bring herself closer to the prominent families at the front – I could see the snake of James's curls and the nod of his wife's fur hat as they prayed and blessed the latest Edinburgh marriage.

Afterwards we gathered outside St Giles' and everyone took

far too long to say goodbye. Johanna and I hopped from one foot to the other, looking forward to going home to bread-and-butter pudding to warm us up. Lillias broke off from a group and approached us. I thanked her for the shawl again – for I had already written the note, but please and thank you were the language that we young girls spoke.

'It was nothing, my dear,' Lillias said. 'You seemed terribly goose-pimpled the other night. Some girls – weaker girls – cannot suffer the cold.'

James looked over and saw his wife with me and watched me squirm.

Lillias was captured by someone and slipped away. Johanna drifted towards Mother to see how long it would be before we could go home. James eased himself from his group and sidled towards me. No one seemed to notice, and they carried on with their conversations. No one except Mother, who glanced over at us from time to time.

'A fine shawl, Lady Christian,' James said.

'I am grateful to my aunt,' I said.

'But there is something you should know,' he went on. 'It was me who chose this shawl. The reds bring out the auburn hints in your hair. It puts you on fire.'

And then he caught someone's eye and headed away, enclosed once again in another group. Mother was laughing at something Father had said. Johanna was linking her arm with Mother's. Mother was looking over at me and pausing, as if there was something she might want to say, a shadow crossing her eyes. But then she went back to Johanna and nodded her head as if to say, *Yes, yes, we are going home soon.* And Lady Lillias pointed her eyes at me like sharp little knives.

# Chapter Fifty

# VIOLET

*A Safe House, Edinburgh*
*September 1679*

I spend that night in snatches of sleep, curled on the parlour chair under a blanket so that I will hear Ginger's murdering bastard if he decides to have a rattle at my door.

My dreams mingle with night-time wakings. The clatter of an ale bottle and the curse of a drunk. Ginger's blood on her wee pink dress. Her hair pin swapped for an abortion. A fumble under a sycamore tree. The hollow scream of a dying man. A courtroom, where I must stand up and recount it all, to the stunned faces of the great and good of Edinburgh, who will gaze me up and down and consider whether I have invented the whole story to save my own neck. The Maiden, the execution machine that I have seen with my own eyes from the parlour at Mrs Fiddes's, standing bold on its scaffold against the Edinburgh skyline, where not even the pigeons dare to perch. I lie awake and think of it, then finally I fall asleep and dream of it.

And how I must send that fine lady to her own death. For they are baying for her blood, there is no doubt, and the sheriff made it clear he had no use for anything that might serve in her defence.

It rattles through me until the morning mist of the Nor Loch, deadly as a sea monster, rises from its banks and seeps under the windowsills; its putrid vapours come to swallow up this wretched town. Whores and ladies and ale bottles and oyster shells alike.

I have nearly paced a hole in the rug by the time Mrs Fiddes returns the next afternoon with steaming parcels of meat.

'I have ordered you a violet silk gown from the dressmaker, and a fine wig too,' she says, stamping the rain off her boots. 'With violet ribbons in the curls. All to match your name. So don't say I am not a generous mistress to you.'

'I have never said anything to the contrary,' I say.

'You can settle the bill once you're finished with this court business,' she goes on. 'But these roasted chicken legs are my treat. Now what, in the name of God, has got into your sour face today? You have a look about you that could turn cream.'

Mrs Fiddes needs two whiskies for medicinal purposes as I spill out the tale of the devil who guarded me last night. I miss out the part where I considered, briefly, knifing the bastard in the throat, as I think it unbecoming, but she is more interested in knowing the timings of his shift than in whatever notions brew inside my head.

'So it's possible he will be back this evening,' she mulls, finishing off one of the chicken legs, licking it clean and scratching under her wig with the bone.

'Perhaps,' I answer, still tussling with my first chicken leg, for my appetite is reduced and the meat quite gristly. Corstorphine Castle has spoiled me: I have forgotten the taste of street-seller food, and will have to get used to the grease and sinew of it again.

'I shall report straight to the constables when I am finished my dinner here,' she says. 'And say I saw him with my own eyes, for there is no use having you dragged into another murder case. It will undermine your reputation. And we need you to remain as sensational as you are.'

Am I? A sensation? Mrs Fiddes must surely think so, otherwise she would be tucked securely in her parlour, replenishing the dishes of prunes in time for the evening rush. She is investing in her prize, expecting a lavish return. And what price will I pay for her assistance? What price will I pay for sending Lady Christian to her death? For that is my role now. The men in robes have tasted her blood and the crowd is baying for her, and I am to be the one to make it happen, for that makes it all the easier for them. Never mind the role the laird played in his own undoing. Never mind that, for he is as untouchable as they are. A titled man. An elder of the Kirk.

'I cannot sleep another night if that man returns to guard my door,' I say, casting away my unfinished chicken.

'There is meat yet on that,' Mrs Fiddes cries, swooping. 'And skin. You will waste away to nothing. Your titties will flop like girdle scones.'

'You are welcome to it,' I say. 'Just assure me that devil will be dealt with and brought to justice. Proper justice.'

'Oh aye, he will that.' Mrs Fiddes slaps her lips together as she picks over the bones, her fingers and chin slippery. 'After this I am straight to the constables. I hope they chop off his ballocks.'

I have the satisfaction of seeing the devil arrested. For he arrives innocent as a lamb for his shift that evening, and as soon as he has eaten a pie and lit his pipe, a gang of constables appear and surround him. I see arms fly and his pipe knocked clean to the ground, and hear yelling and cursing as he is dragged away in the direction of the Tolbooth Jail. The pipe lies not five minutes before it is claimed by a ragged-coated fellow, who pulls it off the street in one deft swoop.

Then a stray dog follows and sniffs the spot, snuffling at the ground for pie crumbs.

Nothing goes to waste in this town, if you have not already noticed. Look around you. Everything picked clean.

## Chapter Fifty-One

# CHRISTIAN

*The Tolbooth Jail, Edinburgh*
*September 1679*

There is a lot of time to ruminate on your childhood when you are in jail.

For that is where the trouble usually begins, for those of us unlucky enough to end up behind bars. Orphans become urchins, who become thieves. I know that from the tutor who came to Roseburn.

But this I have learned for myself: girls who are wronged can become vengeful women. And it matters not whether they are ladies or harlots or maids.

In Roseburn House, where *Hope Lies Within*, family gatherings began to make me feel nervous.

I wondered, when trying on whichever gown Mother had suggested, for whichever dinner or luncheon we were attending, what my uncle would think. Was white too childish? And I was vigilant to see whether he took any special notice of me. Sometimes he did. I would see him across the table or room, larger than life and recounting anecdotes that made the gentlemen boom with laughter; would see his eyes skit to me, to check whether I was taking notice. On other occasions, when he was caught up in conversation, he ignored me completely. I would return to my room despondent, for he was the only man who took any notice of me and, when he did not find me interesting enough, truly I was a lost cause.

And then I would wonder: am I imagining him paying me any attention?

And so it went, from time to time. Months went by without seeing him. Then a letter would arrive, inviting us to something he would surely attend. Or Mother would sigh to Father, 'Duncan, it's our turn to host' and my heart would race. My thoughts were filled with him, even though I did not want them to be. *He was my aunt's husband.*

At Easter, more than a year after that first Christmas, I had recently turned fourteen and James attended a Sunday gathering that my parents hosted at Roseburn. He chewed his roast lamb whilst whispering in his wife's ear and casting glances at me. Lillias suckled at her wine, the glass barely leaving her mouth. She even poured some for herself from the bottle. That was the first time I realized how much she drank.

That Whit Sunday he and Lillias came again, bringing us a skilled new groundsman, whom they no longer had need of at Corstorphine, with Mother wanting someone to tend to the new box-hedge maze she'd had planted, and unaware yet how much money Father was losing at the gaming tables.

As it was such a fine late-May afternoon with bright skies and a soft breeze, James insisted that I show him around the maze whilst everyone else went into the rose garden. It was so close by, and the hedges so low at waist-height, that nobody raised an eyebrow and instead rushed to show Lillias the creamy

Scotch briars coming into bloom. And there we were, alone in the twists and turns of the greenery. I stayed a step ahead of him, flitting anxiously.

'Don't be shy,' he said, following me over the dirt path. 'Slow down. I am not as light on my feet as you.'

'I am just cold,' I insisted.

'Nonsense! This is the best day we have had all year.' He sniffed and put his hands on his hips, stopping at a corner bend. I was opposite him, three feet or so away. We remained there as a bumblebee roamed near our heads before he waved it away.

'I've been watching you,' he said. 'Soon men will start to flock around your sister, but she is all hair and giggles. You are far more interesting.'

I didn't know what to say, or where to look.

'There is no reason to blush,' he went on. 'You don't know how attractive you are, but you are fourteen now – almost a woman. You have an effect.'

Then he laughed, a light laugh, as though we had simply been admiring the foliage, and said it was time to join everyone else, and he turned on his heel and left me standing alone in the corner.

I did not believe him. How could I possibly *have an effect*? I was nothing.

I saw the way gentlemen were beginning to crowd around my younger sister and elbow each other out of the way, and they had never done that to me. And even if James's words were true, what was the effect I was having?

That was when I started looking for answers in the only place that might have them: our library. In the afternoons, after lessons. Eventually, in a hot and tired daze, after reading a pamphlet of sonnets by William Shakespeare full of lines about beauty and love that were both revealing and confusing, I found the marriage manual.

Once I had that in my hands, I knew.


We went to the Lammas Fair at Corstorphine in the summer of 1676 when I was fifteen.

It was an attempt to cheer Father up. He had complained of a racing heart. He drank whisky in the mornings for medicinal purposes. He disappeared in the evenings and was out all night. Johanna said he was betting at card games and had lost some of our savings. Mother said a day out with his family would set him right again. She warned us not to watch the cock-fighting or the bare-knuckle boxing and worried at the chance of a sudden downpour, but we would avoid that and would load the carriage with loaves and confections and even see about a new horse. And afterwards we would be hosted by the Forresters, who had been gifted a curious fruit all the way from South America. Lillias had written of it to Mother and said it would be the centrepiece at dinner.

Lillias did not attend the fair. But we arrived, Johanna and I, full of anticipation after a sweltering hour in the carriage, for the only fairs we had attended were on such a small scale as to be nothing larger than Saturday market days.

Mother and Father said Johanna and I could walk alone for a quarter of an hour, whilst they watched a dull-looking game of bowls. As we idled around the stalls, we bumped into James. He already smelled of ale.

'You ladies must have a chaperone,' he said. 'There are scoundrels making quick work of fine girls like you today.'

Johanna looked irritated. I could see she was torn between

her fear of the robbers and thieves of Corstorphine and the chance to be let out of our parents' sight for a brief interlude.

He produced some coins. 'Here, Johanna, buy ales for everyone,' he said, tossing them to her. She looked aghast, but took her place in the queue. He grinned at me. 'Tell me, Christian, are you any good at backgammon?'

'I've never played it,' I said. The only game we played was chess, for Mother said board games were not for ladies.

'It's time you learned,' he said. When Johanna returned with the ales on a tray, shortly followed by my parents, he made sure everyone had all but finished their drinks before announcing he was taking me to the inn for my first backgammon game, and it was high time I learned, and high time his dear niece saw some of the world, under his chaperonage.

'It is a perfectly respectable inn, run by a fine landlady, and I have the use of a cosy snug at the front,' he said. 'There will be no trouble at this time of the day.'

'If you say so,' said Father, although I doubt he would have said that if I had ever suggested it. 'Look after her, James.'

Johanna's eyes were wide. She looked both horrified for me and relieved it was not her being singled out for this honour. I should have been terrified, but in truth this was the most thrilling proposal I had received in my entire life.

'Christian, I understand your reticence, he said, entirely misinterpreting my wide-eyed look. 'But trust me, if you are to one day be a fashionable lady of this world and have anything interesting to say to your suitors, then you must understand how this world turns. You will entertain everyone with your impressions at dinner. There are even two obedient little terriers you can pet.'

Mother looked doubtful, but would never object to James. Not when the word *suitors* had been thrown into the air.

'She will be in the safest of hands,' he assured them both. 'You are all welcome to return for dinner at your leisure,' he said. 'The pine-apple will be presented at six o'clock.'

'The pine-apple!' Mother was quickly distracted by this news. 'Duncan has talked of these. He read of them in *The Caledonia Broadside*, didn't you, Duncan?'

Father looked sceptical. He was a man of oats and mutton and whisky, whose daughters were safest in their own garden and did not frequent inns. But no one said no to my uncle.

'I hope the pine-apple is not riddled with disease,' he said. It was meant in seriousness, but James guffawed.

'I'll have Cook scrub its spikes clean,' he said. 'But don't worry, Duncan, it is roast beef and gravy for our main. The pine-apple is an amusement. The girls will enjoy it. Now come, let's finish these ales.'

I could not believe the turn the day was taking. I had spent so many years trapped in the confines of Roseburn House, and now this. I had seen the sketch of a pine-apple in *The Caledonia Broadside*, although I was not supposed to read the scurrilous news pamphlet. But never mind the pine-apple. I was headed to an inn!

I had wondered what it would be like inside such a place. In truth, it was far duller than I had imagined. The floor was strewn with sawdust, and men and women sat at tables eating and drinking, but no one was dancing or misbehaving or seemed riotous. Well, it was barely noon, I supposed. The air was full of pipe smoke and the stale tang of ale. All heads turned at our arrival, but James whisked me through the main salon into a small snug, where the three occupants reluctantly left when they realized their laird wanted his favourite spot.

I sat, puffing my skirts around me and feeling quite daring.

'The inn suits you,' James laughed as the innkeeper brought ales. 'You are quite the modern young woman.'

I felt it. Truly daring. I took a deep breath to slow down the pace of the day, so it would not all go by in a rush and I would be home, looking out of Roseburn's windows, before I knew it.

The backgammon was a decent game.

'You are clever,' he said, when I won the third round.

'It's not difficult,' I said. 'Mostly luck of the dice.'

'Luck and talent,' he said. 'I am ordering us a whisky.'

'I don't drink whisky,' I said. But James handed me a glass and told me that it was a skill to be able to drink it without wincing. And the rest of the afternoon became a blur, for the next thing I remember was him watching me, his chin in his palm.

'Look at you, quite comfortable in this environment,' he said. 'Quite beautiful.'

'I am not.' I squirmed, realizing I was slurring. If I drank more, the room might start spinning.

'The thing about gaming,' he said, 'is that it puts two minds together. For a brief spell, our minds are quite entwined. Connected. I have enjoyed that sensation immensely. I think you have too.'

I did not reply. I was not so drunk as to let loose with my words. James rose and straightened his coat. There was a ruddiness to his cheeks.

Was it any surprise what happened as he walked me back to Corstorphine Castle, safely in time for dinner? That he stopped me just at the entrance to its grounds, under the sycamore tree, and whispered the same things into my ear. *I think you are beautiful. I think we are truly connected. Like the branches growing above us, and the seeds forming amongst them. We are two wings of a sycamore key.*

I had drunk four ales and a whisky, and he had drunk even more. Everything was soft at the edges. Only the present moment mattered. I might even have stifled a giggle. The next thing I remember was the touch of his lips on mine, scented and wet, and I jumped back, shocked at how vivid it was.

He had done something he should not have done.

And I had enjoyed it.

He made no further move, but motioned that we should walk back up the avenue to the castle. The road shifted and I could not keep a straight line. I remember the heat as we walked in and then sitting down to dinner, and the pine-apple fizzed on my tongue and Father wouldn't try it, and Lillias had red-wine stains at the corners of her mouth, and Johanna looked bored to tears, and James acted as though absolutely nothing had happened between us.

But I was beautiful.

That's what he said again, just a few years later, when he kissed me during my visit to Corstorphine Castle. The exchange that started our affair.

And I believed him.

Yet those were the same words I heard him say to Violet Blyth when I saw him fumbling at her under the same syca-more tree.

And I realized, at once, that he had called me beautiful and taken everything I had, for nothing more than the sheer game of it. Easy as a round of backgammon.

# Chapter Fifty-Two

# VIOLET

*Edinburgh*
*September 1679*

Mrs Fiddes made sure the man who killed Ginger was dealt with, good and proper. He confessed to the fact, as they found some of her undergarments in his lodgings that he must have ripped from her, and some belonging to other girls too, poor souls. But who these girls were, we might never know, as this is a town that swallows people up.

His confession spared me the embarrassment of being a witness at his trial as well as at Lady Christian's. But it does not spare him the hangman's rope. I am not supposed to leave the safe house, but Mrs Fiddes bribes the man at the door with a free evening at her parlour of delights, and he comes as our chaperone so that we can watch the hanging. Everyone loves a good execution, do they not?

It happens at dawn. We can barely make our way up the street for the crowds. There are at least a thousand at the Mercat Cross. I am shivering under the cape Mrs Fiddes brought. She is next to me, warm as a fireside, hands folded at her chest. I have never seen a mob so silent as when the man walks out of the Tolbooth door onto its execution platform, in chains. Even the chewing of morning bread rolls stops, gobs half full.

*This is for you, Ginger*, I pray. I repeat it over and over, steeling myself as he takes his last steps, lurching over the wooden boards. He looks drunk. He is less of a man than I remember. He is thinner and his face is bruised. He still wears his pea-green coat.

Is Lady Christian shivering in a coat or wrapped in wool blankets? Is she watching? I look up at the windows. I do not see her face.

Will I join her soon, for theft of that sword pin, or even accused of murder myself?

He takes the steps to the scaffold. You can tell the prison guards from the High Constables, for the guards are scruffy and savage-looking and the constables look clean and their buttons shine.

A minister in a long black cloak mutters at the side of the scaffold. I hope he spares a prayer for Ginger.

The man closes his eyes as he is hooded and the noose put round his neck. Mrs Fiddes reaches for my hand. She clutches it. I clutch hers back.

He falls with an almighty crack. He jerks and bounces. I cannot take my eyes off him. Then he is still, and the mob erupts, for that is a good hanging.

I am ushered back to the safe house, the doorman pulling me so that I don't get lost in the crowd. Mrs Fiddes stands, one hand in the air as if to salute me, the other grasping her shawl. Just before she is swallowed up by the mob, I realize she is wearing the sword pin at her throat.

Ginger is at peace.

But I am not.

\*

I am relieved when the day finally rolls round that I am called to appear on the witness stand for Lady Christian's trial, for it brings me one day closer to the day when I can escape the clutches and threats of Mrs Fiddes. I will get my hands on that sword pin and she will never see me again, I swear it.

Before all that, though, I have a task I must do, to everyone's satisfaction.

I am trotted out to the court in a horse and carriage, despite the fact that you could hop the journey on one foot. Mrs Fiddes instructs the carriage to pick me up from the safe house and parade me all down the high street, then into the Canongate as far as the White Horse Inn at Ord's Close, before turning at the gates of Holyrood Palace and making its way up again. This is all in order, she says, to make the hire worth the price, and to give the waiting crowd a sense of my arrival. It is a mockery, of course, but she adores every minute of it, sitting next to me and howling at every bump in the road and pointing out every gawping face in every filthy window.

My dress is so wide and frilled there is scarce room for the broad bawd on the leather upholstery. My violet ruffles fill every corner of the coach. My titties spill atop it like two snow-capped mountains.

'You are like the Pentland Hills in winter,' roars Mrs Fiddes. 'They will worship you in that courtroom. Your likeness will be in the broadsides by morning. Curse these potholes. I can feel myself bruising as I speak. My arse will be purple as your dress.'

There is no sign of the sword pin, thank God. Once I have satisfied myself of that, I try to pretend she is not here with me. I try to compose myself.

But I am in a cold sweat. How will I pay her back for all of this? She has spent a fortune on me.

The carriage halts before the courtroom doors, a vast crowd assembled. They have brought pies and chicken legs, knitting and sketching papers.

'The witness,' they roar, the swell of it rippling through them.

'Ignore them,' hisses Mrs Fiddes. 'And look serious. Don't smile, lest the artists catch you looking frivolous.'

I have never felt less like smiling or felt less frivolous in my whole life. I am dragged in by the waiting constables, and I can hear snatches from the crowd as I go. *The famous witness – his maid. Oh, his maid indeed, she is nothing but a harlot, and look who is accompanying her: mother of the biggest whore-house in Scotland. Not a pair to be trusted. Whose prick has Violet Blyth stroked to get herself off the hook?*

I am put into a holding room, separated from Mrs Fiddes, who is sent to a waiting room for the other interested parties. I wonder where Lady Christian is. If she has to battle through that crowd like me or whether she was held here overnight? Are there secret tunnels between the jail and the court? I have no sense of her arrival or her presence, for I can hear nothing in this room except the rumble of my belly and the gallop of my heart. The morning stretches on. I imagine what is happening in the courtroom, with men in black capes shuffling sheaths of papers and scratching names in books and leaning towards each other in earnest, the whiff of good bacon and coffee on their whiskers, saying, *A splendid play at the Tennis-Court Theatre last night*, whilst two women tremble.

There is a sharp rap, and a young bespectacled man puts his head round the door, followed by the rest of his lanky self.

'Miss Blyth. The order of events is as follows,' he says, as if describing a dinner menu. 'You will appear first – shortly, in fact – and the other witnesses will be next.'

I do not know whether to stay sitting or to stand, for there

are rules about where your arse should be in court. I swallow
and decide to stay on my seat, for he is only a laddie, and we
are not in public.

'Who are the other witnesses?' I had not heard of this devel-
opment. I had assumed I was the only one. He peers at a list.

'Not many,' he says. 'The Reverend Brodie of Corstorphine,
and his men who attended the scene. But there are also some
personages who have been called to give evidence about the
characters of Lady Christian and yourself.'

'My character?' We blink at each other. He in his prim white
collar and me in my blast of purple silk.

'Indeed,' he peeps. 'It is a matter of formality.'

'And who is speaking on behalf of my character?'

He consults his list.

'I wish I could read,' I add. 'Such a skill.'

He coughs. 'Indeed. Now there is a character witness here,
a Mrs Rita Fiddes, who I believe is your guardian? Miss Blyth,
are you quite all right?'

Mrs Fiddes. The sly old boot. Why did she not say she
would also be appearing on the witness stand? *Sensational* –
that's what she called me. I look down at myself, a foam of
ruffles. She has dressed me and wigged me and fed me and
now she will *describe* me, to all and sundry. And the only person
who will profit from her accounts of me is the damnable bawd
herself.

I grab at the top of my dress, pulling it as far as it will go
towards my neck, in a weak attempt to cover as much of my
bare flesh as I can. Rita Fiddes has no interest in defending
my character.

'Miss Blyth? It is time.'

I jump at the sound of my own name. I am trembling with
fury and fear. The laddie is opening the door further, to allow

for the width of my skirts. I stand up shakily and make my way towards him. We turn into a long corridor that is panelled in dark wood and has sporadic high windows that spill yellow sun onto stone slabs. We walk so hurriedly the light hits my eyes in flashes and stabs that make my head spin, as I follow him all the way along the corridor and up a wide flight of steps into the courtroom.

Ma used to tell me a story. The very day I was born, a most spectacular creature was walked through Edinburgh town on a short rope. A 'camel' it was called, cloven-footed and humpty-backed. It had come all the way from the desert sands on a ship to Leith Port and it was on its way to Brounisfield, to the home of a rich tailor who had bought it and built it a stable.

All of Edinburgh stared, she said. From those in the highest tenement windows to those in the lowest puddles of piss. A wondrous teller of the bedside tale, was Ma. Must be where I get it from. Even Ma broke away from her early labours to stand at the top of the close and gawp at this beast, before returning to the throes of agony, for I was born the wrong way round. But more on that later.

For now – this day in the court – I feel like that very dromedary must have done. Cloven-footed like the Devil himself. Exotic. Desperate to escape. As all of Edinburgh stares. A sea of wigs and red noses. That Mr Dalhousie with question after question, trying to trip me up and make me seem an untrustworthy witness. Did I remember the incident correctly? Had I consumed ale at the fair? Had I not once worked in a whorehouse? And is it true that I was in an embrace with the laird with my petticoats up, pardon the description, Your Honour?

Smelling salts are brought to some of the ladies at the back. Fans flap like pigeon wings. Artists smirk and sketch. Gents lick their lips.

I cannot help the fact she killed him.

I tell the court what happened and that I could not stop her. She might have killed me too.

I try to tell the court the things she said to him as he lay there. But Mr Dalhousie is having none of it. He says she denies the whole thing completely. Won't let me speak of it. And the sheriff pulls me off the witness stand as fast as he can, for I am causing all manner of a commotion in the court-room.

Next: enter Mrs Fiddes. Never seen anyone happier to be at the centre of attention. Never seen a room of men so rapt – and that is saying something, coming from me. A character witness *extraordinaire*.

'And how would you describe Miss Blyth's trustworthiness?' Sheriff MacDonald's eyes bulge. You would never think he has lain in Mrs Fiddes's own parlour having his red arse cheeks nursed better.

'Violet is not the smartest girl in the world. But she is honest. I have never heard her tell a lie,' the old bawd coos.

'And how are we to trust either of you,' howls that Mr Dalhousie, 'when we all know the sinful profession you are both in?'

'I know nothing of sinful professions,' claims Mrs Fiddes, voice rising and hands clasped as if in prayer, 'for I am an honest landlady with decent lodgings that simply keep girls off these dangerous streets.'

'Now, now,' Sheriff MacDonald's voice rises over the din of

hoots and whistles. 'This murder is a sorry incident indeed. However, I have no choice but to look at all of the facts, as they are presented to this court, and decide which facts are relevant and which facts are not.'

'One fact is relevant,' cries Mrs Fiddes, pointing a finger. 'My dear friend Miss Blyth has been dragged into scandal. A public embarrassment the likes of which I have never seen in all my days. It is not her fault the laird could not keep his hands off her – why, look at her: her figure and her demeanour are enough to drive any man wild with lust. But that girl should be seeking recompense for her troubles.'

Sheriff MacDonald has not heard such talk in all his days, for his face goes as purple as my dress. I think he is fit to throw the bawd in a cell, when one of the men in robes creeps towards the bench, head bowed, with a slip of paper in his hand, which he passes to the sheriff.

We all watch him read it.

He looks up and addresses the room.

'A matter has been brought to my attention,' he crows, seeming pleased enough with himself. 'Another damning piece of evidence about the character of Lady Christian. From her own Aunt Lillias. From beyond the grave.'

## *THE CALEDONIA BROADSIDE*

### EDINBURGH, 29th September

The unsent letter from Lillias Forrester was found during the preparation of Corstorphine Castle for its new occupants, the new Laird John Forrester and his family. Perhaps she meant to send it before she tragically died?

*June 1679*

*Dear Niece,*

*I am fully aware of your liaison with my husband. Your own uncle. If your dear mother knew, it would kill her. I heard you both in your chamber, under my own roof. When I returned from the healing waters, none of my own staff could look me in the eye. You have made me ashamed to live in my own home.*

*He has always had a notion for you. You must have been aware of it. Foolish of you to succumb to his charms, for you are not his first mistress and you will not be the last. He has always been like this.*

*I would urge you to stop for your own sake, but it would be no use, would it? I barely have the strength to write this letter, never mind beg you to see sense.*

*Your aunt,*

*Lady Lillias Forrester*

## Chapter Fifty-Three

# CHRISTIAN

*The Tolbooth Jail, Edinburgh*
*September 1679*

I believe, now that I understand the world better, that my uncle enjoyed the sport of the long chase. He did not simply want to throw himself upon me that day under the sycamore tree when I was drunk. To risk me getting upset and telling Mother and Father. That would have tarnished his reputation. He thought too highly of himself. And he wanted me desperate for him.

Another gift arrived, on my sixteenth birthday. It was a gold brooch in the shape of a sycamore key. My birthday, in February, was a sombre occasion as Father had died three months earlier and no one wanted to celebrate. We were spared the indignity of being evicted, as Father's brother, who inherited the Roseburn title, decided to remain in Fife at his wife's estate, which was far bigger than ours. But Mother realized that their savings had slipped through Father's fingers at the gaming tables. She would ask Johanna and me if we had taken various necklaces or rings because she seemed to have mislaid them, but we hadn't. Father had lost them at the gambling parlours.

She had her pearls, a simple single string, which she gave me that day as a gift. 'These will give you a luminous glow,'

she said. 'You need them more than Johanna.' I doubt she had
the money to buy jewellery.

Then a parcel arrived from the Forresters.

'This is lavish,' she said, when I had opened it. She looked
taken aback. 'What does Lillias say?'

I read out the note: '"This brooch will look splendid on that
fine navy gown of yours, but you could also wear it with something green, the shade of sycamore leaves."' I held it in the
palm of my hand. It gleamed. Expensive. Sophisticated.

'She is thinking of making you as presentable as possible to
suitors,' Mother said. 'I just wish they would pay equal attention to Johanna.'

'It is more James than Lillias,' I said. It was the first time I
had dared say anything. I closed my fingers over the brooch,
feeling its edges.

Mother's eyes widened. 'What on earth do you mean by
that?'

'I think he is the one paying extra attention to me, not my
aunt,' I said.

*We are two wings of a sycamore key.*

Mother looked at me coldly. 'You are not to complain,
Christian,' she said. 'We need our family, especially now. And
the next time we see them, you will be wearing that brooch
on your green taffeta cape.'


I did not see Lillias for a while, as she became sicker and
could not join her husband at any social event. First she was
limited to Corstorphine village and constitutional walks. Then
the castle grounds. Then the castle itself, unless she was in
her wheeled chair. Which suited James wonderfully, I expect,
for it meant he could do as he pleased. He visited London.

And then he began visiting Roseburn, helping Mother to avoid financial ruin.

'Remember the sycamore brooch,' Mother said, the evening before he was due. 'No arguments.'

She used me. She used me to lure him, so that he would look after her.

I can hardly blame her. What else was she to do?


Andrew sent a white-lace gown to the Tolbooth for my trial. The note said the fabric was imported from Italy and stitched by the same seamstress who had created my wedding gown, but this dress was far simpler. I think he was trying to make me look innocent. I slipped it on and waited for the guards to take me to the court.

# Chapter Fifty-Four

## VIOLET

*Edinburgh*
*October 1679*

I know what you're wondering. What was Lady Christian's reaction to her verdict? When the sheriff pronounced her for the chop, *what did she do?* And if I had a penny for every time I've been asked that, I would be richer than our very own bawd.

It happens on a Friday morning, 3rd October. Just after nine of the clock. St Giles' has pealed the start of the working day and Edinburgh's townsmen are giving a half-arsed attempt at their morning duties, hoping to clock off at noon and head to the oyster houses.

We members of the court, on the other hand, are assembled for the verdict. The room smacks of morning breath and stale wig. The cavorting and gossiping and hysterics will come later, but for now we are straight and tidy as piano keys. All except her. I can see a side view from where I am put. She sits with her arms folded into her belly. She is thin. Her dress creases at the sides. There is grime ingrained into the crumples already. She should not have worn white. It shows the stains. You cannot look pure in it for long. Sweat patches bloom at her armpits.

'All rise,' the bespectacled laddie pips and upwards we sweep. In strides the sheriff. He sits at his bench.

'Lady Christian, you will stand,' he booms, and she does, barely, for her knees knock and her shoulders quake, curls of hair escaping from ribbons.

'On the charge of the murder of Lord James Forrester, I find you guilty,' he says.

She buckles. She is caught by the two men on either side, but they do not let her sit. Instead they hold her up by her elbows whilst she wilts and droops like a flower without water. There are wails from the other side of the room where two ladies with jewelled topknots sit and clutch each other.

The sheriff allows a few moments of this before the gasps become too much of a hullaballoo. He stands. The court hushes. He reads out her death-sentence as she whimpers and denies. She is pulled out of the courtroom before anyone else is given leave. From my bench, which is on a platform, I can see all of it as though it were a performance. Even her last moments are without dignity, for the back of her gown drags after her and there is a long, wet streak down the rear of it. She has pissed herself.

I expect someone from the court, or one of the constables, to come and tell me what to do next, for that has been the way of my life for so long now. But no one does. Those to the left and right of me stand up and leave, but I remain sitting and stunned. For I have witnessed a horror show. And we are all still in the midst of it, for she is to be beheaded on Monday at first light. The courtroom drains of bodies until all that are left are a few stragglers. I cannot move. The temptation to be rid of this gown is sore, but I feel stuck to this hard bench.

Is there anything different I could have done?

Could I have tried to spare her?

I think not.

Would she have spared me if I had been the one to kill her lover?

I think not.

But still, the thoughts whirl inside me and I know that when these gentlemen are steadying their nerves with whiskies this afternoon and shaking their heads at the fate of the adulteress, the murderess, and for each day onwards, I will have Lady Christian branded into my soul. Like a punishment. For where I walk, she will walk with me. She will whisper from every silk gown that floats past me.

'Well, Violet, it is time for you to come home, now.' Mrs Fiddes looms over me, her face graver than I have ever seen it.

Home. The whorehouse. What choice do I have? I stand up and take her arm and we leave the courtroom like two old lovers. In the panelled hallway stands a group of high-society ladies and gentlemen, hiding from the crowds. The family. They all stop to watch us as we go. Mrs Fiddes has down to a fine art the skill of sweeping past disapproving stares. She glides, chin wobbling, but head held high.

I cannot say the same for me. I am drawn to the waiting eyes of a blonde-haired lass whose radiance is at odds with the ugliness of the occasion. Despite her beauty, she has a wretched look. Her face is blotched, and she is fanning herself and breathing rapidly. She says nothing, as folks of their rank never do like to disturb the peace, but she watches me. Her eyes bore into me as I walk out at Mrs Fiddes's slow pace. I can feel her curse me. I can feel her mourn.

# Chapter Fifty-Five

# CHRISTIAN

*The Tolbooth Jail, Edinburgh*
*October 1679*

They won't do it. It will be too obscene. I could just tell them I would be grateful to stay here, in this cell, until my natural death. Andrew would pay. More than was needed. He could ask the Forresters to write a letter to Sheriff MacDonald, an appeal. We are family, after all.

Then I remember what Mr Dalhousie said. That a crime of this nature – the killing of a man of such high standing – could never be punished with a light sentence.

But I didn't tell the court everything that happened.

How he really died.

I should have taken the risk and told them. That would have silenced Violet Blyth.

Mr Dalhousie will be here any minute. There has been so much commotion that the mice and rats have scattered to the furthest edges of their network of tunnels and now the cell hangs in silence. I can still feel the presence of that guard, filling the doorway. He will have a weekend of delights with me, I could see it in the pulse of his neck, in the snarl of his leer.

*And remember, you can have anything you want here. If you're willing to pay the right price.*

Anything I want.

What do I want if these are to be my final days? Who can help me? Mother has not once visited me in this cell. Johanna has her own family to look after.

I will be left here to think of nothing but what happened with James.

I never knew him.

I thought I did. I thought that knowing the familiar touch of him was enough to know him completely. *Oh, James*, I would think to myself, *there is that persistent curl that never quite sits right, there is that scar on his arm, there is that rough patch of hair on his chest. I know my lover so well. I have always known him.*

I never knew about the other half of his life. The half when I was not there. When I was sitting by the fire, embroidering Andrew's name into a kerchief. Writing letters to my sister. Thinking of James. His curls and scars woven into my embroidery and my handsome script.

What were you doing, James? You had so many opportunities.

Rutting Oriana the kitchen maid when Lillias's back was turned? And Violet Blyth. A harlot from Bell's Close. One of the rouged girls Johanna and I would gawp at before clutching each other's hands. No wonder Violet had such a sensual touch that day she attended to me. Her hands have been down every trouser leg in this wretched town.

And the way she stood on that witness stand, pretending to be innocent.

There is a scream inside my head, and if I let it escape it won't stop until they sever it. *This is all your fault, James Forrester. You have done this to me. My earliest days and my final days, governed by you.*

My mouth is numb from biting my lips to keep myself from screaming.

I think I hear Mr Dalhousie coming.

There is only one person who can help me now.

I know what I am going to do.

# Chapter Fifty-Six

## VIOLET

*Bell's Close, Edinburgh*
*October 1679*

Men are queuing at the door of Mrs Fiddes's apartments already. The line is so long we can scarce get inside.

'Make way,' she shouts, returning to her full vigour at the promise of so much coin.

'The whore witness,' they cry. 'Extra pennies for your gory tale.'

'Enough!' Mrs Fiddes has her back to the door, my arm grasped firmly by her hand. We are tussled and tumbled, and hands are flying up my skirts and roving over my flesh. The door opens a crack and Mrs Fiddes pushes me inside, following me herself, and I land in the arms of Flora and the girls, who greet me as fondly as a long-lost sister they had given up for dead.

'Dear Violet,' they cry, 'what horrors you must have suffered. You are trembling fit to burst.'

I can barely stand the touch of them on my arms. I have had enough of being crowded and poked and prodded and judged. I put my fingers in my ears and close my eyes, screwing them tight shut. I have not done this since the day Ma died.

'Leave her alone,' says Flora. 'She is about to have a misadventure.'

I breathe. One. Two. Three. I open my eyes. The girls are all boggling at me.

'Doors open in twenty minutes,' Mrs Fiddes cries through the keyhole as she dusts down her skirts and straightens her wig.

'I am just back from sending a woman to her death,' I say. 'You cannot put me to work in twenty minutes.'

Mrs Fiddes puts a hand on each of my shoulders and walks me into a corner of the hallway.

'Violet Blyth, you are *considerably* in my debt,' she growls. 'All I did in that courtroom was make sure no one will ever forget you. And these here fellows are paying good coin for a tea party in the parlour this very afternoon, with you as the star-turn. Now don't worry if you are rusty. Flora and the others are there for assistance, to keep the tea-kettles boiling, so to speak. And there is a spare room, as Mollie has run off with a customer.'

My mouth opens and closes, but nothing comes out.

'Come now, I have a carriage fetching your things from that apartment, but until then there are dresses in the armoire. Wear something red, to give them a taste of the blood she will shed on Monday. They will enjoy the theatrics.'

I follow her to the spare room Mollie has left. I can barely remember who Mollie was. Her old room is in the middle of the corridor, opposite the parlour door, which means I will never get a minute's peace, with all the toings and froings. Mrs Fiddes shuts the door, leaving me alone. A wash of grey light filters through the window. It smells of musty sheets. I lie down on the bed. It sags beneath me. She will really make me work – today of all days.

I have eaten nothing since last night's dinner. I could not stomach a breakfast and now I am rattling with hunger pangs.

I have done the right thing, have I not?

I am not sorry Lord James is dead. Not really. Not after that sore whipping he doled out, which left marks on my arse for days. Fellow like that was always dabbling in trouble.

And I told the sheriff what he needed to know. No point in adding in any superfluous detail.

Oh my God, they will behead her on Monday. They will do it. I have seen enough death at that Mercat Cross. They had the taste for it, the wigged men. And then she will become a legend. A fireside story. And I will return to being a ghost, for that is all I ever was. Lingering in these closes. Hanging in his turret, not-quite-real. Unacknowledged by the men who own this town, unless they need a quick fumble or an unpleasant murder tidied away.

I still keep seeing him, lying there on the ground.

And my own stab of guilt. I know what I did.

I put my fingers in my ears again and screw my eyelids tight shut until all I can hear is a low hum and all I can see are black swirls. Sometimes red bleeds into the black and I fight it by rubbing my eyes until the bleeding stops.

# Chapter Fifty-Seven

# CHRISTIAN

*The Tolbooth Jail, Edinburgh*
*October 1679*

*You did kill Lord James Forrester in cold blood.*

Lammas Day. Everything that happened keeps turning in my mind. I wake in the night with it, sweating and shivering, hay scratching my face and rats nudging my feet. It follows me as I pace the cell.

It starts with me walking back from the fair, the sun beginning to burn through my coif. Reverend Brodie's sly words rang in my ears, pointing out how James had become *a regular companion* in my husband's absence.

The scent of the roasting hog gave me hunger pangs, but I could not eat a plate of street-cooked meat in public. The poor herbalist was hanging in the branks, and I was set on pleading with James to order her taken down before she perished. If anyone could help, he could.

But I knew, in my heart, he would not.

He would not step in to save a harmless woman. He would say something like it was up to the Kirk Session, or that these things were out of his hands, or that lessons needed to be learned and it was the best way to keep women in order.

And then I remembered Oriana, sitting on her punishment

chair. My anger at her. But when I'd caught them, that day, and James had said that she had *carnal lusts*, I had known deep down, hadn't I?

It was James's carnal lusts, not hers.

I passed the inn where he had taught me backgammon. Something clicked. The memory of dice rolling on a board. Ale after ale.

I was agitated. Andrew would not agree to a divorce. He would be horrified. He would interrogate me and force it out of me. He would make me confess how it began, how young I had been when James started to pursue me. I could picture Andrew's face, aghast as it all came out, and he would shake his head and say there were decades between us, and James took advantage.

I could not deny that.

As I made my way towards the castle gates I realized something.

I was simply a piece in James's game. He had the power to rule my life, and always had, and could choose to adore me or slap me down. Just as he had the power to cut a woman from the branks or leave her there to die.

And when I entered the grounds, passing the sycamore, the most horrifying shock of all.

He was there, with Violet, hands everywhere and telling her, *Come on, my beautiful, we cannot resist each other – we are connected.*

Flashes of skirts and skin.

It was a repeat of what I had seen with Oriana. Watching him being intimate with another woman. The shame of it. The horror engulfing me.

I was nothing to him.

I did not know him at all.

What else had he done, behind my back, and not told me?

Shooed me home after an afternoon together and gone straight to one of his maids? And the maids had watched me come and go. Both of them. Gazing quietly from beneath their frilled caps.

The sycamore leaves rustled and shimmered, but I was still. Silent. James and Violet did not know I was here.

He tilted his head back. 'You are beautiful under this dress,' he said.

I flinched. *Beautiful*. How many women had he said that to?

When he said it to me, I'd believed he meant it. But he didn't, did he?

He just craved female attention to make him feel wanted, and that had almost cost me my marriage and my reputation.

*You are beautiful*. Who had heard that from his lips? Lillias? Perhaps he had no need, for their marriage was arranged. Oriana? Perhaps he had no need, for he believed he owned her.

It was a flare of rage, rising from my belly and engulfing me. Making my head boil. Then something else happened between them, for he stopped midway pawing at her petticoats and seemed to inspect them before he went back to nuzzling her ear again.

I don't know what alerted them to the fact I was there. Maybe they sensed my fury.

He saw me first. Gasped. Backed away from her.

Violet scampered out of the way, righting her skirts.

'Christian. This is not what you think. She is always trying to tempt me, this one.'

'You have ruined me,' I screamed. 'You would have married me and kept another mistress as though you were a king.'

'Oh, come on,' he said. 'It's Lammas Day after all – the whole village will be fucking each other by sunset.'

'You are despicable,' I said. 'I thought you were in love with me.'

'You were desperate,' he said. 'You came begging.'

Violet laughed. 'He cannot help himself,' she cried.

'This is none of your concern,' he warned her. 'Get back to the fair.'

She shook her head.

I looked him straight in the eye. 'You are filthy,' I said.

'He is filthy indeed.' But this was a new voice. Someone else had joined us. I did not recognize her at first, without the white frilled cap she wore around the dining room, for her hair was in unruly plaits about her shoulders now and she looked unwashed. And the look of hatred in her eyes was new. I had not seen that before.

His ruined maid, Oriana.

## *THE CALEDONIA BROADSIDE*

### EDINBURGH, 4th October

### CHRISTIAN NIMMO: GUILTY

The fate of the Lord James Forrester is now known. He died at the hands of his mistress and niece, Lady Christian, who now languishes in the Tolbooth Jail awaiting execution on Monday at first light. Our writer-at-large, Mr Nicholas Thomas, who has brought you these broadsides by working tirelessly through the night, will be at the Mercat Cross, where the terrifying Maiden looms for all to see, to relay an eye-witness account of the drinking and drunkenness expected, and the last dying actions and words of the unfortunate condemned.

# Chapter Fifty-Eight

# CHRISTIAN

*The Tolbooth Jail, Edinburgh*
*October 1679*

A man has been lingering, staying just at the edge of my line of sight. I noticed him outside the jail when I was first brought here. He wears a dark coat and a dark hat and so he is like almost every other man in this town, except that he is a half-head taller than most and carries a writing box.

I saw the same man, in the courtroom, scribbling onto it. Now he is down on the street.

He is the man who is writing all the gossip about me in the broadsides. I wonder why he does it. I wonder if I wave at him, or stare at him, whether he will report that in his scurrilous sheet or keep it to himself, like a prize.

He will stand down there and watch the blade slice me, and will lick his lips and dip his quill in his ink and write: HER FINAL STEPS, or maybe something more theatrical.

Perhaps I should invite him up. Tell him to bring a best mutton pie and two ales. He can write a ballad about me.

Oriana looked as shocked to be standing there as we were to see her. As though she had not quite expected she would be brave enough. She trembled. Hatred and fear, I know both those feelings well.

Violet gasped again. I had the urge to slap her.

'How long have you been here?' James demanded, the blood draining from his face.

'Long enough to know the kind of devil you are,' Oriana said. 'But I always did.'

'Leave, or I will have you put on the repentance stool again,' he warned.

'I have only come for what I deserve,' she said, her voice shaking. 'We are all starving in my family because I can't work. No one will have me, not even to rinse out their chamber pots. Give me more money or I will go to the Kirk Session and tell them all about you and your women.'

James was outnumbered. But he showed no fear. Slowly and calmly, he drew out the sword that had lain at his side. It rasped against its sheath. Violet gasped. My fingers touched my own sword over my gown; it was instinct. He pointed his sword at Oriana. 'They will not believe you,' he said.

'Reverend Brodie will believe me,' she said. 'He suspects you already. All the village gossips about you. You are the talk of the inn. Women coming and going at all times. Especially this fine lady. Perhaps it's her turn on the repentance stool.'

She was looking at me.

'I will not be threatened,' I said. I drew my own sword. I trembled at its weight in my hand, as I had never done such a thing before or even dreamed I might have to brandish it.

'Go on, then, stab me,' Oriana taunted. 'For that is the only way you will silence me. But you will hang for it, with these witnesses here.'

'Give her some money, James,' I said. 'It's your fault she lost her job.'

He swung round and pointed his weapon at me. 'You ordered me to dismiss her. Thinking yourself Lady of Corstorphine.'

'I knew it,' Oriana said, walking towards me. 'The adulteress. You are a *hoor*. Don't pretend you're anything else. Do you know how he treats women? Whips them, doesn't he, Violet?' Ignoring the sword at my side, she shoved me hard on the shoulder, enough to send me staggering back. She looked wild.

I straightened up. Pointed the blade at her.

'You don't even know what to do with that,' she taunted. 'You couldn't fight with it if you tried.'

I swiped at her. I did not mean for the tip to even go close, but James intercepted to push her out of the way. And he caught its full force in his arm.

He buckled, falling to his knees, dropping his own sword, blood spreading through his shirt, a bewildered look upon his face as though he had taken a punch in a fight. My mouth opened and I screamed in shock, a scream that was echoed by Violet and Oriana.

'You have killed him,' said Oriana.

James looked up at us, shock turning to a fury I had never seen. His face was white. I had seen him rage before, but never like this. His other hand grasped for his sword.

'You stupid, stupid bitch,' he said, his voice low and controlled. 'You are all stupid whores. Thieves and liars and whores. Get off my property, all three of you, before I do something I regret.'

He looked at his arm. His sleeve was crimson.

'You will pay for this,' he said. 'Each of you will regret this day.' He looked directly at me. 'How on earth will I explain this wound to Andrew Nimmo?' he hissed.

Then it was Violet who spoke.

'You have not killed him, Lady Christian,' she said, shakily. 'But now is your chance before he ruins us all. Before he puts Oriana in the branks and me in the whorehouse, and beats you to death for slashing his good shirt, and tells your husband and all of Edinburgh what a desperate whore you were for him.'

I knew James.

I knew he could.

I could see them all gossiping about me, my husband fleeing back to sea with the shame of it, and my uncle losing no time in making a marriage proposal to someone else, like Miss Mariota Blair, and me spending the rest of my days wilting among the orange and lemon trees in my glasshouse, shunned.

'Do it,' Violet urged again.

And so I grabbed his sword before anyone else could. Now I had two weapons in my hands. One light, one heavy. I can still feel the weight of them. I can still feel the power of that moment. Violet was right. We were all in danger. I dropped my own sword as he made to take it from me, and stabbed him with his blade until he stopped moving. It was as though I was seized by an impulse and I could not stop. I did not just stab him once, I did it again and again, as though I had to finish what I had started and finish the deed properly. The next thing I remember is that I was kneeling at his feet and shrieking, and Violet was gently taking the sword from my hands, saying, *'Enough, now.'*

How will that tale go down with the man from *The Caledonia Broadside*? How would he write it: THE THREE WOMEN WHO ALL PLAYED THEIR PART IN THE MURDER? Woodcut prints of us, glowering down from the coffee-shop walls. The betrayed lady who stabbed him. The whipped harlot urging her on. The shamed maid who threatened him and caused him to draw his sword; who called me a whore and taunted me into making that first swipe.

But of course I could never have told anyone that. Not Mr Dalhousie or Robert Gregor or Andrew or Sheriff MacDonald. They would have found Oriana, and she would have been another witness to my crime. And if I had said Violet told me to do it, that would have been a direct admission of guilt.

But she is as guilty as me.

I would have watched her hang for this crime and she knows it.

There is something I can do. Flee. Create my own punishment of banishment. It is not what the sheriff has in mind, as he scribbles my death warrant. But I have come too far and suffered too much to take his sentence. I wait for Mr Dalhousie.

Do I regret stabbing my uncle? Yes, bitterly. But only for the trouble it has caused me and the fact that a blade now awaits my neck. He deserved what he got and I know this, because every time I think of him my blood boils.

# Chapter Fifty-Nine

# VIOLET

*Bell's Close, Edinburgh*
*October 1679*

I drag myself off the bed and into a red gown, then into the parlour. I need to get this afternoon over and done with, so I can get back to my own company and carry on with my thinking. Trying to make sense of it all.

I know, I know. I should not have goaded her into stabbing him. It is the worst thing I have ever done. It was revenge for the whipping. I cannot deny it. And who knows what Lord James would have done with me, when he realized I had taken that sword pin? He could have thrown me out onto the streets or had me removed by the constables, or put me on the repentance stool or just kept me as his whore, but treated me worse.

I seized an opportunity. I had to make a choice, without having the time to consider it, and that was the choice I took. And look at what a coward I am myself with a weapon, for I could not avenge poor Ginger's murder, could I? Despite my tall tales and my bravado, Lady Christian is a far more coura-geous woman than I. Who would have thought, from the peely-wally look of her and all those ribbons and ruffles?

And now look what I have done to her.

But she would have done the same to me.

*

In the parlour I stop dead in my tracks.

Who should be standing warming her arse by the fire? Oriana herself. Except gone is her maid's wool skirt and in its place is a yellow silk dress.

We stand, surveying each other. She looks ashamed. I don't know what I look like.

'There was nowhere else for me to go,' she says. 'And you did say to come here, if I was in a fix.'

So this is one of the new girls Mrs Fiddes talked of. I laugh. I cannot help it. 'A fix?' I cry. 'You bolted from that stabbing faster than I have seen anyone run. Left me to try and save the poor bastard's life – not that I could.'

'You should have bolted too,' she says. 'And the lady.'

She's right. We should have.

'You were lucky the lady did not drag your name through this trial,' I say.

'And what use would that have done her?' Oriana says. 'The last thing she needed was me as a witness, for I saw it all. Easier to try to blame you. She thought she would get away with that. The gents who come into this parlour have been entertaining us with the tales from the broadsides.'

'You were listening to check whether your name would be mentioned,' I say.

She shrugs. 'And you? Why did you not mention me?' She looks just as translucent in this room as she was in that turret. I wonder whether many gents fancy her.

'You remind me of someone,' I say. 'Another girl from this very parlour who I could not protect and who ended up murdered by a customer. When you bolted away that day, his purse in your hands, I knew I had to give you a chance. Otherwise you might have been accused yourself.'

'Well, that may be true. Or maybe you were scared I would say you told Lady Christian to kill him,' she says.

'Oh, but I did not really mean that,' I say.

'Oh, but I think you did,' Oriana says.

Yes. In the moment, I did. But who can honestly say they have never felt the red rage? And I will not dwell on it, for what is done is done and the way Lady Christian attacked him was more than just defence.

'Well, after all the meals I brought you and the piss pots I emptied, it was the least you could do,' she adds.

Oh, that girl's language has soured since she fell from grace.

'I am grateful to you for looking after me when I had my abortion,' I tell her, for I had not thanked her at the time, and she had kept her eye on me through those sorry days.

Oriana does not meet my gaze. 'You were not the first. I told you that.'

And that is when I realize.

'You had used the herbalist yourself, hadn't you? That is how you knew what to do and is why you did not judge me. The laird made you pregnant too.'

She says nothing. But she does not deny it.

And that is where some of her own fury came from, isn't it? Forced to go against God's will in order to avoid having a bairn that would see her jobless. I am struck by the power of it. Fury. Revenge. For look at the trouble it can wreak.

I am lucky that neither Oriana nor Lady Christian saw what the laird saw that day under the sycamore tree. The sword pin in my petticoats. I am lucky that it was too small to be noticed from where they were standing, and that they did not hear the words he whispered in my ear when he saw it. But it makes me fearfully uneasy that Mrs Fiddes has it in her possession and has no desire to hand it back to me.

I have one more question for Oriana. I will ask her later.

'Come on, girls,' bustles Mrs Fiddes, walking in and nudging Oriana from the warm spot at the fire. 'My arse is numb from that court bench. It is almost time for the show. You can save getting acquainted till afterwards.'

And some show we put on for those gents. Six of them in total that afternoon, entertained by cups of tea and marzipans and Mrs Fiddes's girls. Flora and her flogger. Oriana who, I learn, can contort herself backwards. But mostly me, for a star-turn I truly am now, there's no disputing the fact. The most infamous girl in all of Edinburgh town.

I do not stop to think of the lost bairns and the bloodshed and the lives ruined, for what good does that do?

On Saturday it is more of the same.

On Sunday morning I wake to the news that Lady Christian has escaped.

## *THE CALEDONIA BROADSIDE*

### EDINBURGH, 5th October

### SPECIAL EDITION

Under constant guard, just how did Edinburgh's most infamous murderess manage to flee? She is slender, but not slender enough to have slipped through the Tolbooth's bars. She must have had some help. The speculation in the coffee houses is that this renowned seductress used her feminine wiles to obtain this help! The speculation in the oyster bars, where the tongues are even looser, is that she will no doubt have thoroughly enjoyed deploying her feminine wiles. No doubt at all!

# Chapter Sixty

# VIOLET

*Bell's Close, Edinburgh*
*October 1679*

The broadsides are full of her escape. The gents read the story to me in the parlour.

Mrs Fiddes's house is also mentioned. A report about the best pleasure palace in Scotland, to rival those of London. With women stripped to their bodices and bold Scotsmen going in and out of its rooms at all hours, with notorious ladies such as Fiery Flora, known for her insatiable appetites, and Holy Oriana, who will dress as a nun if you wish. But none to top Mistress Violetta, former whore of a murdered laird, who will whet your whistle with her tawdry tale of blades and blood under sycamore trees.

Oh God, it is an awful time. My heart thumps so hard I think it must be in tune with the hooves of the horse the lady is galloping on. Oriana is no better. We glide past each other in our jewel-coloured dresses, our eyes meeting over wigged heads and purses of coin, each hoping for news. She slips down to the coffee house each hour, to see if news of the lady has been posted. Sightings. Speculation. She comes back and shrugs in her nonchalant way. If she says, *I don't know* one more time, I will slap her.

I cannot eat.

I cannot sleep.

I cannot get near Mrs Fiddes's chamber to hunt for that sword pin, for she keeps the door locked day and night.

I hope Christian is on a ship. I lie in the small hours, before the poultry market squawks into life. If I screw up my eyelids and put my fingers in my ears, perhaps I can feel the waves beneath her.

Oh, Violet Blyth, go to sleep and stop blethering shite to yourself. It will do you no good if you have not slept a wink.


The knock at the door becomes as fearful to my ears as a death-rattle, so it is with no joy that I answer it one Monday morning, dreading another customer.

Instead a smartly dressed gent stands looking as disgusted with me as I feel with myself. His nose wrinkles at the sour piss that steams off the sides of the close where the gents relieve themselves outside, after they have relieved themselves inside.

'I am here with an important delivery for a Miss Violet Blyth,' he announces, with a face as sour as a trout.

Well, I tell him that is me and bring him to the parlour, into which he drags himself reluctantly.

'Miss Blyth,' he says, 'I hereby reunite you with your box of belongings retrieved from Corstorphine Castle.'

He hands me the parcel. I had thought I would never see it again. I open it straight away, for I do not trust anyone not to have poked and pilfered. I am overjoyed to see it contains all my bits and bobs from Ma and Da. And the bairn's bonnet. Dear wee sister, I crave the sweet, milky innocence of you. A sob heaves from my throat. I feel my body start to buckle, but I catch myself just in time.

The gent coughs to get my attention. 'I also hereby present you,' he says in a voice that sounds like he has plums in his gob, 'monies owed to you from your time working as a maid with Laird Forrester, which has all now been accounted and settled.' He hands me a brown parcel.

He could have slapped me in the face with an old shoe and I would be less stunned.

'Monies owed?' I am agog at this trussed parcel, for I had truly come to the conclusion that I would never see those wages he promised that he was putting aside for me. The girls gather at the door, come to see the latest commotion, but I shut it in their faces as I quickly realize this is no business of anyone else's.

'Correct – he was most fastidious in his accounting, if a little over-generous in the wages he was paying you.' He frowns, producing a piece of parchment and a quill from a black leather case. 'Now sign for it here, if you will. Sign with an X, for that will do if you cannot write your name.'

I bid the man goodbye. There is no man I have ever seen happier to take his leave of Mrs Fiddes's apartments than this one, leaving me – when I count out the money – a decent pile of pounds Scots.

Mrs Fiddes does not try to take a cut of it.

'It is blood-money,' she says, 'with a streak of bad luck running through it. Besides, we are doing well these days.'

I count it and hide it away.

That night is another busy one and, after it goes quiet, some of us sit up a while with wine and speculation about where the lady has run off to and whether she will ever get the chop. I sit beside Oriana, who gets good and pissed, her eyes half closing as she listens to Flora sing a bawdy ditty.

'Oriana,' I say. 'There is something I have wondered.'

'What now?' she slurs.

'When I was in the turret and you were coming and going, did you leave the door open on purpose?'

She laughs. Her lips are red from wine. She should not drink, it does not go down well.

'Maybe,' she says. 'Once or twice, if I thought the laird wouldn't be coming to you. Just to see what trouble you might cause.'

'Because you were too scared to cause trouble of your own,' I muse.

She does not reply. Simply laughs again and sips her wine.

When dawn comes and we traipse off to our beds, I lie awake a while, looking through my box of precious things and listening to the cockerels. That is a sound I do not like. The mournful squawk of it. Always too early; the sign of another miserable day. I've always lived on Bell's Close, but when I lived with Ma and Da, our room was on the other side.

I have already said I was born the wrong way round, right foot first, scaring the midwife half to death, but I came out all right and that has been the story of my life. The plagues had long gone by then, but there were other ills brought by these putrid miasmas that would see a whole tenement stair of folks off in the night. They coughed, did Ma and Da. They hacked through the winters, their breath silver puffs in the damp air. I had a doll made of rags that I clutched to my chin, for Ma had taught me softness and gentleness in the way she held me and the bairn.

Oh, Ma, if you could see me now. The sketch of them that the tattie-seller did for their wedding day is so thin it could disappear to nothing but dust. But it is like them. The sharp edge of her jaw and the sticky-out ears I got from her. The ridge of his eyebrows. Two broad grins.

I remember things from those days like dark oil paintings or half-sketches where the details are missing, so you find yourself trying to make them out. A room in a close, up big stone steps. Once I might have tripped and clattered down them, for I remember going knock, knock, bang, bang and the world upside down, and being scooped up and Ma screaming. A fire in the corner that terrified me, for it reeked and bellowed like a dragon. Flat cakes cooked to black. I don't really remember Da. Just the scuff of a beard, so there must have been kisses and closeness.

I remember lost babies. My sister and maybe some before her, for I remember Ma delivering more than once. The howls and the huddles of women. And not being allowed near her. I remember the cough, the great hacking cough that took Da first, then the bairn and then Ma.

It never got its grippy fingers round my throat, and the neebours said I must have some magic about me; and one of them, a big man with red hair, waited till Ma's body was taken off. Then he arrived at the door with his own wife and bairns and took my hand, and walked me down the road to the chapel where the orphans are dumped. I still feel his palm, coarse and pulling at my own hand, slowly but surely.

I fold everything back into the box, ever so careful.

The doll is long gone, but that soft side of me must still be there somewhere.

They buried Ma and Da and the bairn all together up at the Burgh Muir, where they put all the paupers in a big pit. I don't know where precisely, for not a stone marks their grave. It was warmer in the chapel than it had ever been at home. Warm with the crawling stink of unwashed bairns, bawling and red-faced and toothless. I could not stand to look at them, for every time I did, I saw my own dead sister. When I got too big, they cast me out, for I was able-bodied and not in need of chapel funds. Time to find work and lodgings, they said.

I would walk the length of Edinburgh town. Looking in the windows of the goldsmith's and peering at the feathered hats for sale in the Luckenbooths. Watching ladies and gents open purses brimming with coins. Wondering how God had made a world where there were rich and poor, for it never seemed right. I tried for work, asking fleshers and vegetable-sellers if they needed a hand, for I was good at shouting for customers and watching for thieves, but no one wanted me. Turns out I was trying to sell the wrong skill.

Where is Lady Christian? Is she stowed away tight on a sailing ship, like they say? Whispering curses of me to the mermaids and the sea monsters? Is she hiding at the bottom of Bell's Close, getting ready to take her revenge on me too? Will I ever have a sound night's sleep again, with her alive or dead?

## THE CALEDONIA BROADSIDE

### EDINBURGH, 6th October

The reward for the return of Christian Nimmo is now DOUBLED to TWO HUNDRED POUNDS SCOTS. There have been several potential sightings of the Murderess, at Leith Port, at Musselburgh, on the road north to the Highlands and even in the North of England. She may be in disguise.

# Chapter Sixty-One

# CHRISTIAN

*England*
*October 1679*

I have definitely slept, but it feels as though I have simply slipped from hour to hour. Until this escape, I had never slept under the stars. I had not realized how the cold air would settle in my chest and keep me halfway between waking and dreaming. William has kept my skin warm. Our breath has mingled. He has heard my story. All of it. And he has not left me.

He opens his eyes and looks at me.

'How much are you being paid for this?' It bursts out. 'I'm sorry, it is not my business.'

'Enough for a new life,' he says.

'We could meet in France,' I say. That bursts out too.

'We could,' he says. 'But first we have to get you there safely.' We hold hands for one long moment, perhaps as long as half a minute, his hand rough and warm and mine soft and warm.

'I might be with child,' I admit. 'With no mother or sister to assist me.'

'Then we will have our hands full,' he whispers. 'Why did you not tell the sheriff this? You could have been spared until the baby was weaned.'

'I did not realize,' I tell him. 'And my advocate did not ask.'

'Your advocate is a fool. Come. I will wash at the river and then we should be on our way,' William says. He lets go of my hand and I watch him get up and walk down to the river, disappearing behind the trees on its bank.

And then a stirring in the woodlands, which starts with a crackle of branches and ends with the whinnying of our horses, alerts me. We are no longer alone.


They rip me from the ground like a weed. They hoist me onto the back of a horse. They tie me with ropes, and the ties sear into my wrists. There are several of them. I don't know how many. They shout and slap. Their nails catch me and their boots thud at me; there will be so many scratches and bruises. They are too many, and too strong and too furious, to fight. They call me a murdering whore who fucked my own uncle. They laugh. The sound caws and echoes between the trees. I don't know what has happened to William. Whether they have found him too or whether he had enough time to escape. They tell me the Maiden is waiting for me. I hope William is running for his life and that he is not captured and following in my wake.

I am used to the threat of my own death. Now I carry the threat of William's death all the way back to Edinburgh. The ropes gnaw. My wrists bleed. I pray that my womb does not.


I am back in my Tolbooth cell as though I had never left it. They had not even tidied it or emptied the chamber pot. The men were given two hundred pounds Scots for me. They were rogues who had taken the chance that I was headed for England and hunted me down for the bounty. I sit on my hay bale, a prize at a country fair. There is no word on William. I trust he is long gone. I hope he is on his way to France.

There is a raw feeling of sickness at the back of my throat that does not go away. Sometimes I retch. I see stars when I stand up.

It is Tuesday afternoon. I am supposed to be dead. I am on borrowed time and the only thing I have done since my return is demand a physician.

The first person I ask is the new guard. The one who let me escape has vanished. I hope they find him and punish him well. I hope it hurts him, whatever they do.

I never used to think like this.

'A physician?' the new guard says. He has teeth that are too big for his mouth and lips that gather spittle at the corners.

'Immediately,' I say.

Then to Mr Dalhousie, who comes to see me later that day. 'It is vital,' I tell him. 'I have not bled for two months.'

He flinches so many times at the words in that sentence that I think he might fall into a convulsive fit.

'I will pass the message on, my lady, but I am afraid I am here with the news that your new execution date is two days from now,' he says. 'They will not waste any time, now that you have shown you are prone to escaping.'

The feeling of nausea gathers in my throat.

'Then bring the physician today,' I rasp, swallowing it down. 'Would you see an unborn child sacrificed?' He bolts, promising he will seek *urgent assistance*. Perhaps we can raise a petition to the court. I scratch lines in the cell walls with my fingernails. I watch the beggars sleep under blankets on the high street below and wish I could swap lives with them. The man from *The Caledonia Broadside* has disappeared. Perhaps he is at his writing desk.

Reverend Raeburn floats back like an apparition and tries to persuade me to pray with him.

'The Lord forgives you for your desperate escape attempt,' he says.

I can barely focus on him. I have not eaten.

'I think I am with child,' I say. 'The Lord would not want this child harmed. I pray you carry out your duty. He is watching over this child.'

The good reverend cannot disappear fast enough, whipping away down the steps, the tail of his robes descending after him. 'I will seek advice immediately,' he says. 'Continue in your prayers.'

I do. I pray for the first time in a long time.

*Dear Lord, I pray I am with child.*


It is a Dr Pringle who comes, black-hatted and bespectacled, with a habit of saying *hum* between sentences and into silences. He tells me that he is, *hum*, an eminent physician with expertise in the *fairer sex*. He takes my pulse and stands staring at me whilst his fingers press my wrist. I wonder if he is looking for signs of pregnancy in my face or if he is trying to peer into my soul, to see what the Devil looks like.

I have not seen my face since the morning of the Lammas Fair. I wonder if I would recognize myself. I wonder if I am pregnant.

'You last bled two months ago. Do you have any nausea?' I can hear the tick of his fine gold watch.

'Constant,' I say. 'I feel I might faint at any minute.'

'That might be the terror,' he says. 'Regardless of the, *hum*, outcome of these tests, you should eat,' he goes on. 'And can you provide me with a sample?'

I am perplexed. A sample of what? Then he produces a small glass flask and hands it to me, turning his back.

I lift my skirts and, after some moments of trying, I produce a paltry offering of my own piss. It trickles over my hands. The side of the flask is wet with it. Dr Pringle inspects the dark amber liquid, holding it up to the window.

'You are dehydrated,' he says. 'And perhaps there is a hue to the urine that suggests pregnancy. But it's difficult to tell, because your nerves are compromised by your current situation.'

I feel opened up and inspected.

'And now to the physical assessment,' he says. 'With apologies, my lady, but it is the best way to ascertain your situation.'

He instructs me to lie down on the hay bale, facing the window. He lifts my skirts. I am naked from the waist down. I close my eyes and wish it all over. What is he looking for? Are there signs? I open my eyes again. He spends a long while regarding my private parts. He is intent on his task. I lie there; I am nothing any longer, no more than a piece of meat. Then I feel his hands. They land on my belly, firm and cold and entitled, and work their way down.

By the time Dr Pringle is finished with his proddings and pokings the sun is dipping below the high-street tenement tops, casting darkness and cold into the room, and I am as wrung out as a dishrag. I may or may not be with child; it is difficult to be absolutely sure at such an early stage, before the quickening, but it would be too high a risk of infanticide to have me executed immediately and he will support a bill to the Privy Council asking for a month's stay of execution.

'For it is not the fault of the unborn child,' he says. 'Should one exist.'

Afterwards he will return and examine me again to see if I have progressed to a more visible pregnancy. Or not. Sometimes the menses can disappear if a woman is under duress, or undernourished.

He utters this, *hum, hum*, as I return my skirts to their rightful place and he wipes his hands with a white kerchief. He looks at his watch, which has a floral engraving on its lid. Then he snaps it shut.

'Who is the father of the child?' he asks. 'Or don't you know?'

He does not wait for an answer, but puts his watch in his pocket. He takes the flask of my piss and pours it into the chamber pot, drying the flask with a kerchief and wrapping it, before putting it carefully into his bag.

## THE CALEDONIA BROADSIDE

### EDINBURGH, 10th October

The Privy Council of Scotland has accepted a request for a stay of the execution of Christian Nimmo, 'In order to determine she is with child, in which case she will remain in custody until after the child is weaned and executed shortly thereafter.'

And who is the father of this unfortunate child? Husband or uncle? Or are there any more gentlemen this hot-blooded young lady has also seduced?

# Chapter Sixty-Two

# VIOLET

*Edinburgh*
*October 1679*

She is all the talk of the oyster bars again. I cannot go to the water fountain without hearing about it. I cannot stroll the Luckenbooths without seeing the seller wifies knitting bonnets for the unborn soul. Her likeness is splashed on every coffee-shop wall. I'll wager she is no more pregnant than the withered Mrs Fiddes could ever be.

Canny, though. I will give her that.

I snort at the speculation over who the father might be. Her husband would not touch her, the laird said.

His other bairn – my bairn – was aborted into a piss pot with none of these theatrics.

I am outside the Tolbooth again. Its chimneystacks and turrets rise at the end of the Luckenbooths. I find myself here more and more. I lean against a tenement wall and look up. I know which window she is at, for I have seen her pale face peer out.

If it was me found guilty, I would have been hanged from the Mercat Cross here, like they did with the man who killed Ginger. All the men who have fucked me would have come to watch me hang, and Mrs Fiddes would have held a wake in my honour, hosted by all her best girls.

I think about knocking on the jail door. Asking to see her.

More than once I have approached it, a great wooden door that opens out onto the high street, two floors beneath the execution platform. But I stop short, pushed and bumped against by gentlemen in feathered hats and fur capes who make it their business to go in and out of these cells.

What would I ever say to her, if she even received me? *I am sorry. They made me testify against you. I am sorry I was fucking him, but I had no choice.*

For that makes me sound like I am as much a victim as she is, and despite what's happened in my sorry life, I think I have been far luckier than she has.

I try my appetite with a fresh morning roll and a jug of milk. I eat and drink, watching her cell window. The roll is soft and gluey and warm. The milk is tolerable. I wonder if she gets fresh rolls or if she is being served fruits and nuts carted up from the Leith Port ships. The high street is quiet, which means she might chance her luck for a breath of air.

I finish the roll. I finish the milk. I put the jug on the ground.

Then she appears.

She is slighter than I remember. Paler face and darker hair. She keeps still, for movement attracts attention. And that is why I shift position. I plant my feet on the ground and put my hands on my hips and tilt my face up.

She sees me. She puts her hands to the window bars. Everything between us disappears. It is just she and I.

*It is not your fault*, I whisper.

I don't know what she says in reply, if anything. Then she disappears. And so must I, for there is work to be done.

\*

I knew the moment would come when Mrs Fiddes forgot to lock her chamber door. It happens that afternoon when she is in the foulest of moods because Flora, sent for a bottle of damson tonic, comes back saying Mr Saltoun had none left on his shelves.

'And did you not think to ask him if he had any in the storeroom?' squawks Mrs Fiddes, nursing a whisky headache with a cold cloth.

'There was a terrible long queue,' says Flora, but that just makes Mrs Fiddes all the worse, for she stomps out of the door, muttering curses on lazy girls who can't do anything for themselves, saying she is quicker going herself.

The whole of the pleasure house is utterly silent for a minute or so, hardly daring to believe she is gone. Then I am at her door handle as fast as lightning and, when it clicks open, I am finally in her chamber.

A gloomier, sourer room I have never stepped into. Curtains and petticoats and stockings galore. The scent of powder and armpits and unwashed hair.

She will be like the laird. She will keep that sword pin close to where she sleeps. Trying to hold in my breath, I pick my way around discarded shoes, wig-curlers and crusted plates, to a walnut chest next to the bed. Her drawers are in chaos. I spend minute after minute pulling handle after handle, raking through papers – I see she has kept copies of *The Caledonia Broadside* – and scent-bottles and feathers and brooches.

She has hidden it good and proper.

I stop. I will not find it like this. I cast my eyes about the room. Mess everywhere. I sigh. Perhaps she wears the pin hidden in her petticoats, as I did, and then I will never find it. My eyes find a coat-stand in the corner, which ought to be piled with hats and gowns, if it were anything like the rest of the room. Instead just one item dangles from it. It is the cape she wore the day they hanged Ginger's murderer. I make my way over to it.

Tucked into its folds: the sword pin. Hiding in plain sight.


Now I am in possession of cash and valuables, and am free of Mrs Fiddes's threats. For the first time in my life. And that is how I manage, finally, to walk free that very day, into decent lodgings in the Canongate, a first-floor apartment in White Horse Close. The sword pin alone was worth enough in rent to keep me here for a year or so. And I am being offered work everywhere that gents congregate for stories and song. The oyster-house owners and the coffee-house men say they'll teach me all I need to know about shucking and brewing, if I will keep their customers entertained with my gory tale. All things considered, this is a decent ending, bearing in mind where it began.

But wait. Do not think this former whore's performance is over yet. More is yet to come.

The finale, if you will.

# Chapter Sixty-Three

# CHRISTIAN

*The Tolbooth Jail, Edinburgh*
*October 1679*

I am torn from my wretchedness by a visit from Johanna. I have not seen her since the trial, when she sat on a bench at the back of the courtroom with Mother, never taking her eyes off me and trying to soothe me with motions of prayer. The court is only a few steps from the place where we shopped for my wedding gown, hopeful as two snowdrops.

Now she is back in Edinburgh, but in its bleakest corner she is terrified. I can tell by her deathly pallor. She had come hooded, dressed like a hag, so no one would recognize her or realize she came from wealth.

Our fingers touch at the bars.

'How is my new nephew?' I am desperate for news of something happy.

'He is red-headed just like his father,' she smiles. 'And we are smitten.' Then her smile fades. 'I have come in secret,' she says breathlessly. 'Robert has forbidden me from coming here. Not because of you,' she hastens, her yellow ringlets bobbing behind the door bars. 'But because of the undesirables.'

'Perhaps I am an undesirable,' I whisper. I sound ragged. Like a crone.

'Nonsense. Look, I have brought you marzipans,' she says. 'To bring you some sweetness. They are in a bag at your door. The guard said he would give them to you.' The marzipans are wrapped in white paper.

Oh, darling Johanna. As if I were recuperating from a sickness. As if they will ever cross the threshold. 'You are my sweetness,' I say, brushing her fingers. 'You are all the joy I need.'

'And for the little one in your belly,' she says. 'The little one will enjoy the marzipans too. You might feel him kick if you eat them.'

Truthfully I feel nothing but the cold strokes of Dr Pringle's hands on my belly.

'Mother is struggling,' she whispers. 'I was not sure whether to tell you, but she is a shadow of her former self, uninterested in the baby, and I don't know what to do.'

'Of course you must tell me. I must know everything,' I say. I wish Johanna had said nothing, but this is my punishment too: to acknowledge the harm I have caused everyone. To suckle on it, in the absence of sweetness.

'She barely leaves Roseburn. She has even stopped going to kirk. The only people she will receive are me and Andrew.'

'Andrew?' I imagine him and Mother, hunched at the walnut table in the parlour, trying to take tea and unravel everything that went wrong with me. Perhaps it was the fanciful idea of the China seas. Or being the plainer sister. If only Father had still been alive, to watch over me a little more closely than anyone else could.

I wonder if Mother ever blamed herself. If she regretted using me as bait to assure her own future.

'Tell her I love her. And that I think of her all the time,' I say.

'Of course. She knows this,' Johanna says. 'And she would be here in an instant if she could.'

I think she could. There is nothing stopping my mother from visiting. It would be undignified, but it is not against the laws of the land. She managed the court. She could bring a chaperone, if she wanted to feel safe. Johanna has managed to come. Has my mother buried me already? Is that easier than facing me?

'Am I like our great-great-aunt?' I ask.

'Lady Warriston,' breathes Johanna. 'They are talking of her in the broadsides.'

I shut my eyes.

'You are nothing like her,' whispers Johanna. 'She had her husband murdered in cold blood. By a servant.'

'But they talk of her to this day,' I say. 'And that is what will happen to me. They will say murdering runs in the family. I will become notorious.'

'But they do not know you,' says Johanna. 'Don't think about what they say. Concentrate on how you will manage. What else can I bring? For you and the baby. You will need fresh milk and meat. I shall send our own physician. We shall pay for anything you need.'

Never have I felt less in need of fresh milk or meat. Whilst my sister bloomed in pregnancy, I feel nothing.

'I want something to help me at the end,' I admit. 'To dull the senses. Should it come to it.'

She flinches, but she does not try to deny that my execution still looms.

'I will see to it, my love,' Johanna says.

Her eyes are red-rimmed with grief and sleepless nights and shame. I have caused this.

'I shall make sure you do not suffer.'

'I'm afraid the gossips were right,' I say. 'But Andrew was no husband to me.'

'But of all people, Uncle James?' She begins to cry. 'After the way he stalked you when we were girls?'

I remove my hands from my sister's.

'You knew,' I say. 'You and Mother both knew and did nothing.'


Johanna takes diligent care of me from the safe distance of her impeccable home. I receive a bottle of milk each morning and meat twice a week. I am sent fresh hay bales, to replace the sour ones, and blankets. A writing set and thick stockings. I wrap myself in everything and yet I am always cold. The chill is inside me now. It has rained on and off for days, and the damp makes it worse. I feel that I will never be warm or dry.

The days form a torturous routine. I usually receive any visitors in the morning – either Mr Dalhousie, checking on me on behalf of Mother and Andrew, or Johanna's physician, taking my pulse and fretting that the air around me is too foul for a healthy pregnancy; and sometimes the minister, Reverend Raeburn, his hands pressed together at his lips.

Reverend Brodie of Corstorphine has not dared visit. Perhaps he thinks I will cast curses on him or seduce him. Perhaps he is too busy with his branks and his repentance stool and telling tales of me to his congregation. I sometimes wonder what happened when he took Violet Blyth aside that day, to take her witness account from her, and what she did to ensure that she was never accused.

Not that it matters now.

Often there are unsolicited visitors. Men who have read the case in the broadsides, and send requests via the guard, see me. A woman claiming to have a message from James from beyond the grave. A dressmaker wishing to gown me for the Maiden, for *Mary, Queen of Scots wore a dark-crimson petticoat to her chopping block, the colour of martyrdom, and it was all they talked about for years.* A childless couple wishing to adopt the baby, for even the news of my possible pregnancy has made it into the printed rags that are pasted on the coffee-house walls.

I reject them all.

Then I see Violet, standing bold as brass on the corner opposite my window. She is eating food in the street.

I gasp, putting my hands on the bars to steady myself. She will not dare come any further, surely?

I wonder, briefly, if I should spit at her through the bars, like the other criminals in this hellhole do. Screech, *How dare you come here? How dare you fuck my lover?* Cause another commotion, when all she ever did was what I did, which was do as we were told.

It was not her fault. So I duck away and leave her there. Her fate is not my concern.

In the afternoons I write to Johanna, Mother and Andrew and sometimes there are letters in return, all via Mr Dalhousie. Mother telling me to take care of myself. Johanna with news of baby Robert's napping and fussing and smiles. Nothing from my husband.

Perhaps he is lying low, I tell myself. Distancing himself from me. The constables interrogated me about my escape. I said I had organized it all myself. Planned it in advance of the verdict, and bribed the guard for contacts to aid me. I would never have betrayed my husband. But Andrew will be fearful he might be found out. I know, from his silence, not to ask for his help again. I wonder if he will eventually go to sea one day and never return.

It's a distraction, of course. Thinking of Andrew and the rest of them whilst I wait for nature to take its course in my womb.

I still think of William. I hope he can feel the warm rays of a French afternoon on his head and see lavender fields. I hope he has not forgotten me.

The Maiden has been silent since I returned. They have no need for it yet. There have been hangings of men who were common criminals and not of high enough standing for the privilege of an execution machine.

Painless, they say. But how can it be?

*Regardless, I am glad James is dead.*

I jump at my own thoughts.

But I am glad. I realize this as a gust of wind snaps at the window bars. Glad that his loud boots no longer stamp their way into rooms, that no more gifts or letters will come. Glad that he no longer has the power to summon me to him or put his hands on me, in passion or in anger.

I am free of him, even if freedom is another hell.

I doze. The milk helps me rest in fitful spells. The rain drips. Day slips into night. I twitch and jerk in my sleep. My hands reach for my belly and I wonder if something is growing there, and if I should whisper to it. In the grey hours I give up on sleep and drag myself to the window, blanket-wrapped and shuddering, to watch the sun rise. I have the urge to urinate, but I hold onto it as the sun comes, triumphant, over the tenement tops.

This will be my last view if they execute me.

I get the urgency to shit and piss; it comes from me in waves of terror. Johanna has sent rags scented with rosewater and I can wipe myself clean. Afterwards I hug my knees to my belly on the hay bale. I feel more pain ride its way through me and wonder if the milk was on the turn.

Then I recognize the familiar heaviness in my belly. The top of my legs cramp. I lift my skirts and put my hand to my private parts. When I look, there is blood.

# Chapter Sixty-Four

# CHRISTIAN

*The Tolbooth Jail, Edinburgh*
*November 1679*

I hide the blood.

I wipe it on hay, then put the hay at the bottom of the bale. I put kerchiefs under my skirts, and hide them under the hay bale when they become soiled.

I am not sure if it is menses or a miscarriage, but the bleeding is heavy and my insides ache. I am careful to stay in the shadows when food is brought, and I remain lying down as much as I can, because standing up or pacing around makes it worse.

And I manage. I manage for two days, and I am beginning to think I might get away with it, if Dr Pringle stays away long enough. Perhaps that will give me a month's grace.

It has rained all week. A fog hangs over the tenements that stink of the foul bottom of the Nor Loch: of dead drunks and animal carcasses, and all the shit that runs down the closes.

There is a constant drip of rain at the window.

It seeps into my thoughts. I find myself waiting for the next drop in the pauses.

How much more of this? Another miserable month as winter grips and men are hanged on my doorstep, and frost turns the Maiden silver and my bones ache, and I shit myself in fear and live in my own stink. How long before the new guard licks his lips at me as the old one did? Or slips his key into the lock and lets someone bad in? How long before Robert Gregor sees the bills Johanna is racking up and says, *Meat once a week only and apples, not candied fruits. I know she is your sister, but think of what she did.*

Then Dr Pringle returns.

At the sight of his black hat I know the only thing I can do is admit that I bleed, for what would be the point in suffering the indignity of having his cold fingers seeking me out? Watching him wipe my womb blood onto his pristine white kerchief and shaking his head sombrely? I have had enough of men's fingers and stares and pushing and shoving and leering.

I have had enough of the stink of shit and the fear of the blade. I need it all to be over. I don't even wait for him to come into the cell.

'My menses came this morning,' I say.

He looks shocked. 'Ah, *hum*, are you sure?' He remains at the door, undecided about whether he should now proceed into the room. The guard is behind him, listening.

'I know my own blood, Dr Pringle,' I say. Then I turn from him and face the window. I do not want to see the uncomfortable look on his face as he bids me goodbye.

'I must inform the Privy Council,' he mutters.

'Tell them I want it done as soon as possible,' I say. 'The waiting is torture enough.'

'Indeed, madam. I will tell them your nerves will not cope with a long wait.'

*Madam*. He does not even call me 'my lady'.

*

Things move swiftly. A flurry of bills and letters via Mr Dalhousie. He excels at administration. He has segments within his portable writing box for everything. He is at his most comfortable seeking out a particular parchment, knowing where it is and declaring, *Ah!* I wonder if, afterwards, he will write a pamphlet on my case, or submit it to a journal.

'My goodness, I have not even considered such a thing.' I realize, at his look of embarrassment, that I have uttered my last thoughts out loud.

I never used to be like this. I am losing control.

'Perhaps you ought,' I say. 'But don't portray me as anything other than composed. Don't tell them I was weak.'

'You have never been weak,' he says, stopping to survey me. 'You have shown a fortitude many men could not manage.'

'Mr Dalhousie,' I say. 'If I had confessed the murder at the outset, and explained that my uncle had tried to seduce me since I was girl and had then been violent towards me during our love affair, do you think I might have been spared?'

My advocate stares at me. His fingers float above his writing box, as if seeking out a file with an answer to this question.

'Spared on what grounds?' he whispers.

'On some kind of leniency,' I say. 'For he was most cruel indeed.'

'But did you murder him?' Mr Dalhousie's eyes are hard.

'I did,' I say. 'But I was most provoked.'

'It is irrelevant how provoked you were. Murder is murder,' he says. 'You carried a sword about your skirts, did you not? Ladies do not carry swords about their skirts for no reason. And there were many, many stab wounds in your uncle's body. That was no self-defence. It was a frenzied attack.'

He is just like all of them. All the men in this world. For it is their world.

'I must see my husband,' I say. 'Please ask him again.'

Mr Dalhousie nods. 'Mr Nimmo is getting through the days,' he says. 'Much as you are. I feel that he does want to see you, but he is fearful of the emotions it will reignite.'

'We need to say our goodbyes. Tell him this will be his last opportunity. And say the same to my mother.'

'Your mother,' he says, 'I fear she will not listen. She ails. She is all but cast out by her circle and is preoccupied with thoughts of her own plight. She fears that if she is seen visiting you, then she will be seen as sympathetic. She fears being removed from Roseburn unless the matter is seen to be settled.' Mr Dalhousie's head disappears into his piles of papers. He gasps on. 'Ah,' he pronounces, 'I knew I had put it at the front.' He hands over the parchment:

*To: Christian Nimmo*

*This letter is to inform you that the date of your execution will be 12th November 1679 at forty-five minutes past the hour of seven in the morning (sunrise).*

*You will be taken from your cell at half past seven and you are permitted one minister of the Kirk to accompany you.*

*Following the execution, your remains will be handed to your family. You have been spared the posthumous punishment of having your head displayed on a spike at the Mercat Cross, as it is considered that would draw too much of an unfavourable crowd.*

> *Privy Council of Scotland, on behalf*
> *of King Charles the Second,*
> *by the Grace of God, King of England,*
> *Scotland, France and Ireland*

Today is 9th November. I have three more days.

*

Mr Dalhousie leaves. The guard returns. 'There is a girl come, by name of Oriana,' he says.

I had wondered if this would happen.

I nod my head. I tell him I will see her.

She stands a few feet back from the door. She wears dull paste jewels around her neck. Her hair falls in greasy ringlets. She is rouged. Her cleavage peeps white and marbled over a yellow dress. I would hardly recognize her, but I can tell what has become of her.

'I have come to pay my respects,' she says.

'I am not dead yet,' I tell her.

'I know you did not mean to stab me that day. I should never have gone back to the castle. I have thought of nothing since.' The bottom of her dress is dark with dirt.

'Look what has become of you,' I tell her. 'You always seemed so meek and well mannered.'

'I blame him for all of it,' she says, the gleam of tears at her lashes. 'He forced me. My family had the highest of hopes when I got work at the castle. I was just turned fourteen and I knew how to wash and wring bed sheets and how to scrub a floor.'

She weeps fully now, but it is not self-pity, I can tell.

'I was such a good maid. Never late out of bed, always said my prayers at night. Then one morning when Lady Lillias was still in bed, as he finished his eggs, the laird said to meet him in the storeroom near the kitchen.'

I close my eyes. I do not need to hear more, for I know how it would have gone.

'He told me I was quite beautiful,' she whispers. 'Quite beautiful. And not to believe everything in the Bible, for some of it is at odds with modern life; and that if I did him favours, he would pay me extra. And he did.'

'He told me I was beautiful too,' I say. 'When even my own husband could not bear the sight of me.'

'Oh, but why ever could your husband not bear you?' Oriana looks astounded. 'At Corstorphine Castle you were radiant. I would wait on you and admire your grace and your poise, and in my own chamber I would practise holding myself as you do – so effortless.'

I am speechless.

'Please do not think you are ever anything other than beautiful,' she says. 'Even now you shine.'

I know it is a trifle. And matters little now. But a small part of me is relieved to hear that in some sense I was beautiful, and it was not just words.

'He's ruined you, as he has ruined us all. But at least you can do me one favour,' I say. 'Make the very most of your life.'

'I will,' Oriana vows, looking more serious than I have ever seen anyone.

But I doubt she will. What chance does she have?

I realize that although I was angry about James turning to other women for sex, that is not the worst of it. It was the fact that he turned to these women despite all I did for him. I was there for him at his whim. I listened to him. I forgave him when he hurt me. I wore the dresses he bought me. I would have left my husband and endured shame, for him.

Johanna comes. She is shrouded in a long scarf. We touch hands at the cell door.

'I wish I could hold you, Sister,' she says.

'You have done so much for me,' I say. 'Your parcels kept me feeling alive.'

'I am sorry Mother has not come,' she says. 'I think it

would destroy her. She was mocked in the broadsides, and
she refuses even to attend kirk. But she has written you
another letter.' Johanna hands it to me. I will read it later
when I am alone.

'Mother is in limbo,' I say. 'Things will get better for her
once I am gone. People will feel sympathy for her.'

I cannot believe I am talking about myself like this.

Johanna strokes my fingers. 'I think constantly about what
James was like with you. I blamed you. I thought you were
attracting him. I even wondered why he favoured you.'

'He was the only man who did,' I say.

'Nonsense,' she says. 'Andrew was besotted. No, really, he
was, in his own way. Remember all the pleasure trips he took
you and Mother on. And the oranges. He just could not love
you physically.'

'James saw my weaknesses,' I whisper.

'He did,' my sister says. 'And now are we going to waste our
hours talking of that devil or shall we walk our minds through
the garden at Roseburn again? Do you remember it in winter?
When we would slip on the paths and skate on the pond?'

'And Fiona would make chocolate,' I say, closing my eyes.
'But keep it secret from Mother and Father.'

'In case we got excitable,' she says. 'They were terrified of
that.'

'That's why we were never allowed coffee,' I say, opening
my eyes again, to see as much of my sister as I can. 'They
thought it would make us misbehave.'

'Do you know what I have realized?' Johanna's face is full
of light now. 'This will shock you, Sister. It is the most absolute hoot.'

'Tell me?' I am ready to be shocked. I am ready to be
distracted.

'It's about the marriage manual. Mother knew we were reading it! And she put it on the library shelf *deliberately*!'

'Oh no!' I say. 'She knew! Oh, she must have been very familiar with it herself.'

'She told me after I got with child. She said she was happy I had found out how it all works, and that she had left instructions for us because it was not a topic she would ever discuss.'

'Oh Lord,' I say, remembering looking at the illustrations by candlelight. The men clambering aboard the women. The legs and arms everywhere. I laugh, I cannot help it. Johanna laughs too. 'I wonder if Father obtained it for her?'

'Oh, *Sister*,' Johanna shrieks. 'Do not make me think of them poring over it together. Copying the pictures.'

We laugh. We are light. We are sisters. We are back at Roseburn. We remain there, touching hands and tasting chocolate and picking roses until night falls and Johanna must take her leave.


Eventually Andrew visits again. I had assumed he would not. Johanna had said she doubted it.

When I see him, my heart soars with happiness, then sinks with grief.

'I was going to write you a final letter,' I say, trying not to let him see the tears in my eyes. 'In case you did not come.'

'We could not part without saying farewell properly,' he says. 'It would not be decent.'

Andrew. So decent. Like his good wines and best quills and excellent table manners. To be forced to discuss the details of our marriage in court must have shamed him to his very core.

'Please continue to look after Mother,' I plead. I know he will, but I need to say it.

'She will want for nothing,' he says. 'She will remain comfortably at Roseburn House for the rest of her days. I will settle any bills.'

'You are a good man,' I say.

'I will be busy. There's much trading. I will be away even more. You would have been very unhappy,' he says. 'I should not have asked you to be my wife. I am not suited to marriage.'

'Perhaps you will find someone, one day,' I say.

I can tell he dislikes this turn. He chews on his lip and clears his throat.

'I am sorry I could not help you to escape,' he whispers. 'I could not have risked a second attempt.'

I raise my hand. 'It was never your responsibility,' I say.

He fixes on me. 'You were mine. And I let you down. I will not let your mother down.'

'I have something else I need you to do.' I have dreaded this request. 'When it is done – when I am dead – ask for my body as soon as possible. Do not let it remain in the custody of the men here.'

Andrew looks appalled. Realization dawns on his face.

'Have you had an ordeal in here? Has anyone taken advantage?'

'Nothing I have not been able to cope with,' I say. 'But you must not let them defile my body, Husband, for there are men that would.'

He looks sorry for me now, and that is the first time I have seen pity on his face. I hate the look – the taut, searching bewilderment of it.

'I am at peace with it,' I say.

He turns away and rummages at his feet. 'I have something for you,' he says. 'It is up to you what you do with it.' He holds up a large parcel. 'I will leave it at the door for you. I hope it gives you some dignity.'

And then we say our goodbyes, as though we were two strangers who had been sitting next to each other in a coffee house. We depart with a nod and an embarrassed smile. And then Andrew is gone, leaving no scent or last words, as though our marriage had never existed.

## THE CALEDONIA BROADSIDE

### EDINBURGH, 10th November

To All Gentlemen: A Warning!

A wife is a great responsibility, for women are not capable of making sensible decisions, being ruled by their fragile emotions and humours. The burden, then, comes to the husband, to ensure that his wife is well fed, but not overly fed. That she is well rested, but not allowed to laze. That she is brought to social occasions, but not overly indulged. That she is kept obedient, but entertaining enough so that she does not bore. The balance is fine. The journey treacherous. If your friends fail in their endeavours, do not judge them harshly, for there but for the grace of God go you.

## Chapter Sixty-Five

# VIOLET

*Edinburgh*
*November 1679*

First, let me show you around my new hoose. Forgive these two big dogs lolling by the fire. Strays they were, sniffing for scraps at the bottom of the stairwell. Well, was I not sorely reminded of how I once did that, so I coaxed them up the stairs and into my apartment. An indulgence, I know. But I like the company, and I am not in the mood to find myself a husband. I think I never will be, for my heart has been filled with too much hope and too much sorrow. What sort of wife would I make for a decent gent who wants to live in the countryside and keep chickens and go on carriage rides? I have seen too many horrors. I would sit forlorn and stare at the fireplace and eventually he would slip from me to the nearest whorehouse, and though the irony would not be lost on me, I would feel most betrayed.

I have a fine bedchamber, all done up in red curtains, and a window that looks out onto the close. And I am never cold, for I have blankets galore that I scent with Carmelite water all the way from France.

Next is the parlour, with a gold-framed picture of my own good self on the wall, painted by one of the court artists. All purple-gowned and skittish. Cost me a few pennies, but I was damned if he was going to sell it to some filthy gent wanting to pleasure his prick at my image every morning. Ho, no! Gone are those days.

I am not the only one of Mrs Fiddes's girls to have retired. Oriana lives with me too, rent-free, for she has taken a job in an alehouse and sends her wages home each week. Well, I could hardly charge her rent when she took the blame for stealing that sword pin, could I? Not that she knows where my new money has come from. I just said it was all the wages due from the laird. Mrs Fiddes has said nothing to me about missing the pin, for she knows she's profited plenty enough.

Also retired is my harlot friend Flora, all flogged out now. She married a customer who lives on the other side of White Horse Close. A flock of pretty birdies here, and a decent life we have made for ourselves, have we not? And, of course, the bonniest flowers decorate poor Ginger's grave.

And if we girls spend our evenings lazing at the fire, talking of the old days, and sipping Flora's husband's good French wines and eating leftover slices of alehouse pie brought home by Oriana, feeding scraps to these two soppy mongrels, then what of it? We deserve our comforts.

Do I ever take a stroll up the road and gaze at the dark mouth of Bell's Close? Well, that is my secret. But fair to say that the Devil makes work for idle hands, and I know the day will come when I must do more than wander and I must take that job in the coffee house or the oyster bar. One day I hope to make something more decent of myself – a home for waifs and strays that does not involve the selling of their flesh. Perhaps.

But I am afraid this was only a fleeting visit, for we have somewhere important we must be.

We have an invitation.

# Chapter Sixty-Six

# CHRISTIAN

*The Tolbooth Jail, Edinburgh*
*November 1679*

The final hours slip, like abacus beads. When Father was dying, he took to his bed until his skin mottled and we placed posies on his pillow. My body has slowed as his did, as though I am dying too. The chill of the stone walls slows my hips and my spine. I ache so much I spend my time on the hay bale rather than pacing. My breathing has become shallow. My vision is full of spots and stars. Johanna's physician had come with a laudanum tincture. I tried it some time ago and it left me sleepy and foggy. I will take it at the end, but for now I need my thoughts to be clear.

I will not go to my death without thinking over my own history. I must catalogue and organize it, so it rests in my own mind as it should, not as others will tell it. For their tales will be full of judgement and dishonesty as they pore over the scandal of it. The guilt and blame. Ignoring the humanity of me.

I have read Mother's letter over and over:

*My Darling Daughter,*
    *Of course you are my darling daughter. You always were.*
*Johanna was the quicker one. Faster to walk. Faster to talk.*

*But you, my firstborn, were my pride and joy. You saw the world differently. You were curious. You were daring. You were fascinating.*

*I knew he had his eyes on you. I told Lillias to keep her husband on a tight leash, but there was nothing she could do. You were not the only one. But you were the most exciting one, for you were illicit. Some men are never content with what they have.*

*I feared Andrew would not make you happy, but he was the right choice for our circumstances. Another failing of mine, I am afraid. But you always wanted more. You wanted to sail the seven seas, and how could that really have happened? In a way, you and James were similar. That is not to forgive my brother-in-law for seducing you, but merely my observation.*

*Please destroy this letter once you have read it, for I am saying things for your eyes only. I am risking so much even by writing to you. Rip this letter to pieces. I cannot be seen to be sympathetic to you, because everyone will shun me. But know that I am sorry. Truly, deeply sorry. And know my love. Know it now, and when you are in your final moments.*

*Your loving mother*

I rip up the letter into tiny shreds and put them in the chamberpot.

She could have come. Instead the steps remain quiet. My family grieve behind their own closed doors. They grieve for themselves, leaving me alone in my final hours.

At just after eleven strikes of St Giles' bell I hear footsteps. The guard appears and tells me there is a man who wishes to see me. When he tells me the man's name, I agree to the visit.

A figure appears and I do not recognize him at all, at first.

Then he comes closer to the candle lantern. It is a man who is simple and plain. A man who has none of the gowns and wigs of my family or my circle of acquaintances. It is the man who put his life at risk to try to help me escape. William Watson.

'Come, come,' he hushes, as my tears stream. We are clutching each other's hands through the bars. His fingers are rough, his nails bitten down, exactly as I remembered them.

'I thought you had escaped to France,' I say, kissing the tips of his fingers.

'I will leave in a few days,' he says. 'I could not leave without seeing you again.'

'I have thought of you,' I tell him. 'Our hours together feel like a dream.'

'When they took you, I had no choice but to run,' he says. 'I could not have saved you. I keep going over it in my mind. The route we took. Whether we could have avoided detection. It haunts me.'

'Nothing is your fault,' I say.

'And the behaviour of James Forrester is not your fault,' he whispers. 'I absolve you.'


Another hour; another abacus bead. William has brought ale and I drink mine with him. He coaxes me to eat the bread and meat on the plate that have lain untouched, and I do it for him. I tell him about the laudanum and he nods, saying that is wise and that I am to take it, knowing that I will leave him in spirit before I leave him in body.

'What will it be like at the end?' I ask. As if he would know.

'It will be quick,' he says soothingly.

'Will I die straight away as soon as the blade hits?' I have thought about this. I cannot stop thinking about it.

'Perhaps not,' he says. 'Perhaps you will be aware for a few moments.'

'I cannot bear the thought.' I shudder. I begin to cry and feel myself losing control again.

'Hush, hush,' he says. 'A few moments, half a minute or so. You will bear it. Use it. Use your last half-minute to think of everything that is most important to you. All the people you love and the things you have done.'

'I cannot bear to talk of it any longer,' I say. 'Or say goodbye to you.'

'Our goodbye will be sweet,' he says.

But before all that: oh, there is something particular about an Edinburgh night! Perhaps it is the cold slice of wind that blows up the high street, with its whispers of the Firth of Forth tides. Perhaps it is the ghosts of the plague-dead making merry in the closes. Or the living: the rattle of drink bottles and drunken laughter. It holds us in its spell. As if we were lovers sharing the night in an oyster house. As if the throng below the window, jostling and cawing, was not here to see me die. As if we were only beginning our journey together, touching hands, full of the magic of darkness, not at the end of it.

All of those who left me for dead on my final night on this earth: my husband, my mother, my sister. They will never know I spent some – precious – moments of it more content than I had ever been. In the thick of night, before the grey fingers of first light steal their way into the cell and the guard returns to usher William Watson away.


He slips back into the darkness like a shadow, leaving just the taste of ale on my lips.

And now I am truly alone. A pause, before men come to

escort me down. The crowd has gathered strength overnight and now it is a roaring throng. I hear the shout of 'Best mutton pies' and whoops and screams. They sing and wait. The High Constables bellow at them to behave. I do not look down on them. I do not want them to know my face. I know the man from *The Caledonia Broadside* will be there. Telling my story to the world. But only those closest to me know the true Christian Nimmo.

I wonder again at the point at which things could have been different. If I had been less showy in the blue dress that Christmas Eve when I was thirteen? If James had chosen Johanna instead? If my jealousy of her had not been so unsettling that I took his attention as a sign I was not so plain after all?

If my husband had made love to me like the men in the marriage manual?

If James had not promised me a brighter world, then mocked my leap of faith by kissing Violet under the sycamore tree?

If Oriana had never come to work at Corstorphine Castle? If I had not had her dismissed?

But I don't have any more time for questions, now.

I open the parcel Andrew delivered. The clothes are exceptional. A black silk gown. A white taffeta hooded cloak.

I shake as I put them on, but I am undeterred. The crowd is loud and restless and there is only one way to silence them.

I have had enough. I need the noise to stop.

The laudanum is bitter, but I swallow it.

They are not burning me at the stake, like they do with the witches and the poor. I will not smell my own burning flesh. It will stun, and then it will be over. Like the tooth-puller. At the very worst I will be alive for half a minute more, that's what William said.

The cell is getting lighter. The magic of the night is fading. I hear voices. Nervous coughs. The rattle of keys. Boots.

My body begins to convulse. I don't think the laudanum is working. I am too aware.

The men stop at the door, as though they cannot take in what they see. There are too many of them to count and the trembling is overtaking me, into my fingers and my teeth and my knees. I have pissed again. The guard, High Constables. The prison minister, Reverend Raeburn. There is the murmur of a prayer. I tell them I cannot come, that I cannot walk, that I must wait for the laudanum tincture to take effect, for I do not feel that I am close to blacking out yet, and that is what I had hoped for. But they move towards me, in slow motion. Some of them take my arms and walk me out of my cell.


We descend flights of steps and I am half carried. We follow corridors that are dark and full of raucous prisoners. The floor is uneven. I stumble two, three times and I hear one of the men curse and another blame my staggering on the tincture. I hear their voices overhead, but the words are snatched by the candle-lantern flames and I cannot understand all that they say, except mutterings of prayer and directions. Left here. The Lord Is My Shepherd. Right here. Careful with your footing, my lady. They are back to calling me 'my lady'. I hear words leave my own mouth, fluttering up to the stone ceiling. *I am absolved. He took my innocence. He cannot hurt anyone else now.*

Then there is an oak door.

And I am pushed through it, into the blaze of morning light.

As soon as the door opens, the crowd roars. I hear my name, over and over again.

We are so high up I can hear every word as my sins are read out. The Maiden is before me, her dark beams towering above me, her blade hoisted high.

When the minister has finished praying for my soul, my fingers move of their own accord and take off the white taffeta cloak, to the gasp of the crowd. I bare my own shoulders, for men have touched me enough in my life and I want no more hands on my skin. Below me, right at the front, I see a familiar face with both hands raised towards me.

William Watson is here, to help me take my final steps. I walk towards him.

## Chapter Sixty-Seven

# VIOLET

*Edinburgh*
*12th November 1679*

Back at Mrs Fiddes's parlour for one last time, and look at the spread! Her finest party yet. They will talk of this for years to come.

Platters of oysters sprinkled with fish sauce from the Orient! Not to everyone's taste, but the sharp sting makes for a salty dance on the palate, I declare. Washed down with the best French wines. A top-up? Don't overdo it – the old flavours of Edinburgh are being forced to make way for the new and it takes some getting used to. This exciting age, brought by ships docked at Leith Port brimming with velvets and spices and traders, is hauling the city onwards from its plague-ridden past.

Now we have stagecoaches departing for London once weekly from the White Horse Inn. A physic garden at Holyrood filled with myrtle and melon; hairy kidney-wort and hound's-tongue to cure all ills, from piles to madness. The city of fifty thousand souls rises upwards to its castle, a city of kirks and physicians and merchants and coin.

This very dress I wear today, imported from Italy with its matching lace choker. Red again, for I have flowed from violet to scarlet these past weeks, forgive the indulgence. I thought a red lace choker a fitting fashion for this morning's event, and does it not become me? A red slash across the neck, as I swish and swirl about the room.

Dawn peeks over the top of St Giles'. The moon hangs on for dear life, a silver slipper set with cold stars. A restless mob has amassed in the high street overnight and it knits gloves and drinks ale and munches pies and heckles *murderess* and waits.

I have seen it all through keeks behind Mrs Fiddes's curtains, as we have the bird's-eye view, right over the high street from her parlour. But it is not time to open the curtains yet. The gents are not quite assembled. The bawd herself is rallying the stragglers and I do declare it will be one of her last tasks, as I have heard a rumour that justice is coming for her too, soon, and that the branks by the door of St Giles' are waiting for her, on charges of running a house of ill repute. Bribes will only get you so far in this town when you have let your gob run loose in court, havering and slavering away for the attention of it. A boarding house, indeed. The Kirk did not take well to that. She will be hoisted from this very parlour and dragged across the street to be gripped by an iron tongue, and there are few souls that would survive three November days and nights in the branks.

But *shhh*. Nothing to Mrs Fiddes on that subject now. Let her enjoy her last great party and chew on her last chicken leg.

In traipse the gents, some half-dressed from their hours in the girls' rooms, some smart as pins with their shirts fully tucked into their breeches and eyeglasses polished clean, to join those of us who have kept vigil in the parlour with the cheeses and the wines, listening to 'Fine Knacks' on the piano – once Ginger's tune, now played by Oriana, but not so smoothly.

I, Miss Violet Blyth, have not so much as touched a pecker all night. I am risen above that now. The petticoat has stayed firmly on. The stockings up. 'Tis such a relief. Alas, I have been called in by our dearest bawd for one final job to do. One last task, and I reluctantly agreed, for I am the best-placed person to do it properly, to tell the story as it happened. And I did so fancy the thought of the Parmesan wheel and the spiced sauces and mingling with the great and good of the town, for they all have the best gossip and the finest connections.

As I pull back the curtains, we can finally cast our eyes onto the street below and the platform of the Tolbooth Jail, which is dewy in the first rays of dawn.

And atop it, the Maiden.

I am so accustomed to being the star-turn in this parlour it feels strange that Lady Christian is the one you are here to see. Oh, do not boo and jeer; I have kept you entertained enough, have I not, through this long November night, with the tale of how it all came to be? Come, Oriana, hold my hand, for you must watch too, my dear, even though I know you would rather run to your room and pray.

And now, glasses refreshed and raised, let us all be upstanding and fall silent and watch Lady Christian lay down her head and kiss the Maiden. Which she does now, with seeming courage enough.

# Chapter Sixty-Eight

# CHRISTIAN

*The Tolbooth Jail, Edinburgh*
*12th November 1679*

Morning ruptures in a flash of sunlight off the Maiden's blade. Pigeons screech and take flight, crashing into each other's wings. The throng roars. Faces stare from tenement windows, horror etched on them. Glasses raised as if they are toasting my health.

*If you only had half a minute left, what would you remember?*

Roseburn. Johanna running ahead in the garden. Laughing softly and blowing dandelion heads. The pages of the marriage manual tucked into my petticoats. *Hope Lies Within.*

A stiff swatch of silvery silk. The ripple of a ship through a foreign tide. Andrew sailing away from me, facing south.

A swirl of black hair, a pomander trailing cloves. The fizz of pine-apple flesh, the juice running down my chin, the same bright yellow as the gorse that flows across Corstorphine Hill. The way he stared at me. The brush of his fingers. The heavy sting of his hands. Seeing him with Oriana. Seeing him with Violet. *We are connected.* I am glad he is dead. *I am glad he is dead.*

The throng is wild now, hooting. Blood on straw. The sky is bright as glass, yet darkening at the edges. The sun is glorious today. Andrew will be pleased, as that is fine sailing weather.

France. William Watson kissing me in a field of lavender. The life we might have had. *I absolve you.*

Johanna again, this time she kisses me on the cheek and slips away. She has always been one hop ahead of me. Doesn't she look divine? One day she will have six boys and girls at her knees, of that I am sure, and she will adore every one of them and name her last daughter Christian. She will take her to Corstorphine Woods one day and share her cherished memories of the aunt that no one else dares speak of. She will watch autumn leaves fall among her daughter's red curls and feel so alive in that moment that she will weep.

Mother. That peacock-tail hat. Doing all she could to save herself and her daughters. I hope she does not spend the rest of her days despairing, but I know that she will. I am sorry you did not come to say goodbye to me, but that is your cross to bear. Darling Mother.

The crowd seems quieter. All I can hear is the thump of my own blood. William Watson is here. William Watson held my hand for half a minute, knowing who I am. I am absolved. I am ordinary. I am beautiful. There was not another path I could have taken. I am decent. I love the sea and December frosts, and I hate pine-apples and whisky.

The sky is darkening now. Turning the shade of *Deepest Noir*, but the sun still dazzles like a piece of gold on the city. It is going to be a triumphant Edinburgh morning. A glorious future for those who survive this city's plagues and poverty and curses and gossip. I can see it all now, I can see the coins jangling in the innkeepers' pockets and the buttons shining on the advocates' coats. I can see the Kirk ministers preaching from their pulpits, and the fornicators' heads bowed as they sit on the repentance stools. I can see the witches they burn at the castle hill and the ones they drown in the Nor Loch. The rouged girls in torn petticoats, the maids straightening their aprons. The polished young ladies waiting for suitors.

I watch it all, fluttering above it, light as a sycamore key, at the mercy of the wind.

# AUTHOR'S NOTE

*The Maiden* is inspired by true events, and an attempt to lay old ghosts to rest.

Christian Nimmo was executed at the Maiden in Edinburgh on 12 November 1679 for the murder of her lover and uncle, Lord James Forrester. She killed him with his sword under a sycamore tree in the grounds of his home, Corstorphine Castle, on the day of the village Lammas Fair on 26 August 1679.

The Maiden is a guillotine-type execution machine that was used in Scotland between 1564–1710 to behead more than 150 convicted criminals, and is now on display at the National Museum of Scotland.

I came across the story of the murder of Lord James Forrester as a child growing up in Corstorphine, now a suburb of Edinburgh. The ghost of Christian Nimmo, known as the 'White Lady of Corstorphine', is said to haunt the scene of the crime.

As a child, I found the story enthralling and terrifying in equal measures. As an adult, I became intrigued by who the real Christian might have been. Not the hot-blooded murderess as she is portrayed, but the woman behind the ghost tale. Whilst the Forrester name is synonymous with Corstorphine, Christian Nimmo is a dark sidenote in its history. The Corstorphine Sycamore Tree, under which the murder occurred, survived from around 1600–1998 and was once claimed to be the largest sycamore in Scotland. The dovecote still stands.

I took as a reference point for *The Maiden* a scathing account of Christian's life and trial from the manuscripts of John Lauder, Lord Fountainhall in *Historical Notices of Scottish Affairs*, published in 1848, in which he describes her as leading a 'godless' life. I didn't believe that. Instead, I imagined what really may have led a woman in 1679 to have an affair with her uncle by marriage and eventually take a sword to him.

*The Maiden* is not a history book or a biography, but simply takes some of the elements of the story that I found most intriguing and imagines a fictional scenario with a cast of characters who I felt might have lived in Edinburgh at that time.

In the historical records, there is no mention of a Violet Blyth nor an Oriana, nor a Mrs Fiddes. But I do imagine women like these existed in Edinburgh's poverty-ridden tenement closes, all struggling to survive against the odds that were stacked against them, just as Christian Nimmo was as good as executed the minute she killed James Forrester, regardless of the circumstances that led to the fateful moment.

As a journalist, I have had the privilege of unearthing interesting stories. In this case, I make no attempt to present the case as a miscarriage of justice or Christian as innocent of the crime or present fiction as fact. Rather, I revisit her execution and the grounds upon which she was convicted in a twenty-first century light, using my own imagination.

Researching and writing *The Maiden* also meant I could revisit and reimagine my much-loved childhood home of Corstorphine. I hope that this novel finds a place in its heart, with its historical inaccuracies forgiven. And I hope that readers will give a thought to the real Christian Nimmo, whoever she truly was.

# ACKNOWLEDGEMENTS

I am incredibly grateful to everyone who has helped me create this novel and put it out into the world.

Thank you, Sam Humphreys and Alice Gray, my amazing editors. You championed Christian's story from the moment you read it and helped me shine a new light onto a dark Edinburgh ghost tale. Thank you also to Maria Rejt and the Mantle team, Rebecca Needes, Mandy Greenfield, Chloe Davies and Natasha Tulett.

To Viola Hayden, my fantastic agent at Curtis Brown, I am indebted to you for helping me shape this novel with your insight and wisdom. It's a joy to work with you. And thank you to Nadia Farah Mokdad as well.

I also owe significant thanks to the Bloody Scotland crime writing festival, which gave me the platform to showcase this story at its Pitch Perfect competition.

Much of *The Maiden* was written on a Curtis Brown Creative novel writing course under the expert tuition of Lisa O' Donnell, who helped give Christian and Violet their voices, and Andrew Michael Hurley, who encouraged its sense of place. Early drafts were read by Kirsty Witteveen, Laura Shepherd, Celia Sutterby, James O'Neill, Andrew Watson, Nadia Shahbaz, Gary Clark, Julie Fison, Jeanie Keogh, Liz Mills Campbell, Anitha Sundararajan,

Elfriede Atwal, Rachel Dunbar and Elizabeth Ingram Wallace. Support and advice were given by Jennifer Kerslake and the CBC staff.

Thank you to writing consultant Sam Boyce, the most enthusiastic reader in the world, for forensic manuscript insight, pitching tips and coffees at Summerhall. And to Magi Gibson, for helping me find my writing voice.

Thank you also to the Corstorphine Trust, which manages the Corstorphine Heritage Centre's museum and archive, including an exhibit on the sycamore tree and the murder of Lord James Forrester.

I am indebted to those who have supported me to write, work, and raise my family. To Darren, Jim and Pauline. To Simon, Jane, Jasmine and Sophie. To David Foster, the best dad and granddad in the world and in loving memory of Margaret Foster, my mum, who was with me in spirit throughout this writing journey. And, of course, to Tom and Ruby. I am so proud of you both.

I am grateful to anyone who has listened to me talk about this novel. Alison Simpson, Cara Chambers, Fiona Young: my friends and book club veterans, thank you for the joy you bring. To my colleagues at the *Scottish Daily Mail* and my dear Stirling Chums, Linda, Chris and Andy. To Sarah Macpherson and Lesley Brydon, I am so glad you are in my Coven.

And, finally, to Sarah Phillips. You have encouraged me in both my writing and my life, with unwavering support and loyal friendship. Thank you.